The Takers

Also by Robert Ackworth

The Moments Between
The Blood of My Brother

THE TAKERS

Robert Ackworth

The Bobbs-Merrill Company, Inc.

INDIANAPOLIS   NEW YORK

Published by The Bobbs-Merrill Company, Inc.
Indianapolis   New York

Designed by Gail Herzog Conwell
Manufactured in the United States of America

First printing

Library of Congress Cataloging in Publication Data

Ackworth, Robert C
     The takers.

     I. Title.
PZ4.A183Tak   [PS3551.C54]   813'.5'4   77–76875
ISBN 0–672–52298–5

To Rita

1

Having a dry run the day before the event seemed a little stupid to the pilot, because it would take the element of surprise out of it tomorrow; but, having lived around Hollywood for a long time, he knew how crazy these movie people were, so what the hell? It was just to give the brass at Regency Pictures a preview of what it was going to look like having a silver Piper circling the lot at five hundred feet, trailing a streamer of two-yard-high letters and figures that spelled out, "Regency Pictures, 1922–1962—40 Years of Glorious Past, 40 Years of Glorious Future."

The pilot took off at ten forty-five, since they expected him to start circling around eleven, and the airport was thirty miles from the studio in Hollywood. A slight smog sullied the thin November sunshine, but the pilot had seen it a lot worse. At two minutes to eleven he passed over the range of hills where letters perhaps twenty feet high set against the side of one hill spelled out "Hollywood" so hugely and garishly that it could be seen for miles.

A minute or two later he was over the Regency Pictures lot. He noted that the back part looked like a wasteland, and that wrecking crews and bulldozers were working there. Farther on, he began circling over the front part, where the huge sound stages and other buildings formed neat rows down parallel streets. There was practically no sign of activity, although there were some automobiles parked here and there in mostly empty parking areas. It seemed strange to the pilot that the place could seem so dead when there was such a big celebration taking place there tomorrow.

Actually, there was considerably more activity going on inside the stages and buildings than there normally was at Regency Pictures these days. The company even had some production in progress. Regency Television was shooting episodes of three television series on two stages and a fragment of the back lot that wasn't doomed to demolition to make way for the large apartment and shopping complex scheduled to rise on the two-hundred-acre site. There were even theatrical pic-

1

tures in production on two stages, though they weren't Regency productions. They were films of independent producers who were renting the studio's facilities. The studio regime was thankful for their presence, for they helped to absorb some of the overhead. Regency Pictures executives would have liked all the empty stages brought to life with new Regency productions on the scale of twenty years ago, when there were five or six pictures in production at all times, but that was just wishful thinking nowadays.

The bulk of the activity at the studio today was special, in preparation for tomorrow's one-of-a-kind event. Stage seven was the hub of much of it. Two areas were set off in the cavernous sound stage for the reception and the luncheon. Carpenters, juicers, grips, set decorators, cameramen, and various other production people generally employed in setting up scenes for filming were hard at work, for the whole thing was going to be filmed tomorrow by Regency Television for a documentary. There was going to be a lot of still photography, too, for the record and, more important, for the publications that were doing the spreads. As Noel Jordan had told the board of directors when soliciting their reluctant approval to bear the expense of this celebration, Regency Pictures was going to get a sorely needed million dollars of free publicity from this.

Down several streets from stage seven in the carpenter's shop, men were still working on what was to be an outsized replica, as big as an elephant, of a silent movie camera of nineteen twenties vintage, mounted on a platform with wheels. Tomorrow, six chorus girls were going to be packed inside it while the exterior was covered with papier-mâché through which they would burst at the proper moment.

In a rehearsal hall down the way, those six chorines were practicing their routine under the instructions of a dance director while a pianist plinked out "I'd Like to Make a Movie of You" from the 1929 early talkie *Regency on Parade*. The girls were costumed as movie cameras in black and white satin, just as in the movie, and they were going to perform the tap routine exactly as it had been done in the film.

In the commissary three streets over, not far from the administration building, the silent-movie-camera motif had been extended to Regency Pictures' birthday cake, a six-foot-tall white and pink confection lovingly constructed by the company's sole surviving baker, who was putting the final touches on it with his frosting gun. The cake looked slightly insecure on its frosted tripod legs, though presumably the frame around which it had been baked would bear the weight.

Also in the commissary, caterers were making preparations for tomorrow's sumptuous luncheon. The menu was fish dumpling with

2

truffle sauce, lobster soufflé, stuffed baby pheasant, cauliflower Polonaise, Spanish red wine, Italian white wine, mocha torte with ground almonds, cheese strudel, and pear brandy, and it was being listed by hand on parchment right now in the art department on more than two hundred souvenir cards to be placed by the plates tomorrow.

In the administration building nearby, in projection room one, studio head Noel Jordan and Regency Pictures' only current contract star, Wells Corlen, were viewing the final cut of Corlen's new movie, *The White Indian*. Jordan was thinking again, as he had many times recently, that they had a potential smash hit here, and it certainly wouldn't hurt to release it concurrently with all the hoopla about the studio's fortieth birthday coming out in *Time* and *Life* and other magazines.

In another part of the administration building, the publicity director, Peter Ribley, was conferring with the most important people from the media who were going to be present tomorrow, including the representatives and photographers from *Time* and *Life*. He'd already outlined the schedule of events for them, had named the famous and even some of the not-so-famous who would attend, and now proposed that they stroll over to stage seven to see the environment they would be working in tomorrow.

As they emerged from the offices in back into the lobby, newly resplendent from the addition to its walls of thirty-some portraits of stars in gilded frames, there was the usual comment from visitors that this was certainly a touching vista of nostalgia. Ribley nodded. The portraits of the major stars who had made this studio what it was (and whom the studio had made what they were) from the nineteen twenties well into the nineteen fifties had lined the galleries of the opulent Regency Grand in New York City ("Even more splendid than the Roxy!" was its heyday boast before it had been torn down to make way for an office building).

The group stepped outside and at once observed the plane circling overhead. "Forty years of glorious past and forty years of glorious future," murmured the *Life* reporter tonelessly as he watched the streamer float across the sky. He said it in a way that made Ribley think he took it as a joke.

"We mean that," Ribley said, smiling stiffly. "Regency Pictures' future is all mapped out."

The *Life* man only smiled, and the group proceeded on to stage seven, where a red carpet was being laid to the stage door from the special parking lot that had been set up between the stage and the adjacent building, the costume warehouse of the wardrobe depart-

3

ment. The *Life* reporter commented that you didn't see much red-carpet treatment around Hollywood these days.

"No," Ribley agreed, and reminisced about the red carpets that had been laid at the Sante Fe station in Pasadena when stars had arrived on the Super Chief in the twenties and thirties, and about the red carpets at big premieres at Grauman's Chinese in the same period. Ribley knew all about it. He'd been around for the whole rise and fall.

They entered the stage, and Ribley took them to the reception area near the stage door, where the guests would be loosened up with champagne before the luncheon. The floor plan had been laid out in the form of a huge five-pointed star, and ten-foot-high stars had been raised around it to form walls. The stars were faced with blown-up stills from some of Regency's most famous pictures over the years and featured its biggest stars—stars like Howard Stanton, Tracy Gordon, Michael Baines, and Mona Gaillard. The *Time* and *Life* people agreed that this was a good way to create the right kind of ambience for the celebration.

They moved on toward the center of the cavernous stage, where there was a flurry of activity, much as if a scene were being set up for shooting. What was being set up was the lights on the catwalks above; and below, the last of the tables for the luncheon. They were arranged on three sides of a square so that all the guests would have a view of the theater-sized motion-picture screen forming the fourth side, where scenes from Regency pictures over the last forty years—including some from the latest one, *The White Indian,* yet to be released—would be shown by rear-screen projection—"without sound, of course," Ribley pointed out, "so as not to interfere with the talk at the tables."

At that moment, Jordan emerged from the administration building with Wells Corlen. They both looked up at the plane circling the lot, proclaiming Regency Pictures' past and future.

"Crap!" said Corlen with a cynical smile. "If Regency Pictures has any future, it's only because I'm making movies for you, and your future will go down the drain when I stop making them."

The studio head found it extremely difficult to smile back, for the young star had expressed a disagreeable truth. "We want you to stay with us forever," Jordan said with pseudo jauntiness. "You're our favorite star."

Jordan continued smiling as he looked at the beaming blond youth who'd been called "the new breed of star" and the "new James Dean." "Obnoxious twerp!" was what he was thinking.

4

2

Howard Stanton had lived in the same Tudor mansion in Beverly
Hills for over a quarter of a century now, and had owned his beach
house in Malibu almost as long. The furnishings and decorations were
little changed from the beginning years, a tribute to the star's taste,
since three Mrs. Stantons had come and gone in the interval without
finding much reason to change things.

Howard enjoyed both his homes immensely, and usually he could be
found spending quiet days at one or the other of them these days, seven
months after his recovery from a bad heart attack. Today he'd risen
early, breakfasted, phoned his broker about some stock transactions,
and looked over a script an independent producer had sent him through
his agent. It was the first script he'd been sent for a very long time, but
one he would certainly reject. He needed no more bad roles. He was
rich, and although he hadn't made a picture for five years, he'd
certainly proved his durability. His major Regency pictures of the
thirties, forties, and early fifties were among the most popular on
television these days.

Since lunch he'd taken his two German shepherds for a walk through
his two acres, with its forest of oaks, maples, and sycamores out front
and its eucalyptus and palm grove out back, its big gardens, and its tall
privet hedges setting the estate off from neighbors. He thought about
Tracy and Mike coming in by plane later today—the studio was putting
them up at the Beverly Hills Hotel, he'd learned—and he thought about
the big celebration on the lot tomorrow. He had mixed feelings about
the prospect of seeing Tracy and Mike again, but his feelings about the
affair at the studio were definite. He'd rather not attend, and he was
sorry he'd said he would. He'd owed everything to the old regime at
Regency Pictures. He owed nothing to the new.

When he came in from the back garden with the dogs, he was
surprised to find two representatives of the new regime waiting for him
in his living room—Noel Jordan, studio head, and Vincent Kale, head
of Regency Television. He was surprised at this unannounced call. He

5

hardly knew Jordan, who had succeeded another deposed studio head a couple of years earlier in what seemed the natural order of events nowadays, and he'd never met Kale until now. They could have come out of the same mold. Both were in their middle thirties, bright-eyed, toothy-smiled, and bristling with energy.

"Naturally you're surprised to see us," Jordan said, his smile widening, "but Vince and I decided not to wait, because this is such good news, and there'll be too much excitement going on at the studio tomorrow to talk about it then."

The good, and surprising, news was that the studio had decided to develop *Westward the Men* into a television series and wanted Howard to play the lead, and they'd brought along a detailed treatment of the proposed first thirteen episodes for him to study.

Howard thought about *Westward the Men.* It had been one of his early big pictures, released in 1937 to critical acclaim.

"One of the few sensible things my predecessors did was not sell that picture to television," Jordan was saying.

"Not that we couldn't do a series from it anyway," Kale put in, "but it's just as well that the theatrical version hasn't been exposed in recent years."

"Westerns are still the favorite fare of Americans and probably always will be," Jordan said. "Yes, I know we're getting into a new type of Western these days, like *The White Indian,* but that sort of thing is largely for the theatrical film audience, and the classic approach is still best for a television series, since it's aimed for a general audience and has to stand the test of time. A good television series can go on making money forever."

Kale was smiling again. "It would be impossible to visualize anyone else but you in the role of Jared."

Howard was silent. He'd played the role of Jared more than a quarter of a century back, and now they were talking about his playing the same role at age fifty-two. It seemed absurd.

"I can't picture myself as Jared now," he finally said, a little cautiously, and then was annoyed with himself for his defensive tone. They knew how old he was.

"Oh, the series will be based on the *mature* Jared," Kale said. "After all, it was the maturing and mature Jared who helped to build America's silver empire, not the youth, and the series will be focused on that."

"Besides, you don't look your age," Jordan said. "You could pass for forty."

"Forty is the age we visualize the mature Jared," Kale added.

6

Howard wondered if they'd considered the possibility that he could have another heart attack anytime, even though, as his doctor had told him, the odds were in his favor, since he'd come out of the first one with apparently little damage. But of course they'd considered it. They wouldn't go unprotected. They would probably take out a ten-million-dollar insurance policy on his life.

"I don't know about it," Howard said.

"Naturally you'll want to think about it," Jordan said, "but we're both confident you aren't going to disappoint us." He smiled. "Our slogan for Regency Pictures' anniversary is 'forty years of glorious past and forty years of glorious future.' You're an important part of that glorious past, Howard Stanton, and you can be an important part of our glorious future, too, if you want to be."

Tracy Gordon was coming into Los Angeles by plane from Georgia, where she'd visited her mother for an uncomfortable few days after flying over from Rome. The seat belt sign would probably go on at any moment, so she took a last look at her face in the washroom mirror. Though her scar was visible to her, it was barely so, and she was aware that it probably wouldn't show in any candid shots they got at the airport unless someone caught her at the wrong angle.

The scar was rather long, shaped like a half-moon, and extended from beneath her left cheekbone almost to her mouth. The wound that had caused it had been so skillfully repaired by one of the best plastic surgeons in the world that it could be detected only at close inspection and in the cruelest light. But Tracy could see it when no one else could.

The seat belt sign below the mirror started flashing, and Tracy took a final look at herself and returned to her seat. Shortly before they set down, the stewardess told her the tower had radioed a request that she remain on board until all the other passengers had deplaned, since there was a welcoming party waiting for her. Tracy went tense at the thought of what she would have to face. She wished she could have a drink.

A few minutes later she descended from the plane toward the group of a dozen or so men waiting below. There were reporters, photographers, and the two representatives of Regency Pictures, who between them had six dozen red roses for her. Red particularly complemented Tracy's brunette coloring and the tasteful gray Chanel suit she was wearing. She posed for the photographers with three dozen in each arm and a radiant smile, as if she were enjoying this and wasn't worried about the candid shots that were being taken in uncontrolled lighting.

The questions began, and Tracy girded herself for the onslaught. She had a justified reputation for trying to evade reporters because of the scurrilous stories that had appeared about her. But she couldn't turn and run this time, not now, and not tomorrow at the studio, where it might be even worse. She was here for one purpose, a purpose she would certainly not reveal to the press, and she intended to see it through.

The first volley was fired at her.

How do you like living in Rome, Miss Gordon? *Fine*. Will you ever return to live in Hollywood again? *It's doubtful*. Well, the old Hollywood seems to be gone, and there's no need for a star to live here anymore, is there? *No*. What do you think of Regency Pictures' fortieth birthday celebration? *It's something to celebrate! Forty is old age in the movie business*. Why did you come clear from Rome for it when you're no longer under contract to them? *Regency Pictures did a lot for me when I was*.

A moment of pause, then another volley.

How will it be for you to see your former husband, Michael Baines? *Pleasant, I'm sure*. And what about your old co-star, Howard Stanton? *I'm looking forward to seeing him*. What do you think of Wells Corlen? They call him the new breed of Hollywood star, you know. *Yes, I know. I wouldn't know what I think of him. I didn't see his first movie, and I've never met him*. Do you think it's possible you'll ever co-star with him? *It's doubtful*. (My God, what a question. She was twelve years older than Wells Corlen.)

The final volley was fired.

Do you ever see Juan Olivares these days? *No*. Would you marry Carlo Martinelli if he weren't still tied to his estranged wife by the divorce laws in Italy? *I have no comment on that*.

She expected them to close in for an assault when she became elusive, but the rest of the questions were comparatively mild. Still, she was trembling a little by the time the barrage ended.

A studio limousine waited to take her to the hotel. The two Regency Pictures representatives accompanied her. She'd already forgotten their names. They were both bland and eager, and probably nothing more than glorified errand boys. They expressed Noel Jordan's apology for not meeting her at the airport, but he was sure she would understand what a busy day this was for all of them at Regency Pictures. She understood, but she didn't believe that was the reason. She doubted that studio heads did such things as meet incoming stars anymore. The eminent and forbidding Augustus Dalton had met her once or twice when she was at her box office peak, but his successors had never given her special star treatment.

Driving through Los Angeles brought back a lot of unwanted

8

memories. Tracy tried to be polite to the studio men, who kept reciting banalities. She even told them, when they asked, that she was happy to be back in California, that it was like coming "home," although nothing could have been further from the truth. The contrived, unnatural talk among the three of them made the trip to Beverly Hills seem endless, just as trips in California had always seemed to Tracy.

The Beverly Hills Hotel was unchanged. It looked exactly as it had when Tracy had first seen it seventeen years ago, in 1945, when she was newly under contract to Regency Pictures. It was a sprawling structure of pink and green stucco set in a palm grove off Sunset Boulevard in the heart of Beverly Hills. The hotel management treated her like visiting royalty as they ushered her to her bungalow. Today was the first time she'd been treated like a star of magnitude for quite a while, and it was a good feeling. It wasn't true that the panoply and trappings of stardom had never meant anything to her, as she'd sometimes claimed in the past.

Her bungalow was filled with flowers, and there was a magnum of champagne in an ice bucket. She had a glass of the champagne with the hotel manager and the studio representatives. The studio men said there would be a limousine at eleven tomorrow to take her and Michael Baines to the lot. Mr. Baines had the neighboring bungalow, the hotel manager informed her. Tracy nodded. She'd expected as much.

The manager and the studio men bowed themselves out. A maid came, unpacked Tracy's bags, and left. Tracy sat with a glass of champagne and stared at the phone, wondering if she should call Howard or wait for him to call her.

They were coming in to L.A. Michael Baines was in the washroom, looking at his still handsome but dissipated face in the mirror and taking the final nips from the almost empty flask he'd brought along on the flight in his pocket. The flask had been full when they'd set out from Idlewild International Airport in New York five hours earlier. Mike's illicit nips in the washroom, added to the two legally allowed cocktails he'd had in the cabin, amounted to considerable alcoholic intake during the trip.

Still, he wasn't drunk, for his capacity for alcoholic consumption before drunkenness set in had increased over the years, along with his drinking. He was a little woozy, but he was fairly confident about facing with a certain amount of aplomb whatever reception awaited him at Los Angeles International Airport. Still, he did need these last nips for courage.

The little sign began flashing, "Return to seat, fasten seat belts," and Mike took a last look at himself in the mirror. There was no getting around it that he looked forty-two, which he was, but there was no good reason why he still couldn't play leading men in the movies. With the right lighting and the right cameraman, they could peel the years off anyway.

He took a last nip and returned to his seat, resigning himself to a final spate of talk from the bore sitting next to him, a fat businessman who hadn't immediately recognized Mike and hadn't even known that he'd been awarded a Tony for his acting on Broadway last season. The bore had talked mostly about baseball and the great things John F. Kennedy's administration was doing for the country, and it had taken all of Mike's control to refrain from telling the creep he didn't give a goddam about any of it.

He learned just before they set down that there would be a reception party waiting for him on the ground. He was relieved that he was being welcomed. He seldom knew what to expect these days, because everything was so different from what it had been.

He deplaned smiling. There were about a dozen men present. They were all reporters and photographers except the two sycophantic types who presented themselves as the studio's representatives. He wasn't surprised Jordan hadn't come. He was glad that the welcoming party was as large as it was and that he wasn't falling-down-drunk and liable to make an ass of himself.

He got through the reporters' questions. Some of them were pretty stupid, and he almost told the truth when one of them asked what he thought of Wells Corlen. "I think he's a good actor," he said stiffly, when his true thought was, "I think he acts like an egoistic prick."

On the way to the hotel, as he only half listened to the empty talk of the studio representatives, he thought of his wife back in New York. He knew Sheila was hurt because he'd left her behind on the excuse that this affair wouldn't interest her, since she wasn't in the movie business. The truth was that everything he did interested her.

He was sorry now that he'd accepted the invitation. Why should he give a damn about Regency Pictures' "glorious future" when he was only a part of their dead past?

He supposed he was really here because of Tracy and Howard, and perhaps to get away from Sheila. But at least he'd be spared facing Mona and a possible stirring up of that emotional hornet's nest, for Mona had declined the studio's invitation.

He wished he'd had the sense to do it himself. He could hardly wait to get to the hotel so he could have another drink.

10

3

In her bungalow at the Beverly Hills, Tracy Gordon was drinking another glass of champagne as she listened to a transcription she'd brought along of an interview gossip columnist Aster Bigelow had conducted with Howard Stanton on her "Here's Hollywood!" radio program in 1948.

Aster Bigelow: "With television making the inroads it is, what's the future of Hollywood?"

Howard Stanton: "It's got a great future as long as we continue to make movies that entertain people the way they want to be entertained, and as long as Hollywood finds new stars like Tracy Gordon."

Aster Bigelow: "Yes, it certainly looks as if Tracy Gordon has quite a future after the smash hit she made in *Heat of Passion.* How is she to work with? You just finished a picture together, didn't you?"

Howard Stanton: "Yes. It's called *Love on the Loose,* and I hope it's just the first of a lot of pictures Tracy and I make together. She's wonderful to work with."

Aster Bigelow: "You mean she's not temperamental. Maybe she can't afford to be. After all, she isn't quite a full star yet. You know how that is, Howard. You aren't a star until it's proved you're going to last."

Howard Stanton: "She'll never be temperamental. And she's going to be a very big star."

Aster Bigelow: "But how good an actress is she?"

Howard Stanton: "She's good. She doesn't think she is, but she's wrong. She doesn't see her talent for what it really is. She's good, and she'll get a lot better."

Aster Bigelow: "I can't think of a better judge than you, Howard. You've been in the business for almost twenty years, and you've been one of our biggest stars for fifteen. If you have that much confidence in Tracy Gordon's future, then I'd be willing to bet that she's going to be one of the biggest stars Hollywood has seen for a long time."

Tracy shut off the machine and removed the record. She hadn't played it for a long time until the day before she'd left Rome, although she'd played it periodically over the years, particularly during the first few years after the broadcast was made. The record had gone with her everywhere she'd lived, and had even survived a room collapsing around it in a hurricane. To this day, Howard didn't even know she had it, and she wasn't sure he even remembered making the broadcast.

She poured the last of the champagne and drank it, frowning at the phone. She was getting a headache.

As soon as he got rid of the hotel management and the studio representatives who'd picked him up at the airport, Mike went next door to Tracy's bungalow, bearing his bottle of champagne. He noticed when she opened the door that she was a little heavier and that there were dark shadows under her eyes, but what the hell? Nobody looked as fresh as two years ago, and it would take a lot more emotional pummeling to make Tracy Gordon anything less than ravishing.

He put down the champagne bottle, picked her up, and turned her around as he kissed her. It was the way they'd played their big love scene in *Smith's War* eight years ago. He wondered if she remembered that.

He set her down and smiled at her. "Tracy, why did we ruin our lives by getting divorced?"

Tracy smiled back. "Why did we almost ruin them by getting married?"

"It was just the wrong time."

"It always would be for us, Mike. Our marriage should never have happened. It almost spoiled our friendship."

"That hurts, Tracy."

"I don't think you hurt that easily." She smiled again. "You got married soon enough after I saw you last. I understand that your wife is lovely, intelligent, and an aristocrat. What a marvelous combination!"

"She's all of that. But don't ask whether we're still happy together."

"All right, I won't."

They looked at each other for dragging moments before Mike spoke. "I think we just had a pregnant pause, didn't we? All right, Tracy, let's get this off right by not talking about things we don't want to talk about, and see how long we can keep it that way."

"Probably not long, Mike. You know how it goes with us."

"Sure. In the meantime, let's drink a toast to our reunion, shall we?" He looked over at her empty champagne bottle on the coffee table. "I thought you might have finished yours, so I brought mine."

He poured two glasses. They raised them.

"To our reunion," he said.

"To our reunion," she said.

They drank. He poured two more glasses and they sat down with them.

"What made you decide to come back for this, Tracy?"

"To feel like a star again. But mostly to see you and Howard."

Mostly to see Howard, he thought resentfully.

"I was a coward when Howard had his heart attack," Tracy went on. "I should have flown over at once, but I hesitated, and then hesitated some more, and then it seemed too late to come, as if it would have just been an afterthought. The truth was, I had this unreasonable fear that if I came he'd die, but if I stayed away he'd live. I just wasn't rational about it."

"We all get paranoid, Tracy."

"That's not a good enough excuse for my inadequacy."

"Don't feel guilty."

"Guilt is my trademark, Mike."

Yes, and his too, he was thinking when the phone rang. He suspected it would be Howard, and it was. There was a quality of both sadness and gaiety in Tracy's voice as she spoke to him. She didn't say much, and she spoke in clichés and conventionalities, which was untypical of her unless she was nervous. She kept glancing at Mike as she talked. He knew she would rather he weren't present while she talked to Howard, and he resented that.

She finally put him on with Howard. Mike spoke clichés and conventionalities, just as she had. He said it was great to talk to Howard again and to hear that he was coming along so well. Howard thanked him and said he was certainly looking forward to seeing both of them at the studio tomorrow.

Mike hung up. He'd watched Tracy drink a glass of champagne in the course of the minute or so he'd talked with Howard, and she was pouring another glass now, her hand trembling a little as she raised it to her lips. Her face was rigid. Mike understood. She'd hoped she was going to see Howard this evening.

Mike was glad she wasn't. He took up the bottle and refilled his own glass.

"I think we ought to go out and raise a little hell together tonight, Tracy."

Tracy raised her glass. Her eyes were angry. "I'll drink to that," she said tensely.

13

4

Howard Stanton stood naked in front of his bathroom mirror, shaving with the old straight razor he still used. He rinsed off the residue of shaving cream and patted his face dry with a towel. Then he stood and looked at his face and body for a long time, as he often did. That face and body had meant a great deal to him during his life. At fifty-two, they still did. He liked to think that in spite of crow's feet and a little sagging, he would continue to look good for a long time to come. And would continue living.

Today he didn't look rested because he'd spent a nervous, mostly wakeful night. It was certainly a bad day to look tired, because in a few more hours he was going to be glaringly on view and irretrievably recorded on film.

Guilty thoughts about Tracy had kept him awake last night. He'd wanted to see her last evening, but he'd avoided it because he'd been afraid of what his emotions would be.

He was afraid of her, he realized. Considering the decision he'd forced on her years ago, something that had caused her far greater hurt than it had him, it was surprising that she didn't hate him.

Maybe she did.

Yet how could he be sure about anything until they talked? Until they were together again?

He wanted to see her so badly that it hurt, and yet he was afraid to.

As Howard approached the studio, he saw the plane trailing the long streamer flying rather low in a circle over the front lot.

The plane would probably circle the area all day, Howard judged as he approached the east gate of the back lot. It was strange that Regency Pictures was touting the studio's future when three-quarters of its huge back lot, where some of its biggest pictures had been filmed, was being bulldozed to secure an entirely different kind of future for the company as an entrepreneur of real estate.

Howard had come early in order to take a last look at some of the

14

back lot standing sets he'd worked on, such as the French street that had been built for *The Young Soldier* thirty years ago and the castle façade that had served for *Ivanhoe* and others of his costumers.

But they wouldn't let him in to look. Safety precautions, they told him. Besides, almost everything that was coming down was already down, including the French street and the castle façade.

Howard drove around to the front gate. The guard was one who'd been around since the old days, somehow having survived the retrenchments and changes of personnel the studio had gone through every time there was an economy wave or a change of power at the top.

The man waved Howard in cheerfully with a bright "Good morning, Mr. Stanton!"—just as if it had been only yesterday when he'd last driven in here.

He was far too early to head for stage seven, where the ceremonies were going to be, so he decided to park temporarily in the visitors' lot adjoining the dressing room building, where parking spaces for the stars and principal contract players had once been provided. Howard Stanton's had been the first on the extreme left for well over two decades. The sign that had read "Reserved for Howard Stanton" for so many years now read "Reserved for Wells Corlen."

Wells Corlen! Howard found it difficult to comprehend the likes of Wells Corlen at the pinnacle of Hollywood stardom and as the savior of Regency Pictures. Like Elvis Presley, currently the top star of a rival studio, Corlen had come to fame as a singer, and like Presley he possessed a good voice, good looks, and abundant personal magnetism. But to Howard the magic quality was missing.

Howard had a feeling that if he walked into the dressing room building and went up to the second floor, where he'd occupied the largest suite in the place for many years, he would find that it now belonged to Wells Corlen.

He didn't go into the dressing room building but walked quickly away, down the street. As he passed the former writers' building down the way, he remembered that you could always hear clacking typewriters through open windows in the days when the studio had maintained a staff of contract writers. The building was silent now. The sign in front announced that it housed the offices of Regency Television.

Television. Certain pundits were saying that the scourge of the movie industry for the last fifteen years was now its only hope for survival. It certainly seemed significant that Noel Jordan had developed his career in television, had been a very big man in one of the television networks, and now was distinguished as the first man from the enemy camp to head a movie company.

15

And now there was a chance that Howard Stanton, at one time Regency Pictures' biggest movie star, might become its biggest television star. But being a television star was not the same as being a movie star. Deciding what to do about the television series was going to take a lot of thought.

Howard reached stage one. The red light wasn't on, meaning there was no production inside. He opened the door and stepped into the vast place. Except for a few scattered lights, the stage was an empty panorama of darkness clear over to the other side, where a huge square of light was framed by the open double doors. A truck was pulled up and things were being unloaded.

The big sound stages like this one were still here, even though much else was gone from the old days. The studio ranch in the San Fernando Valley and the British studio near London were gone. And even though the stages remained, most of them were dark and empty, and Howard supposed the company would like to get rid of the bulk of them, too.

He walked out and backtracked to the administration building, which remained the largest building on the lot, just as it had been when Howard had first walked through the front gate in 1930. The building was distinguished by statues of the Regency page—a symbol as familiar to the public as the M-G-M lion—on either side of the main entrance door, clarion suitably raised to his lips to announce that a Regency picture was about to unfold.

Howard entered the deep central hall. For years, at the far end, on the wall between the two doors leading to the executive suites in the rear, portraits of the two men who had founded the company and had determined its destiny in its great years, Augustus Dalton and Nicholas Smetley, had hung side by side. Dalton's portrait had been removed the day he was forced out of the company, and Smetley's had been removed immediately after his death. Howard had felt it a sad statement on the times that successors had so hastened to remove all traces possible of the giants who'd created this once towering enterprise.

The portraits of Regency Pictures stars that had hung on the damasked walls of the Regency Grand in New York before its demolition now hung on stucco walls on both sides of the hall here. Howard walked along, looking at the portraits, pausing particularly at those of Georgina Fox, Leni Liebhaber, and Tracy Gordon.

His own portrait was the last one on the wall on the right side, painted in thirty-five or -six, as he remembered, when he'd been at his physical peak, ranking right up there with Robert Taylor as one of the handsomest men in pictures. It was a good likeness of the young Howard Stanton, but he didn't look at it long. He moved on to the

16

portrait that occupied the place of honor: Wells Corlen, Regency Pictures' golden boy.

The shining smile seemed to mock Howard. He turned away from it and left the building.

It had been a long time since Mike had wakened trembling from head to toe, but he did today. He lay in bed for a while, and then got up and faced himself in the bathroom mirror. As he'd expected, he was bleary-eyed and bloated.

He'd made a fool of himself last night, of course. He remembered bits and patches of it as he showered; and the more he remembered, the angrier he got. He was angry with those customers in the Polo Lounge who had seen and heard him make a fool of himself. And he was angry with Tracy for shutting him out. The memory of Tracy's closing her bedroom door on him early this morning and his return to his bungalow, almost tearful with humiliation, was particularly painful.

He got out of the shower and patted himself dry with the huge towel in front of the mirror. He let the towel drop and surveyed the reflection of his body. He looked at himself critically because he was sober. When he was drunk, he could look in the mirror and see himself as he once was, not as he was now.

Actually, considering the abuse he'd handed himself, he didn't look bad. He would still look good in tight cowboy pants if the chance for a Western came again. But everything was relative, and he wasn't blind to the slight sagging in the pectorals and the little roll of flesh around the waist that would worsen if he didn't take measures.

He went to the living room and poured himself a small Scotch. It brought a quick burning moment of relief, and he poured himself a larger one. He sank down in a chair beside the phone. He knew he should pick up that phone and call Sheila, but he just couldn't do it. What he really wanted was to get the hell out of here. He wanted to be anywhere but here. He shouldn't have demeaned himself by coming back for this stupid so-called celebration, and he wondered now why he'd decided to come. He foresaw a miserable day ahead of remembrances he would rather not remember, of unhappinesses he did not want to relive.

And he hadn't the least doubt that Wells Corlen would be dominating everything today. Wells Corlen, superstar. Wells Corlen, the new breed of Hollywood star. Wells Corlen, horse's ass.

He downed the Scotch and poured himself another one.

Tracy wasn't quite ready yet, and she could tell, from the sharp way his glass clanked as he put it down on the marble-topped coffee table, that Mike was getting restless waiting for her in the other room. But she didn't intend to hurry, for there was still plenty of time before they had to leave for the studio.

Tracy had spent much of the morning looking at herself in one mirror or another, watching as the hairdresser put the final touches on her coiffure, watching as the maid helped her to dress. Both were gone now, and she rose from her dressing table to look at herself again in the full-length mirror on the closet door.

She decided there was nothing more she could do to make herself look better. Her hair was perfect, and the classic dress, cut like a Greek chiton, that she'd had designed in Rome for this occasion was the type of high-style gown she looked best in, even though it didn't wholly conceal the five pounds she'd put on in the last six months. Neither did her careful makeup entirely hide the darkness under her eyes.

She moved up closer to the mirror and examined her face. It had been said often enough that she was one of the most beautiful women in the world. Aster Bigelow, before she'd turned on her, had written in her column, "Tracy Gordon's face is her future."

Others had been more specific, had described her broad forehead, naturally arched eyebrows over almond-shaped golden eyes, straight nose, and generous mouth all put together in complete harmony on an oval-shaped face framed by luxuriant sable hair. Much in particular had been made of her skin, and of the dewy quality of the amber eyes that so often seemed to be verging on tears of sadness or joy. Most of all, in speaking of Tracy Gordon's beauty, they'd talked of "glow."

Tracy turned away from the mirror. She was thirty-five years old, and although most people thought her as breathtaking as ever, she was full of fear about the glow going and the shadows coming.

She paused at the slightly open door. Mike sat across the room in profile to her, a little flushed, jaded-looking, but still a study in rugged handsomeness. It occurred to her that the casual observer looking at Mike would undoubtedly conceive of him in life as he was on screen, the strongest man in the world, in total control of himself and all situations. Yet the glass of Scotch being lifted to his mouth before eleven in the morning was a clear statement of how not in control of himself he was. He looked as strong as Howard, but he was weak—as weak as *she* was. How mercilessly they'd kept proving that to each other in their life together a few years ago.

She walked into the room. Mike looked over, hesitated a moment, put his glass down on the table with a slightly trembling hand, and stood up as she reached him. His smile came slowly. She understood.

18

He resented the ultimate ending last night—himself alone in his bungalow, her alone in hers.

"Shall we call the car and go?" she said.

"What? And arrive early? That wouldn't be at all starlike."

"We weren't very starlike in the Polo Lounge last night," she said. "We acted like fools."

"Sit down. Let's talk about that."

They sat down and faced each other across the coffee table.

"It's a little late to talk about a fait accompli," she said.

"What did we talk about last night?" Mike asked.

"We talked about the so-called good old days in Hollywood, and we talked about them far too loudly. I'm afraid it might get into the columns."

"I certainly hope so. Some tidbit wrapped around a question like, 'Were Tracy Gordon and Michael Baines whooping it up because of plans to remarry after he sheds wife number four?' "

"Don't joke. I don't want publicity like that."

"A good scandal is the best thing we can hope for. Why, my career got a whole new lift when that scandal magazine published a story about my stag movies."

"I don't want them writing about me at all. I want them to leave me alone."

"If they do, you're dead. I want them to keep talking about me, good or bad; and you do, too, even though you say you don't. You don't hate it any more than you hate making movies. You wish the same thing I do, that it would all be like it was ten years ago."

"No, I don't want to go back to it. Time goes on and we change. I wouldn't want it to be the same as it was. I don't think you would, either, if you weren't drinking your breakfast."

"Don't tell me *you* are going to moralize about drinking before lunch."

"Of course not."

"I wish I didn't *have* to do this, Tracy." He put the glass down and stared at it. "Where did my guts go?"

She didn't answer.

"I think my marriage is coming apart," he went on, "and I want to talk about it."

"But I don't. I don't know the lady involved, remember? And even if I did, I'm not qualified."

"If I can't talk it over with you, who can I?"

"I don't know," she said. "Maybe Howard."

He scowled, and she was sorry she'd suggested that. His relationship with Howard was uneven. He was resentful of and jealous of Howard at least part of the time, and though she didn't like it, she understood it.

"I wouldn't have tried to go to bed with you last night if my marriage weren't coming apart," he said.

"Mike, I don't believe that."

He raised his glass and took another swallow. "You're right. I wanted to go to bed with you again, and it wasn't just for old times' sake."

"I don't believe that, either."

"God, Tracy, you have an infinite capacity to hurt!"

Did she? She would have thought she had an infinite capacity to *be* hurt. Besides, she didn't believe she'd ever really hurt Mike. Not his soul, anyway. Just his ego.

5

Photographers representing various publications, the news services, and Regency Pictures' publicity department were posted with a scattering of reporters along both sides of the wide red carpet leading up the studio street to stage seven. The motion picture camera crew shooting the proceedings for the documentary was located near the stage door.

The luminaries and slightly lesser lights had been arriving up the carpet from the parking lot for the last twenty minutes, escorted by slim young men outfitted in the crimson and gold costume of the Regency page and carrying a replica of his medieval trumpet.

But the novelty of the page escort, a touch suggested by a bright young man in publicity, soon wore thin, and some, like Howard Stanton, found the processional to the stage door as embarrassing as it was nonsensical. Cameras clicked in his face and lenses pointed at him like gun muzzles as he was led down the carpet by a page toward Jordan and his "receiving line" of studio sycophants at the stage door, above which the red light was incongruously burning, signaling that shooting was going on inside and no one should enter. To Howard, the whole thing seemed irredeemably outlandish already, even for this business. The march of stars, featured players, directors, producers, and a whole potpourri of other movie types to stage seven was reminiscent of arrivals at Grauman's Chinese and the Cathay Circle on premiere nights during the nineteen thirties, except that there were no searchlights sweeping the skies and no ranks of police to prevent fans from storming the arriving celebrities.

Jordan reminded Howard of one of those old-time premiere hosts, too—those sleek-haired and shiny-toothed masters of ceremony who would ask celebrities to stop at the microphone and say a few words of cheer to the fans at home glued to their radios.

But those old-time premiere hosts had never failed to recognize everyone on sight. Jordan did, and it made his job of greeting the arriving guests eminently more difficult. Having come comparatively recently from New York television, he didn't recognize more than a quarter of the people approaching on the red carpet. There were two older publicity men, Hollywood people through its rise and decline and knowledgeable of who was who, posted behind him to whisper identifications when needed.

The guest list was by no means restricted to those who'd been associated with Regency Pictures along the forty-year route of its destiny, logical though that would have been. Important outsiders such as big independent producers and heads of rival studios had also been invited, plus a disproportionate number of network television people, the latter because of Jordan's desire to push the studio in that direction. As often as he could, Regency Pictures' current studio head made a point with the press that although the movies had made television what it was, it was now up to television to make the movies what they'd been.

The photographers were shooting all arrivals, from the most obscure former Regency contract player right on up, though no one was fooled into believing that many of the shots would appear anywhere. In the published accounts of this joyous occasion, the public would be interested chiefly in the pictures of the stars.

Certainly they would be interested in the shots made of Tracy Gordon, gorgeous in her chiton and turban, smiling radiantly, a little heavier perhaps, but becomingly so. She posed outside the stage door with the bouquets of calla lilies Jordan had just presented her, a dozen in the crook of each arm, the petals languishing against each famous breast.

And of course they would be especially interested in the shots of Wells Corlen, currently reigning god in filmdom's Olympus, who had the good showmanship to arrive in the buckskins he'd worn in *The White Indian,* due to be premiered in the wake of a flood of publicity about today's doings.

In fact, with Corlen's dramatic and late arrival, the important ones were deemed finished, and latecomers were denied the opportunity for a photographed grand entrance, for Jordan and his party and the battery of photographers and reporters moved inside to the star-shaped reception area not far from the stage door. Champagne and conversation were flowing and the king-sized blown-up stills from Regency films forming the walls of the area were being looked at, laughed at, wisecracked about, and even, in isolated cases, seriously discussed.

Jordan soon fell in beside Tracy, who was being questioned by a reporter and snapped in a series of those candid photos she hated. She answered the reporter's questions with feigned enthusiasm while she thought about Howard and their unsatisfying reunion in the parking lot just before they'd been separated, to be paraded down the red carpet. A hug and a kiss and a spoken very-glad-to-see-you mixed with an unspoken I'm-really-very-nervous-about-it, and then they'd broken away from each other. She was left with the sad feeling that there wasn't going to be much more to it than that—that she would leave California in a day or so with her emptiness still unfilled.

But she smiled grittily and told the reporter she was sure the movies were going to make a comeback, a remark that pleased Jordan, who said he was looking forward to that day soon when she'd be back on the lot making a Regency picture again. Tracy doubted that would be very soon, but that wasn't what made her want to cry. She'd never cried in public in her life, and it occurred to her that it would be a bizarre item for the press if she broke down in tears at Regency Pictures' fortieth birthday party. But she didn't. She smiled and laughed instead, and Jordan's foolish ego led him to believe it was because he was being witty. But Tracy wasn't even listening to him. The reporter and the photographer had moved on, and she was sipping champagne and wishing for oblivion.

Mike was way across on the other side, near the buffet table, looking at the famous full-length still of Mona Gaillard from *Lisa,* the one of her in a black satin gown with her long hair flowing over her perfect bare shoulders. How many, many times in his life Mike had looked at this still. A framed eight-by-ten of it had stood on the piano in his house in Pacific Palisades for years. How many different thoughts he'd had about her since she'd appeared in his life twenty years ago, and how much she had affected his life—probably more than any single other person.

22

He was glad she wasn't here today. He supposed she'd refused the studio's invitation because she was still smarting over the failure of her "comeback" a few years ago, and blaming Regency Pictures for it.

Mike turned from the still and looked around the room. He saw Tracy talking to Wells Corlen. Tracy was smiling as if she actually enjoyed listening to him. Mike hoped he would be able to avoid meeting Corlen today. He acknowledged to himself, but only to himself, that he was jealous of Corlen for his spectacular success. Corlen was absolutely sitting on top of the world, a superstar already at a stage of life when Mike had just been getting his start.

Tracy was half listening as Corlen told her that she and Marilyn Monroe had been his favorite female stars in the early nineteen fifties, when he was growing up, as if that were a century ago. He said it as if it were a concession on his part for her to have been a fantasy figure to him, as if here he was, a real superstar, when she was only a fading memory like all the other has-beens crowding the area, getting giddy on the champagne and their rehashed memories of much better days. But perhaps he wasn't really saying it that way, she acknowledged. Perhaps it was the champagne that was doing it to her.

"I'd sure as hell like to make a pass at you, Tracy Gordon," the golden boy suddenly said, and Tracy smiled stiffly. She wished he would go away. She wished Howard would rescue her. She wondered where he was and what he was thinking about. She looked around for him and saw him at a far wall, looking at the big still from *Safari* of him and herself caught in a stampede of Cape buffaloes. That still was a cutting reminder to her of a close brush with death, and a poignant remembrance of another frustrating stage in her relationship with Howard. She wondered if Howard was thinking the same thoughts.

Fortunately, Jordan appeared and spirited Wells Corlen away; but, not so fortunately, just as Tracy was about to go over and join Howard, Mike appeared. He looked flushed. Tracy doubted that it was just the champagne. Knowing Mike, she thought it was probably also his seething emotions.

"Jordan will be handing out accolades to Corlen during the luncheon, sure as hell," Mike said, "but you can bet he won't mention my Tony."

"Probably not," Tracy said. "They think Hollywood, not Broadway, Mike. You know that."

"They've never given me credit out here for being a good actor."

"Yes, they have. You were nominated for an Oscar."

"But I didn't get it, and that was a goddamned cheat."

She didn't answer, and he was irritated when she turned her head from him, as if she found the crowd around them suddenly irresistibly fascinating.

"You've never fooled me," he went on in an ugly tone. "No matter what you've said about not caring, you want to be a good actress."

She turned back to him. "As long as we're being so frank, let's face it that an Oscar would be more appealing to you than a Tony anytime. All you really want is to be a big movie star again, Mike."

She turned away again, shocked with herself for having deliberately hurt him that way. But it had simply been building up in her, she realized. She didn't know how to undo it, so she wouldn't try. She would only be silently sorry, as she had been about a million other things over the years.

Mike himself had turned away. He didn't want to talk with her now. She'd hurt him. She'd said that all he wanted was to be a big movie star again. It was the word "again" that made it hurt.

Howard was looking at a still from *The Young Soldier,* the picture that had made him a star thirty years ago. It was a still of himself in a muddy trench, looking young, bewildered, and full of fear. He supposed the scene expressed how he'd felt about life in those days. He was three decades older now, but he was still sometimes bewildered and full of fear.

Suddenly Tracy was there, slipping her arm through his. "It's good to remember some things, isn't it?"

"Yes. It's good to remember my first big picture." He smiled at her. "And it's good to remember about you and me, Tracy."

Her arm tightened around his, and the moment hung tautly between them, but it couldn't continue. It was time for the luncheon to begin.

It was two-thirty in the afternoon, and the gourmet luncheon being served to more than two hundred celebrants at tables covered with fine linen tablecloths was being well enjoyed by those whose taste buds hadn't been too severely blunted by overindulgence in champagne and hors d'oeuvre at the reception.

Conversation, buoyed by an inundation of exotic wines, proceeded headily at most tables despite the continuing distractions of clicking and flashing still cameras, the probing lens of the roving movie camera recording the documentary, the anachronistic and mostly unmemorable music and background scores from old Regency movies played by a small orchestra near the head table, and the unrolling on a large screen within everyone's view of a montage of scenes from Regency movies.

Jordan talked a lot, but most of it was lost on the others. Wells Corlen, regretful that he was seated between Jordan and Howard

24

Stanton, was twisting his head and smiling at Tracy Gordon whenever he could. Michael Baines was brooding over Corlen's skyrocketing success in a world that seemed to have strange notions of what gods and goddesses should be these days. Tracy Gordon was finding it increasingly hard to pretend to be happy that she was here or hopeful that she would be able to put it behind her without more scars on her psyche. Howard Stanton wished he could reach down the table and touch Tracy Gordon.

At the conclusion of the serving of the cauliflower Polonaise, the pouring of the red wine, and the unrolling of a scene from *The White Indian* in which blond white captive Wells Corlen performed a Cheyenne war dance in a breechclout, the screen went dark for a special event.

"Wells Corlen," Noel Jordan announced over the microphone at the head table, "will now re-create his most popular number from *The Performer,* his first Regency picture and our biggest box office success last year! 'I Love You Still' remains the number-one pop hit in America today, over a year after the release of the film. The song was written by Wells Corlen especially for the film; it was recorded by him for Regency Records and earned him his twelfth gold record."

Corlen went to the center of the area and began to sing and gyrate to the accompaniment of the orchestra. Mike wished he could close his eyes and ears and shut out the sight and sound of the young man. He kept his hands clasped tightly in his lap and declined to join in the substantial applause at the end. Wells Corlen, the reality of today and the promise of tomorrow, beamed at his audience and sat down.

The orchestra struck up a tune with an antiquated Charleston quality to it. The papier-mâché replica of the nineteen-twenties silent movie camera, over a dozen feet tall, was rolled in. Six chorus girls, dressed as movie cameras themselves, came ripping through the paper and went into a kicking tap dance to heavy applause.

Afterward, Jordan smiled lavishly as he said into the microphone, "Probably few of you remember that this number was originally performed in *Regency on Parade,* the nineteen twenty-nine picture that kicked off the all-singing, all-dancing, all-talking phase at Regency Pictures."

Few remembered it, Howard reflected, because it had been the very worst of all of Regency's movies.

"It introduced the great era of the sound film at this studio," Jordan went on, "and today we're introducing yet another era, the greatest of all."

Jordan went on far too long about Regency Pictures' future, presenting few facts to give substance to his colorful rhetoric. When he had finished, to lukewarm applause, the huge frosted silent-camera birthday cake was rolled in, its forty candles burning brightly on top. When Jordan put the knife in to cut the first piece, the cake collapsed on its insecure legs. Nervous and mirthless laughter swept the place.

Howard had told Tracy and Mike after the celebration that he was too tired to make a big evening of it with them, as Mike had suggested, and had invited them to come out and spend the next day at Malibu with him instead. He realized that Tracy would prefer to come alone. But it was emotionally safer for them the other way.

It was true that he was tired. The unleashed flood of memories today had taken its toll. But it was not the kind of tiredness that would let him sleep. He decided to walk the beach to unwind from his tension.

As he headed through the sand he asked himself how many times he'd walked the beach of Malibu over the years. A thousand times? Two thousand? Why should it seem different tonight?

The externals were certainly the same. The ocean was dark and shining in the moonlight. The breakers fell on the beach, leaving a spumy deposit, then rolling back out to the depths with a rushing sound. Lights beamed beckoningly from beach houses here and there along the way. Occasionally he passed someone else walking.

The externals were the same, yet it seemed so different, and perhaps, he thought, that was because he was thinking about so many things he hadn't thought about in a long time. He thought about Leni and Georgina and Penelope and Tracy. He thought a lot about Tracy.

The scenes that went through his mind were short, swift, wordless. He felt breathless, not from his walk but from the multitude of thoughts he had, the almost forgotten images he suddenly had to cope with.

He turned back, aware again on the periphery of this relentless reminiscence of how tired he was. When he reached the house, the fire he'd built before setting out had died down. He stirred it up with the poker and watched the glitter of flame revive itself. Suddenly an image of Rudolph Valentino came to mind.

Rudolph Valentino! He hadn't thought of the silent-screen star for a long time. But he thought of him now, for in a sense it had been Valentino who had started it all for him.

26

6

On the twentieth of November, 1921, eleven-year-old Howard Stanton had an experience destined to influence the rest of his life. On that crisp, sunny Sunday afternoon Howard asked for and received permission to travel to Central Park for sledding with his school friend Oscar Pendleton. But he did no such thing. Instead, he walked from the brownstone on East Thirty-sixth Street where he lived with his parents in a large apartment occupying the second and third floors to the Rialto Theater at Broadway and Forty-second Street to see Rudolph Valentino in *The Sheik*.

Howard's parents would have been horrified if they'd known, and his father would most certainly have strapped him with his belt. Howard's father, a bank executive, had come from England as a boy, and he felt that his British origin made him infinitely superior. To Howard his father's unsmiling pomposity was as disagreeable as his mother's brooding bitterness. He didn't like to be around his parents, and kept to his room or left the apartment whenever possible. His favorite escape was the movies, usually on Sunday afternoons when it was presumed he was doing something with Oscar. His parents looked down their noses at motion pictures, thinking the theater the only worthwhile dramatic art, and weren't aware that their son had ever seen one.

Today's visit was Howard's first to the Rialto, which was called The Temple of the Motion Pictures—Shrine of Music and the Allied Arts. He was already impressed with the theater's marbled grandeur as he waited for the next show with hundreds of others behind a gold-braided rope in the lobby.

Howard had a fifteen-cent seat, which was at the top of the gallery, but he liked the location because of the sweeping view of the movie palace. A magnificent, elaborately decorated circular dome was overhead, inset with an enormous chandelier in the center and a dozen smaller ones on the circumference. Below was a sweeping stage set in a semicircle behind the orchestra pit, fronted by a looming proscenium.

27

The organist at the grand pipe organ filled the auditorium with a variety of thrilling sounds while the audience settled itself for the treat to come. The lights dimmed and the curtains opened, and the organist introduced a theme resembling a horse's hooves in gallop as titles flashed by and faded to the first scene, a view of a vast expanse of desert with a woman rider in white riding togs appearing over a dune, galloping her horse as fast as possible. The title announced that this was the English maiden Diana, played by Agnes Ayres.

In the distance was a pursuing rider. A closer view revealed a dashing figure in burnoose and flowing jeweled robes astride a handsome Arabian stallion. According to the title, this was the desert chieftain Sheik Ben Ahmed Hassan, played by Rudolph Valentino.

Howard gripped the arms of his seat, and the organ music reached a new crescendo as the sheik's horse overtook the young woman's and the sheik reached over and lifted his intended captive out of her saddle, swinging her over to his own horse. She struggled fruitlessly against him, beating his chest with her hands.

She continued to struggle as his swift Arabian carried them to his desert encampment. There, the sheik bent her to his will, in spite of her pleas.

Later, his lust and her hate gradually turned to mutual love. After an exciting interlude in which she was kidnapped by a rival desert chieftain and recaptured by the sheik, they came to the only decision possible for their future happiness. Although she was free to return to England if she wished, she would never do that now. Her place was with the sheik, as his wife.

And so, as the love theme rose from the mighty organ to fill the auditorium, the picture ended, the lights came up, and the audience applauded. Howard rose reluctantly to leave. He would have liked to stay for another performance, but he couldn't afford to arouse suspicion.

When he got home, his father was sitting stiffly in the winged mohair chair beside the fireplace, reading one of the leather-bound classics from his shelves—books that Howard was not allowed to touch because of their expensive bindings. His mother was sitting equally stiffly on the mohair davenport, knitting.

His father looked at him and said nothing. His mother asked, "Did you have a good time, Howard?"

She said it in the way a teacher might ask him if two plus two made four. He answered "Yes" and, excusing himself, went up to his room, lay down on his bed and thought about the scene in the tent between Valentino and Agnes Ayres. He knew what men and women did when

28

they were naked together in bed, and he knew from what he'd learned from the boys at school that he would want to do it as badly as anyone else someday. What he couldn't picture was his mother and father doing it. They must have done it once, or he wouldn't be here. But he didn't think they did it now.

He lay back on the pillow and closed his eyes. In his mind, he saw a burnoosed figure with flowing robes on an Arabian stallion approaching swiftly over the desert sands. But as it got closer, the figure that took shape was not Rudolph Valentino but Howard Stanton.

Howard would have preferred seeing movies in the grand manner on all occasions, at the Capitol or the Rivoli or one of the other palaces that had an orchestra and a big stage show to complement the picture. But his pocket money, earned on Saturdays in the stockroom of Abel and Stern's Haberdashery on Third Avenue, didn't go far enough to cover expensive tickets, and if too much of his money was missing, his father, who banked a set amount from it each week for him, would be suspicious. So Howard saw most of his movies in a small neighborhood house where he could get in for a nickel at matinees and a dime evenings.

Howard liked Douglas Fairbanks, Wallace Reid, Richard Barthelmess, and a number of other stars, but after he saw *The Sheik,* Rudolph Valentino became his favorite actor. During the next five years, Howard saw the Valentino movies over and over. When Valentino didn't make new pictures for a year because of a dispute with his studio, *The Sheik* was reissued, and Howard saw it six times.

It was all Howard's secret, even from Oscar, for to have expressed an admiration for Valentino at school would have invited being called a pansy. Although the girls revered Valentino, the boys hated him. It was obvious to Howard that they hated him because they were jealous of him for his handsomeness and his finesse with women. Howard was handsome himself, although of course he wasn't as dashing as Valentino. But he had fine strong features, deep gray eyes, a head of thick black hair, and what promised to be an athletic build when he filled out more; and the boys at school, except for Oscar, envied and disliked him for his physical superiority. Howard didn't care. He had his dream, and it made up for his unpopularity. He wanted to be like Rudolph Valentino, and he wanted to do with his life what Rudolph Valentino was doing with his.

Howard followed Valentino's on-screen and off-screen lives as closely as he could, picking up any magazine that had the idol's picture on the cover, reading the piece over and over until it was virtually memorized, then disposing of the magazine because he couldn't risk having it found in his room at home. He relished the star's glittering fame, his opulent way of life—the extravagant mansions, Voisin motorcars, stables of horses, and personal costuming worthy of a prince—and in particular his hypnotic effect on the women of the world. More than one article Howard read suggested that when women watched Valentino make love on-screen, they often imagined themselves in the place of the heroine. The idea of that was wicked and exciting, and Howard's wish was that one day the women of the world would watch him with the same desire. It was true that he wasn't experienced in making love, but surely Valentino hadn't been, either, at Howard's age.

But the talk around school wasn't of "making love," anyway, but of "getting a piece of ass." Howard didn't believe that half the boys who boasted of getting into some girl's pants had actually accomplished it, but the day finally came, when he was fifteen, that he could have truthfully boasted himself if he'd been the type.

On that fateful day Oscar informed him, "Jane Willoughby's going to be home alone tonight and she wants us to come over."

Jane Willoughby was reputed to have the hottest pants of any girl in school, and that evening she lived up to her reputation. When Howard and Oscar arrived, they found two other boys there from another school. It was a hot night, so Jane had a big pitcher of lemonade set out in the parlor. The room was filled with Tiffany lamps and hideous furniture with clawed feet.

She didn't waste time. She took one of the boys from the other school into the bedroom and closed the door, and a minute or so later the sounds of ecstasy leaked through, including a few dirty words.

"She just can't get enough," Oscar said with a grin. "She has to have it all the time."

Howard knew there was a word for that, but he couldn't think of it at the moment. He was a little worried about what lay ahead. He knew what he would be expected to do, for he'd seen it all graphically illustrated in the cartoon books handed around school, but he was sure that with all the experience Jane Willoughby had behind her, she'd know it was his first time, and he'd hate it if she kidded him about that. Still, maybe she wouldn't care that it was his first time if she had to have it all the time.

The first boy came out, looking sheepish, and sent the other boy in, and in a couple of minutes there were sounds of pleasure again, and then the second boy came out, and he and his pal said, "See you," and left.

30

Jane, wearing a black kimono and a smile on her face, appeared in the murk at the slightly open door to her bedroom.

"You come now, Oscar," she beckoned.

Oscar went. Howard wished he had the nerve to get up and walk out, but he would never live it down with Oscar if he did. He had another glass of lemonade to take the dryness out of his throat. All too soon Oscar emerged.

"Jesus," Oscar said as he sank down on the couch, looking as if he'd spent all his energy for the rest of his life. "Go on in, Howie. She's waiting for you."

There was nothing to do but go. He walked into the netherworld of her bedroom and closed the door, determined that he was not going to make loud breathing noises or say four-letter words that would find their way through the wall to Oscar.

Jane lay on her bed with her legs apart.

"Come on over here," she said. "It's you I want more than anybody else. That's why I saved you for last."

He walked over, hoping she wouldn't see that he was trembling. She seemed a thousand years old: a woman, not a girl. He stood beside the bed and looked down at her. She had an ordinary face with a pug nose and thick lips. Her lipstick had been partly rubbed off in her passion with those who'd preceded him. Her figure was plump and she had big breasts.

"Get undressed," she commanded, and then turned up the light beside the bed. "I want to *see* you while we're doing it."

He would have preferred it with just the languid light from the street lamp coming in through the curtains, helping to hide his embarrassment and fear.

Somehow he got out of his clothes. He'd managed to get his trembling under control, and he was hard.

"Wonderful," she said, getting up on her elbow and leaning over quickly to kiss his penis as he got on the bed with her. "The biggest and best prick I've ever seen!"

He was perfectly all right then. He lay down on her and found that it was much easier than he'd expected. He kissed her nipples and listened to her moan, and he kissed her mouth as he slipped into her. She was wet and warm and wonderful down there, and he'd never known a more joyful feeling than being inside. He would have liked it to last forever, but very quickly he could feel himself being drawn toward the end as he plunged deeper and faster into her.

"Fuck me, fuck me!" she said as their bodies slapped together, and Howard cried out from the intensity of the effusion, a far greater

31

explosion than he'd ever experienced in masturbation. For a moment he thought he was going to die.

He removed himself from her and lay beside her, wondering if he would ever breathe normally again.

"It was wonderful," she sighed. "You even made *me* come."

The important thing, he thought, was that she hadn't guessed that it was his first time after all.

When he was sixteen, two important things happened in Howard Stanton's life. He fell in love, and Rudolph Valentino died.

The Valentino tragedy occurred in August. His new picture, *The Son of the Sheik,* had just premiered in New York, and Howard, among many others, stood in line to get in to see it. Once inside he saw it three times, thus compensating for having paid the admission price of a first-run theater.

His attention didn't flag for a moment, even through three sittings. Valentino was magnificent. He had great personal magnetism, he had a perfect face and body, and he was a good actor on top of it. Howard left the theater that Sunday hoping that when he was a star, he'd be just one-half as good as Valentino was.

When he got home he went straight to his room, where, to his surprise, his father appeared at once. The last time his father had come to his room, more than a year before, it had been to reprimand him. From his frown it looked as if he were about to do it again. How old he looked! thought Howard. He was forty-one, only ten years older than Valentino, yet in Howard's eyes he looked old enough to be Valentino's father.

"Where have you been, Howard?"

"Oh, around," Howard said, aware that his tone was surly but unable to control it. He hated talking to his father.

" 'Around' is not an explanation. I want specifics."

"I was at Oscar's," Howard said, which was not a lie, for he'd stopped there for a few minutes before going to the theater.

"Do you have your homework done for tomorrow?"

"No. But I'm going to do it now."

"Why do you leave your homework until the last minute all the time? When are you going to learn that it's the man who's prepared who gets ahead in this world?"

"You can't complain about my grades."

"No, I can't complain about them in general, but the fact that you consistently get ninety in English, history, and civics and only eighty in mathematics disturbs me greatly. Mathematics is the foundation of the banking business, Howard. I want you to get ahead quickly in the business, so you are to give greater attention to the subject of mathematics in the future. I want to see that eighty climb to one hundred. Every time I see one hundred on your report card for mathematics, I'll put ten dollars in your savings account." He paused. "Howard, do you understand?"

Howard nodded, but he knew he would make no extra effort in mathematics, a subject he hated simply because it was, as his father had said, the foundation of the banking business, which his father expected him to enter right after he graduated from high school. Howard had no intention of holing himself up in a teller's cage, but he certainly couldn't tell his father so.

"Another thing, Howard. You're a big boy now, and I'll not tolerate any funny business with girls. Do you understand?"

Howard almost smiled. It was crazy that his father was just getting around to something that should have come up two or three years before.

"I know that it's hard to control desires," his father went on, "but you must. I don't need to tell you what consequences you can expect from me if you ever get a girl into trouble."

No, he didn't need to tell him, but it was hard to understand how his father had managed to bring up this subject at all.

But the episode with his father soon faded from his mind, for Valentino was ill. The papers were full of it. The actor—who had come to New York to promote the opening of *The Son of the Sheik*—had fallen ill after a party and been rushed to a hospital, where his appendix had been removed. For a while the reports were encouraging. But then peritonitis set in, and the star's condition was sinking, according to the gloomy headlines.

Howard was troubled. It couldn't be that Rudolph Valentino was going to die, could it? Such a possibility seemed incredible. He couldn't believe that Valentino wouldn't live forever.

But Rudolph Valentino did die, and Howard lined up with thousands of others in the procession that filed past the bier before the funeral. Howard had only the briefest glance at the waxen but handsome dead face, because the police kept the line moving constantly.

On the day of the funeral, Howard was in the streets with the large crowd that had turned out to see the cortège pass by. Then the body was shipped to Hollywood for burial, with the newspapers faithfully reporting the daily progress of Valentino's journey to his crypt.

Howard continued to grieve, and his parents couldn't understand what had happened to his appetite. He felt as if he'd lost a very dear friend.

Jeanette Bixby was a stunning girl. With her delicate and exotic beauty, she had some of the qualities of the movie actresses Howard admired most—Gloria Swanson, Greta Garbo, Mae Murray, and Nita Naldi. She was a sensation the minute she transferred into school, and there was hardly a boy in the class who wasn't dying to take her out.

"She's still got her cherry, too," Oscar said knowledgeably. "I can tell."

Naturally a beauty like Jeanette Bixby wasn't going to lose her cherry to just anybody, and Howard couldn't blame her for that. What disturbed him was the way he kept thinking about her. He didn't want to tie himself down with a girl. He had too many other things to do and think about.

One day in study hall, Jeanette asked bluntly, "Why haven't you asked me for a date?" So he did. He took her to see Warner Baxter and Gilda Gray in *Aloma of the South Seas*. That night in bed Howard had a vision of himself and Jeanette making love in pareus on a tropical beach.

He took her out on more dates, and usually they ended up at the movies. He'd always gone to the movies alone before, and it took getting used to, having Jeanette beside him in the dark theater, wanting to put his arm around her shoulder but not doing it.

But he soon found he enjoyed taking her to the movies, and he was disconcerted when one day she suggested that they see a play.

"The theater is vastly superior to moving pictures," she said superciliously. "The actors are much better, and so is everything else. The theater is *art*."

Howard thought Jeanette said that because she thought she should, for she was quite snobbish. She was particularly sensitive about what location they sat in when they went to the movies and, after Howard reluctantly consented, to plays. She felt that the galleries were beneath her dignity, yet Howard couldn't really afford to squander his earnings on orchestra seats.

Jeanette liked to say around school that she'd seen this play or that one, so they began going more and more often to plays. Their classmates listened to Jeanette in awe. Though she wasn't liked, she was greatly admired for her beauty and her haughty manner. She was considered remote, like a movie star, and that quality about her was what appealed to Howard most.

"No, Howard, *no!*" she said the first time he tried to kiss her, on their third date. On their fourth, when he was insistent, she slapped him, though not terribly hard. On the fifth date she let him, and after that she would neck with him during the last five minutes of a date, if there was a convenient place for it, which there usually wasn't.

But he was still conscious of a certain coldness.

"Howard," she said one evening when they'd been to a school dance and had impressed everyone with their skill at doing the Charleston, "we mustn't vulgarize our relationship by being too passionate."

"I can't help it," he said. "I feel passionate." He wondered what she'd think if she knew he lay on his bed after their dates with his eyes closed, visualizing their beautiful bodies grinding against each other in the act of love.

"I like you, Howard; I like you a lot," she continued, "but I won't go the limit. I'm saving myself for my husband."

But *he* was going to be her husband, he thought, although he didn't say so then and there. That would come later. He loved her, and he intended to marry her. He'd thought a lot about it and had decided that their marriage wouldn't interfere with his career. Maybe she might even have a movie career herself. The movie magazines were always pointing out that although some Hollywood marriages failed because of conflicts over careers, others worked out fine—the one of Mary Pickford and Douglas Fairbanks, for instance.

Howard liked to envision himself and Jeanette as big stars, married to each other and living in a mansion like Pickfair. It wasn't even out of the realm of possibility that he and Jeanette would replace Doug and Mary as the king and queen of Hollywood. After all, Doug and Mary weren't getting any younger, were they?

Howard didn't reveal these dreams to Jeanette, because he didn't feel she was ready to hear them yet. He hadn't even told her that he loved her, although they'd been going out together for six months. He decided he'd tell her the night of the junior prom, which was only a month away.

"*I love you, Jeanette,*" he would say (he could find no better way to announce it, despite all the thinking he'd done about it), and she would say, "*I love you, too, Howard.*" Then he'd take her, and she wouldn't have to feel guilty about it, for it would only be another year until they got married and left for Hollywood.

But during that month before the junior prom, he became aware that something was wrong, that something was different about her. But when he said, "You've changed—what is it?" she laughed and said, "Don't be silly."

But he wasn't being silly. For a long time they'd been going out every Friday and Saturday, and when she said one Friday that she couldn't make it that evening, that an aunt was visiting, and then used the same excuse the next Friday, he was suspicious.

That evening he decided to drop over to her apartment unannounced. Just as he was turning the corner, he saw her come out of the brownstone where her family lived. He almost called out her name as she headed down the street in the spring dusk, but an intuitive feeling of dread stopped him. Instead, he followed her.

There was a boy waiting for her at the next corner, a swarthy boy who talked loudly with an accent. Howard followed closely behind them for several blocks, listening to the boy carry on and Jeanette laugh. The boy's hand was on Jeanette's rear, patting it all the while.

Howard wondered later, as he lay numbly on his bed, why he hadn't grabbed that boy and knocked him down.

The next evening when he called for Jeanette, after working over in his mind for hours what he should say to her, he said simply, "I saw you with that guy last night."

She paled. "It doesn't mean a thing, Howard. I can explain."

But she couldn't explain, for she didn't understand any better than Howard why she would want to go out with the crude, untutored boy and have him paw her when the handsomest boy in school was her steady.

Except that he wasn't anymore.

He never went out with her again, even to the junior prom, and it wasn't long, after a few days of hurt pride had passed, before he was asking himself how he could ever have thought himself in love with her.

He went back to going to the movies alone and doing other things alone or just with Oscar, and he had a good summer. That fall, in the first part of his senior year in high school, he saw Al Jolson in *The Jazz Singer*. He thought the singing and talking parts of the picture were sensational.

Jeanette Bixby didn't come back to school that term. The news soon made the rounds that she had gotten herself pregnant by some boy from the Lower East Side and been sent away to the country to have her baby.

Howard had a calendar on which he marked off the days. It seemed a long time until next June, when he would graduate. But he'd decided that he'd stick it out, that he would get his high school diploma for the sake of his parents, even though a diploma was certainly not necessary in the field he intended to enter. But the moment he graduated he would get out. He didn't tell his plans to anyone, even Oscar. He studied, worked hard at his Saturday job, and put away every possible penny, for he would need it all in June.

He saw as many pictures as he could, and he studied the way the actors acted and the way the pictures were put together, for he wanted to know as much as he could when he reached Hollywood. One picture he particularly liked was *Flesh and the Devil*. Howard found the love scenes between Greta Garbo and John Gilbert tantalizing. He imagined himself in many a scene like that, and he decided that he was much handsomer than John Gilbert or Charles Farrell, who had played with Janet Gaynor in *Seventh Heaven* and was the latest idol. Howard was often told these days how handsome he was, and although he pretended it embarrassed him, it didn't.

But his father and mother weren't impressed by the magnificence of his profile and his body. They looked at him and saw only the vision of an ordinary young man in a blue serge suit smiling in a teller's cage. In April it was arranged that Howard would start at the bank the Monday following his graduation from high school. In the meantime Howard made other plans.

His appearance in the senior class play was his last gesture at school. He wasn't crazy about the stage, because the theater wasn't nearly so exciting to him as pictures, but he thought that acting in the class play would be good experience. The English teacher who directed the play told him that she'd never had a better romantic lead in all the years she'd been doing the plays.

"The play was crummy," Oscar said afterward, "but you were great, Howie. Know what? You'd make a good actor!"

Howard smiled. He was still glad he hadn't told his parents he was in the play. They wouldn't have thought it dignified for a future banker to appear on stage, and it would have meant trouble.

He wanted no trouble, and he had none. The day after graduation he simply slipped out of the house with a suitcase, went to the train station, and bought his ticket to Los Angeles.

7

It took Howard a week to get to Los Angeles. Along the way he slept sitting up in the coach and ate sandwiches peddled in wicker baskets, and he saw a good deal of scenery before they reached the baking sands of the California desert.

On the way out he had periods of uneasiness about what he'd done and feelings of guilt for having vanished without a trace. His parents would be terribly worried, and after he reached Los Angeles he was tempted to write and let them know where he was. But he decided against it, for he was convinced that it would only bring his father straight out here to take him home.

He wasn't much impressed with Los Angeles, except for the eucalyptus trees, which were everywhere, and the consistently sunny weather. He was initially disappointed in Hollywood, which he found more garish than glamorous, but he was greatly taken with sumptuous areas like Beverly Hills, which he toured on a sightseeing bus. He sat rooted with fascination as the guide pointed out one palatial home after another. When the tour reached the Valentino mansion, Falcon Lair, Howard found it to be everything he'd expected.

"Rudolph Valentino had unusual decorating tastes," the guide said through his megaphone as they passed the estate. "He had black walls, black draperies, and black furniture. He even had a black bathtub."

Howard wondered how much of that was exaggerated. He also wondered what the guide would think if he knew that the next owner of Falcon Lair was sitting right on this bus.

Howard rented a cheap room in a boardinghouse in Los Angeles and got a job jerking sodas evenings in a drugstore nearby. The evening job meant that he could use his days for breaking into pictures. He knew it wasn't going to be easy. He'd read countless stories in movie magazines about how hard it was, and about how many failed along the way.

He tried going to the studios directly, although it soon became obvious that he didn't stand a chance of seeing the casting director at any of them. The guards at the gates were polite but firm.

38

In August he visited Rudolph Valentino's grave on the anniversary of his death. There was a flock of mourners on hand to pay respects, and Howard wished he could have afforded some flowers to add to the splendid sprays that were laid at the crypt.

Howard wanted to meet compatible people whom he could talk to about the picture business, so he moved from his boardinghouse in Los Angeles to one in Hollywood that was filled with movie aspirants. His immediate neighbor, with an attic room as plain and uncomfortable as his own, was a man named Barney Flugle.

"This crazy name's my good-luck charm," Barney said when he introduced himself. "Great name for a comedian, eh, kid? I'm not going to let them change it, and that's all there is to it!"

Barney was twenty-five and seemed to believe Howard when he said he was twenty-one, a fib Howard told everyone who asked his age. They became friends immediately. Barney often dropped in on Howard after he got home from his drugstore job late in the evening, to chat or to try one of his vaudeville routines on him. Howard laughed at Barney's routines, but he didn't think Barney was a better comedian than Charlie Chaplin or Buster Keaton, as he boasted.

"You'll see," Barney insisted. "With sound coming in, they'll need comedians of my style. Sound will change everything."

It hadn't changed much yet. Here it was 1928, and most of the movies were still silents. But Howard had no fear that his own voice wouldn't be suitable for sound pictures, for one of the first things Jack McCall, his drama coach, said to him was, "You'll wow them with that rich baritone!"

Howard had started lessons with McCall after reading his advertisement in *Daily Variety* boasting that most of his students went on to fame and fortune in the movies. Jack McCall had come out to Hollywood in the earliest days of the industry, and had appeared in several pictures, including *The Big Parade* and *King of Kings*, but his roles hadn't been significant.

"You either make it or you don't. And, brilliant as I am, I didn't. That ad's wrong about my students becoming stars, Howard, but I think *you* will make it."

Jack got him started in fencing and gymnastic classes, too.

"Your build is great already, Howard, but fencing will help you to move better, and the workouts will make your body even finer. A face is important for a star, but a body is almost as important. When you've got both, you've got practically everything. Remember what a beautiful physique Valentino had? They took full advantage of it. He had a dressing scene in just about every picture he made to show off his marvelous bare chest. As for Fairbanks, he has his shirt off half the time. There's nothing more enticing to see than a physically compelling person almost naked and ready for action."

Jack also helped Howard to get registered with Central Casting, although he pointed out that he could count on the fingers of one hand the stars who had risen from the ranks of extras.

"I don't intend to make a career out of being an extra," Howard said. "But at least it will get me inside the studios."

Getting inside was still a long time to come, and in the meantime Howard worked, watched, and waited. When he'd been in Hollywood three months he still had no real friends besides Barney and Jack, and he'd seen two girls and one man move out of the boardinghouse to return home, their hopes having run out. Their rooms were soon rented to three others with fresh dreams.

Howard quit his evening job at the drugstore and started working afternoons at a men's clothing shop on Hollywood Boulevard. It worked out fine. He had his mornings free for making any rounds he cared to make and for his lessons, and he had his evenings free to go to the movies or to bum around with Barney.

It began to bother him that he still hadn't let his parents know where he was. So in the middle of December he wrote them a long letter explaining that an irresistible compulsion had brought him to Hollywood, and he hoped they would understand. But understanding between him and his parents was just as impossible as it had always been. He received a reply from his father full of lashings for his "lack of appreciation for all I've done for you!" and a demand that he pack and come home at once. Howard angrily wrote back that he wasn't coming home until he "made good," and then he would come only for a visit.

But his feelings of guilt were somewhat assuaged by having let his parents know where he was. He even sent them his new address when, the following June, twelve months from the day he'd arrived in California, he and Barney moved out of the boardinghouse into an apartment in a place called Paradise Court. Barney was moving ahead faster than Howard was, having done three bits in the last six months. One had ended on the cutting-room floor, but the two that survived eventually got Barney consideration for a contract at Universal.

So far, Howard had worked a grand total of three days in the studios, in crowd scenes where his face had been swallowed in the great mass of other faces. Yet with only those small results to show for his efforts, he'd still accomplished more than many hopefuls who'd been around here trying to break into pictures longer than he had.

He felt he was making progress. He looked older and dressed older than he was, and he seemed to be developing professional finesse.

"You're going to be a good actor," Jack McCall kept telling him, and Howard knew that Jack was sincere about it. Howard worked hard on the acting, vocal, and bodily movement exercises Jack gave him, and he kept improving week by week. "You *really* want it, and you're willing to work to get it," Jack went on. "Most of them say they're willing, but they aren't. They'd rather sit around talking about what they want to become than put in the work that's necessary to get it. Your voice is much better than it was, because you've worked to make it that way. And when you read a line now, you get meaning into it. In the beginning, just words came out. It takes brains and work to get meaning into what you're doing."

Howard was pleased with Jack's appraisal, and didn't think it was exaggerated. He intended to keep on working and get even better.

But his life wasn't all work. One night he attended his first Hollywood party. It was given by a character actor who'd made a fair success in pictures the last few years and had bought a gaudy little villa in the Hollywood hills. Barney was invited and was told that he could bring a friend, so he asked Howard to come along.

"Of course," said Barney when they were on their way to the party in the rumble seat of a 1926 Essex, having bummed a ride with an acquaintance, "these Hollywood parties aren't anything like they were in the old days. They used to fill the swimming pools with champagne and have Roman orgies going on while a twenty-piece orchestra played to keep everybody in rhythm."

Howard knew that Barney didn't speak from experience, for he hadn't been around Hollywood much longer than Howard had, but as usual he let Barney think he was awed by his knowledge.

The host, already full of gin and high spirits, greeted them effusively at the door. His living room was filled with young people who were gaily drinking gin out of coffee cups. As a joke, a bathtub filled with gin had been plunked right in front of the fireplace.

"Why coffee cups to drink from?" Howard asked in puzzlement. "Why not glasses?"

"Are you kidding?" said Barney with a laugh. "He's making like this is a speak, Howie. Don't you know they drink from coffee cups in speaks?"

Howard was embarrassed at his ignorance. He supposed Barney probably realized that up to that moment he'd never had a drink in his life. But he certainly wasn't going to admit it. He dipped his coffee cup into the bathtub and took his first sip as if he knew what he was doing.

41

The gin stung his lips and throat, and he had to restrain a cough. Fortunately someone came up to speak to Barney, and Howard slipped away, saved from having to try another sip of the stuff before he'd recovered from his first one.

He wandered around for the next few minutes, observing how people were drinking. The ones who were not wobbling at this point were taking the gin slowly, as if they were indeed sipping hot coffee from their cups. Not the way men slugged down drinks from shot glasses in saloon scenes in the movies, but the way they drank champagne in drawing-room scenes.

He took another sip and then another. It wasn't so bad, he decided. It stung less as he sipped more. He began to feel a little light-headed even before his first cup was empty, and he got into the dancing. He danced with a girl with red hair and a flat figure who reminded him of Clara Bow. He had another cup of gin and danced even more energetically with a brunette than he had with the red-haired girl. He felt wonderful.

He remembered suddenly that he'd come with Barney, and looked for him. But Barney had vanished. He could be anywhere. The party, from the sound of things, and from the flow of traffic up and down the stairs and in and out of the room, seemed to be going on all over the house.

There was a hand on his shoulder, squeezing. "Hey, how about you and me taking a walk in the garden, Sheik?"

It was a surprise to be called "Sheik," for the term hadn't been used much in the last couple of years, now that memories of Valentino were fading. Howard would have been pleased to be addressed that way by a woman, but it was a man who was smiling at him, a blond, good-looking man of about thirty. Howard glared at him and shook his hand off. The man disappeared, still smiling as he went.

Ten minutes later, when Howard rather unsteadily made his way along the upstairs hall, looking for the bathroom, he blundered into a bedroom where a couple were copulating in the full glow of the bedside lamp. They were breathing heavily as Howard entered and didn't protest his brief presence.

There was another revelation when Howard opened the bathroom door. The blond man whose advances Howard had rejected downstairs was in there embracing a brown-haired young man.

"Won't you join us?" the blond man said cheerfully. "We're about to have the world's best fun."

Howard smiled stiffly, shook his head, and closed the door. As he turned away, he faced the red-haired girl who'd reminded him of

42

Clara Bow. She was smiling glossily. To his surprise, she reached out and felt his groin. He hardened at once.

"That's the kind of reaction I go for," the girl said. "The bedrooms are jammed, but nobody's screwing in the linen closet down the hall. We can do it in there."

He didn't see how they were going to, after she opened the closet door and turned on the light. There were shelves on both sides and across the back, and little space in the center for them to stand in. But she pulled him inside, shut the door behind them, and leaned against him, lifting her face to be kissed. She forced her tongue between his lips and began a long, tart kiss, bitter with the taste of gin. Her arms were around his neck, her groin pressed up hard against his, and he wondered if he would be able to get inside her standing up. There seemed to be no other way.

But she had something else in mind. While she was still demanding his kiss with her lips, her fingers were unbuttoning his fly, pulling his penis out, stroking it. Soon she slid down to her knees. Purring like a kitten, she kissed the head of his penis and then the shaft. He looked down, rooted in fascination as he saw her bring her lips back to the head of his penis, kiss it again, and then close over it. He watched his penis being drawn into her mouth. Back and forth she went on it, slowly, deliberately, caressingly, and he started toward his peak immediately. What he'd heard was true. This was even more sensational than the regular way!

She seemed to know that his climax was rising in him, and she went faster. In no time, he was coming. His teeth clenched and his hands pressed down on her head. Her arms were wrapped around his thighs, and she clung to him and kept him in her mouth until he subsided.

He leaned back against the shelves for support, trying to get his breath back, wondering how she would expect him to satisfy her. But she didn't expect anything. She rose to her feet, smiled at him again, opened the door, and was gone.

When he was reasonably steady again, he went back downstairs. He had another cup of gin and then still another. There was a group singing "Margie" at the piano, and he joined in with them, but he didn't stay long. He felt squeamish. He decided to go out for some air. He stepped out onto a terrace, where he heard a giggle from the depths of a porch glider. As he was passing, he saw a girl's face, her exposed breast, and a man's face against it.

A hand came out to his thigh and stopped him. "Come on down here," the girl said, giggling again.

The man's hand came out to Howard's other thigh and squeezed. "Let's make it the three of us," he said. "It's best that way."

Howard didn't even answer them. He felt very sick. He brushed their hands off and staggered off the terrace into the garden. He took deep breaths of air, but he only felt worse. Suddenly he was bent over and the vomit was pouring out of him.

When it was over, he went to the swimming pool nearby and scooped up some water to try to rinse the terrible taste out of his mouth. Then he sank weakly onto a chaise longue beside the pool and hoped that a few minutes of rest would restore his strength.

The next thing he knew, he was being shaken awake. He looked up at the grinning Barney. It was dawn. Barney's eyes were bloodshot and his breath was incredibly bad.

"Party's over, Howie. Hope you got your gun off before you passed out."

"Oh, I did."

A few minutes later, with the new day's sun glinting on the windshield, they were being driven home in the Essex.

Barney signed a contract with Universal for four years starting at two hundred dollars a week, with options every year and an escalation clause that would raise his salary fifty dollars a week every time the option was picked up.

"Of course," Barney said confidently, "we'll tear this one up and sign a new one for three or four grand a week as soon as I prove my worth at the box office. That's the way it's done. They only give you a little until they see if you prove out. Well, I'm going to prove out, Howie."

Howard had no doubts about that. Barney had a lot of talent. And the top comedians made big money. Charlie Chaplin and Harold Lloyd had made millions. Of all the estates Howard had seen on his sightseeing tours, he thought Lloyd's the most splendid.

Howard was glad for Barney's success. But he was envious, too. He had been in California for almost two years now, and he was no nearer to getting a contract than he had been the day he'd arrived. Of course, he was a decidedly better actor than he had been, but that was of little consolation when he couldn't put it into practice.

It worried him that Barney might want to get an apartment of his own now that he had his contract and could afford it. Howard couldn't cover the rent of the Paradise Court apartment by himself. But Barney soon put him at ease.

44

"We'll stick together until you've made it, too," Barney said generously, "and then we'll each buy a private palace."

But when was he going to make it? Howard saw the inside of a studio only on the rare occasions when he got a call for work as an extra.

Then he had an idea one night when he lay awake worrying about whether he was ever going to get anywhere in his efforts to become a movie star. He told Barney about it in the morning.

But Barney shook his head. "It's crazy, Howie. It'll never work. They hire *office* workers for the studio offices, not guys who want to be actors. Besides, they're never going to select an actor from the studio office. You're wasting your time."

But Howard thought it was worth a try, so he started going to the studios mornings before he reported in at the men's shop. He couldn't get through the gates at M-G-M, Fox, Paramount, Universal, or Radio Pictures. But at Regency Pictures he managed, after the studio guard unwillingly called the office at Howard's persistent urging, to get in to see the office manager.

The man was named Zimbaldi, and he was dressed so conservatively that Howard was glad he'd decided to wear his blue serge suit. Zimbaldi gazed at him through his pince-nez with obvious suspicion. He reminded Howard of the type of man who worked with his father at the bank, and he would have walked out without even trying except that he was running out of studios.

"I suspect," Zimbaldi said, "that you came to California with the idea of becoming a motion-picture actor."

Howard nodded. There was no use denying it. He could tell that Zimbaldi was exacting, and he knew he'd have to account to him for every moment of his time since his arrival.

"What have you been doing since you've been here?" Zimbaldi asked.

Howard told him, and the office manager grimaced, as if he'd just swallowed something unpleasant.

"Jerking sodas and selling clothes don't qualify you as an office worker," Zimbaldi said. "Besides, why have you given up the idea of becoming an actor?"

"Because the odds are against it. I've given it enough of a try. If I were going to make it, I'd have done it by now."

Zimbaldi nodded, but his eyes still held suspicion. "Why do you want a job with a studio?"

"Because I like the business. I don't think a man has to be an actor to get somewhere in the picture business."

45

That impressed Zimbaldi. "As a matter of fact, Stanton," he said, drawing himself up slightly, "a man can often get much further in the picture business if he is *not* an actor."

Zimbaldi gave Howard short tests in spelling and arithmetic, and when Howard didn't make any mistakes, he offered him a job as office boy.

"You can work yourself up from that if you do a decent job. I'm not an easy man to work for, so you can take it or leave it. However, I don't believe I need to remind you that we're having hard times, and jobs are scarce."

No, he didn't need to remind him. Howard took the job on the spot.

8

Howard quit his job at the men's clothing shop and went straight to work at Regency Pictures. Barney mused that it was a peculiar way to try to get into pictures, but added, "Maybe it'll work because it *is* crazy."

Howard knew one thing for certain from the beginning. He loved going to the studio. He always arrived for work at least a half hour ahead of time, and that pleased Zimbaldi. It also pleased him that Howard seldom forgot to add "sir" when he addressed him.

"I'm going to be careful around him," Howard told Barney. "If I get out of line, he'll kick me out, and I can't have that. Now that I'm finally inside a studio, I'm going to stay until I get what I want."

Besides being early to work and late to leave, Howard dressed neatly, did his work conscientiously, and remembered always to be respectful to Zimbaldi. Of course, the office manager earned his respect, for he managed his small staff of clerks so efficiently that there were few mistakes. Their office was in the white stucco general office building, not far from the much larger white stucco administration building, where the studio head and other important persons had their offices. Zimbaldi's office handled a multitude of detail work and record-keeping that Howard found boring.

He was glad he was the office boy and not a clerk, for when Zimbaldi wasn't using him for one odd job or another in the office, he would send him on errands around the lot, and Howard soon knew the grounds well.

It was a wonderful studio, not as big as M-G-M, but growing toward that level, with a large back lot, eight sound stages, and dozens of departments. It was like a miniature city, in a way, and almost every kind of craft and trade was represented within it. Howard was amazed to learn from Zimbaldi that there were almost three hundred different trades involved in running the studio and making pictures.

The first day he was at the studio, Howard saw the noble-looking Augustus Dalton, head of the studio and second in power only to Nicholas Smetley, who controlled Regency Pictures from the New York headquarters. Howard was sent over to the administration building to deliver a message to the production chief's secretary, and he'd just come out when the Dalton limousine pulled up. He looked with interest at the gray-haired tycoon who emerged from the black Rolls Royce and passed inside, but the man didn't seem to see him. Howard didn't allow himself to be disappointed. This was his first day at the studio. He'd been waiting for almost two years to be noticed by someone in Hollywood who could help him. He could afford to wait a little longer.

In the meantime, he would learn everything he could about making pictures. It was soon clear to him how complicated it was to get a picture into production. After Alexander Renfew, the production chief, and Dalton approved a script, a hundred things had to be done before the first scene was shot. The first step was to turn over copies of the scenario to the set and fashion designers and to the casting, makeup, wardrobe, location, transportation, research, music, sound, publicity, and auditing departments, so they would all know what they were to contribute to the picture.

It was usually weeks or months before the preliminaries were completed by the various departments and the picture was ready to shoot. It was rare that an errand took Howard to a set during the actual shooting or rehearsal, but on one occasion he saw a scene being rehearsed between Regency's biggest stars, Rex Walters and Denise Carroll. It was said that these two detested each other, but from the passion they generated in rehearsal no one would have guessed it. Howard watched Walters with special interest, for this was the man he hoped to replace as Regency Pictures' top male star someday.

He looked over Walters' file in the publicity department one day when he was on an errand there. Walters had come to Hollywood in 1926 after working in the theater for more than a decade and had

47

immediately carved his niche as the studio's leading actor. His contract had recently been renegotiated and extended, with his salary greatly increased. That worried Howard. The studio wouldn't have granted Walters such generous terms over a considerable period of time if it didn't feel that he was going to stay on top for a long time yet.

The trouble was, there could be only one top star. The others were subordinate. The top star got the top money and the best roles and was the hardest to dislodge from his perch. No, it wouldn't be easy to take over Walters' position!

"Walters' pictures make money," said Zimbaldi, who got more and more confidential with Howard as the days went by. "He gets twelve thousand a week, but that isn't publicized. In these times, it wouldn't sit too well with the public."

"Hard times don't seem to be affecting the studio much," Howard said.

"Business hasn't fallen much yet, because sound is still new enough to make it a novelty to see a talking picture. But we might see some tightening of belts around here soon if conditions in this country don't improve."

Three months after he started to work at Regency Pictures, Howard went with Barney to see the first picture Barney had completed under his contract with Universal, a B comedy that Howard didn't think was very funny, although he thought Barney was very good in his supporting role to W. C. Fields. The sound was good, too—much improved over the squeaky reproduction that had prevailed in 1929.

"Yes, sir," Barney said as they emerged from the theater. "I can't see anything but a beautiful future ahead, Howie."

Howard managed to conceal his envy of Barney's progress, but Barney's success only accentuated his own failure. Being an office boy at Regency Pictures wasn't getting him onto a foot of film. Every day producers and directors walked right past him without seeing him.

"You've done good work, and someday you'll have *my* job," Zimbaldi said to Howard when he'd been at the studio for six months.

The idea was appalling, and Howard considered quitting. It was torture to remain unnoticed while new players were being added to the contract list periodically. Howard was certain that he was as talented as most of them. As for the actors the studio was importing from the New York stage for their good voices and acting ability—necessary qualities for the motion picture performer, now that talkies were here—not many of them had good screen personalities. Yet they were signed and he wasn't.

One evening he stayed late and walked the studio streets, trying to decide what to do. He ended up in the back lot, where he came to his decision on the Western town street, the setting for a noisy gun battle scene that afternoon but now silent in the moonlight. His mind made up, he went back to the office to get his hat. Tomorrow he would tell Zimbaldi he was going to quit.

He was just about to leave when a fluttery man from the story department came in with a scenario that the studio head had ordered brought to his house at once. The man was obviously a new employee who didn't know much about how things were done; he thought mistakenly that someone from the office was supposed to deliver the script.

Howard suddenly had an idea. He decided not to enlighten the man. "I'll take the scenario to Mr. Dalton," he said, and called the studio garage. Since he didn't have a written order from anyone with authority, it took considerable persuasion to obtain a car and driver.

They rolled out into the Hollywood night, with Howard in the back seat, holding the scenario. He liked the idea of being driven by a chauffeur, and he wasn't afraid of what the consequences might be. He'd planned to quit tomorrow anyway, so if this didn't work, it wouldn't make any difference.

The studio chauffeur drove up into the reaches of Beverly Hills where the estates got progressively bigger and grander the farther they went. Finally they reached the Dalton gates and wound up the long driveway between an avenue of trees. The heavy vegetation that screened the house from distant view was suddenly behind them, and a palace appeared before Howard's eyes. Every window was lighted.

Howard clutched the scenario more tightly as a butler opened the door. "Mr. Dalton is expecting this script," he said, and then, when the butler extended his hand for it, added, "I'm supposed to see him personally. I have a message for him."

To his surprise the butler didn't question him but invited him into the large central hall, which had a white marble floor and a staircase that rivaled the one in the "palace" set that had served as part of a royal residence in a recent Regency picture. Howard followed the butler past a pair of tall doors, partly open, that led into a room from which voices murmured. Howard had only a glimpse of the sumptuously furnished room and the group of richly dressed middle-aged persons sitting near a great fireplace.

But Augustus Dalton was not with them. The butler led Howard back beyond the staircase to a large carved door opening onto a library with a magnificent oriental rug on the floor and several oil paintings on the one wall that wasn't occupied by shelves of books from floor

49

to ceiling. Dalton sat in dinner clothes behind a very large carved desk. He looked surprised to see Howard with the butler.

"You could have sent it in," he said. "You didn't have to bring it yourself. Or did you want a look at my house?"

The butler waited, obviously annoyed that he'd been used.

"I had to come in," Howard said unsteadily. "I had to tell you about myself, Mr. Dalton."

"Let me tell you what you want to tell me and save us both time. You're an actor and you think you should have a screen test."

"I'm a *good* actor, Mr. Dalton, and I took a job months ago in your office, hoping that someone inside the studio would notice me and give me a chance."

"That's a new approach," Dalton said without changing his impassive expression, "but not a very good one. And it's a mistake for you to come here and try this. I'm a busy man."

So it hadn't worked. Well, he'd lost nothing, had he? Yet he couldn't remember when he'd felt emptier than he did at this moment.

"I'm sorry I intruded on you, sir," he managed to say, hoping the thickness in his voice wasn't noticeable to Dalton.

"Just a minute," Dalton said as Howard quickly turned to follow the butler out. "What's your name?"

"Howard Stanton," he said, with a final look at the studio head before he walked out. He was sure that Augustus Dalton would not fail to see that he was fired in the morning.

Howard almost decided not to go to work at all the next morning. He considered quitting by mail, even though that was a coward's way out. He expected Zimbaldi to be waiting with a pink slip and a stern lecture when he arrived at the studio, but nothing was different, and the office manager and the rest of the office staff were acting normal. Then Howard realized why the blow hadn't fallen immediately: Dalton never arrived at the studio before ten o'clock.

Ten came and went, and so did ten-thirty.

"What's the matter with you today, Howard?" Zimbaldi asked as the clock inched toward eleven. "You don't seem yourself."

"I haven't been myself any of the time, Mr. Zimbaldi," Howard said, and saw the office manager frown in bewilderment.

Shortly after eleven, the phone on Zimbaldi's desk rang, and Howard watched as the office manager's face showed his growing stupefaction.

"I don't believe it," Zimbaldi said as he hung up his phone receiver. He looked at Howard. "That was Mr. Dalton's personal secretary. Mr

Dalton wants to see you. Now what would he want to see *you* for? How would he even know who you are?"

"We're old friends since last night," Howard said, already halfway to the door. "I guess he wants to fire me personally."

But he didn't really believe that. The studio head would never stoop to firing an office boy personally. No, it must be that Howard's desperate venture last night had worked in his favor after all.

Howard hurried across the street to the administration building and entered the white double doors leading to the studio head's suite. A receptionist sat behind a handsome desk. She sent him through another set of double doors to a larger office, where Dalton's secretary, the formidable Miss Engleman, sat behind an even handsomer desk. Miss Engleman informed Dalton through the intercom box that Howard had arrived, then nodded him through another set of double doors into an office whose extravagant beauty would have made a greater immediate impression on him if his attention hadn't been so arrested by the sight of Dalton and the production chief, Alexander Renfew, sitting there waiting for him. Dalton sat erect in a large leather desk chair behind the largest desk Howard had ever seen. Renfew sat in a deep leather chair beside the desk. The rest of the vast room registered only vaguely in the periphery of Howard's vision, but he was aware of heavy white draperies, many oil paintings on the walls, a giant fireplace, and leather furniture everywhere.

"So this is the fellow who thinks we should give him a screen test," Renfew said harshly as Howard stood uneasily at the desk.

Dalton nodded. "Tell Mr. Renfew why you think we should give you a screen test, Stanton. And please don't use your unusual approach at my house last night as a reason."

"I want a screen test because I can act and because I've got a good voice and because I look good and because I've got star quality." Howard marveled at his own audacity.

Renfew obviously marveled at it, too. "Star quality. Tell me, Stanton, what *is* star quality?"

"Has anyone really been able to define it properly, Mr. Renfew? I just know I've got it."

Renfew laughed. "So you know you've got it." He turned to Dalton. "What he's got is a damned lot of nerve." He looked back at Howard, his eyes angry. "Do you know how many people would like us to give them screen tests, Stanton? Hundreds, thousands. We only give a few dozen a year, and only a small percentage of the people we test get contracts. I can't think of a single good reason why we should give you one."

"I've already given you several good reasons," Howard said. "If you let me get away, you'll be sorry."

"Or perhaps," Dalton said with a smile, "you'll be the one who's sorry."

"And I think," Renfew said, "we *will* let you get away."

But Howard had hardly been back with Zimbaldi for ten minutes when he was called to the phone.

"Mr. Zimbaldi," he said when he hung up, "this will surprise you. I won't be working here much longer. I'm being given a screen test."

9

Howard wondered if Alexander Renfew was trying to ruin him at the outset by giving him a script for his screen test that would show him at his worst. The scene he was handed and told to prepare for quickly—for the test was scheduled for the next day—contained no action and very banal dialogue.

"It's a typical test script," Jack McCall said that evening when Howard frantically went to him for help. "And you're lucky they're letting you see it in advance."

"The production chief wants me to fail," Howard said. "When I met him, hate for me stuck out all over him. He reminds me of my father."

"That's too bad. But maybe you're wrong. Production chiefs have to be tough, Howard. They've got to make the right pictures with the right people or they're soon out of a job."

Yes, he knew that. But he still thought Renfew just plain didn't like him. Still, the important thing was that Augustus Dalton did.

He spent a very bad night and in the morning was sure he had circles under his eyes, but Barney told him it was his imagination.

At the studio it seemed strange to report to the makeup department instead of the office, and he wondered, as a man worked delicately on his face with a makeup brush, whether Zimbaldi had recovered yet from the shock of what had happened. He also wondered if Zimbaldi expected him to come back to his job in the office if he failed his screen test.

No! he told himself as he walked to the stage where the test was to be shot; no matter what resulted from the test, he could never go back to that office again.

The set was simply an ordinary little parlor with a sofa, an armchair, a reproduction of a painting on the wall, and some unstylish tables and lamps, the kind of parlor that could be found in almost any second-class bungalow. Howard didn't like the looks of the set any more than he liked the script, or the fact that he was wearing an ordinary suit for this scene instead of a doublet, plumed hat and boots, or some other dashing costume.

A girl named Kathleen Mintor was being tested with him. He was glad to see that she was far more nervous than he. She was a sexy Denise Carroll type, and she was going to look even sillier playing a housewife than he was going to look playing her husband.

The director was a young man named Forest who seemed uninterested, even bitter, and Howard wondered if he'd been relegated to this job after proving incompetent as an assistant director on feature productions.

They rehearsed the scene quickly. Howard came through the door on the set and kissed the girl. They said a couple of inconsequential things, and then she accused him of not loving her. He argued back that he did. This led to a quarrel. At the end they made up and kissed again.

It wasn't the most exciting material, but Howard hoped they could improve upon it by trying it a few times. He was surprised when Forest ordered the scene shot immediately after the rehearsal was finished.

"But shouldn't we have another rehearsal?" Howard asked. If for no other reason, they needed it to get Kathleen Mintor unwound a little. She was as stiff as a board.

Forest looked at him with open hostility. "No, we shouldn't have another rehearsal," he said coldly. "What do you want to do, lose your spontaneity?"

There was nothing Howard could do but comply, but he had a sinking feeling that this screen test was going to turn out miserably. Still, he couldn't just walk off the set, so he took his place and waited while the electricians shifted the lights and a makeup man appeared to put a few final touches on Kathleen Mintor's beautiful but vacant face. "Light them!" the cameraman called, and the battery of lights went on. Howard blinked for a moment under their awesome brilliance before his eyes became adjusted. "Everybody quiet!" someone said. A boy appeared with a clapboard showing that this was a test of Howard Stanton and Kathleen Mintor.

"Quiet, please. Roll them. Action." Forest gave the final order, and the scene progressed. Howard felt wholly inadequate and extremely nervous, but he wasn't nearly so nervous as Kathleen Mintor was. Her face was damp with perspiration as he kissed her, and her body trembled against him.

The scene was completed in one continuous shot, and then they performed the same action again for close-ups. To Howard, the second and third times seemed worse than the first.

"Wasn't it *awful?*" Kathleen Mintor said after it was finally over.

"Yes," he agreed.

He went to the apartment in Paradise Court and waited. He knew it would be a long time before there would be a decision, for they first had to print the film and show it to the persons who mattered, but he didn't expect it to take days.

On the third day that he sat by the phone waiting, he decided to call Zimbaldi and apologize for walking out the way he had. Zimbaldi had recovered from his initial shock, but he wasn't at all happy about Howard's abrupt departure. The office manager was cool and wary on the phone, but not rude. Obviously he wasn't taking chances. He was no more certain of what Howard's future status would be at Regency Pictures—if there was to be any status at all—than Howard himself was.

The next day the phone finally rang. In an ominous tone of voice, an assistant of Dalton's named Haskell instructed Howard to come to the studio. Haskell turned out to be a tall, thin man of about thirty, with thick steel-rimmed glasses and a commanding air.

"You are to see your test," Haskell said, and took him to a projection room, where they sat side by side while the test was run off.

Howard was in agony from the beginning. He could hardly believe that the person he was watching on the screen was himself. The face he saw up there didn't seem nearly so good as the face he saw in the bathroom mirror. As for his voice, it was godawful. How could he ever have thought it rich and powerful, and how could Jack McCall have said it was? And his acting seemed grotesque! In spite of her empty face, Kathleen Mintor was twice as good as he was, and she was terrible.

It finally ended. Haskell had sat stoically through it, and he made no comment when the lights went up.

"Tell me," Howard said, "has Mr. Dalton seen this test?"

"Of course. So has Mr. Renfew. You don't think they'd let you see it before they did, do you?"

"Has Kathleen Mintor seen it?"

"No, but you needn't let that concern you. You're to come with me now to Mr. Dalton's office."

Howard dreaded facing Dalton, but there was nothing he could do but accompany Haskell. The scene at the studio head's office was the same as before with Dalton behind his desk, Renfew in a chair nearby. Even the hostility in Renfew's eyes was the same.

Dalton simply nodded at Haskell, and the assistant vanished wordlessly. "Sit down, Howard," Dalton said, and waved him to one of the deep leather chairs near his desk.

Howard had never felt more awkward than he did as he crossed the great carpeted expanse to the chair, which somehow seemed a mile away. He wished he could just disappear.

"What did you think of your screen test?" Dalton asked.

Howard shook his head. He couldn't speak.

"Still think you're a great actor with star quality?" Renfew asked with a sardonic smile.

"I think I could be—in time," Howard managed to say.

"Mr. Renfew doesn't think you have a chance," Dalton said. "But I do. Something came across on that screen besides your gaucheness. I'm going to give you a one-year contract and see what you can do. I don't believe I need tell you what will happen if you don't improve a great deal in that period of time."

Howard sat there in numb disbelief.

"You can tell your agent to see us about the terms," Dalton said.

"I don't have an agent," Howard said.

"You'll have to get one. It's part of the game." Dalton paused. "We'll have the contract drawn up at two hundred dollars a week."

Howard nodded, trying to conceal his delight. Two hundred dollars a week was a fortune!

He got an agent whom Jack McCall recommended named Emory Deems. That Jack spoke for him was enough, for Jack was extremely honest. He even admitted to Howard that he couldn't do anything more for him in the way of training, that his future development would now come from actual experience.

"But just because you won't be coming by for lessons anymore," Jack said, "I hope you won't stop coming by altogether."

"Oh, I won't," said Howard.

Jack smiled sadly. "I'm sure you mean that. But when you're a star, you'll change. You'll have a new group of friends."

"No, I won't," Howard assured him, but he thought that Jack was probably right.

55

Emory Deems was young and enthusiastic and, like Howard, a comparative newcomer in the business. They signed a contract for one year, and Emory said, "We'll renew it only if I can improve your lot when your studio contract comes up for renewal. I don't expect you to pay me ten percent unless I can do something for you that you couldn't do for yourself."

Barney was glad about Howard's contract and insisted upon taking him out to celebrate. Along with them went Alice Sanders, the latest in a procession of girls in Barney's life, and a girl friend of Alice's. Howard didn't like the girl, and he didn't have a good time, but he managed not to show it.

Alice, a comedienne with a nightclub act, showed up at Paradise Court with increasing regularity. Barney didn't cut up much when he was around her. The seriousness of the situation became evident one night when Barney said nervously, "Howie, you are about to become a best man."

Howard was prepared to move out of the apartment in Paradise Court after the wedding, but the newlyweds moved instead into a larger apartment on a palm-shaded little street off Hollywood Boulevard. Howard felt lonely only briefly. Actually, it was a relief to be alone.

At the studio he was assigned a small room on the third floor of the dressing room building, where the lesser contract players were quartered. His room was a far cry from the sumptuous suites on the stars' floor, but it was perfectly satisfactory, and he hoped to be moving downstairs in the not-too-distant future anyway.

Very little happened to him during his first six weeks at the studio. He ran into Zimbaldi with embarrassing frequency, and he completed his official biography for the publicity department, which listed his age as twenty-four instead of twenty, the correct figure, and, to give the impression that he had an "adventurous spirit," falsely stated that he'd been a sailor and a cowboy before coming to Hollywood.

"I want to wish you luck," Zimbaldi said rather tensely the first time they met after Howard had signed his contract, and after that, whenever they met they simply nodded and walked on. Howard had an idea that Zimbaldi considered him a traitor.

A week later Howard was told to report to the office of Louis Epstein, the studio's senior producer who was usually in charge of the pictures starring Rex Walters and Denise Carroll, either together or apart.

"I've seen your test," Epstein said. "I think you have possibilities, but you have a long way to go. It's probably foolhardy to consider you for a featured role for your first picture, but we have something here that might be all right for you."

The proposed production was based on a play that had been a recent success on Broadway, about a dashing man-about-Manhattan, his society wife, his mistress, and his younger brother who at the end of the picture takes his mistress away from him. The role of the older brother didn't seem right for Walters, in Howard's eyes, but the star accepted it readily enough. The role of the wife went to Iris Morley, who'd been imported from Broadway because of her fine voice and exceptional acting ability; and the role of the mistress went to Madeline Tremont, who'd been signed to a contract just shortly before Howard had. Her real name, she informed Howard, with whom she was friendly at once, was Susie Fuldheim.

There was tension on the picture from the beginning. Rex Walters developed an immediate antipathy to Iris Morley—probably because she greatly outperformed him—and to Howard. But the picture moved along well, within budget and on time, in spite of Walters' growing sullenness. Howard had only a few scenes, but he worked hard on them and did them well enough to earn a nod of approval from the director, who was known for being choosy about the quality of his actors.

The picture was finally wrapped up, and there was a champagne party on the set to celebrate its completion. Dalton and Renfew dropped in for a few minutes, and Howard was pleased when Dalton singled him out.

"You've done all right with this, Howard. Keep up the good work."

Howard was exuberant. After he had three glasses of champagne, he asked Madeline Tremont if she'd like to go out and do the town with him. She'd had four glasses of champagne herself, so they went straight to her apartment to bed instead.

Madeline confirmed the rumor that Rex Walters took each new contract starlet to bed at least once for testing purposes.

"He took me to the Hollywood Hotel the same week I met him," she confessed. "He must keep a suite there all the time. We went straight up."

Howard was pleased when she told him that he was better in bed than Walters was, for Walters had a reputation for sexual prowess.

Madeline was frank. She called herself a nymphomaniac, and she certainly had a great appetite for sex. Howard learned a lot from her. She had a book describing all possible positions of the sex act. They laughed over the book and tried many of the positions, sometimes unable to finish properly when a particularly ludicrous position sent them into paroxysms of laughter.

Sex was fun between them, and that was all they wanted from it. There was an understanding from the beginning that their relationship would endure only as long as it remained fun. They talked about love only once.

"I'm a lot more interested in becoming a star than falling in love," Madeline said.

"That makes two of us," Howard said.

"There's nothing that hurts more than love going wrong," Madeline went on, looking serious for the first time since he'd known her. "I know from experience."

"So do I," Howard said, and turned away from her, thinking of Jeanette Bixby, the only person he'd ever loved, the girl he'd dreamed of marrying and bringing to Hollywood, where they would reign as screenland's new "king and queen." But Jeanette had preferred a lowborn type from the Lower East Side, and it had ripped him apart. It still pained him to remember it.

He wanted no more of that kind of hurt. He just wanted to be a big star, loved by everybody, loving nobody. He turned back to Madeline. "Let's fuck," he said.

After the picture was released and the fan mail started coming in, the studio decided that Howard and Madeline should be seen together in public for publicity purposes.

"This will just make it more convenient, since we'd be seeing each other anyway," Howard told her with a laugh.

They'd both come out well with the reviewers, and so had Iris Morley. But Rex Walters hadn't. Howard worried that Walters wouldn't like his having won praise in a small role while he himself had been disparaged. Walters might see that Howard was held back.

But that worry lessened considerably when Augustus Dalton phoned Howard one Friday morning and asked him to his estate for the weekend.

10

Augustus Dalton's weekend gatherings at his estate in Beverly Hills were sometimes likened to William Randolph Hearst's at San Simeon, although they were on a much smaller scale. Howard was greatly surprised to be invited. Minor contract players were seldom on the guest list, which was usually dominated by stars, directors and producers, top novelists and playwrights, and sometimes segments of European royalty.

But that weekend Howard found himself the solitary guest.

"I hope you don't mind," Dalton said. "There are times when I don't feel like having a lot of people around. I thought this might be a good chance for Mrs. Dalton and me to get to know you better."

Howard was delighted that they would want to know him better. He was given a handsome room furnished in heavy dark pieces. The room was wonderfully masculine. Eunice Dalton seemed to sense that it was just right for him, for it proved to be his room for all subsequent weekends he spent at the estate.

The house was incredibly beautiful. "Forty-four rooms," Eunice Dalton told him when she took him on a tour of the house. He liked her immediately. She was dignified yet warm. He thought she would make a good mother, though there were no Dalton children.

They sat beside the swimming pool late Saturday afternoon after Howard had swum its length a few times to show Dalton the handsomeness of his physique.

"What do your parents think of your chosen career?"

His parents. He didn't like to be reminded of them. They'd given him very little but coldness and disapproval in his boyhood, and he could remember no unqualifiedly happy times they'd spent together as a family.

But there was no use trying to explain to Dalton what he didn't understand himself. He said evasively, "We haven't talked much about it, but they don't like it."

Dalton smiled. "My father didn't approve of my going into the

59

motion picture exhibiting business, either. He wanted me to be a lawyer.''

But even without his father's help, Augustus Dalton had managed to get backing to open his own theater in 1915. The following year he formed a partnership with another ambitious man, Nicholas Smetley. By 1920 they owned six theaters, two of them large houses in New York City. The next year, they owned twelve.

"We soon faced the same problem that Fox, Mayer, and other exhibitors had already faced," Dalton said. "We were going to have to produce pictures to show in our theaters or close down."

So Regency Pictures had been formed in 1922, and Augustus Dalton had come to Hollywood to run the studio, while Nicholas Smetley remained in New York as the final arbiter in the company.

"I hope I'm not boring you with all this," Dalton said.

"It's very interesting," Howard said.

"I thought you'd be interested, although most actors are interested only in themselves. They don't seem to realize that this is the most fascinating business in the world."

Howard carried away with him that weekend an invitation to come back the following weekend, and the feeling that Augustus and Eunice Dalton somehow looked upon him as the son they wished they had.

"Oh, God, oh, God!" Madeline moaned.

Howard kissed her nipples again and tongued her skin down to her stomach. Then he straddled her near her face, and she took him into her mouth and worked his penis with her lips. They had both found this position especially stimulating, and the sensation was so intense that he soon had to withdraw or it would have been all over entirely too quickly.

He lay on top of her for a while then, just kissing her, not going into her immediately, but she soon urged him to finish it.

"I'm so hot I'll burn up if you don't fuck me this instant!"

He wasn't embarrassed by her frankness anymore. He entered her and they writhed together for a few moments before they came. Then they lay back, breathing heavily.

"It's wonderful when we do it," she said after a while. Her hand came over and rested on his groin. "That's a beautiful thing you have there, and it's getting hard again."

"What do you expect, with you touching it like that?"

"Let's do it again, right now."

"But I couldn't come again this soon."

It wasn't true, as he found out less than five minutes later.

There were three other guests besides Howard at the Dalton estate his second weekend there. One was Alexander Renfew, who stayed overnight both Friday and Saturday. Howard felt uncomfortable with Renfew around. He couldn't shake his feeling that the production chief didn't like him and wouldn't hesitate to try to curb his progress at the studio.

He was also a little uncomfortable with the other two guests: Norman Sutter, the New York playwright, who was by reputation and behavior a pansy; and Elizabeth Beck, Eunice Dalton's niece. Elizabeth was a recent graduate of Bryn Mawr, and Howard's immediate fear was that the Daltons hoped he might develop an interest in her.

She was a plain-looking and dignified girl, as conservatively dressed as her aunt and uncle. Howard felt uneasy that they didn't have anything in common to talk about, but it didn't seem to bother her. She contributed something to his education that weekend by pointing out various Monets, Renoirs, and Matisses on the walls that he couldn't have identified on his own.

"These are the best of the Impressionists," she said. "My aunt and uncle have such fine taste! It's really very difficult to identify them with Hollywood."

She was obviously a snob, but that didn't matter to him as long as she didn't get any romantic ideas about him. Or sexual ones. He couldn't imagine going to bed with a mousey stick like her who didn't even wear lipstick.

She continued his education by having him roam the lavish rooms of the house with her while she identified the periods of furniture in them, mentioning such terms as Regency and Louis Quatorze, which he promptly forgot. Finally they parted to change into swimming suits, then met again by the pool. She wore a plain black suit that accentuated her own plainness and the flatness of her figure. But she seemed no more impressed with his figure than he was with hers, although Norman Sutter, ostensibly listening to Renfew talk on the other side of the pool, apparently was. But Howard had no fear of Sutter. When the playwright's eyes had asked the silent but obvious question earlier, Howard had answered by turning his own eyes away. He knew Sutter wouldn't pursue the matter. Intelligent homosexuals took "no" for an answer without question.

The dramatist's new play had been purchased by Regency Pictures, and during dinner Dalton spent most of his time trying to persuade Sutter to write the screenplay version.

Sutter laughed and shook his head. "Hollywood just isn't for me.

Making pictures is a matter of collaboration, and I couldn't collaborate comfortably. I'm simply too independent for it. I couldn't stand seeing my work pieced in with the work of other writers and then refashioned still further by producers and directors. No, not even for all your beautiful, shining Hollywood gold."

After dinner, Howard went for a stroll with Elizabeth in the garden.

"I admire Norman Sutter," she said. "He refuses to be lured by the false life out here."

"It's a good life," Howard said defensively.

"It's all glitter and no substance. What do people do here but eat, drink, and talk pictures? I think it's so tiresome!"

He didn't answer her.

"Really, Aunt Eunice and Uncle Augustus don't fit in with it at all. They're cultured and educated. They're not like the rest of the Hollywood hierarchy." She looked at him. "I have a feeling you're terribly unsuited for it, too. Oh, Howard, there's so much that's exciting and worthwhile to be learned in life! Don't get trapped in this nothingness!"

He didn't know what she was talking about, and he didn't really care. "I'm content with the way things are going."

They'd made a circle of the garden and had reached the pool. They stopped there, and when she moved a little closer to him, he knew she wanted him to touch her. She was interested in sex after all.

But fortunately they were called into the house then for the showing of a new and elaborate musical from Metro-Goldwyn-Mayer.

"We have our own personality at Regency Pictures," Dalton said, "but we like to know what the competition is doing, too."

That night, as Howard lay in bed, he wondered if Elizabeth was waiting for him to come to her in the pink Marie Antoinette guest room down the hall. He hoped not, but the possibility kept him awake. An hour later his door opened and her spindly shadow appeared against the light from the hall. She hesitated, then entered and closed the door behind her, crossing ever so slowly to the bed, where he lay wondering helplessly what to do.

She leaned down over him. He couldn't see her very well, but he thought he detected fear in her widened eyes. "You wouldn't come to me, so I came to you," she said, her voice edged with tension, daring him to send her away.

It was certainly what he wanted to do, but he couldn't, for she was the Daltons' niece, and Augustus Dalton controlled his destiny. He would have to go through with this and pretend that he liked it and hope that sex would be enough to satisfy her; that she wouldn't want romance, too.

He forced himself to reach out and feel her thigh. It felt as bony as it looked. "Take off your nightgown and come to bed," he said with difficulty.

She dropped her nightgown while he slipped out of his pajamas. She got into bed and lay flat on her back beside him, her arms rigid at her sides. He was glad he could hardly see her, and he was glad she didn't reach for his penis right away, the way Madeline always did, for he wasn't hard. It was the first time he'd ever been in bed with a girl and hadn't gotten immediately hard. He knew it was because he didn't like her and didn't want her.

But he had to do something, so he bent over and kissed her. Her lips were dry. He stroked her skin, and it was dry, too.

He felt her small breast. He knew he didn't want to suck her nipples any more than he wanted to kiss her lips or go into her.

His hand went down. Her vagina felt much the same as the others he'd felt, a little triangle of hair over a mound of skin with a slit, but the lips were smaller, and it didn't respond to his fingers the way the others had. It seemed to be shutting him out rather than inviting him in, and he wondered if she really wanted to go on.

But she didn't say anything, and somehow he had to get hard and perform. He closed his eyes and thought about screwing Madeline. He even thought about screwing Jeanette Bixby, whom he'd wanted so much to make love to and never had. The hot little scenes in his mind made him hard.

He spread Elizabeth's legs, entered her, and lay flat on her, his face against hers, his eyes still closed. She was very tight down there, and he wondered if she was a virgin and if there would be blood when he withdrew. Oh, how he hated this and wished it would end quickly! She didn't seem to be responding, but whether it was out of inexperience or lack of pleasure he couldn't tell.

He managed to come. He lay panting against her for just a moment, then withdrew and lay beside her. There didn't seem to be any blood, but that was the only good thing about it.

There hadn't been a sound out of her all through it. Now she said, "I can't stay all night."

He'd expected anything but a remark like that. "No, you shouldn't," he responded quickly. "We might get caught."

She got out of bed and pulled on her nightgown, saying, "You thought I didn't know you were pretending I was someone else."

"I wasn't."

"Yes, you were," she said. "We won't have to talk about this in the morning. We'll pretend it didn't happen."

In the morning he told the Daltons he wasn't feeling well and left before Elizabeth appeared. He didn't see her the next weekend, either. Eunice Dalton said that her niece had decided to cut her visit short and return home sooner than expected. Howard found it hard not to show how relieved he was.

11

Howard was cast next in a college musical, which the studio hoped would start a cycle of simple musicals that could be produced on low budgets by omitting the big production numbers that had proved so costly in *Regency on Parade*. Howard's role was second in importance only to that of the lead, Ron Baxter, but in his view being cast in a B picture after starting his career in an A production wasn't really making progress.

"You must always remember," Dalton said, guessing Howard's doubts, "that every picture gives you added experience, and it's broad experience more than innate ability that polishes an actor. Furthermore, you must realize that if you become a star, it will take more than one picture to make you one. You don't become a star without a following, and you don't get a following until you've had sufficient exposure."

That seemed logical enough, and Howard tried to inject enthusiasm into his performance even though he didn't like the script or his role. He found working with Ron Baxter much easier than working with Rex Walters, but Ron wasn't a star of Walters' magnitude, and he could afford to let other cast members give good performances.

But if Howard felt at ease with Ron, he didn't with Timothy Briggs, who had a smaller role than Howard but was obviously going to do a lot with it. Briggs had made his initial success as a juvenile on the New York stage in one of Norman Sutter's plays. The story went that Sutter had gotten Briggs into the play, whatever that might mean. But the

64

playwright could not have had anything to do with Briggs' talent. He was a good actor. And he had a radiant kind of blond good looks.

"I don't think my competition at Regency five years from now will be Rex Walters," Howard told Barney one evening when he was visiting him and Alice. "I think it will be Tim Briggs."

"I think my competition is and will remain W. C. Fields," Barney said. "Lloyd and Chaplin have yet to make their first talkies, but when they do, they'll fall flat on their faces. You'll see."

Howard was silent. He wouldn't dream of saying so, but there was no doubt in his mind that Barney was completely outclassed by a genius like Chaplin.

He left earlier than he'd expected to, discontented with the evening. He didn't enjoy being with Barney as much as he had before. Barney's marriage and the lengthening periods between contacts seemed to be affecting their friendship. Yet aside from Barney, Howard hadn't found any lasting friends in his three years in Hollywood.

Still, what did it matter? He didn't need close relationships. All he needed in his life was movie stardom. And he had an increasingly optimistic feeling, from the way Dalton seemed to like him and was pushing him along, that it would soon be in his grasp.

Howard's first car was a 1931 Model A Ford roadster with a rumble seat and spoke wheels. It was a far cry from the Duesenberg touring brougham with fancy wire wheels that Rex Walters usually showed up in at the studio, but Howard intended to have one of those, or something superior to it, as soon as he could. In the meantime he drove the roadster around the hills to see the great estates of movie people and dreamed of owning a big place himself when he was a star.

One day he drove up to Falcon Lair and spoke to the caretaker, who told him that the place had been empty since Valentino's death, although someone had made a down payment on it several years ago but had never completed the deal.

"I don't blame him," the caretaker said. "It's a haunted place. A lot of people feel *him* still around."

Howard didn't believe in such nonsense, although the story went that Valentino himself had believed in it. The idea of ghosts wouldn't have kept Howard from wanting to own the estate, as he once had. What kept him from wanting it now was a lessening of interest in the whole Valentino idea. It embarrassed him now that he had tried so hard to emulate Valentino. Much had changed in the five years since Valentino had died, and the extreme romanticism the star had represented seemed outmoded and unreal in these times.

65

Besides, Howard became convinced that his mirror and his personal conception of himself had been deceiving. He was Howard Stanton, not some diluted Valentino, and that was all right. In Hollywood you made it not because you were like someone else but because you had your own brand of personal magnetism, and because you got the breaks and developed a following.

Howard was developing a following. His first picture had brought him considerable fan mail, the college picture even more. He dropped in periodically at the fan mail department to read some of the letters that had come in for him, most of them requesting his autographed picture. The girls in the department said they could tell from his mail that he was going to be Regency Pictures' next big star. But he wondered whether Tim Briggs got as much fan mail as he did. He was afraid to ask.

In 1931, Regency Pictures had a dozen stars, headed by Rex Walters and Denise Carroll, and almost a hundred featured contract players, a score of whom hoped to be stars themselves someday, the remainder being character actors who would never be stars but whose careers promised to endure longer than the average of seven years allotted to movie people in general.

"We are bettered in our contract list and physical plant only by M-G-M," Dalton said one weekend. "We're exceeded in theater ownership only by Loew's and Paramount. Where we go from here depends on us. The industry got complacent in the mid-twenties, and even the top producers were turning out mediocre stuff on the theory that in prosperous times the public would go to see anything. It was a theory I never subscribed to, and I was proved right. Sound saved us and brought the audience back to the theaters, from which it had begun to flee. But sound won't continue to save us. Only good pictures will. Our country is going through painful times, Howard. Last year there were over four million people unemployed. This year it will certainly get worse. Hollywood people like to blind themselves to facts like that. I refuse to hide from them."

Howard was pleased that Dalton continued to take him into his confidence. It had become a pattern for him to be invited to the Dalton estate on alternate weekends, and he became increasingly and genuinely fond of Augustus and Eunice Dalton. The weekend gatherings were stimulating, and Howard was glad that he was usually the only actor on the guest list. Hollywood was entirely too clannish. Generally, producers mixed with other producers, directors with other directors, actors with other actors. Howard saw plenty of other actors

66

during the week. He used his weekends to broaden himself. Besides, he was meeting important people at Dalton's that he wouldn't have met otherwise. He certainly didn't like all of them, but he pretended he did. It was necessary to make as good an impression as possible on important people in Hollywood, because you never knew whose help you might need next. Howard didn't intend to let any opportunities slip out of his grasp.

Dalton's favoritism caused some resentment among stars and lesser lights on the studio's contract list. Unfriendly stories circulated about the frequency of Howard's visits to the Dalton estate, and he supposed that the stories would have been even more vicious if so many of the disgruntled hadn't stood in fear of the consequences they might suffer if they incurred Dalton's displeasure.

"I don't care what they say," Howard said to Madeline when she reported some of the nastier things being said about him, the least offensive being that he was playing Dalton for a giant fool in opportunistic moves to get to the top.

But he did care. He wanted Rex Walters and Alexander Renfew and other important people around the studio to respect him, even if they didn't like him. He didn't want them thinking he was using Dalton, although he realized he was. Dalton seemed to think of him as the son he'd never had, and Howard was playing on that feeling. But in addition he sincerely liked the older man.

He knew the talk would really sizzle when, after he'd been with the studio just a year, he was awarded a choice role that could just as logically have gone to Tim Briggs or any of several other young men around the studio who were talented and attractive.

"I think *The Young Soldier* could very well be the making of you," Dalton said the weekend he revealed the exciting news to him. "Renfew felt you'd be better for the second lead, but I disagreed."

As it turned out, Tim Briggs was assigned the second lead, and since Tim was a fine actor, Howard would have to work all the harder to make a favorable showing. The studio was spending a lot of money on this production, and Howard knew that although the picture could be the making of him, it could just as easily be the breaking of him if his performance didn't stack up.

Still, everything seemed in favor of the gods' being on his side, and on the studio's side, with this picture. As Dalton pointed out, the public was predisposed to favorable reception of a war picture because of the recent great success of *All Quiet on the Western Front*. Besides, the story had been received enthusiastically by the public, first in book form, then on the Broadway stage the previous season.

"The same emotions are involved here," said Dalton, "as in *All Quiet*. The difference is, the lead in that one was German, and you are an American soldier. You'll have wonderful opportunities for acting."

Dalton was right. The young soldier was a coward who found his courage in the end, only to be killed in the last battle of the war. The part called for a level of acting that Howard wasn't sure he was up to. Lew Ayres had come across with just the right quality of pathos in *All Quiet on the Western Front*, and Howard hoped he could do as well. But he wasn't confident that he could. He'd convinced himself, during his instruction from Jack McCall, that he'd become a good actor, but now he wasn't at all sure that was true.

The director on *The Young Soldier*, Herman Small, was a martinet and a perfectionist, and that, as Dalton told Howard one weekend, was why his pictures were so good. To get the perfection he demanded, he would shoot twenty takes of a scene if necessary. It was impossible for him to keep within a budget or on schedule, but the pictures that resulted were worth the extra expense and prolonged shooting. They were beautifully photographed and ingeniously edited. And, miraculously, they were a successful union of art and commerce.

Three weeks before the picture started, Small talked to Howard about preparation for his role.

"We have to create the illusion that you're a soldier," he said. "Actual experience would be your best background for this, but you were in knee pants when the war was on."

"I think I have a feeling for what it's like from war movies I've seen."

"There've been some good war pictures and some good interpretations of soldiering," Small said. "I'm thinking especially of John Gilbert in *The Big Parade* and Lew Ayres in *All Quiet on the Western Front*. Aim for doing as well as they did. Shoot for something big, and it's easier. Read *The Red Badge of Courage* and imagine yourself as the youth. That's based on the Civil War, but the character has the same qualities and problems this young soldier has. *Think* yourself a soldier, and you'll do a good job."

Howard tried to the limit. He cut out his social life completely—which considerably annoyed Madeline—and spent his evenings going over the takes for the next day, trying for the best nuances possible as he rehearsed, a little self-consciously, before a mirror.

The final scene was shot on a hot day in August. Afterward there was a champagne party on the set at which virtually everyone, including the demanding Herman Small, congratulated Howard on a job well done.

12

Howard had chosen to see none of the daily rushes of *The Young Soldier,* but he accepted Dalton's invitation to see the rough cut in projection room one. He was the only actor present. Besides Dalton and himself, the other viewers were Renfew, Small, the producer, the assistant producer, and the studio's publicity director.

The lights dimmed, and Howard gripped the arms of his velvet-covered seat and prepared for the worst. He continued to sit up straight in his chair through the first scene, which showed Howard saying good-by to his girl before leaving for army camp.

A few minutes later, when that scene faded to the next, Howard's tenseness subsided. He felt it was going to be all right. He looked right and he sounded right, and the picture was working. A few more scenes into the picture he was sure, and he gave silent thanks to Small. The care that the director had taken showed subtly in every scene, and he'd drawn maximum efforts from the whole cast.

After a sneak preview in Pasadena brought enthusiastic audience response, relatively few changes were made in the final cut, and the picture was premiered at Grauman's Egyptian Theatre in Hollywood six weeks later. When it opened in New York and other major cities in subsequent days, the reviews were favorable. To Howard and Tim, the important observation a number of reviewers made was that with *The Young Soldier* two new stars had been born.

Howard's fan mail tripled almost immediately after the picture went into general release, and if it kept on growing he would reach the point where he would have to have a special secretary to handle it instead of the staff of the fan mail department. Reviews from cities all over the country were clipped in the publicity department, where a clerk mounted clippings in a special pressbook for him. He was becoming famous; he was becoming important.

Dalton withdrew him from the next picture he'd been scheduled to do. "We'll hold you for a better role. You've made a hit, so it's important we don't disappoint the public with your next picture. I've seen potential stars ruined by being rushed into the wrong vehicles."

Howard was idle for the next two months. He filled in the time learning to ride and improving his fencing. Tim Briggs was his frequent companion on horseback rides and was an able fencing opponent. Howard had been uneasy about Tim when they'd worked on the college musical together, particularly after the word got around about Tim's sexual predilection for men. But they'd become friendly during the shooting of *The Young Soldier* after Tim made it clear that though he would enjoy a sexual relationship with Howard, he was more interested in being his friend. Recently Tim had told Howard that he was going to marry his high school sweetheart from Nebraska. Howard hoped that meant he was going to give up the dangerous homosexual existence he'd been leading in Hollywood.

Howard's riding and fencing sessions with Tim ended when Dalton asked him along on a trip to New York. Dalton was going there to consult with Nicholas Smetley, the chairman of the board, for a few days, and he suggested that Howard might like a look at his hometown after his long absence. Howard felt no urge to see New York right then, but he supposed he had to face his parents again sometime, and it would be easier to do it now that he'd scored his first big success in the movies.

Besides, the trip would give him a chance to know Dalton even better, although they'd be calling him an opportunist more loudly than ever around the studio since the word got out. He'd heard that Rex Walters had scornfully labeled him an "ass kisser." Someday he hoped to make Walters eat those words, though in a sense they were true. Although he continued to like Dalton more and more, and through him was at last learning what a good father-son relationship could be like, he recognized that he was using him more and more, too. He reasoned that he'd be a fool not to take advantage of any chance to better himself through his growing influence on Dalton. After all, how many people in Hollywood were lucky enough to have a studio head take such great personal interest in them?

They took the Super Chief from Pasadena to Chicago and the Twentieth Century Limited on to New York. Dalton occupied the largest compartments available on both trains. Howard spent more time in Dalton's compartment than he did in his own on the whole trip, and the two men became even closer than before.

It seemed incredible to Howard that the countryside rolling by was the same countryside he'd seen a few years ago coming the opposite way. It looked so different. Maybe it seemed different because these were different times. Dalton talked soberly about them.

70

"I refuse to close my eyes to national problems the way some people do in our industry. People are on public relief, and people are selling apples on corners. They are not attending Regency theaters at the level they were in 1929 and early in 1930. It didn't seem as if things could get worse than they had by the end of 1930, but they have. Someone must be elected next year who will save this country. Otherwise, we'll all go down the drain."

Nicholas Smetley's chauffeur met them at the station in New York and drove them to the Park Avenue apartment the studio maintained for Regency executives and stars when they came east on business. The place was opulently decorated and furnished, and the feeling of it contrasted greatly with the general feeling of the city, just as the well-dressed and apparently happy men and women on Park, Fifth, and Madison avenues seemed so unlike the shabby, desperate-looking people away from that part of town. It gave an entirely different impression of hard times from what Howard had experienced in Hollywood, where the shabbiness, when it was present at all, was concealed in fantasy.

He waited two days before he called his parents, and that evening he went to see them. Not surprisingly, nothing had changed in the brownstone apartment where he'd grown up. It was still furnished with the same dark furniture and still permeated with the same dark atmosphere. Walking in, seeing his parents in the familiar cheerless environment, he was assailed with a rush of unwanted memories of his childhood and adolescence. He saw himself alone, avoiding them and being avoided by them. They had never wanted him and he had never wanted them; it came down to that.

The greeting was awkward. He couldn't remember ever shaking his father's hand before. The handshake didn't last long. He kissed his mother's cheek very briefly. Her cheek was rigid, her skin cool. They both looked unchanged, middle-aged and handsome, and it occurred to him that at least he could thank them for passing along their fine looks to him, if for little else.

It surprised him when his mother said they'd gone to see *The Young Soldier* and thought he was good in it.

"I'm glad you liked it," he said, and looked at his father, wishing for a miracle, wishing his father would say that now they understood why he'd run away to Hollywood. But his father didn't say that, and Howard realized he never would, even if Howard became as great a star as Douglas Fairbanks in his heyday.

What his father did say was that the executives at the bank had taken a ten percent cut last year and would have to take another ten percent this year, and that they all prayed the bank wouldn't have to close, as

71

hundreds had throughout the country since the crash. And on and on. His father's life was the bank—he didn't have anything else to talk about—and throughout the recital Howard kept remembering that the bank would have become *his* life if he hadn't run away from that fate.

His parents didn't ask about his life in Hollywood, and he didn't offer to tell them about it. Howard was glad to leave them after an hour and return to the comforting company of Dalton. He almost tried to talk with Dalton about his strange, loveless relationship with his parents, but nothing came out. He supposed he would never be able to talk with anyone about it.

Howard was a little disappointed that Dalton didn't ask him to go along to one of his several meetings with Nicholas Smetley.

"You're not big enough yet," Dalton said. "Smetley doesn't like actors, and he refuses to meet any but the biggest stars. He comes to Hollywood once or twice a year for short business visits, and if, as we hope, you become really big, he'll ask to meet you. You won't like him. He's eminently unlikable. I dislike him myself. Always have."

"Yet you were partners in business for years, and you started Regency Pictures together."

"Of course. And now he controls slightly more Regency stock than I do, and I suppose he could topple me if he wanted to. But he doesn't want to. We may not like each other, but we work well together. Sometimes men who don't like each other work better together than men who are friends. He runs the business end well, and I run the studio end well. Each of us would prefer to do it all alone, but neither of us could. Even Caesars need help, Howard."

Dalton was silent for a long moment.

"I suppose you remember that Caesar was betrayed. I don't intend to be, Howard. Not ever."

During the next three years Howard's stature in Hollywood increased steadily. He made four pictures each year from 1932 to 1934, and most of them were well received. His contract was renegotiated each year in line with the growing box office returns of his pictures, and in 1933 he moved into a large apartment on Hollywood Boulevard and acquired a valet. When he bought a house in Beverly Hills a year later he also acquired a Swedish couple to serve as cook and gardener and a set of black Alsatians which guarded his property with the ferocity of lions. His garage held a new Pierce-Arrow.

That year he was making as much money as Clark Gable, and a secretary worked on his fan mail full time. When he made a costume picture based on a Rafael Sabatini novel, he was at last able to show his flashing style with a sword, and when the reviews came out, he found himself likened to Douglas Fairbanks at his peak a decade earlier in *The Mark of Zorro*.

Howard was quite aware that the Depression continued out there, albeit somewhat alleviated by the emergency measures taken by Franklin D. Roosevelt, but he felt remote from it.

The motion picture industry had been having its own economic troubles, but it was running. Radio Pictures had avoided bankruptcy through the popularity of Fred Astaire and Ginger Rogers. Mae West had rescued Paramount. Shirley Temple and Will Rogers had saved Fox, and *Frankenstein* and *Dracula,* Universal. M-G-M had weathered bad times, and Regency Pictures had scarcely faltered under the guidance of Augustus Dalton and Nicholas Smetley. Regency wasn't even affected when, after 1932, the Production Code was enforced.

"We've always made clean pictures," Dalton said. "We'll continue to do so."

But the studio was disturbed about the unfavorable reputation Hollywood had as a Sodom, and sought only "clean" publicity in these sensitive times. Morals clauses were inserted into all contracts, and Dalton made it plain that they would be enforced.

Howard wasn't worried about himself on that score. He felt no urge to try dope or to make love to children. His life as a star was quieter than it had been before. His greatest enjoyment was in the home his success had acquired for him, and he was at home more than most stars were. He spent far fewer weekends at Dalton's than before, but there seemed little lessening of the closeness between them.

Other relationships changed considerably. He'd stopped seeing Madeline Tremont a few months before she married an assistant producer at another studio. Regency Pictures hadn't picked up her option, and Howard doubted that another studio would sign her, since she'd failed to make a hit with the public.

Howard's relationship with Barney changed even more drastically. Universal failed to pick up Barney's option, and his agent couldn't get him placed with any other studio. Howard found it harder and harder to stop by and see his old friend, for Barney was becoming increasingly depressed. He'd aged a decade in the last year.

"What the hell," he said on one occasion. "All good comedians are natural-born pessimists, Howie. Before you can be funny, you've got to be morbid. I ought to be hilarious from now on. My wife went home to her mother."

Barney's wife never returned, and Barney left Hollywood soon after, heading for New York and, he hoped, the big time. He wouldn't accept the money Howard offered to lend him.

"But I promise I'll keep in touch, buddy," he said, and then disappeared from Howard's life.

Howard felt a certain guilty relief that Barney had left. Things had changed between them in recent years because things had changed for them. They'd started out at the same end of the spectrum and were now at opposite ends.

Howard's closest friend now was Tim, who fenced with him, rode horseback with him, and taught him to hunt. When Tim took up flying, he wanted Howard to try it, too.

"No, it scares me," Howard said honestly. "I get dizzy just looking down from a tall building."

Tim's marriage was well into its third year, and he seemed happy with Phyllis, the bride he'd brought back from his hometown. They'd bought a small ranch out in the San Fernando Valley and had settled down to what appeared to be a stable existence. If Tim was pursuing any homosexual interests on the side, Howard didn't know about them.

Tim was doing well at the studio, too, ranking just behind Howard—who ranked second only to Rex Walters—in box office returns among Regency's male stars. Denise Carroll maintained her lead among the women.

"But we need a prestige female star," Dalton told Howard one evening when they were having dinner together. "We need a Dietrich or a Garbo. Have you ever seen Leni Liebhaber?"

"I've seen stills of her. She's beautiful."

"And exciting. She's the Germans' biggest star, you know. She's even Hitler's favorite." He smiled. "Liebhaber isn't her real name. It was chosen for her by a director. It means 'lover' in German."

" 'Lover,' " Howard repeated. "It sounds as if it fits her."

Dalton nodded. "I think it would be worthwhile for me to make a personal trip to Berlin to try to sign her."

74

13

While Dalton was in Europe, Howard's mother died, and Howard wondered, after learning that there'd been no physical illness involved, whether she'd simply given up the struggle because she found life intolerable after fifty years of bitterness and unfulfillment. Howard wished he could cry for her, for a person who had never found happiness deserved tears, but he couldn't. He'd never loved her in life, and he couldn't love her now, as he looked at her for the last time, serene against the white satin lining of her coffin.

A few months later, while Dalton was still in Europe, there was another telegram, and Howard went east again, this time to bury his father. He felt even less inclination to cry this time. As he stood before the coffin, he was ashamed to find himself relieved that he would never have to worry again about what his father thought of him.

He was surprised at the large number who turned out at the funeral home to pay their last respects to his father: an unexpected revelation that this dour, intractable man had been well respected, perhaps even liked, by his associates at the bank.

Howard wasn't surprised at his father's will, which left him one dollar, with the estate designated for distant relatives. He was glad about it. His attitude was that he wanted nothing from his father in death, since his father had wanted nothing for him in life.

"But don't you want anything as a remembrance?" an ancient cousin named Genevieve, who'd been left the household things, asked him as he prepared to leave the old apartment for the last time.

"No," said Howard, and walked out. He wanted no memory of any of it. He didn't even want to see the front of that brownstone ever again—or the street or the neighborhood.

Back at his hotel, he lay awake wondering about his incapacity to feel deeply for others. There was no denying that he *wanted* to be unloving and unloved, to remain self-contained. Despite his special relationships with Dalton, Tim, and Barney, he still kept a certain distance between himself and each of them. He supposed that some of this was rooted in the absence of normal family feeling as he was growing up. He wasn't sure. But his continuing doubts made him wonder if he would ever love anyone enough to want to marry. He supposed the studio would rather he didn't. A romantic lead was a better box office draw if he was a bachelor.

He had a hard time getting to sleep that night, but in the morning he was all right again. He made arrangements to fly back to California that day. It was his first flight, and he forgot his initial nervousness soon after they were aloft. He decided that the trip to the Coast by air was quite remarkable. With stops in Chicago, Tulsa, and Salt Lake City, the flight took only eighteen hours.

News awaited him that the property he wanted in Malibu was now available, and he bought it immediately. It was a small white beach house on a level and a half built into a hill, with a jagged set of steps leading from a sun deck down to the beach below.

Dalton returned from Europe after signing Leni Liebhaber and the director with whom she'd made her best pictures, Karl Gurtner.

"Oh, I know the dreary experiences most studios have suffered from importing foreign directors, and that's why we've avoided them at Regency," Dalton said. "Most foreign directors can't make good American pictures, but is that really surprising? You take a man out of his familiar surroundings and stick him where he doesn't really belong, and what can you expect? But I couldn't get Leni Liebhaber without taking Gurtner, too, so I signed them both. I was lucky to get her under any conditions—she's definitely Hitler's pet."

"Do you mean she goes to bed with him?"

"No, I don't think so. But Hitler admires her tremendously as an artist. Anyway, we're lucky to get her. And Gurtner, too, I suppose. If they can do for us what Dietrich and von Sternberg have done for Paramount, we'll be all right."

Howard asked Dalton to come out and see his place at Malibu, and the studio head had his chauffeur drive him out one Sunday. He looked as dignified as a Wall Street banker stepping out from the hulking Rolls Royce, which looked completely out of place sitting behind the small beach house.

"Cozy and in good taste," was Dalton's comment about the place. "Taste is one of your hallmarks, Howard. It's an unpurchasable asset, so be glad you were born with it. It's like being a star. Either you are or you aren't. I'm glad you are."

Howard nodded. "It's wonderful, and it's going to get better. You'll see. I'm going to be bigger than Walters."

"That will be something for the public to decide," Dalton said.

76

"Rex Walters has made a great deal of money for Regency Pictures. He's still king."

"But he's a drinker, and he's getting worse."

"Big stars have been drinkers before. I'm not willing to write Rex off yet. We have a big investment in him, and he has a big investment in himself."

"I'm going to topple him from his so-called throne, no matter how," Howard said.

"You really want to be king, don't you? So badly that it's probably the first thing you think of when you wake up in the morning. And you want it just for yourself." Dalton smiled. "I guess we could call that the ultimate in ego."

"I suppose so."

"You don't want to be anyone's husband or lover or anything," Dalton went on. "You just want to belong to yourself."

Howard knew that Dalton was speaking only reflectively, not critically, and he didn't resent his observations.

"You're wrong," Howard said. "I want to belong to my fans."

"Not belong to them," Dalton said, smiling. "Just be worshipped by them. But don't get me wrong, Howard. I understand."

"Yes, you do. And you especially understand ego. Let me ask you a simple question. For whom did you build Regency Pictures?"

"For myself," Dalton answered.

Howard didn't understand why his new picture kept being postponed until he was summoned to Dalton's office one day and found that he was to go into an entirely different production. Renfew was there. So were Rex Walters and Tim Briggs. Tim smiled at Howard, but Walters simply looked away.

"We're going to do a very big picture," Dalton said. "It hasn't been publicly announced yet, but we've succeeded in purchasing *Westward the Men*. I don't know whether any of you have read this book, but you should. It's an epic rendering of the winning of the West. It's had wider readership than any other book in the last two years. That makes a bigger audience for us. Not that we wouldn't have a big audience with it anyway. There's never been a Western that hasn't made money."

"But a Western as a *big* picture?" Walters said doubtfully.

"*Cimarron* was an epic Western and a very big picture," Dalton said. "Do I need to remind you that it won the Academy Award for best picture in 1931? We intend to win it this year with ours. We have three top men on the script, and John Edsel will direct. I'm convinced after seeing *Becky Sharp* last year that Technicolor is the most natural color process we'll find for a while. I think that certain types of pictures—such as spectacles, costume dramas, and musicals—will eventually be made in color for the most part. We intend to lead the way. The Depression isn't over yet, gentlemen, despite Mr. Roosevelt's efforts, and only those in the vanguard of progress will prosper. We intend to lead the way in our industry in as many ways as we can."

"There are three main male parts in the picture," Renfew put in.

"And it's only fitting that Regency Pictures' three leading male stars be awarded those roles," Dalton said.

There was silence, and Howard supposed that Walters and Tim were thinking what he was—that the three main roles were undoubtedly not of equal importance. It was probable that one of them had a considerable edge over the other two, since that was the way it was in most books, plays, and movies. But Walters could be confident about one thing. No matter what role he got, his name would be above all others in the billing, and in larger letters, as specified in his contract.

"But I still can't see doing a Western as a big picture," Walters said.

What was he afraid of? Howard wondered. That he wouldn't be able to stand up physically to this type of role? That he wouldn't look pretty enough with a stubble of beard and dirty buckskins to satisfy his legions of women fans? That the competition of both Howard Stanton and Timothy Briggs in the same picture would be too much to handle?

"The Western is the most beloved of all movie forms," Dalton was saying to Walters. "The movies virtually began with the Western, and Westerns have always proved enormously popular with the public. Don't worry, Rex, we know what we're doing here. We can't be absolutely sure about anything, of course, but I'd be willing to bank my reputation on this picture. I predict that ten years from now we'll look back and count this picture as a milestone for all of us."

But Walters still looked doubtful a half hour later when Dalton closed the conference with the announcement that production would begin in six weeks.

Howard wandered restlessly in his eucalyptus and palm grove at the far end of one of his gardens, wondering how long it would take for the girl to arrive. Perhaps he should have gone straight to Selma's, except that he didn't like to take the chance of running into someone from the studio there.

Besides, stars seldom went to Selma's house. They had Selma send a girl out, or they arranged to go to the girl's place.

Howard started toward the front, thinking he heard a car coming up the drive. But no. The night was hushed. He'd found that only out on the desert was the night more silent than it was in Beverly Hills.

He reached the swimming pool, flanked on one side by two cabanas and an outside bar and surrounded by a tall hedge of privet. The house was remote from those on adjacent estates and sat well back from the street, with only parts of its handsome Tudor façade, with the tall leaded windows, showing through the screening of old oaks, maples, and sycamores.

The pool was lighted from below, giving the water an eerie effect. Howard stared into it and wished the girl would hurry. He wanted and needed sex. On top of that, he was melancholy and didn't want to be alone. This happened seldom, but it had been happening more often than usual lately. He supposed if he were more gregarious socially, he wouldn't get into a state like this. Perhaps he should give some parties and show off this place.

The distant noise of a car motor grew in the night. Howard came around in front just as a little roadster pulled up before his massive carved entrance door. A lovely girl stepped out, smiling, and he opened the door and let her into the house. He took her into the library to give her a drink, and she commented with admiration on the heavy masculine furniture, the work of the decorator Howard had hired to do the place.

"Do you read any of these books?" she asked as he poured drinks, and when he nodded, she said, "That makes you different from most movie people with libraries. They buy books just for their bindings, or because they're first editions."

"I suppose so." He wished she wouldn't talk so much. She was apparently trying to get acquainted, and he didn't want or need that. After all, they'd probably never see each other again after tonight, so why get involved in something like that? He functioned best sexually when things were impersonal.

While they had their drinks, she talked about coming from Idaho, where she certainly never intended returning, grand though nature was there. Then she laughed and said, "I've been rattling on, and I forgot to tell you my name is Willa. Believe it or not, I didn't come to Hollywood to break into pictures. I want—"

He stopped her by taking her drink out of her hand, bending her back, and kissing her. She responded wholeheartedly. He was fully hard and very hot and thought of giving it to her right here, maybe screwing her standing up against a wall of books. But he decided against it. "Let's go upstairs."

"We can't yet. Rose isn't here."

Howard was surprised to learn that another girl was coming, and wondered if Selma had misinterpreted his instructions. But he dismissed that, for Selma never made mistakes. Selma had probably phoned Willa and told her to go to Howard Stanton's, and Willa had thought it would be a lark to get a friend in on the act.

The doorbell rang. Howard admitted a girl with red hair. Rose was as beautiful as Willa, and as they had drinks in the library, Howard asked himself how he could be sure he didn't care for three in a bed if he didn't try it.

They went upstairs to his bedroom, with its heavy carved canopied bed and several heavy carved chests. They shed their clothes and lay down together on the big bed, Howard between them. He wondered which one he should turn to first. He selected Willa and leaned over and closed his mouth on hers. As he kissed Willa, he felt Rose's tongue moving down his side, and then her head was buried in his groin and her lips were around his penis.

Rose was making him hot too fast, so after a few moments he pushed her off and moved over on top of Willa, who sighed as he kissed her mouth and her neck and her nipples. He felt Rose's tongue on his skin again, moving down his back to his buttocks, then down the backs of his legs, then up again. Willa's legs parted beneath him and he inserted his penis. She kept saying, "Wonderful, wonderful, wonderful," as he moved back and forth inside her, and Rose kept tonguing him behind as he thrashed. He came heavily and lay panting on top of Willa, and Rose stopped tonguing him and pressed her face against his shoulder.

He lay back between them. No one said anything. The girls seemed to be waiting for him to get his strength back. Sometimes that took an hour. This time it took just ten minutes. When Rose leaned down and started sucking on his penis, he was immediately hard.

"Oh, it's too big for me to handle," Rose said as she came up with a laugh. "But I love to try."

"I'll bet it's the biggest cock in Hollywood, Mr. Stanton," Willa said, and it occurred to Howard how ridiculous it was for her to be addressing him so formally after he'd just performed the most intimate act possible with her.

"Now it's my turn to have it in my cunt," Rose said, leaning over Howard and kissing him, her long red hair falling all around his face. He started to raise himself to turn her over and lie on her, but she pushed him down flat on his back and then moved back and sat down slowly on him, moaning with delight as she took his penis deep up into

80

her. She did the work, rising up and down on him; he moved his body very little until the tension began to rise in him. She leaned forward then, resting on her hands, and lowered her full breasts to rub them against his chest. Her tongue slipped into his mouth as they pushed more deeply into each other. Their bodies moved together faster and faster and then he was coming, and from the way she was moaning, she was coming, too. She collapsed on him.

"That was beautiful to watch," Willa said, but he didn't see anything beautiful about it except the sharp pleasure at the end. Drained and depressed, he moved Rose off him and closed his eyes. He wished they would get dressed and leave. He wanted to go to sleep.

But then he heard a moan and opened his eyes. Rose was kissing Willa deeply and hungrily. Their bodies were pressed together, with Rose's large breasts melded into Willa's smaller ones, and when their lips finally parted and Rose started tracing a line down Willa's body with her tongue, Willa sighed in greater ecstasy than she had when Howard had been on top of her.

Howard watched as Rose turned her body in the opposite direction from Willa's and her arms went around Willa's buttocks and Willa's went around hers. Their mouths worked on each other avidly as they groaned with pleasure. Finally they both reached climaxes within moments of each other.

Howard got out of bed and put his robe on. They took the hint and got dressed and left, seeming a little annoyed with his attitude.

He went back downstairs and out to the pool and stared into its lighted depths for a long time. He couldn't remember ever feeling so alone before.

14

Preparations for *Westward the Men* were more thorough and lavish than for any other Regency picture in 1936. They were going to shoot the production on the studio's sound stages, on the back lot, on the ranch the studio had acquired in the San Fernando Valley in 1933 when land prices had skidded to a low point, and on location in Arizona and Colorado. A three-month production period, far longer than for most pictures, had been allocated, beginning in May.

"But we can't let the picture run much over deadline," Dalton said at a meeting he held with the producer, the director, and the three stars. "We must get it edited, promoted, and into the Regency Grand in New York by December. We want an Academy Award for this, and we're all going to work together to see that we get it. We haven't had our share of Academy Awards, but that's going to be changed in the future."

John Edsel, who had been assigned the direction of the picture because of his skill in handling epic themes and big scenes, went to greater lengths than most directors in preparing the actors for their roles. He asked the principals to come to his office daily during the preproduction period to read the script from beginning to end, in strict continuity. It was as if they were preparing a play for the stage. It was Edsel's conviction that the use of this procedure would allow the actors to develop a far better understanding of their roles before the picture began than the usual way of leaving it more or less to chance. Howard and Tim both thought they were getting a lot of benefit from the readings. Rex Walters' opinion of the procedure was expressed in his failure to show up for them morning after morning. When his absence continued into the second week, the question arose as to whether or not he would ever show up, even when production began.

"If I had the role of Jared," Tim said, "I'd make damned sure I was here to see that nobody got it away from me."

It was true that the role of Jared was the strongest of them all, and Howard would have liked it for himself. He was playing Joseph, and Joseph and Jared both ended up empire builders, Joseph in ranching, Jared in mining. But the role of Jared came across more compellingly. Tim was to play Victor, who was cut down in mid-picture, before he could prove out as an empire builder, too. The role had less meat to it than the others, but Howard knew that Tim would compensate for that by turning in a better performance than he and Walters did.

Rex Walters showed up for the last reading in Edsel's office. He arrived at eleven o'clock, two hours after they'd begun, with several days' growth of beard on his face and a strong suggestion of whiskey on his breath. He stumbled so badly over his lines that Edsel, in obvious disgust, released them without completing the session.

Production was to begin the next day. Howard went to bed at nine that evening, as he always did when he was working on a picture, but nervous anticipation kept him awake. His thoughts drifted from one thing to another, and eventually he found Leni Liebhaber on his mind again.

He'd been thinking a lot about the foreign star ever since he'd seen one of her German pictures run in a projection room the week before. Images from the picture kept repeating themselves in his mind. He kept seeing the beautiful woman throwing her head back and tossing her mass of blond hair as she laughed. Her laugh was feminine but with masculine heartiness. He kept hearing her talking in that throaty, husky manner that forever suggested sex.

And he kept thinking of her love scenes. She didn't so much accept love as make it herself. Her love scenes suggested total sexual abandonment. Howard wondered if this obviously uninhibited woman, used to the artistic freedom permitted in European pictures, would be happy about the restrictions the Hays Office put on Hollywood movies.

Leni Liebhaber would probably hate Hollywood, Howard decided just before he dropped off to sleep.

The next morning Howard and Tim, made up and in costume, were waiting in Howard's portable dressing room on stage twelve a half hour before production was to start. At ten minutes before nine they stepped onto the set. Everything was ready for the rehearsal that would precede the filming. The next ten minutes moved slowly, and then it was announced that Rex Walters hadn't arrived at the studio. Neither had he arrived home last night, it was determined from his valet by phone a few minutes later. It was soon obvious that it was futile to wait for him, so Edsel shot around Walters that day.

Rex Walters didn't show up the second day of production either, or the third, fourth, or fifth day. At that point Dalton ordered production closed down until further notice.

The next day news came that Walters was in New York and about to sail for Europe. The studio immediately announced that he was suspended and that his role in Regency Pictures' new epic production in Technicolor, *Westward the Men,* would now go to Howard Stanton.

Howard was glad to get the role of Jared, and hoped that Tim would be advanced to the role of Joseph, a much bigger part than he had as Victor, but the studio arranged to borrow Clinton Bendell from Fox for Howard's vacated role. Production was scheduled to start again in ten days, after Bendell finished his current picture.

"We'll be exactly one month behind schedule," Dalton said worriedly as he and Howard were driven to the Pasadena train station that day in Dalton's Rolls Royce. A retinue of studio executives followed in other limousines, and one limousine at the end contained nothing but flowers. "But somehow we'll make up for lost time without sacrificing quality. Somehow we'll meet the Academy Award deadline this year."

On the station platform in Pasadena, they arranged themselves in ranks like a military receiving party, with Dalton and Renfew up front with Howard. Four studio pages waited with their arms full of blooms from the flower car, and four photographers were ready with cameras and flash guns. They were certain to get good pictures, for there'd never been an occasion when Leni Liebhaber, the woman with the most photogenic face in the world, had ever taken a bad one. The pictures in the newspapers a few days earlier, showing the German star debarking from the *Bremen* in New York, had been striking.

And now she was here, stepping down from the train, smiling mistily from behind her veil, followed by Karl Gurtner, her director, a dapper man with a small moustache. The scene was quickly set for the photographers. The star stood with both arms filled with flowers, furs towering around her cascade of blond hair, as the flash guns popped.

Dalton said, "This is Howard Stanton," and Howard shook the slender gloved hand and thought that he'd never seen such eyes as hers before—violet eyes, liquid and omniscient, with the knowledge of the ages buried in them.

Cameras clicked on and Leni Liebhaber continued to smile. Her violet eyes kept returning to Howard, and Howard knew already that the beautiful star was going to affect his life dramatically.

15

Howard believed he was in love with Leni Liebhaber from the moment he first saw her. It seemed incredible that he could even *be* in love, much less so suddenly, yet here it was, and he was utterly helpless.

Work had started on the picture, and he couldn't allow his fascination with Leni to affect his portrayal or keep him from the rest he needed to get through the long days of rehearsals and shootings. But he saw her whenever he could, and whenever she let him. He tried to conceal from her how annoyed he was that she spent so many of her evenings with Karl Gurtner, for he didn't want her to know she had such a hold on his emotions. But he doubted that he was successful. The violet eyes remained omniscient.

Gurtner moved into the Garden of Allah, as the studio had arranged, thereby forestalling the awful possibility that Leni might ask him to move into a guest room in the Brentwood house the studio had rented for her. Leni immediately acquired a fat German cook, a dour German butler, and a spindly German maid to look after her. Howard found all three forbidding, but not nearly so much as the secretary-companion Leni hired and put in a guest room, an American girl named Adrienne Gremley. She was cold and ruthlessly efficient. She would have been pretty, Howard supposed, if she hadn't dressed so severely—usually in a plain gray or black suit—or worn her hair drawn back so tightly against her head.

The house of early American style that had been rented for Leni couldn't have been more unsuitable for her. It was filled with colonial furniture and braided rugs, against which Leni's chiffons, satins, jewels and furs seemed ludicrous. She should have been established in exotic surroundings—such as one of those Moorish or Spanish places in Beverly Hills—but the fact that she hadn't been did not seem to disturb her.

So they would dine on sauerbraten on a Duncan Phyfe table, with Leni dressed in some stunning creation that she'd picked up in Paris. She seemed made for night life, yet one trip to the Trocadero was enough for her where Hollywood nightclub life was concerned. That excursion invited published speculation on their "romance" from all the Hollywood columnists, which of course delighted the studio.

"So the American public will think that the European star and the American star are in love," Leni said in her excellent, lightly accented English. She laughed. "Let them think that. How can it hurt?"

Yes, how could it hurt? he thought, pained at her flippancy. He was in love all right, but she wasn't. Yet he had to make her fall in love with him. Everything depended on it. Nothing mattered more, not even the picture.

He took her to his house, and she said she was enchanted with it, but he did not believe her. It was decorated for a man, and when he married her—and he *must* marry her—the house would have to be done over to reflect her femininity.

She said she was enchanted with the house at Malibu, too, but he doubted that as well. It seemed unlikely that she would feel at home in such simple surroundings.

He didn't think she looked natural in the simple white sports dress

85

she wore the first time he drove her out to the beach house, for he was used to seeing her in high-fashion silks. Yet at the same time, sports attire wasn't out of place on her. To a degree, she was a sportswoman. She told him that, like many Germans, she skied. She was also a strong and expert swimmer, as she proved to him that day. It was harder to look like a skilled swimmer in the ocean than in a pool, but she managed it.

When they came out of the surf together that first time, they lay down in exhaustion side by side on beach cots. While she lay with her eyes closed, her incredibly long and thick eyelashes resting on her high cheekbones, he propped himself up on an elbow and looked at her. God, she was beautiful!—even with her glorious hair tucked away out of sight beneath that bathing cap. Could anyone possibly have more nearly perfect bone structure? Even when she was old, she would still be stunning.

To Howard, her slender body was as nearly perfect as her face, though she was small-breasted. She looked almost boyish in her black two-piece swimming suit. When Howard had commented that he'd never seen a swimming suit before that revealed a woman's midriff, she'd laughed and said that women had been wearing two-piece swimming suits in France for over a year, and why was America so late in picking up styles?

She opened her eyes and found him looking at her.

"You want to make love to me, do you not?" she said. "But you do not try. Is it because you are afraid I will not let you?"

He smiled warily but didn't answer. He wasn't sure why he'd restrained himself.

"How many men have been in love with you?" he asked.

She smiled. "Are you sure you really want to know?"

"No."

"Then we will not talk about it. Any more than we will talk about the women who have been in your life."

"Would you be jealous?"

"I do not believe in jealousy."

"No?" He was surprised, and wondered if she was telling the truth. He suspected that she didn't always tell the complete truth, in spite of her ingenuousness. "I think you're a woman of deep passions, and jealousy is a part of passion, isn't it?"

"It is if you love someone enough. Perhaps I have never loved anyone that much."

He hoped that was so. He wanted to be the first man she ever loved.

"Gurtner loves you and he despises me," he said.

"He very seldom likes men who interest me." She smiled again. "I like that."

"I'm sure he's asked you to marry him. I'm glad you didn't."

"Why would you be sure? Perhaps he does not want to marry me. Some people do not want to marry. Some people should not marry. Just because you love does not mean you should marry."

He didn't like the sound of that. Had she built up a case for herself against marriage? That might take some undoing. She was strong in her convictions.

"I think Gurtner would marry you in a moment if you'd have him," he said. "Why did you insist that he come along to Hollywood with you?"

"Because he has given me my best pictures. Because he knows how to use me in a picture, and how do I know that an American director would use me properly? I would be afraid without Karl here."

"Why did you come? You're the biggest movie star in Germany and Scandinavia—probably in all of Europe. Isn't that enough?"

"Nothing is ever enough. Have you not learned that yet? I am here to make a million dollars, and then I will go home. A million dollars will convert to countless German marks."

"You want something more than money here. You'll know that in time."

Howard and Karl Gurtner together escorted Leni to the party given in her honor by Augustus Dalton. It was an even more lavish affair than most of Dalton's gatherings, and the guest list included important producers, directors, and stars from all the studios. To Howard's relief, Gary Cooper wasn't present, although there was no doubt that the Paramount star had been invited. It was said that Dalton wanted to borrow Cooper to co-star with Leni in her first picture, since he'd proved such an appropriate foil for Marlene Dietrich in her first Paramount pictures. It was true that Gary Cooper and Leni Liebhaber would make an electric team, and Howard hated the idea of it. He hated the idea of Leni's being teamed with anyone but himself, in pictures or out.

He doubted that Dalton realized how he really felt about Leni. Dalton would have no good reason to suspect that the "romance" being publicized about two of his stars amounted to anything more than ballyhoo. After all, Howard had led Dalton to believe that there was no room in his life for any kind of love but that for his career.

When Dalton failed to consider him for the co-starring role with Leni in her first picture, Howard's disappointment was keen. The way delays were occurring, the picture wouldn't go into production until the following year, long after Howard had finished *Westward the Men*. Surely Dalton would see the advantages of co-starring him with Leni—if only to reap the benefits of their current publicity.

His thoughts revolved around that for a while as the party buzzed around him, intruding with a melange of chatter and laughter and music floating in from outside, where an orchestra played near the pool. He listened to Leni as she talked intelligently with a half dozen persons clustered around her. They were wholly engrossed in her conversation, an unusual circumstance in Hollywood, where most persons were more interested in listening to themselves than to others. Leni was a star who cast a spell on other stars, a real phenomenon.

"Oh, Howard!" A hand tugged at his shoulder, and he turned to face Eunice Dalton. "You remember Elizabeth, our niece, don't you?"

He turned reluctantly to face her. He managed to smile and look pleased to see her, but he found her as distasteful now as he had four or five years ago, when he'd unwillingly gone to bed with her. She was even less attractive now, and her eyes looked hostile. She also seemed to have had a lot to drink. To make matters worse, Eunice Dalton went off and left him alone facing her.

"Have you met Leni yet?" he asked awkwardly.

"Why would I want to meet that Nazi vampire?" she said coldly.

"Miss Liebhaber is not a Nazi and not a vampire," Howard said stiffly, trying to control his anger.

"Is she a good screw?"

He looked around. No one seemed to have heard, thank God. He turned back to her. "Elizabeth, you're not going to gain anything by embarrassing us."

"I don't *care!*" she said. "What embarrasses me is that I *wanted* you so badly, and you weren't worthy of my desire. You're empty. All you are is a beautiful piece of nothing. And there'll come a day when you won't even be beautiful anymore, and then you'll be less than nothing. Just like that Nazi. I can just see her as a shriveled-up old crone with no teeth!"

She started to laugh, but it ended with a choke, and he saw tears as she turned and rushed out of the room. He didn't follow her, and she didn't return, but her remark about his emptiness disturbed him for the rest of the evening.

The axiom was that you couldn't tell whether a picture would be a hit or a flop until you got it before an audience, but Dalton and Renfew were convinced from the first day of production that *Westward the Men* would break box office records. Howard hoped so. Starring in a smash hit could make him a bigger star than Rex Walters. And of course there was the matter of the Academy Award. If *Westward the Men* was voted the best picture of 1936, Regency's prestige would rise greatly in the industry.

But what was most important of all was the returns a big hit would bring in. The picture had the biggest budget of any produced in these precarious times except for a couple of super-productions Thalberg had turned out at M-G-M. If it failed and lost money, Dalton would be in trouble with New York. Howard knew that Nicholas Smetley had been skeptical about "putting so many eggs in one basket" in a period when, after a start toward economic recovery, the country seemed headed for a dip again.

But the first rushes had convinced them all that they were on the road to a smash hit, and the consensus was that Walters' absence from the picture wasn't going to be as important as they'd thought.

The location trip loomed closer, and Howard no longer looked forward to it, not liking the idea of leaving Leni for six weeks. He didn't feel at all secure about his hold on her. Sometimes, to his despair, he had the inescapable feeling that she wouldn't care if she never saw him again. At other times she seemed genuinely interested in him and everything he did.

He was pleased when she expressed a growing interest in his picture and even asked him to tell her the story of it one day.

"It's part of the epic story of the American Western movement in the first couple of decades after our Civil War. The picture begins with a wagon train going west, full of people who want different things—freedom, their own land, success—"

"Love?"

"Yes. That's part of most stories, isn't it?" he said with a smile. "I play the part of Jared, who is ruthlessly ambitious. He and Joseph both love Priscilla, who is on the wagon train. She marries Jared, so Joseph marries Sarah, his second choice. The third major character, Victor, is killed."

"Jared sounds the most interesting. I am glad you are Jared."

"Jared is what Renfew calls a good villain—the type who walks all over everybody to get what he wants."

Leni smiled slightly. "There is nothing that appeals more to a woman than an evil man."

"If you feel that way, then you must worship Hitler."

He thought he saw a flicker of anger in her eyes, but if it was there at all, it passed in an instant.

"But of course I do," she said coolly. "He has saved our country."

"Many people think Roosevelt has saved ours."

"The ancient Greeks and Romans needed their gods, and so do we, five thousand years later. There is nothing wrong with that."

"That's the point of our picture. We need these heroes."

"Go on with the story," she said.

"There's a lot of trouble with the wagon train on the way west. There's an attack by Indians that takes many lives. There's an avalanche that takes many more. Joseph saves Jared's life when he's attacked by a bear. Victor, who helps Joseph acquire the beginnings of his cattle empire, is killed in a cattle stampede."

"And what happens to our good villain? What happens to you?"

"Well, Jared finds silver, makes a fortune from mining it, and builds a Victorian mansion in Denver. Joseph later finds out that Jared had played a terrible trick on him that he can't allow to go unavenged. He goes to Denver and almost kills Jared. He gets the satisfaction of doing that and of facing Jared's wife and finding that he never really loved her after all."

"And Jared lives through it?"

"Yes."

"A happy ending." She laughed. "American pictures must always have a happy ending. I do not believe I like your picture, Howard."

"That's all right, Leni. Over here we're allowed to like what we want to and not like what we want to."

"And you think we are not in Germany?"

"I think you are not."

"You are right. But it is for our good, Howard, and we must do it, just as we must make our kind of picture and you must make yours. But I do not think we should talk about it anymore. It has caused a coldness between us. Do you feel it? Yes, of course you do. We will not talk about it anymore."

So they didn't talk about it anymore.

While Howard was on location, he wrote Leni almost every day, but she didn't write him often, her excuse being that she couldn't write English as easily as she spoke it, which was true. Howard wouldn't have minded that so much if she'd been home more often in the evening when he phoned.

"She's out dining with Herr Gurtner," Adrienne repeatedly explained in her self-satisfied manner. Howard managed to dislike the young woman just a little bit more with each new contact.

The location shooting was being conducted in a country of grass, desert, and mountains of almost virginal purity in the heart of Arizona, and Howard would have enjoyed being there if he hadn't missed Leni so much.

After the location company moved from Arizona to Colorado for special scenes, they returned to Hollywood two weeks behind schedule. By the time retakes were completed and the scoring and final editing got under way, the picture was two hundred thousand dollars over budget and a month behind schedule.

"We won't be able to release the picture this year," Dalton said, "so we'll have to wait an extra year to win our Academy Award. But the important thing is that we have a really fine picture."

When he saw a rough cut of *Westward the Men* a few weeks later, Howard was well satisfied that it was indeed a fine picture, that it would reap glory for Regency Pictures and top stardom for himself.

That weekend he drove Leni to Mexico, ostensibly to take her to a bullfight. She wanted to ask Adrienne to come along with them, but Howard talked her out of it. Still, as they crossed the border, Leni pointed out that Howard had been stuffy in refusing to let her invite her secretary-companion to accompany them. After all, Adrienne would greatly enjoy a trip like this.

"I don't want a third party along on our honeymoon," Howard said. "We're not going to a bullfight. We're going to get married."

At first, when he saw the look on her face—he didn't know whether it was fright or delight—he thought she was going to refuse. But two hours later they were married, and one hour after that he lay naked with her for the first time.

He'd had fears about it. He'd thought about it many times, about how it would be to make love to someone he loved, and he'd feared that something would go terribly and irreparably wrong and leave a psychic wound that would never heal. He'd feared that they wouldn't be able to function together, that he would find her frigid or that she would find him impotent.

"You are beautiful," she said as he came into the room from the bathroom, a towel around his midriff. She lay naked on the bed, her arms at her sides, her legs slightly apart and slightly raised, her shining blond hair fanning the pillow. "You are beautiful," she repeated. "Come to me quickly."

He dropped the towel and went to the bedside, and before he could lie down with her, she raised herself and kissed his groin. He lowered himself beside her and began kissing her. His lips traveled from her lips to her nipples and then to her belly and finally to her vagina. He'd never

91

thought he would kiss a vagina, but he did. He kept kissing and licking the lips of it, and she kept moaning, and he supposed she would have come right then if he'd gone on with it, but he stopped and mounted her and they carried each other to the top.

He kept thinking, every time they did it that wonderful first night, that there was nothing better than this in the world when you were in love.

16

Michael Baines had been sitting in the Mayfield Theater for four and a half hours on this damp autumn Sunday afternoon. He had viewed the new Howard Stanton picture twice, though he would never have admitted that to anyone. If you said you had a favorite male movie star, you were tagged as a fruit.

So Mike had never told a soul that Howard Stanton was his favorite star because he was handsome and athletic and came across on the screen like someone you would like to know. Mike could never confess to anyone in Grove Center, Indiana, that he liked Howard Stanton better than Clark Gable, Errol Flynn, Johnny Weissmuller, Rex Walters, and any of the other handsome heroes out in Hollywood, California, where Michael Baines intended to go one of these fine days, at least on a visit, although he never mentioned that, either, or told anyone that he secretly read *Modern Screen, Motion Picture,* and *Photoplay.*

While he watched the Donald Duck cartoon for the second time, he reflected on the Howard Stanton movie. He'd liked it a lot, but in his view it hadn't come close to Stanton's greatest picture, *The Young Soldier,* which Mike had seen when he was twelve years old and which remained, four years later, in 1936, his favorite picture of all the hundreds he'd seen.

Mike rose from his seat as the Previews of Coming Attractions announced that Mae West was coming in *Go West, Young Man*. He walked to the back and paused to look down at the people sitting in pairs and in larger groups all the way down to the screen. He couldn't understand why people went to movies with other people. It was much better to go alone. If there was anything he hated, it was being distracted during a movie by someone talking to him or touching him.

He walked home. When he got there, he found Uncle Vernon's 1934 Chevy sitting in the driveway. That disturbed him. He liked his mother's brother all right, but he didn't like Aunt Minnie or their stupid little twin boys of eight who always pestered him to play games with them when he didn't feel like it. He visualized the evening ahead. First they would have supper, accompanied by a lot of talk from Uncle Vernon about what Roosevelt was doing wrong, countered with talk from Mike's father about what Roosevelt was doing right. Then they would listen to Walter Winchell broadcasting to his "fellow Americans and all the ships at sea," and then to Drew Pearson, who would give his "predictions of things to come." If the predictions were good, they would be happy while they played Monopoly, turning the radio back on when Eddie Cantor came on and informed them how he loved to spend "this hour with you."

He went in and said hello pleasantly enough to his aunt and uncle. His aunt beamed back broadly, for she thought he was the politest boy in Grove Center and kept saying so aloud, to Mike's embarrassment. The twins immediately started to pester him to help put back together their model airplane, which they'd dismantled down to the last screw.

The call to supper saved him. The food was good. Mike's mother was a wonderful cook, although she didn't look like the type who would be. She was very beautiful still, even though she was over forty. He wondered if she'd dreamed of going to Hollywood when she was young. Surely she could have been a great silent screen star. But she'd married her high school sweetheart, and her life was centered around cooking and cleaning their five-room house. Often, when she seemed sad, Mike wondered if she was regretting lost dreams. But she didn't share her secrets, any more than Mike did.

The evening unfolded as Mike had predicted—the political talk at supper, the radio programs, the game of Monopoly, with his mother somehow remote from it all, as if she could endure it only because she kept her mind on something else. Mike was soon itching to get away. When Ira phoned and said conspiratorially that he had something to show him and asked him to come over, Mike jumped at the chance, though he had no wish to see Ira. He fibbed that Ira wanted his help on a geometry problem. Once outside, he took his time walking the six blocks to Ira's house. He certainly didn't consider Ira a close buddy anymore. They'd begun to drift apart about a year earlier when Mike had decided that he didn't want to be close, really close, to anybody.

Being too close, having somebody looking inside you, was too uncomfortable. People who got close managed to find out what your dreams were, and Mike didn't want anyone knowing his.

Ira was waiting on the porch swing. His parents' 1936 Terraplane was gone, and Ira said they were out playing Bingo at the Elks Club.

"Wait'll you see what I've got in my room," Ira said, bounding upstairs. Mike followed uneasily, suspecting that Ira had something horny to show him. He felt both excited and reluctant.

Ira had three cartoon books and a photograph. The cartoon books showed Dick Tracy, Tillie the Toiler, and Maggie and Jiggs in various sexual situations. The photograph was of a man on top of a woman, obviously having intercourse.

They sat down side by side on the bed. Mike contemplated the cartoon books with mixed feelings. He didn't want to look at them, and at the same time, he did. He started leafing through Tillie the Toiler, and he had a hard-on immediately. He was embarrassed at the way it made his corduroys bulge.

Ira was presumably looking at the Maggie and Jiggs cartoon book, but when Mike glanced over, he found Ira watching him. Ira had his hard penis out and was stroking it.

"Get yours out, Mike," he urged, his eyes on the bulge in Mike's pants. "Let's jack off together."

Mike hesitated. For a few moments, as he stared at Ira's hand working his rigid penis, he acknowledged to himself that he wanted to join him. But he mustn't let himself. "Don't be stupid, Ira," he finally said. "We're too old for that stuff."

He closed the cartoon book and rose to show that he meant business. He wanted to look through the other books, but he knew he'd better get out of there immediately.

"No, we're not," Ira said, although he reddened and stopped stroking his penis. "A lot of guys jack off together."

"It isn't natural at our age," Mike said. "If you want to be a fairy, just keep on doing things like this, and you'll be one in short order."

Ira's face was flaming now, and his penis had shrunken. He tucked it inside his pants, buttoned his fly, and stood up.

"I'm not going to be a fairy!" he said indignantly. "But I've heard talk about *you*."

"Just what kind of talk, Ira?" Mike asked, feeling both angry and uncomfortable.

"Well, you don't date much—"

"I don't date much," Mike cut in, "because I'm saving my money for college. I don't work all day Saturdays unloading stuff at the A&P to earn money just to throw it away on dates."

Ira looked awkwardly at his feet. "I'm sorry, Mike."

"We'll just forget it," Mike said, but he knew that neither of them would forget it and that their faltering friendship was over. Mike didn't care about that. What he cared about was that some of his classmates thought he was a fairy.

He thought about it on the way home. He decided that the real reason they thought he was a fairy was not that he didn't date much but that they didn't like him. And they didn't like him because they were jealous of him. Partly because he was just about the best student in his class, partly because he was the best swimmer in the class—indeed, the school led in intramural swimming competition because of him—and he had a wonderful swimmer's build. And, finally, because he was the best-looking boy in the entire town. They had only to look around them to see that.

When he got home, his relatives were gone and his parents were listening to their mahogany Majestic console radio in the living room. Mike went straight upstairs to his bedroom. On the bedside table were his gooseneck reading lamp and his small Stromberg-Carlson radio. He liked to lie in bed and listen to the radio, his favorite programs being dramatic series like the Lux Radio Theater, Gang Busters, Suspense, and Inner Sanctum. Radio was second only to the movies to him, and he sometimes thought that he'd like to be a radio actor, although there was no doubt that he would far prefer to be in the movies.

But he didn't turn on the radio immediately. He stood before the dresser mirror and looked at himself. He had tawny hair, clear blue eyes, and what the magazines called "regular features," a face as well put together as it was possible to be short of being too "pretty." He was lucky. He'd inherited the best possible bone structure from a beautiful mother and a strong-featured father.

He took his movie stills from their hiding place behind some boxes on his highest closet shelf, where his mother couldn't reach when she cleaned. He'd been sending to the Hollywood studios for years for stills from his favorite movies.

He began with the stills of Johnny Weissmuller and Maureen O'Sullivan in *Tarzan, the Ape Man,* which he'd seen when he was twelve. The movie had so thrilled him that he'd immediately started reading the Edgar Rice Burroughs series of Tarzan books and imagining himself as Tarzan. He looked thoughtfully at still after still, lingering particularly with the series from *The Young Soldier.* He was fascinated with Howard Stanton's handsomeness. He looked terrific from any angle. He was by far the best-looking man in Hollywood.

Suddenly he was aware that his father had entered his room. There was no time to hide the stills that were spread on the bed all around him. He froze as his father approached, picked up one of the stills and stared at it.

"What kind of nonsense is this?" he said, throwing down the still and looking demandingly at Mike.

"I collect movie stills," Mike explained fumblingly. "It's just a hobby," he added weakly.

"Some hobby," his father said, scowling. "Sometimes I just don't understand you, Mike. I'd expect a girl to keep a movie star collection, but not a boy. I want you to get rid of this stuff. And I want you to get rid of it tomorrow. Is that plain?"

His father didn't wait for an answer. He turned and left the room, his rigid posture showing how angry he was.

Mike consoled himself with the thought that it could have been worse. If his father had been beered up, as he often was when he came home from his weekly poker game, he might have taken a strap to Mike. He hadn't done that in years, but it could happen again anytime. His father had gotten rough with his mother, too, at times when he'd been boozing.

Mike returned the stills to their hiding place, hoping his father wouldn't ask about them so he wouldn't have to lie about having thrown them away. He wished his father would forget this incident, but it was unlikely. It might even give him the same idea about Mike that some of his classmates had. Or he might put two and two together and guess that Mike wanted to be an actor. That would make him angry, for he was determined that Mike was going to be an accountant someday.

Mike had a hard time getting to sleep that night. When he did, he dreamed that he was a small boy again and his father was strapping him.

An unexpected opportunity came to Mike the following week. He was approached by Miss Brendler at school one afternoon about the prospect of appearing in a school play. Miss Brendler taught English at Grove Center High, and she was also responsible for producing and directing the senior class play.

She was now going to expand her activities by occasionally putting on one-act plays, with sophomore and junior actors, for presentation at school assemblies. She thought Mike would be perfect for the male lead in the first play on the program. She gave him a script to take home and read to see if he'd be interested. She as much as said that he would be offered the part, although formal tryouts would be held at school, in fairness to the other students.

Mike was exuberant. The only way he'd know whether or not he could act was to try, and now he wouldn't have to wait for a chance to see. He laughed frequently as he read the play, *Maneuvers,* in his room after supper. It was about a buck private in the Army who was standing guard outside the colonel's house and got into one scrape after another involving the colonel's daughter. Mike read some of the lines aloud and liked the sound of his own voice saying them. He practiced every day before tryouts, and he was by far the best of the dozen boys who showed up.

Marianne Sellers was so much better than the other girls who tried out for the part of the colonel's daughter that Mike wondered if she hadn't had some advance study, too. He was surprised that she'd turned up for the tryouts. She'd seemed so aloof and standoffish that it was hard to imagine her wanting to be in a play. She'd come new to the class this fall and had immediately discouraged the immense popularity she could have had by turning down every boy who asked her for a date. Hardly anyone could resist asking, for she was unquestionably the most beautiful young girl in town with her long auburn hair, which swept to the small of her back, and her extremely white skin. When she kept rejecting would-be suitors, she was disparaged around school as a snob, but she didn't seem to care.

Mike found her easy to work with, and one day after rehearsal he asked to walk her home. On the way they decided to stop at the drugstore for a soda. There were some very surprised looks from various of their classmates as they sat down in a booth together.

Marianne sighed as she looked around. "I certainly don't like our silly classmates."

Mike nodded. "I know what you mean."

"But I like *you,* Mike. After working with you in the play, I think we can be friends."

"Well, sure," Mike said, uncertain as to what she was getting at.

"I need a friend. I don't need, and don't want, a *boy*friend. The pattern that's set for everybody is that you're supposed to fall in love, go steady, and then get married and have kids. I don't like the idea of that. I don't think I'll *ever* want any of that."

"What do you want?"

"Right now, to learn as much as I can. Then, when I graduate—and you mustn't mention this to anyone, for I don't want anyone to know about it, least of all my parents—I'm going straight to New York and try to make a career for myself on the stage. Not just try. I'm going to *do* it."

How wonderful! He had found someone with a dream similar to his. He told her his secret then. He said that although his folks expected him to have a business career, what he really wanted was to be in the movies.

"You'd be perfect!" Marianne said. "You're the best-looking boy I've ever seen, Mike."

"And you're the most beautiful girl I've ever seen."

She laughed. "If we weren't more interested in other things, we'd probably be sweethearts."

But there was certainly more safety in what they were, and even though he wouldn't have minded being more physically intimate with Marianne, Mike was glad to have a compatible friend at last whom he could talk to about what interested him most in life. He and Marianne were seeing each other quite often outside rehearsals even before *Maneuvers* was enthusiastically received at a school assembly in the middle of December. They liked each other so well by the time the play was presented that it helped them to give better performances.

They would often sit together in study hall, and they met frequently to talk in the halls between classes. He walked her home after school a couple of times a week, and sometimes they would stop for a soda on the way. They started attending school parties together. Not once did Mike kiss her or even put his arm around her, knowing that she wouldn't have welcomed such advances, but their classmates certainly didn't realize that they were only friends. The talk buzzed around school that they were going steady, and Mike hoped the speculation that he was a fairy had ended.

Miss Brendler drove them to the city one Saturday to see a matinee performance of Katharine Cornell's touring company. From the moment the play started, Mike was spellbound. The fine acting made him forget that this was a play and not life. When the final curtain fell, breaking his spell, he found it hard to believe that he was merely sitting there in a theater seat. He had been completely lost in another world.

He decided that maybe it would be better for him to aim for the stage first before the movies.

Mike no longer needed to prove to his classmates that he wasn't a fairy, but he hadn't yet proved it to himself. As much as he didn't like to think it, he sometimes asked himself if his admiration for such physically compelling stars as Howard Stanton might mean that he actually did harbor sexual desires for men. And sometimes he wondered if he

98

used Marianne's lack of interest in physical contact as an excuse to avoid pressing her on it.

He was normal, he told himself.

But telling himself wasn't enough. He knew he was going to have to prove it. He could have tested himself with any number of eager girls around school, but suppose he failed? He'd never be able to live down the talk.

There was one way of finding out about himself without anyone at school knowing. There was a girl on the other side of town named Loretta Angelo who was a whore. Ira had pointed her out on the street once to Mike, and he'd admired her prettiness and had wondered that she sold her body. It was said that the police let her operate because she gave herself free of charge to members of the force.

It was also said that she charged four dollars, more than Mike made for a whole day of work at the A&P, but he decided to make the expenditure. When he phoned her to make a date, she immediately said, "You sound like a kid."

"I'm eighteen," he lied.

"All right, come here tonight at eight-thirty. But you'd better be of age."

When she opened the door to him and let him into her garish little apartment that evening, she said, "I can tell you're not eighteen, but I'm going to risk it with you anyway, because you're so good-looking."

"So are you," he said truthfully.

"Kiss me," she demanded, and pulled him against her, pressing her big breasts against his chest. He put his arms around her and hoped she didn't notice how nervous he was. She forced apart his lips with her tongue, and as it darted into his mouth, all he could think of for a moment was a snake's fang. But it wasn't bad, and he used his tongue, too. It was a long kiss that ended only when she reached down and felt the bulge in his pants. "I like that a lot," she said, and led him back into her bedroom.

She was wearing a kimono. She slipped out of it and lay down on the bed, which was already turned back in readiness, and watched him while he awkwardly undressed. He was even more nervous now, could even feel himself tremble, and hoped she would mistake that for passion.

He went to the bed. She smiled as she extended her hand, took his, and pulled him down beside her. She put his hand on her breast. They kissed again. She reached down and stroked his penis. She spread her legs and urged him over on top of her.

"Hug me, kiss me, rub your cock on my nest!"

He did as she commanded, and then she put her fingers down at her slit, spreading it, inviting him in. He inserted his penis easily, and she wrapped her legs around him and locked him in that warm, meaty place, and it felt glorious, absolutely glorious, and he closed his eyes and pumped irresistibly, knowing from the drawing in his groin that started almost immediately that he wouldn't last long before he came.

"Oh, oh," he said as he neared his climax. He kept groaning as he came and came.

When he'd stopped, he couldn't wait to slip out of her. He felt terrible. He wanted to get dressed and leave at once. But he sank back weakly beside her and lay there breathing heavily.

She said, "It was your first time, wasn't it?" He frowned at her, about to deny it, but she smiled before he could and said, "It's all right. You can really give a girl a thrill."

As he walked home a few minutes later, he was still depressed, but glad of one thing. He was no fairy.

17

Howard's discontent had really begun long before his hour of triumph with the highly successful world premiere of *Westward the Men* at the Regency Grand in New York City on February 22, 1937. Looking back upon it, particularly after Leni went off to Germany without him later that year, he realized that the roots of his unhappiness lay in scattered incidents going back almost to the very beginning of their marriage, incidents that had seemed insignificant at the moment of their occurrence.

But it had all built up, and Howard was more and more on edge, even on the day after the premiere, when both the picture and his performance were lauded by the important newspapers. The day after, it was publicly announced that he was to co-star with his wife in her first American picture, which was scheduled to go before the cameras in the near future. Howard blew up at the news.

100

"You might have told *me* about it before you told the world!" he exploded at a meeting with Dalton and Renfew.

"But we thought it was understood," Dalton said. "And we thought it was what you wanted."

It was true that he'd wanted it, although he hadn't liked the idea of being third choice after the studio had failed in their attempts to borrow either Gary Cooper or Cary Grant from Paramount for the role. But he had eventually decided that he didn't want to co-star with his wife in *The Lady from Tangiers*. He feared being overshadowed by Leni in the picture, and he doubted that he could work well under Gurtner's direction. He didn't bring up those reasons with Dalton and Renfew; he offered instead what he thought would be in their view a better argument.

"The role is too sophisticated for me," he said. "Cooper and Grant are fine for sophisticated parts, but I'm not."

"How do you know?" Dalton asked. "You've never tried one."

"It's time you started tackling roles like this," Renfew said.

"If you want to remain a star," Dalton said, "you can't limit yourself."

"Why not?" Howard demanded. "Most stars limit themselves to a certain range of roles, except for the few that are truly good actors."

That was true, and Dalton and Renfew both knew it, but nothing would change their minds about Howard's co-starring with Leni in *The Lady from Tangiers*. Suspension was even suggested as a possibility, in case Howard's obstinacy continued.

"If you want to get down to the rock-bottom truth about it," Dalton said at the end of the disagreeable interview, "we don't have another male star of suitable stature for this role. And we can't have further delays in starting the picture. It should have gone into production six months ago."

Gurtner's dissatisfaction with the script, which had been rewritten a dozen times, and his later dissatisfaction with certain set designs and with some of Leni's costumes had caused the delays.

Even though it had been many months since her arrival in Hollywood and she was yet to start her first picture, Howard's wife hadn't faded from the headlines. Their marriage was still a topic of interest to the fan magazines, and their appearances in public always brought the photographers running. Leni was frequently photographed at the racetrack, which she had found to her liking because, as she commented, "the horses' beautiful bodies thrill me." No matter what angle the camera caught, the results were always breathtaking. "The world's most

101

beautiful face," more than one important columnist said of her, to the studio's delight.

But they were not delighted with the story resulting from an interview Leni granted to a writer for one of the most widely read fan magazines. The writer, a rather plain middle-aged woman, came to the house for the interview and was disarmed the moment Leni appeared. As usual, she entered like a queen arriving at court, wearing a ravishing smile and stunning gown. The writer's jaw slackened and her eyes widened. Leni Liebhaber on film was staggering, but Leni Liebhaber in the flesh was unbelievable.

"My couturier?" Leni smiled at the first question her interviewer asked and named a German, although Howard knew that almost her entire wardrobe had come from Paris. She'd reluctantly admitted to him that the French triumphed over the Germans only in the realm of women's fashions.

"And what do you think of American fashions?" the woman asked.

"I do not think the American housewife looks as chic as she should in spite of mass production and low prices," Leni said.

"I'm surprised," the writer said. "I've interviewed foreign stars before. They love American fashions. They love *all* things American."

"They say that," Leni said, "but they do not mean it. They say it only while they are making pictures here. When they go back home, they laugh about how they told such lies."

Howard knew he should interfere, should say something to divert the conversation from the direction it was going, but he was helpless.

"Don't tell me you don't *like* America?" the writer asked.

"But of course I do. I would not have stayed otherwise. But I do not think America is as great a country as it could be with the right leader. I do not think the leaders of America have done nearly so much to make this a great country as our Fuehrer has done to make Germany great."

The writer frowned. "I'm surprised at you, talking like that."

"Why should I not speak the truth?" Leni said. "Is this not the country where one says what one wishes?"

"Yes, of course, but it seems strange that *you* would say it. You were brought over here to star in pictures for a great deal of money. You've accepted American largess, and you've married an American, yet your loyalty still seems to be to Germany." The writer's tone was now very cold. "It's an outrage, considering what's going on in your country today under Hitler."

"What are you talking about?" Leni said. "The Fuehrer saved our

102

country from ruin. We were worse off economically than even America at the beginning of the decade."

Howard broke in weakly, "Leni, we're getting away from the subject. We aren't here to discuss the world's woes but the picture we're going to make together."

"You're right, of course, Mr. Stanton," the writer said stiffly. "Shall we get on with it?"

The rest of the interview proceeded grimly, but with politics omitted. Leni said little and was sullen after the writer left, claiming she had a headache and retiring to her room. Howard tried to control his anger, but it didn't help when he went upstairs to talk to Leni and found Adrienne with her. It was difficult, as usual, for him to conceal how much he disliked Leni's secretary-companion. He supposed he was suffering from some kind of distorted jealousy, but he didn't like Leni's lavishing so much attention on the woman. It was true that Adrienne was intelligent and knowledgeable and answered Leni's need for a friend on her own intellectual level, but Howard was annoyed at the extent of the young woman's invasion of his life with Leni. He'd thought it a mistake that Adrienne be permitted to live with them, but Leni had insisted that she needed her nearby.

Right now he detected resentment under Adrienne's mask of indifference when he sent her off with the brisk comment that he wanted to talk to his wife alone. Leni seemed to resent his intrusion, too, but he felt that the matter of the unfortunate magazine interview must be discussed immediately and resolved, not left to smolder into a growing misunderstanding.

"But I *must* say what I feel," Leni said angrily when he tried to explain how her words to the magazine writer could backfire on her.

"You don't have to talk about politics."

"I must say what I feel," she insisted again. "Loyalty and honesty cannot let me deny what the Fuehrer has done for me and my country, no matter what you think."

He felt like a scolded schoolchild. Her logic and intelligence frightened him. There were times, as now, when he felt himself too small a man to cope with her, yet she was what he wanted most from life. He'd thought once that there was nothing he wanted more than stardom. Now he knew he would give it all up for her if necessary. Yet he felt so insecure about her! It frightened him that she'd moved in here and hadn't made a single change in the decor. It was a house decorated to fit his tastes as a bachelor, and he'd fully expected her to change many things. When he'd asked her why she didn't, she'd said she liked it exactly as it was. But a fear persisted with him that she didn't change the house because she considered it only a temporary stopping place in her life.

"Tell me this," she went on. "If you went to Germany, would you not at heart remain an American?"

He nodded.

"Then there is nothing wrong in my loving Germany."

"No, of course not, but you should love your new country, too, Leni, and you should make that point if you're going to talk about this for publication. You see, it's the system of government in Germany, the dictatorship, that people here are against."

"But what is wrong with the system? It has rebuilt Germany. We are better off under the Fuehrer than you are under Roosevelt."

"Leni, people here are afraid of your Fuehrer. They're afraid he's going to make war. They hear about things like the persecution of Jews in Germany—"

"Jews!" she interrupted with a grimace. "You talk nobly about saving Jews, but you hate them, too."

He frowned. "That isn't true. Whatever made you think that?"

"I know you hate them, inside yourself. Americans who are not Jews hate Jews."

"That's absurd."

She smiled. "We will not talk of it now. No more talk. I want you to make love to me."

She reached out and took his hand and drew it to her breast. He knew this was no way to settle it, but he couldn't help himself. He bent her back and made love to her.

The magazine article was remarkably frank for a fan magazine. The writer had implanted her resentment of Leni plainly in her copy, and her editor hadn't seen fit to soften it. Dalton was upset. It was bad publicity. The piece appeared only a little more than a month from the time of the interview, apparently having been rushed to press to fill a gap in the latest issue of the magazine, and unfortunately it appeared on the first day of production of *The Lady from Tangiers*. That day was bad enough, with not a single foot of usable film shot, due to Gurtner's fussiness, but it worsened as word of the article made its way around the studio and more and more people read it.

The following days were little better. The production of *The Lady from Tangiers* quickly became a nightmare for Howard, although Leni took it in stride.

"But this is how Karl works," she said when Howard complained

104

about the maddening delays that put the picture a little more behind schedule each day. "We will have a beautiful picture when we are finished. It will be a picture that matters. And *we* will matter, and it will be because Karl is the greatest artist the motion picture industry has ever seen—greater than Griffith and Eisenstein and Pabst and Dreyer and all the rest. Being so great himself, he makes *us* great."

She still insisted that Gurtner was entirely responsible for her success, although Howard insisted that her beauty, talent, and personal magnetism were, that she would have risen to stardom under anyone's direction. But she refused to accept that.

Howard couldn't remember ever disliking anyone so much as he did Gurtner, not only because he felt that the pompous director's hypnotic influence on Leni was unhealthy but also because he made the cast and crew suffer without relief under his fanatical tyranny.

Gurtner obviously disliked Howard, too. That had been evident from the beginning, and his antagonism had intensified after Howard and Leni had married, with Gurtner setting out to make himself as obnoxious to Howard as he possibly could.

But it had come as a considerable relief to Howard to affirm in his own mind that Leni had never been Gurtner's mistress. Indeed, Gurtner appeared to be alienated from sex, which would explain his failure to marry and his propensity to spend most of his time away from the studio brooding in his villa at the Garden of Allah. But Howard's relief was offset by his concern over the fact that Gurtner still dominated Leni intellectually, that she was his goddess and he was her high priest.

It would have been better, thought Howard, if the director's response to their marriage had been overt jealousy, something Howard could have dealt with openly. Instead, Gurtner satisfied his rancor by doing all he could to belittle Howard on the set and in the picture. He deliberately designed shots to show Leni in a lofty position and Howard in a subordinate one, the mistress looking down on the one who should have been master. Leni at the top of the staircase, gorgeously gowned and jeweled, looking down at Howard far below, half hidden in a pool of shadows. Leni on the deck of a ship, looking down at Howard on the wharf, half hidden by a cartload of luggage. Leni, laughing as she pulled Howard up from the floor by his hair after he'd fallen to his knees to beg something of her.

It was demeaning, and jarred with the character of the sophisticated and aggressive man Howard was playing. The humbling shot angles weren't script directions but part of Gurtner's campaign against him.

Howard's nerves worsened by the day. Most of each day was consumed in waiting around while Gurtner adjusted and readjusted and then readjusted again each setup to get the pictorial effect he wanted. At the end of two months of production they were where they should have been at the end of one. Renfew's office kept putting budgetary pressure on Gurtner which he ignored, obviously calculating that the studio was now too deeply committed to this expensive movie to stop production and shelve it. Besides, Regency Pictures had all the money in the world to waste, didn't it?

Except that it didn't. There was a general box office slump as the year progressed that had all the studios wondering what they were doing wrong. Dalton was solemn and concerned about it. The dipping box office returns had put the company in the red for the first quarter of the year, and they were even contemplating taking *Westward the Men* off a road show basis long before expected because of declining revenue.

There was also more bad publicity to deal with when Rex Walters was convicted in criminal court of statutory rape of a girl whose child he'd fathered. She'd only been sixteen at the time he'd seduced her. A storm of outraged letters poured into the studio, and the item got flaming publicity in the newspapers. Aster Bigelow, whose columns were sneaking up on Louella Parsons' in popularity with the public, kept the matter alive in a series of stinging attacks on Hollywood hijinks, with Walters starred as the major character.

"Walters is so thoroughly identified as a Regency star," Dalton told Howard worriedly, "that whenever people talk about his sordid situation, the studio is brought to mind, too."

Dalton was so distracted with other worries that he seemed almost indifferent to Howard's complaints about the way Gurtner was handling the picture.

"You're being oversensitive about it," Dalton said after Howard had brought up the matter several times.

"Damn it, I'm not only wrong for the part, I'm being swallowed. I'm being upstaged by Leni in every scene. Not because of her," he added quickly, "but because of Gurtner. I'm not coming across the way I should in this picture because he's changing the aspect of the character I'm playing."

"You're wrong, Howard. I assure you, this picture will do nothing worse than make you a bigger star."

Howard didn't believe Dalton really felt that way. Dalton had seen from the rushes what Gurtner was doing. But Dalton was concerned about how far behind schedule and how much over budget the picture was, and rather than admit the truth and take Gurtner off the picture—which Leni would assuredly not tolerate, anyway—or force him to reshoot part of it, he was sacrificing Howard.

106

He thought about what he could do about that. The most dramatic argument he could make would be to walk off the picture. That would show Dalton he meant business!

But it would be a big risk. Even though the studio had a large investment in him and he was an established box office attraction, Dalton might be angry enough to drop him. Dalton had cooled somewhat to him lately, and Howard recognized that the studio head's special interest in him in the past wouldn't help much now if Dalton decided he wanted to break him.

No, he couldn't risk it. If he walked out in the middle of an expensive picture like this and Dalton suspended him, or worse, the doors of every studio in Hollywood would be forever closed to him.

Worse yet, if he walked out on the picture, his marriage would be finished. He'd just have to bear it to the end.

It was June, and *The Lady from Tangiers* had been in production almost four endless months.

"Gurtner would never get away with stretching out production like this in Germany," Howard said to Leni. "He's doing it here because he's determined to waste as much of the studio's money as he can. And he knows that he's making me more and more nervous with all his nitpicking and delays, and he's succeeding in getting the rotten performance out of me he's after."

"That is not true," Leni said, frowning.

But she wouldn't allow herself to be led into a real talk about it. She was elusive nowadays, usually retiring early to her room after dinner on the excuse that it had been a difficult day at the studio. It irritated Howard that she often called Adrienne in to read to her until she fell asleep. Sometimes that took an hour or more. Howard was resentful because Adrienne had more access to his wife's company than he did, and it worried him that on the fewer and fewer occasions that he and Leni made love, there was something withdrawn about her. He attributed their difficulties in communication largely to the strain they were both under at the studio.

They seldom went to Malibu, because shooting was a six-day week, and Leni didn't like the beach much anyway. Still, one Saturday they decided to drive out and spend the night and all day Sunday. But when they stopped at the house to pick up the overnight bags Leni had phoned Adrienne to pack, Howard was annoyed to find that the secretary-companion expected to go along with them.

"I don't understand," Howard said to Leni.

"I thought it would be nice for Adrienne to see the beach house," Leni said with a smile.

107

"Oh, dear," Adrienne said with what Howard was certain was false concern. "I thought Mr. Stanton knew you'd asked me."

There was one advantage to Adrienne's coming along to the beach. She occupied the second bedroom, so Howard and Leni slept together. He would have preferred sleeping with her every night, but she didn't rest well when someone was with her, and he'd learned right after the honeymoon that when the lovemaking was over, he was expected to retire to his own bed.

Tonight they slept little anyway. He made love to her three times, and for the first time in many weeks he filled his need of her. The third time they made love, she took him in her mouth and he took her in his. The first time they'd done this, she'd been surprised when he told her he'd never done it before. It was common in Europe, she said. He supposed it was common enough here, too, but he'd never wanted to do it with anyone before Leni. It was wonderful doing it with her. It was wonderful and beautiful doing it any way with her because he loved her so much.

18

It was just shortly after dawn when Howard wakened, yet Leni was gone. Strange. She always slept late when she could, and she certainly could have today. He found a pot of coffee, half emptied, still warm, on the stove. She must have decided to take an early walk on the beach.

He decided to dress and go after her. He frowned as he passed the closed door of the guest room, reminded that the unwanted Adrienne was in there. Outside, he looked up and down the beach, wondering which way Leni had gone. He took a chance that she'd gone south. As he walked along the beach, his glance kept passing back and forth between the sleeping beach houses and the subdued early morning sea, and it seemed almost as if he were alone in the world. It was so peaceful at this moment that it was hard to believe that life offered so many problems.

He wished he could send Adrienne away and isolate Leni and

108

himself in this peaceful place forever, away from Hollywood and the rest of the world. How he loved her! He wanted children by her, and hoped that the time would come soon when she would be willing to stop taking precautions when they made love. He wanted with Leni what he thought he would never want with anyone—a normal family life.

A horseman appeared, galloping down the beach toward him. A boy of fourteen or fifteen, he recognized Howard and pulled up. He was the son of a producer at Columbia who had a place down this way.

The boy beamed at Howard. "You're looking for your wife, aren't you?" He pointed behind him. "They're back there sitting on a rock. Just keep walking. You'll run into them."

Them! He didn't know why it hadn't occurred to him that Leni would have asked Adrienne to go along on her walk.

Leni smiled at him when he came up, saying, "I did not want to disturb you because you were sleeping so peacefully."

He didn't believe that. Suddenly he didn't believe a lot of things. He didn't know what was wrong, but something was. Something was very much wrong.

The shooting on the picture was finally finished, three months behind schedule. There was still the editing to do, and the scoring, and then the sneak preview would be held. There might be some reshooting after the first public reaction was in, but Howard hoped not. He didn't think he could stand ever doing another scene under Gurtner's direction.

Leni's next picture was being planned in Renfew's department, but little had gone past the story treatment stage at this point.

"I'll tell you very frankly," Renfew said to Howard when he called him in to discuss his next picture, "that we simply can't risk getting in any deeper on Leni until we see what kind of reception the public gives *The Lady from Tangiers.*"

In the meantime, Howard was set to go immediately into a picture designated a "screwball comedy," a term invented by another studio that had found considerable success with pictures of that nature.

Howard's co-star was to be Denise Carroll, who remained the queen of the lot, although it was naturally said she was worried about the competition from Leni Liebhaber. Howard looked forward to working with her because she was a real professional and a good actress.

While that picture was in production, the studio was making preparations for him to step into the two major productions that had been awaiting Walters' return, a remake of *Ivanhoe,* which had been Regency's biggest silent film a decade back, and *The Great Typhoon,* a romantic adventure that the studio planned to film partly in the South Seas early in 1938.

The studio had invoked the morals clause to cancel Walters' contract, and it was unlikely any other studio would use him now, either. Howard felt a sense of satisfaction that Walters would never get in his way again.

Although there were fewer problems at the studio for him now than there had been when he was making *The Lady from Tangiers* with Leni, there were still too many at home. He had the inescapable feeling that Leni was bored with him and that if he didn't find a way to make himself more exciting to her, as he must have been in the beginning, she would simply walk out on him one day. She was still ardent in bed, but their unions weren't nearly frequent enough for him, and she was becoming more and more elusive.

They were seldom alone together anymore. Usually he would come home from the studio and find her having cocktails with Adrienne and Gurtner. Then there would be an interminable discussion on something that bored him, such as Gurtner's observations about the Russian director Eisenstein, whom he considered his only real peer, and then an equally interminable dinner.

Dinner often ended as late as ten or afterward, and he would have to go straight upstairs to bed or risk being tired on the set the next day, but too often he had to take a pill to get to sleep, because it distressed him that the conversation continued downstairs until the small hours, with him excluded.

One night he couldn't stand it any longer. When they rose from the dinner table, he took Leni's arm and said firmly to Adrienne and Gurtner, "She's coming upstairs with me."

Leni froze, and her arm stiffened in his grasp as she tried to pull away from him. But he tightened his grip and turned her toward the door, noting as he shoved her out into the hall that Gurtner and Adrienne had been struck speechless with incredulity.

"I do not understand this," Leni said as he pushed her toward the staircase.

"Oh, I think you do," Howard said. "You're going to get loved, and I'm going to get loved back. There hasn't been enough of that in our lives lately, and we're going to do something about it right now."

He picked her up in his arms and carried her upstairs, putting her down only when they were in her room. She stood there uncertainly as he went about locking the doors.

"That's to keep Adrienne and Gurtner out, just in case they get any

110

cute ideas about trying to rescue you. Get out of your clothes," he went on as he shed his coat and ripped at his tie and shirt, popping a couple of shirt buttons in his haste.

"You are acting like an animal," Leni said, looking at him wonderingly, as if she were seeing him as he really was for the first time.

"I think animals are what you really like," he said, stepping forward and gripping the neck of her dress, which plunged low to reveal the cleft between her breasts. She cried out as he ripped the fabric and tore the dress so far down that it fell to her feet. Then she laughed. He'd hit a true chord in her. This was what she really liked. As mental as she was, she was even more physical. The best thing to do with her was not to ask but to take.

So he did. He tore off her underclothes and shoved her roughly to the bed. He lowered himself on top of her.

"I'm too hot for the preliminaries," he said as he pushed her legs apart and inserted himself. "We'll have those for dessert."

He made love to her more often that night than he would have thought possible of him. There wasn't a part of her face and body that he missed. If there was any stiffness or reluctance in her in the beginning, it was soon gone. He wouldn't let her get out of bed for an instant, for he didn't want to give her a chance to take precautions. He wanted to impregnate her, he wanted a child of her; and she would want one too, he knew, when she saw how important it was to their marriage. He didn't care that he would be a wreck on the set tomorrow. He didn't intend leaving the bed. They would stay awake all night making love.

When the morning light crept through the openings in the draperies, he looked at her and wondered that she could look so beautiful after being manhandled all night long.

"You are an animal and you are also a little boy," she said.

"I don't care what I am, as long as you love me."

"I love you," she said, but he was disturbingly aware that she hesitated before she said it.

Out of nowhere Barney showed up at the house the week after Howard's picture with Denise Carroll was in the can.

"Those bastards at the studio wouldn't give me your address," he said in his loud voice as he embraced Howard. "I had to take a sightseeing bus tour to find this place."

Barney's voice was just about the only thing about him that hadn't changed drastically in the few years since he'd left Hollywood. He looked like an old man. His rumpled, grease-splotched suit looked as if it might have been handed out by the Salvation Army. His shoes were

111

badly cracked, with rundown heels, and Howard was sure there must be holes in the soles. Barney's smile tried for bravery but didn't quite succeed.

"You look great," Barney said. "Of course I knew that before I came. I've been catching your pictures, Howie. I've never missed a one."

"Why haven't you let me know where you were all these years?"

"I've been busy, and I'm not much for writing." Barney's tone sobered. "I'll tell you very frankly that things are bad with me. Do you know what they say about comedians being the saddest men in the world? Well, here's the saddest of them all. I haven't worked for way over a year. There are a hell of a lot more comedians around than there are nightclubs to work in nowadays. No vaudeville, and very little burlesque, either." He paused. "But I'm not here to put the touch on you, Howie. I was just wondering if maybe you might put in a word for me with the casting director at Regency."

"Why, of course," Howard said after a moment of hesitation. He realized that he wasn't really very glad to see Barney. The truth was that he'd practically forgotten him.

"I knew you wouldn't let down an old pal," Barney said.

Howard felt backed into a corner; he hardly knew what to do next. He decided that the first thing to do was get Barney some decent clothes. They went to a ready-to-wear clothier in Hollywood, where a new sport coat and slacks and new shoes changed Barney's general aspect, but he still had a look of desperation.

There was no thought of asking Barney to stay at the house. Leni would certainly find him crude, and Howard didn't see any reason why they should meet yet.

"I'll take you out to my place at Malibu for a few days," he said, seeing it as a temporary way to handle an awkward situation. "You'll get plenty of rest, sun, and peace there."

"After hitching rides and riding the rails all the way out to California, I could sure use some, Howie."

Howard drove Barney out to the beach house and left him well provisioned, telling himself that he would go straight to the studio the next day and see the casting director. But he didn't. He didn't go the next two days, either. He didn't know why he was postponing it. He only knew that he wished Barney had never shown up and presented him with a big problem he didn't want to handle.

But when he phoned Barney the morning of his fourth day at Malibu, Barney's first question was, "What did the studio say?" Howard gave a fumbling excuse and said that he'd arranged to see the casting director the next morning.

Mort Weinstein was surprised to see him. Most of the requests to the casting office came by phone, and usually from producers and directors, not from stars. As Howard came in, Weinstein was finishing a call to Central Casting, ordering some extras for the next day.

"Well, Mr. Stanton, what can I do for you?" Weinstein asked pleasantly when he'd finished his call.

"I hope you can help me get Barney Flugle a job," Howard said.

Weinstein remembered Barney from his Universal pictures, but he said with a shake of his head, "We wouldn't have anything for him. We don't make that kind of comedy anymore. We were never good at it because we didn't have the right kind of directors or comedians for it. Flugle is the Minsky type of comedian, the old burlesque regular, and that type doesn't go in the movies anymore. Except for W. C. Fields, the radio comedians like Cantor, Benny, and Hope are the only ones Hollywood can sell nowadays."

"Even a non-comedy bit would be a help for Barney."

Weinstein shook his head again as he put his hand on a neat pile of half a dozen scripts on his desk. "These are the screenplays for the pictures going into production next month. I've been over them all carefully to plan casting, and there isn't anything suitable in here for Flugle. But if anything does come up, I'll let you know."

"I'd appreciate that."

"But I'd like to point out that throwing a down-and-outer a bit sometimes does more harm than good, because more likely than not there would be no additional bits to throw him afterward. Sometimes I think that when you hit bottom, it's best to get out of the business. But few do it. Most of them just go on scraping bottom, hoping against hope." Weinstein sighed. "They say that once you've been in the business, you can't be happy doing anything else. I guess that's true."

Howard was able to delay facing Barney about his talk with Weinstein because the weekend intervened. He phoned Barney that he was tied down with unavoidable social obligations Saturday and Sunday, which wasn't true, and said that he would drive out to Malibu on Monday.

"That means you don't have good news," Barney said, "or you'd tell me right now."

"There's plenty of hope," Howard lied. He found himself

exaggerating again when he saw Barney on Monday. "Naturally it's going to take time, but something is bound to come up for you at the studio. It's just that the right thing doesn't come along every day for any of us, Barney."

"Especially not for me," said Barney. "I'm not exactly—what's that big word? 'Versatile,' that's it."

"What you do, you do very well, and that's what matters."

"Don't kid me, Howie. Fields is a genius, Chaplin is a genius, maybe Keaton and Lloyd are geniuses. Me, I'm just a bum. I have to work damned hard to get my laughs."

"Most of us have to work hard to get what we're after."

"You're right. I'm acting like an eight-year-old. I guess I want you to feel as sorry for me as I feel for myself, and that's stupid. That's no way to be with a pal who's trying to help. Thanks to you, I've got a roof over my head and stew in my belly for the first time in a long while, and I'm going to stop squawking right now. So why don't we take a walk together down that big beautiful beach out there?"

Howard changed into tennis shorts before they set out, because he was supposed to develop a deep tan by the time *The Great Typhoon* went into production.

"Howie, you've sure got a build," Barney said with a touch of envy in his voice as they started down the beach. "A build and a face. No wonder you're an idol."

"I'd like to think I amount to something more than that," Howard said a little sharply.

"Don't get touchy," said Barney with a laugh. "You've got a hell of a lot more than that working for you. You've got male 'it,' Howie." He looked out at the ocean. "That big pond's got 'it,' too. It's just about the most terrific thing I've ever seen. It got me to thinking about time, Howie. Time is a funny thing. It goes on, and something like that big pond out there doesn't change at all. Yet we change from day to day. Think back eight years, when we were in the boardinghouse together. You were a kid with big hopes and I was a wise guy with a swelled head. Well, look what a few years have done to us. You've made it as big as anybody could, and I've—"

"Barney, please," Howard interrupted.

"You're right. I was going into the sorry-for-myself routine again. Stop me when I do that, Howie. Anyway, I haven't been able to stop thinking about this time business. It doesn't matter much about time passing when you're young, but when you get in your thirties and forties, it begins to matter more and more. You think back and you wonder what happened to the people who were important to you. For

114

God's sake, Howie, I never went home once after I ran away when I was sixteen. I hated my stepfather's guts, and I took it out on my mom. I never wrote her and told her where I was. It was years later, after I'd made a couple movies, before anyone from home knew where I was. Then a cousin of mine I could hardly remember took the trouble to write and say my mom had died five or six years before and they hadn't been able to find me. Jesus, I was ashamed, Howie. I mean, when they *die,* you stop to think what a crumb you are."

Barney looked at Howard, apparently expecting some comment. Howard had nothing to say. He was thinking of his impassivity when his own parents had died.

"People are so important to us," Barney went on. "Why is it so many of us end up alone?"

"You aren't alone."

"No, you've been proving to me I've still got a friend left, Howie, but I figure it should be more than one. Jesus, I've run through a lot of people in my lifetime. It's been like letting water run through my fingers."

They walked on in silence for a while, and then Barney spoke again, in a choked voice.

"What I've been wondering about most is what happened to Alice. She was my wife, and I was nuts about her for a while, but I never bothered to keep in touch after we split up. That's awful, Howie."

Yes, Howard supposed it was.

Howard felt shaken by his talk with Barney. When he returned to Beverly Hills he tried without success to put it out of his mind. Much as he didn't want it, he seemed trapped with a certain amount of responsibility for Barney's immediate future. He recognized how lucky he'd been in his own career and how unlucky Barney had been in his, but it didn't make him sorry for Barney as much as it made him glad for himself. He knew he shouldn't feel that way, but he did.

He also realized that he should put forth more effort on Barney's behalf than he had, not only because they'd once been close but also because getting Barney back on his feet would help to get him out of his life again.

After two days of thinking about it, he decided to go directly to Dalton and ask for help. But when he phoned Barney to tell him what he planned, there was no answer. When there was still none after several more tries, Howard drove out to Malibu, full of dread.

The note Barney had left read: *I'm sorry I have to make a mess for you after the way you've tried to help me, Howie, but you know and I know there's no hope for me. A dead man is a dead man.*

Barney's body was washed up on the beach a mile down the way barely an hour later.

There was no one to come to the funeral.

That was what Howard kept thinking as he made the arrangements, as he bought a lot for Barney in Forest Lawn and picked out a coffin at the funeral parlor.

There was no one to send flowers but him, so he sent a dozen sprays. They surrounded the coffin when Howard went to the funeral parlor and looked at Barney's corpse. Barney looked serene. Seeing him this way, it was hard to believe he'd ever had problems.

Howard sat alone as the service was read by a clergyman whose manner couldn't have been more sincere if there'd been a hundred mourners. Howard rode out to the cemetery and watched while Barney's coffin was lowered. He kept thinking about Barney ending life all alone. He wondered if his own life would end the same way.

19

Howard had the 1927 version of *Ivanhoe* starring Rex Walters screened for him several times before the studio began its remake. There was no doubt in his mind that they would all have to be thoroughly on their toes to top the silent version, which had with complete justification been Regency Pictures' biggest success in the twenties. The costume picture was an action masterpiece, beautifully performed and directed with pace and high spirits.

The new production was to be filmed in Technicolor. John Edsel had been assigned as director because he'd done such a fine job forming beautiful color compositions in *Westward the Men*. Howard was glad to have Edsel directing him again, for the director had managed to pull out of him the best performance he'd given yet.

He was making careful preparations for the picture. He'd read Scott's novel twice, and while a castle with a drawbridge and moat was being erected on the back lot and the armory was turning out mail, shields, and swords for the picture, Howard was going over the final versions of the script.

But his determination to do a creditable job as Ivanhoe—indeed, to top Walters' interpretation of the role—wasn't helped by his growing concern over his deteriorating relationship with Leni. He recognized that he was paying a penalty of pain and hurt for loving her so much, and sometimes he wished he'd never met her, let alone married her.

Certainly, if he hadn't, he'd be spared his tormenting jealousy over her continuing attentions to Gurtner, to various members of the established German colony in Hollywood who showed up at the house with increasing frequency, and to Adrienne. Adrienne was even learning German from Leni at this point, and it annoyed Howard greatly that his wife and her secretary-companion were becoming closer and closer friends.

But Tuesday was Adrienne's day off, and Howard hoped, as he returned home from a meeting with Edsel at the studio and stopped the car in front of the house, that Gurtner hadn't spirited Leni off somewhere. He was relieved to find her in the big, beam-ceilinged living room, dressed in a classically plain black silk dress with a stiff raised collar around which her beautiful hair fell softly.

"Where are the servants?" he asked.

"I wanted to be alone. I gave them the afternoon off."

He sat down beside her on the huge couch. There was a bottle of champagne in a bucket on the table in front of her, and a half-filled glass. Champagne was all she ever drank. He'd once commented on her custom of drinking in the afternoon, and she'd said that champagne was appropriate at any time of the day for those who took the trouble to savor life.

"I'm glad you gave them the afternoon off," he said. "We need to be together more, Leni. We don't talk enough to each other, and we don't make love enough. I don't like it because you give so much of yourself to others and so little of yourself to me. It's going to stop!"

She smiled. "What do you call that in America? Oh, yes. You are putting your foot down, are you not?"

"Yes. You're married to me, Leni, not to your friends, and you're not free to do what you want to do. Things are going to change."

The smile stayed. "The man of the house," she said softly. "That is very German, very European. There the husband speaks and the wife responds. Women are not partners with men as they are here."

"I like that idea."

"Do you? It is not democratic, is it? I am surprised that you would approve of anything that is not democratic."

"Leni, I've never claimed that our system is perfect."

"I am glad, because it is anything but perfect, Howard. This country is supposed to be so democratic, but is it, really? If that is so, why are

117

there so many poor people? Why have they not been helped more? Why is it necessary for American workers to strike so often? Why—"

"That's what you and your friends talk about in German when you get together, isn't it?" he cut in sharply. "What you think is wrong with this country!"

"Yes. And there is much wrong with it." Her smile was gone and her face was set.

"And there's nothing wrong with Germany? You have Utopia there under Hitler?"

"There is less wrong there than here. I think Germany has a great future. I think the greatness of America is in the past."

"Leni, America *is* your country now," he said in exasperation.

"I will always be a German," she said quietly.

"You're my wife, first and foremost." He paused. "Leni, why did you marry me?"

"Because I had to," she said without hesitation. "I could not have done anything else."

So she'd married him not because she loved him but because she'd had to—whatever that meant. He had no response. Maybe she didn't love him, maybe she never had, maybe she didn't know what love was. And maybe he didn't, either.

"God, Leni," he said with a shudder, "I don't know what to say to you. Why should a man be speechless with his own wife? Why is it you're so different from anyone I've ever known?"

"If that is so, I am glad. I want to be different from everyone else in the world."

"You are," he said. "But I'm telling you, Leni, that things are going to change. You're going to spend less time with Gurtner and your other German friends. I think you get the idea. Right now, I have another idea." He put his hand on her breast.

She laughed. "At three o'clock in the afternoon?"

"You weren't particular about the time of the day when we were on our honeymoon."

"I am ready," she said with another laugh, and leaned her head back against the cushion, presenting her neck for him to press his face against. "I am always ready for you."

It wasn't true, but he didn't care. It only vaguely disturbed him that he was diminishing the effect of his ultimatum by ending it this way. He couldn't turn back. He was burning up. Again, as so many times when they made love, it was as if it were the first time and the last time and the only time.

Minutes later he lay spent and breathless, his face pressed against

118

hers. As his breathing eased, he opened his eyes. She was staring out into the room, and she was smiling.

The Lady from Tangiers was ready for its sneak preview, its editing finally having been completed by Gurtner. The picture had been screened at the studio the previous evening, but Howard had declined to attend.

"I didn't want to see myself," Howard said. "I'm not good in this picture, and that's all there is to it. I can't work with Gurtner."

"But you did, and you did a good job," Dalton said.

"Yes, you come across very well, Howard," Renfew said. "It's a beautiful picture. Leni is sensational."

"I don't doubt that for a moment," Howard said.

"But the final test is whether or not the American public accepts her," Dalton commented. "Just because she's big in Europe doesn't mean she will be here. It's hard to believe that she could miss, but she could. It's very costly to introduce an imported star. You have to put out a lot in the beginning without being sure you're going to get it back. With actors coming up from the bottom, it's different. Look at the slow buildup you got, Howard. You clicked before we'd spent millions. But this is different."

"Thank God you did import her," Howard said, annoyed with Dalton for his attitude. Dalton was like this occasionally, thinking of people as products for exploitation, not as human beings.

"We think it will work out," Dalton said. "We expect Leni to be one of our most popular stars. But her future pictures will have to be brought in more efficiently. We can't take a year, and spend twice what the budget calls for, to make a picture. She's got to have more exposure than one picture a year anyway. Only Garbo can get away with that."

"You'd better talk to Gurtner about that, hadn't you?" Howard said sarcastically.

Dalton annoyed Howard further by insisting that he and Leni attend the sneak preview. Howard couldn't understand why it was expected. Usually only the studio head, the production head, the director, the writer, and the supervising cutter went to the sneak preview, for they didn't want any subjective interference or reactions from the actors.

"But I think it will be a delightful experience," Leni told him as they drove to the studio to meet the others.

"It might be a sad occasion," he said bluntly. "The picture could flop."

"What would that mean?" she said lightly. "Only that I will not be a star in America. But I will still be a star in Europe."

119

"But you're married to me and you're an American now. You're not going to make any more pictures in Europe."

"Perhaps only an occasional one," she said, smiling. "But do not worry. The picture will not fail. Nothing Karl does ever fails."

That wasn't true, either. Howard knew that Gurtner had turned out several flops in Germany. But there was no use antagonizing Leni about it now. They both needed to be as calm as possible this evening.

Limousines were waiting at the studio to transport the preview party. Dalton asked Howard and Leni to ride with him, and the others followed in the other cars. When they arrived at the neighborhood theater in Glendale where the picture was being previewed, the manager hurried forth to greet them and pointed proudly to the marquee, which announced that there would be a sneak preview tonight at eight-thirty. Boldly heralded that way, it couldn't really be considered a sneak preview, but at least the announcement had filled the rather shabby little theater.

After a request from the manager on stage that the audience fill out preview opinion cards as they left the theater, the lights went down and the picture began. Howard watched himself tensely through several scenes before he decided he'd misjudged his performance. He'd risen above the miscasting and Gurtner's abuse and was coming across pretty well.

The picture itself was pictorially perfect. The care Gurtner had taken to compose beautiful pictures was evident in every scene. The stunning images he'd achieved compensated somewhat for the inadequacies of the dialogue and the story line, and for the most part the audience seemed rapt, although they laughed several times in the wrong places, which meant there would be reediting of those particular scenes.

But it was Leni herself, more than all the other elements, who held the audience's attention. There was no doubt of it. She was the woman of mystery that every woman envied and every man wanted.

It was over. The audience applauded as the lights went up, and many of them, already having seen the advertised picture, got up and departed, leaving their preview opinion cards in the lobby as they left.

The preview party returned to the studio with the cards, sending back a chauffeur to bring the cards deposited by those who stayed on to see the second showing of the advertised picture. The studio was dark except for streetlights and a few lighted windows in the writers' building. Buckets of champagne, a buffet spread, and a waiter from the commissary were on hand in Dalton's office. The cards were turned over to a secretary for tabulation, and Dalton told the waiter to pour the champagne even though it was customary to learn the results before celebrating.

"I'm sure already we've definitely got something to celebrate—a fine picture and a great new star for Regency Pictures." Dalton raised his glass and smiled at Leni. "To the world's most beautiful star."

The tabulation confirmed Dalton's high hopes. At least fifty percent of the preview audience had made some favorable remark about Leni—particularly about her beauty, her voice, or her acting ability—in the blank space on the card that asked for special comments. Howard had drawn few comments. Hardly anyone had rated the picture outstanding, but ninety percent had rated it as excellent or good. A very few had marked it as poor. For the performances of the players, Leni won hands down.

"Yes, we have a hit," Dalton exulted, and led another round of toasts. The other batch of cards brought in an hour later simply strengthened the results of the first, and the next day the revisions of the picture started, and new shots were inserted and new cuts made. The premiere was scheduled for the following month.

Ivanhoe had the top budget of the year. No corners were being cut. Good, beautiful pictures cost money, and Dalton was willing to go to battle with Smetley to spend it. The early rushes indicated that Edsel's facility with shooting in color had even improved upon his accomplishments with *Westward the Men*. The picture was going to be handsome and authentic.

Howard felt at home in the role, and he felt much more comfortable playing opposite Georgina Fox than he had opposite Leni. Georgina had been discovered by a Regency Pictures talent scout in New York City while performing in her first Broadway role. She had real acting talent, and she was bringing excitement to the role of Rebecca, a considerable challenge, since the character would have been quiet and unobtrusive with the wrong person in the role.

Howard soon found himself comparing Georgina with Leni. Georgina wasn't stunning in the sense that Leni was, but she was quietly lovely, with vivid, inquiring brown eyes. She seemed as intelligent as Leni, but more open and straightforward. There was an appealing quality of innocence about her. Two weeks after he began working with her, he felt he knew her better in some ways than he did his enigmatic wife.

He felt a physical attraction to her, too, the first he'd felt toward anyone besides Leni since she'd come into his life, and it surprised

121

him. He kept imagining himself in bed with Georgina, and he wondered if she had similar thoughts about him.

He knew he should let well enough alone, but one day he asked her to have lunch with him in the commissary.

"You weren't my favorite movie star before I came to Hollywood," she confessed, "but you are now."

He looked quizzically at her. "What does that mean?"

"That you've been friendly and helpful to me on the set, and I appreciate it."

"How do you know I don't have ulterior motives?"

She smiled, and for a moment he thought she was going to ask him if he did. But she said, "You're making it a lot easier for me in my first movie role, and that's important to me. I want to be a success in the movies. I also want to be a good movie actress."

"You already are."

"I mean *really* good. Not good in the way that Katharine Hepburn and Bette Davis are, but good in my own way. I want to be so good that when people see my name on a theater marquee they won't hesitate to buy a ticket because they'll know I'm going to give them my all. Last year my ambition was to be a great stage star—that to me was the ultimate in achievement. But even the greatest Broadway stars have a limited audience. In the movies, you can reach the whole world, and if you're good the whole world knows it. I think even the most ignorant people know the difference between someone who's good and someone who isn't. They feel it."

Howard nodded. "I could even tell that as a kid."

"I want everybody to feel that way about me. I don't care about having a husband or a lover, but I do care about being a good actress. My career comes first with me."

"I felt exactly the same way once. You'll find there's room for both. Besides, no matter how determined you are against something's happening, you can find yourself so overwhelmed that there's no turning back."

He hadn't expected to say anything like that. He met her eyes uncertainly. They were full of questions.

"I suppose so," she finally said in a very quiet tone.

20

The production of *Ivanhoe* was proceeding as smoothly as the production of *The Lady from Tangiers* had not. Howard felt from the beginning that it would turn out to be a fine picture, and he was most pleased with the strength and depth of his part. There was only one drawback. The studio declined his request to train for and play the jousting scenes himself.

"We must use a double," Renfew said flatly. "The insurance company wouldn't permit us not to. Besides, you couldn't get as good at jousting as the stunt man is without several years of practice, and we hardly have the time, have we?"

Howard went back to the set on the back lot where the filming of the siege of the castle was into its second day. Hundreds of extras were on hand for the storming of the drawbridge and the ramming of the gate. The day before, during one very extended shot, Edsel had used six different cameras operating simultaneously from different perspectives so that the action could be sustained for more than five minutes. During the exceptionally long stretch of action, Howard had stood on the rampart in his armor and mail while arrows, shot by unerringly accurate archers, had flung past him, and a group of castle defenders at his elbow had tipped over a cauldron of simulated burning oil on besiegers scaling the wall from the moat below. Howard had actually felt as if he were in the midst of a real battle.

But the excitement in making movies only came in spurts, as Georgina pointed out when they had lunch together in the commissary that day.

"I'm finding some of this business fascinating," she said, "but I get bored, too. There's too much waiting around while they get things ready."

"That's part of the game. This is a complicated business. It takes a lot of time to set up for a scene. But there are compensations."

She smiled. "I know what you mean. It all gets into your blood."

123

"Yes. That's what makes it hard if you start to slip. The idea of having to give it up is unbearable."

"I'll never let Hollywood take me over that way," she said, "even if I become a star. I don't want to be owned by a system. Or by a person."

"What does that mean?"

"Just that I don't want to be in love. I never have been, you know. Not even in high school."

"Being in love doesn't mean 'ownership,' " Howard said. "It implies a shared relationship."

"Is that the kind of relationship you and your wife have?"

Howard shifted in his seat. Her question had brought him up short. "Do you realize that this is the first time either of us has mentioned my wife?"

"Yes. It surprises me that you don't talk about her."

"I'd be interested in what you think of her," he said.

"I think she's the most beautiful woman I've ever seen."

"What else do you think?"

"What else could I think about her? I don't know her, and you don't talk to me about her."

It was true; he didn't. He'd thought about that. He'd also thought about how Georgina was more and more on his mind, on and off the set.

"I don't think we should have lunch together anymore," she suddenly said. "I don't want any gossip to start about us."

"I don't think that's what really worries you."

"No. What really worries me is that this is taking on a serious tone. I don't think either of us can afford that."

He frowned. He didn't want to stop having lunch with her. What he wanted was to see more of her than he did. But she was right. They would have to stop this from growing. He didn't want to hurt her. Even more, he didn't want to hurt himself.

Howard hated the panoply of premieres, and he contemplated the public debut of *The Lady from Tangiers* with negative feelings. It was opening at the Cathay Circle Theatre in Hollywood on Friday and at the Regency Grand in New York City on Saturday. By Monday the reviews that counted would be out, and Howard was by no means convinced that they would be kind to him. He faced the premiere with dread, unbuoyed by Leni's repeated assertion that it would be a triumph for everyone concerned. He'd never seen her more beautiful than she was when she emerged after hours of preparation for the event, helped by her maid, a studio hairdresser, and the officious

Adrienne. Leni wore a beautifully draped white silk crepe evening gown, her most stunning costume from the picture, and a long, full white wrap bordered with white fox fur.

A studio chauffeur picked them up and drove them to the spot several blocks from the theater where the procession of limousines transporting the studio party was being formed. The cars were arranged to arrive at the theater in a certain sequence, steadily discharging at timed intervals the important persons connected with the picture and those prominent in the studio hierarchy.

As the stars of the picture, Howard and Leni were scheduled to arrive last, when the waiting fans, roped off and held back by the police on both sides of the theater entrance, were at the pitch of anticipation. Finally the time arrived, and they proceeded toward the target in the distance where beams of light from powerful searchlights circled in the air, heralding the premiere.

As they pulled up, Howard looked at Leni. She was glacially beautiful, neither her face nor her eyes revealing the least trace of emotion. But she smiled radiantly as they stepped out and faced the cheering crowd. There were gasps of appreciation at her beauty. Howard smiled into the crowd himself as she took his arm and they moved toward the microphone, but he knew they weren't looking at him, just at her. She was hypnotic. She was not only the most beautiful woman in the world, she was also now the greatest star.

As they stepped up to the microphone, Dalton was finishing a carefully worded announcement tagging *The Lady from Tangiers* as Regency's best picture of the year, the same label he gave each of the studio's major releases. The announcer introduced them, and there was a renewed volley of cheers from the sidelines.

Howard said that he was glad to be here and that this was the most important occasion of his life, which many others had said before. But he got a good cheer despite the lack of originality.

"I love you all," Leni said into the microphone in her husky voice. She got an even bigger cheer than Howard had. She was a queen, all right, and they knew it.

Richly dressed men and women crowded the lobby of the theater, which had been extravagantly done up like a Mediterranean flower garden. This was one of the major premieres of the year, and the most important people from all the big studios had been invited.

It was evident from the beginning that the picture would be well received by the premiere audience. Leni Liebhaber claimed every man and woman present for her own.

Afterward, there was a party at the Cocoanut Grove, and Howard

125

drank glass after glass of champagne, but it didn't help his spirits. The rest of them were exuberant over the success of the premiere, but he was miserable. He was sorry the picture was good and sorry that it would be going into general release, for it meant that Leni would belong to the whole world now. She was no longer just Leni Liebhaber, European star and wife of Howard Stanton. Now she would be an international star, with all it demanded. Would there be anything left for Howard Stanton?

He knew he shouldn't be thinking this way. Why should he begrudge her the universal applause and adulation they all coveted? He didn't think she would begrudge him his.

Yet he continued to feel resentful, and when the celebration finally ended and they were going home, he hoped he'd be able to end his depression by making love to his wife tonight.

But Adrienne was waiting in the living room with a bottle of champagne and one of those tentative, deceptive smiles on her face. Leni sat down with her, to drink champagne and tell her what a thrilling evening it had been. Howard went upstairs alone. He'd seldom felt more discouraged.

Leni told him the following week that she wanted to go home to Germany to visit. "There could be no better time, with my next picture delayed again."

The studio was having casting and script problems with Leni's projected picture, and production had been postponed until spring.

"There might not be a better time for you," he said irritably, "but what about me? *Ivanhoe* won't be finished until the middle of January, and then I go into *The Great Typhoon* a few weeks later."

"That is why this is a good time for me to be away. You will be very busy."

He frowned. "I'd have hoped you'd want me to come along."

"Of course I wish you could. Next time you will. Howard, I must go! I yearn to be home again. Surely you can understand that."

He did and he didn't, and he had an uneasy feeling in the pit of his stomach, which grew when he learned that Leni had invited Adrienne to accompany her and that Gurtner was going along, too.

But Dalton was delighted about the venture.

"It will be good publicity for the release of *The Lady from Tangiers* in Europe," Dalton said. "And we can hope that Gurtner will decide not to come back. He's been anything but content here."

"But Leni wouldn't work with anyone but him," Howard said.

"She'll change her mind about that. Leni is going to be our brightest

126

female star, and she'll do what's necessary to maintain her position. Besides, she realizes that we'll do what's best for her."

Howard shook his head. "You don't know Leni."

"Or perhaps *you* don't know her."

"If I don't, who does?"

"Howard, it's axiomatic that Hollywood husbands and wives are blind to each other."

"I know you don't really believe that."

"I believe it in certain cases." Dalton frowned at Howard. "What's she doing to you? You've changed. Is it because you feel unsure about your marriage?"

"No," Howard said stiffly. "Besides, even if it were true, is it any of your business?"

Dalton looked coldly at him. "Of course it's my business! You're a Regency star. I think you certainly must realize that your life can't be entirely your own. I can't let it be. I owe it to Regency Pictures not to let it be."

"There is a limit."

"Howard, don't make the mistake Walters did. You can't win over us. Nobody can. You're owned by the public and you're owned by Regency Pictures. Don't lose your perspective. It can be dangerous. Don't even think you can't be broken. I could break anyone in this studio. Smetley could break me, and Wall Street could break him. Only God can't be broken. Perhaps it's good that we all have to worry about losing what we have. It keeps us on our toes. It becomes even more important as you grow older. You'll find out."

"We've gotten a long way from what we started out talking about," Howard said.

Dalton looked reflectively at him. "It's the first time for quite a while that we've talked at all." He paused. "Perhaps we've said enough for now."

Howard nodded and stood up. "Just so you understand one thing. I'm not unsure about my marriage. I've never been so sure about anything in my life."

"Very well, Howard. I'm glad to hear that."

Howard turned to walk out. At the double doors, he looked back. Dalton was absolutely motionless at his desk, his eyes fixed firmly on Howard. They said they didn't believe him.

21

It was anything but a private farewell. There were studio and news services photographers and a group of fans on hand when Leni arrived with Howard at the train station, Gurtner and Adrienne immediately behind them. Leni was stunningly appareled in a black traveling suit fringed with fur. She posed smilingly with Howard against the backdrop of the Sante Fe Chief while the powder-flashes popped.

On board, Leni's compartment was crowded with flowers, and a bucket of champagne waited. There was no time for a toast, with the train set to pull out in a minute. Irritatingly enough, Gurtner and Adrienne declined to make themselves scarce at the last important moment. The good-by kiss was unsatisfactory.

Leaving the train, Howard stood among a group of waving fans and watched as Leni's beautiful face, glowing through the compartment window, receded and was gone.

The house was unbearable without her. While she was crossing the continent, he kept sending telegrams to be delivered to her on the train, and when she was ushered into her suite at the Plaza in New York City, he was waiting on the phone for her. He talked to her as often as he could find her during the next two days, and then she was lost to him, swept away on the *Europa*. A smiling picture of her and Gurtner against the ship's railing appeared in the New York *Herald*.

Howard had hoped until the last moment that she would change her mind and not sail, but she was gone, and she wouldn't be back until the end of February. He might as well bear up to it. Perhaps in the long run the trip would pay off. Maybe Leni would get her nostalgia for Germany out of her system for a while. And perhaps, as Dalton felt was possible, Gurtner would decide not to return.

In the meantime, Howard would be busy with work. There was *Ivanhoe* to finish and *The Great Typhoon* to begin. There were only a few weeks left on *Ivanhoe,* and Georgina's scenes were already completed. Howard was glad. If she wasn't on the set, then he couldn't talk to her between takes. What had started between them must be stopped where it was, at the beginning.

But he missed seeing her. She was on the lot every day, because she was attending the acting school the studio had started—to teach motion picture acting techniques to new contract players—but she didn't go to lunch when the *Ivanhoe* company did, and he wondered if that was deliberate. One day he ran into her by chance near the writers' building.

"You look like a schoolgirl," he said with a laugh. She was wearing a white sweater, a red plaid skirt, white socks, and the brown and white saddle shoes that were so popular with the young set. "All you need is pigtails."

"Silly," she said, laughing herself. "Schoolgirls haven't worn pigtails for years. They wear the Garbo bob, just like their mothers."

"I guess I'm not up on what schoolgirls and their mothers are doing."

"Typical Hollywood star. You live in a world all your own."

"How's it going?" he asked.

"It's going very well. I've moved out of the Hollywood Studio Club into a little apartment with a girl I met there. She's under contract to Columbia. You might say that we're at the same stage of development, but we're not rivals, since we're at different studios, so we get along well as roommates. But I think I'm a better actress than she is."

"I don't doubt it. And I don't doubt that you're much more beautiful than she is, too."

"I'm not beautiful," she insisted. "Your wife is beautiful. I'm just pretty. There's a great deal of difference."

Howard frowned because she'd brought Leni up.

"I see I've embarrassed you," she went on. "I'm sorry. You're a terribly moral man, Howard, and I find that admirable."

"But I'm not. You wouldn't say that if you knew what I want to say to you." And *do* to you, he thought.

"Don't say it," she said. "We turned back before. We've got to stay turned back. I don't want either of us to be hurt, and as I said, I don't want to be in love, and I'm not going to be. As for you, you can't afford it, can you?"

She turned and walked away.

It was a regrettable day from the beginning. Howard wasn't in any of the day's scenes, so he didn't go to the studio. He had planned to study the scenes for tomorrow, but he couldn't concentrate. Untypically, he had a Scotch and soda, although it was only a little after lunch, and then he called the office at the studio and asked for Georgina's address.

"We can't give out that information, sir," said the prim voice at the other end. "It's a studio rule."

"I'm Howard Stanton!" he snapped out, then regretted his irritability. He understood why they had to have such rules. He supposed everyone from burglars to rapists called the studios to obtain addresses.

"I'm awfully sorry, sir," the girl said, but still refused to give out the address. It seemed that anyone could call the studio and say he was Howard Stanton. Howard told her to look up his private number and call him back.

"Now will you believe me?" he asked when she rang him.

"Yes, sir," she said contritely, and gave him Georgina Fox's address immediately.

He was already sorry he had asked for it. He could imagine what would happen if the girl mentioned it to anyone. The story would then make its way around the studio, assuming new dimensions along the way, and a distorted version might get to the columnists. He might well have gotten himself and Georgina into a bad situation through his rashness.

But he wasn't going to stop now. Under the stimulus of another Scotch and soda, he started for Georgina's apartment in Hollywood in the white LaSalle convertible coupe he'd bought for Leni. He almost turned back twice. When he got there, Georgina's roommate answered the door. She said that Georgina was at the studio posing for publicity stills and would be gone all day.

"I'll certainly tell her you were here, Mr. Stanton," the girl said, smiling as he thanked her and turned away.

He was sorry he'd come and sorry that Georgina would worry when she found out about it. She was certainly trying harder than he was to keep her emotions under control. Why wasn't he? Was his recklessness an attempt to get back at Leni for going away and making him realize how very much he needed her?

Or was it someone else he needed? Was it Georgina he needed?

God, what *did* he want? he asked himself as he drove on sudden impulse toward an address where he couldn't really afford to be seen. When he looked back on his life, at the youth who'd haunted theater balconies, who'd idolized Rudolph Valentino, who'd worked as a soda jerk, a clothing salesman, and an office boy before brazenly presenting his case to one of the most powerful studio heads in the business—when he thought of what Howard Stanton the youth had won over

130

tremendous odds for Howard Stanton the man, what could he possibly want now that he didn't have?

Didn't he have just about everything? In this Depression year of 1937, nine quick years from his arrival in Hollywood, he owned a fifteen-room mansion in Beverly Hills, had three cars in his garage and thirty suits in his wardrobe, was number eight on the magic list of box office favorites, and was married to one of the most desirable and fascinating women in the world.

He reached Selma's place, and if she was surprised to see him she didn't show it. She asked him what type he had in mind, and he said, "A friendly type—I want to talk more than anything else." She produced a girl named Nan who had modeled herself after Jean Harlow, with platinum blond hair and pencil-thin eyebrows. She told him her story while they drove toward the beach house. It was standard. She'd come here to get into pictures, and three years of trying had gotten her nowhere. You would think they'd need a new Jean Harlow now that the original was gone, she pointed out.

What was he to say? That no one could ever take the place of anyone who had been or was? That she couldn't be another Harlow any more than he could be another Valentino? Or that even if they could, the public wouldn't accept carbon copies? There was no use saying it, for she wouldn't understand. She was too determined to cling to her dream.

Still, it wasn't his worry. He hadn't brought her along to discuss her problems but to distract him from his own. He wondered what she'd think when she found out he didn't intend to touch her.

She loved the beach house.

"It would be wonderful to live forever in a house like this with someone you loved," she said gaily, darting around, examining things.

That didn't sound like a girl with career dreams talking. Neither did it sound like a whore talking. He forgot what she was for a while as they walked the beach together that cool December day, her platinum hair a white corona in the sunlight. Somehow she seemed like an old friend who'd shown up from nowhere to renew their acquaintance.

The walk sobered him somewhat, but back at the house he started on the Scotch again and had finished two highballs before she'd finished her first.

"Why are you trying to get drunk?" she said. "Don't you like me?"

"Yes, I do. Maybe that's one reason why I'm getting drunk. I feel guilty because I brought you here."

"I think I understand. You have a beautiful wife. You feel guilty because of her, I suppose."

"Maybe."

"Maybe? It sounds like you don't really know."

"Maybe I don't. But I do know one thing. I didn't bring you out here for sex."

She took a breath before she answered. "I'm disappointed. I hope it isn't anything I've done."

"It isn't," he assured her.

"Well, from my viewpoint, it's too bad. You're handsome. You have a wonderful build. I know you'd be good at it—I can tell. I enjoy it when I'm with someone who's good at it."

"I brought you here because I needed someone to be with me," he said. "And now I'm tired and I think I'll take a nap."

"This won't be a very flattering story to tell, will it?" she said. "I spent an afternoon with Howard Stanton, but he didn't make love to me. He took a nap."

"Then why tell it?" he said as he rose to go to his bedroom.

"I guess the great screen lovers aren't gods. They're just people."

He stopped and looked back. "I'm afraid so."

"Do you know what the frigid woman said? 'Put it in my icebox.' "

He didn't laugh. "Call me in a couple of hours if I don't wake up by then."

He went into the bedroom, closed the door, stripped, and lay down leadenly on the bed. He fell asleep instantly.

When he wakened, it was abruptly. He was hard and she was crouched on his thighs, nude, looking at him hungrily.

"That's the most magnificent cock I've ever seen," she said. "And those beautiful balls—a stud's balls!"

He felt like telling her to get the hell out, but her cupped hands came gently around his genitals and held them, and she leaned down and licked his penis again and again and pressed her face against it.

Then she raised herself and moved up on him. "I'm going to sit on it. I'm going to put it in my hotbox."

He didn't think that was funny, either. Nothing about this was funny. Yet he didn't stop it. She was sitting down on him and he was going up into her and she was moaning with pleasure.

She collapsed onto his chest, her breasts pushing against him, her hair against his face, her mouth at his ear.

"Fuck me," she groaned. "Fuck me, fuck me, fuck me . . ."

132

22

Toward the end of January, Leni sent word that she'd decided to delay her return from Germany until April.

Her first reason was that since she and Gurtner were still not satisfied with the script for her next picture, regardless of the several revisions that had been sent to them, it was quite obvious that its starting date would have to be postponed again.

Besides, it would be ridiculous for her to return in February as planned if her picture wasn't going to start soon, since Howard would soon be gone. He was scheduled to go to Samoa for location shots on *The Great Typhoon* early in March.

"This is outrageous!" Dalton said in an unusual display of emotion when he summoned Howard to his office to talk about it. "We've introduced one of the greatest female stars of our time to worldwide audiences, and we're being asked for new Leni Liebhaber pictures right away, but we can't get her back here to make her second picture. Howard, you're her husband. Tell her to come home!"

"Don't you think I've tried? I blame Gurtner for her stubbornness. He certainly hasn't loosened his hold on her. And you were dead wrong thinking he'd choose to stay on in Germany and let her come back here and make pictures on her own. Don't you see what this business about unsatisfactory scripts really means? He's trying to wear you down. When you reach the desperate stage, he'll agree to bring Leni back, but only on better terms."

"Leni is just as perverse as Gurtner," Dalton said. "I think she enjoys being a difficult woman. We can't afford to lose her because of our large investment in her, but we can't afford to keep an uncooperative star, either. Make her understand that, Howard."

"I would if I could," Howard said stiffly, "but I can't always get through to her."

Dalton looked soberly at him. "Your marriage *is* going to pieces, isn't it?"

133

"God damn it, that isn't true!" Howard said hotly. "My marriage is fine. Now is that clear?"

Dalton stared at him. "No, Howard, it isn't at all clear."

Howard knew that the best thing he could have done was simply go to Germany and bring Leni back. But it was impossible. Production on *The Great Typhoon* was scheduled to start the second week in February in spite of the fact that the leading lady hadn't been settled on yet.

Three days before production was to begin on stage four and in the new million-gallon tank on the back lot, Howard was informed that Georgina Fox would be his leading lady. He'd suspected she might be chosen. She was dark and lovely, a natural for the part of the beautiful native girl the sea captain falls in love with. Furthermore, Dalton and Renfew were both convinced, after her performance in *Ivanhoe,* that Georgina would be a star, and they were eager to get her into a new picture quickly.

She came to the set the first day of production, although her first scenes weren't due until just before they were to leave for Samoa.

"I'm glad we're going to be working together again," she said.

"So am I," Howard said, smiling at her, but his tone warned her as much as hers had warned him. They were telling each other that they had to be careful, that they couldn't let themselves get carried away.

For use in studio-shot scenes, a large-scale schooner, complete to the last spar, was moored in the waters of the big tank on the back lot. Two weeks of hard work were devoted to shooting shipboard scenes, and then two more to the typhoon scene, with the giant wind machines tossing the ship around in the tank.

Some typhoon shots were also made with a miniature model of the ship being battered in a smaller tank on the tank stage, but the ones that counted most were made aboard the schooner itself while studio technicians created the most monstrous storm possible.

The storm was filmed at intervals that were continually interrupted while camera setups were changed. The terrifying climax, when the ship was driven into the island harbor and broke up under the fury of the storm, was the most carefully planned scene of all. Carpenters came aboard with saws to weaken the ship so it would break up properly. A medical crew from the studio dispensary stood by, because there were certain to be injuries. Six camera crews were on hand to get shots from all angles, because once the final breakup of the ship had begun, there would be no stopping the scene for new setups. The same scene would also be done with the miniature model on the tank stage to fill in the long shots, but it was the big breakup that counted. It was one of the

134

biggest scenes the studio had ever filmed. Even Dalton left his office to see it.

Overhead, an enormous span of canvas cut off the California sun from the dark, raging waters set into motion by the wind machines. The ship rocked and groaned under the lash of the waves. A great wave rolled over the ship, and Howard collapsed under it. It wasn't planned action, since there couldn't be any, and Howard found himself wondering if he was going to live through it. The wind howled, the waves pounded, and the ship was coming apart beneath him. The simulated storm seemed to go on forever, although actually it took only a few minutes. But the director got what he wanted. The ship crashed on the shore and came apart as required by the script, and they were all spilled out.

Two men suffered broken arms, and Howard had never before felt such terrible pain as he did in his right side. But it was only a misplaced rib. In two days it was back in position.

There were several days of interior shooting on stage four, and then the location party took off by seaplane for Hawaii, where they were to continue the journey south to Samoa by another seaplane.

"It's my first time up in a plane," Georgina said as the California coastline receded behind them. "I thought I'd be frightened to death, but I'm only mildly scared."

"Most things aren't as bad as we think they're going to be," Howard said, and then realized that it could have meant a dozen things. She looked at him briefly but didn't try to make anything of it.

"I've decided already that flying is thrilling," she said after a moment of silence. "I think I wanted to be an aviatrix once. Anyway, I admired Amelia Earhart."

"Tell me what you're *really* thinking at this moment, Georgina," he said abruptly.

She looked away from him, out the round porthole into the sky. "I'm thinking that there's a woman named Leni Liebhaber—or is it Leni Stanton?—who's very important in your life." She looked back at him. "Had you forgotten?"

"No," he said. "I hadn't forgotten."

Samoa was the paradise the studio research department had said it was. The second-unit crew, which had been there for a month photographing background shots and planning the scenes they were to shoot with Howard, Georgina, and the supporting players that had been flown down, were already dreading the day they would have to depart.

"These people know how to live," said Ted McElroy, a recently

135

promoted assistant director who had been put in charge of directing the second-unit operation.

Georgina agreed. "They don't know how to be cruel to one another because they don't need to be. They don't have to worry about economic depressions or wars or whether they can afford a new Chevrolet next year. Or any of the other nonsense we worry about."

"I don't think you worry about such things yourself," Howard said.

"Not much. But I will if I get anywhere. It never fails that the more you get, the more you want, does it? These islanders don't get more than the basics, and that's all they want. I hope, for their own good, that they don't ever get any more."

"But their basics are better than our basics to begin with," Howard pointed out.

It was true. The climate was incredibly wonderful, and the natives lived their lives in a beautiful setting. Life was perfectly peaceful, and no one rushed. The heavily forested lands produced enough copra, breadfruit, and bananas for export to balance the few imports the trade ships brought to the lovely lagoons.

The natives were cheerful and handsome, and worked as extras in the village scenes as if they were playing a game. One big scene portraying a village feast and a large-scale native dance was particularly realistic because it was created directly from their way of life.

Production moved forward with such efficiency that they were soon ahead of schedule, and it looked as if they would be finished in Samoa a week ahead of time.

"I'm going to hate to see this come to an end," Howard said one day when he and Georgina were walking on the beach after shooting was finished.

"So am I." Her voice trembled. "Howard, I don't think I ever want to go back home."

He looked at her. Her eyes were expectant as she searched his face, waiting for him to say that he didn't want to go back, either. But he couldn't let himself say it, for his life was back there, with Leni.

"I think I'm going to cry," Georgina said in a stifled voice, and suddenly ran off.

He followed her along the beach, shouting her name as seabirds cried overhead. He was amazed at how swiftly she ran. She still wore the pareu of bright-flowered cloth from the scene they'd just filmed, and her long dark hair streamed behind her as she fled. Somehow it was terrifying, the lonely stretch of beach staring whitely under a dazzle of sun, the great forest looming to the side, the breakers spilling on the sand, the perfect sky, and the two of them utterly alone in the world. It was as if she were running headlong to her doom, and in a moment he would be left all alone, forever.

"Georgina, stop!" he shouted desperately.

But she didn't. She darted off the beach into the forest, and it was only by luck that he found her there, huddled on a patch of grass beneath a cluster of great arching palms. She was weeping so hard that her body shook. He hesitated, then put his hand on her shoulder. Her face turned to him, contorted with agony.

"Howard, I love you! And it isn't going to bring me anything but unhappiness! Because you love *her!* Oh, God, why did it happen? I didn't want to love anybody. But I love you. And I want you to take me. Now."

"No."

"Yes," she said, reaching for his hand, pressing it against her breast. "You're saying no because you don't want to hurt me. I'm already hurt, and it's nobody's fault. I want you to take me. You must."

He was hard. She reached out and felt his erection. He pulled her to her feet and clasped her against him. Their mouths opened and their tongues met.

"I want us to be naked," she said breathlessly.

She parted her pareu and dropped it while he struggled out of his clothes.

"Oh, God," she said, looking him up and down. "You're beautiful!"

She was a virgin—and he was as gentle as possible. He prepared her until she seemed to be burning up as much as he was, and then he made the slow, difficult insertion that obviously at first gave her pain.

They lay there until the sun went down and the chill drove them back to the village, and he lost count of how many times they made love.

The next day she said, "I meant everything I said yesterday. And I know we mustn't talk about it anymore. It would only make it worse to talk about it and remind ourselves that everything is changed, yet nothing is. But I thank you, my darling, for making love to me. It could never be the same with anyone else. It will be hard to stay away from you after that, but I'll have to. An affair is impossible. I've thought it out. We can't; we just can't."

He had no argument to offer. His own feelings were in tumult. He was glad there was less than a week of shooting left. But they got through it. She kept to the bargain she'd made with herself. She was almost a stranger while they shot the last scenes, and at night she vanished into her quarters and stayed there.

The time came to leave. The negatives of the final setups of the last scenes were stored aboard the seaplane that was to transport the cast and the crew away from the island, and the heavy generating equipment, cameras, lights, and cables that had been shipped by water for the filming were loaded on a ship in the lagoon for the return trip.

The natives gave them a feast the night before their departure. Georgina, wearing a pareu and dancing with the natives, had an expression of bittersweet happiness. Howard didn't go near her.

The next morning they sat apart on the plane. As it rose out of the lagoon and winged north, Howard looked down at the golden island receding into nothing. It had been paradise for only a while.

23

It was to be a private farewell, without fanfare or publicity, with just Dalton accompanying Howard to the station. Dalton was grim as his chauffeur drove them through the palm and eucalyptus forests of Beverly Hills.

"You've got to bring her back, Howard. It's been over six months now. We've got to get her into her new picture or she'll lose her following."

"For God's sake, I'll bring her back!" Howard said.

"I hope so," Dalton said, with a dragging note of doubt.

"She's coming back with me, and that's all there is to it, so stop worrying," Howard insisted, but he was immediately sorry for his carping tone, for Dalton had been under the stress of unusual worries since last week's disastrous fire. In spite of the studio's extensive precautions and the heavy equipment it maintained to fight fires, runaway rivers of flame, shooting high into the sky, had gutted stage five the week before at a loss figured in the millions.

This had followed on the heels of Dalton's bitter disappointment over the Academy Awards. The studio head had been exultant when

Westward the Men had been nominated for best picture of the year, but the Oscars had gone elsewhere at the award ceremony.

"We've had a run of bad luck," Dalton commented at the station. "It's bound to change. Life is like that. You have a run of bad luck, then you have a run of good luck. You bring Leni home, Howard, and that will be a change of luck. The problem will be to get her to come without Gurtner. As far as we're concerned, he's broken his contract by refusing to approve the script after we went to generous lengths to revise it in accordance with his endless suggestions."

They shook hands, and Howard boarded the train, watching as Dalton walked away. A year ago Dalton would have looked back and waved, but now he just walked on.

Howard's thoughts settled on Georgina again when he was seated in his compartment and the train started to move. He thought of her entirely too much, and he wished he could stop it. But the image of her moved irresistibly into his mind time after time, and sometimes, as now, her image was mixed with Leni's. In some distant corner of his mind, he seemed to hear Leni laughing, as if she knew about him and Georgina and thought it very funny. What hurt him was the idea that if Leni knew, she wouldn't care.

He'd tried hard to stop himself from seeing Georgina again, and at least he'd succeeded in that. The last time he'd seen her was when they'd parted after the flight home from Hawaii, but how many times since then he'd wanted desperately to call her, to see her! Those countless unrealized temptations were behind him now, and he was on his way to New York, then to Hamburg, to Berlin, and then back home again. With Leni. He hoped that in the process of completing this long trip, and with the passing of more time, the problem of how he and Georgina felt about each other would become less pressing. Besides, how could he be sure how he felt about Georgina until he saw Leni again?

He tried to think of other things. He looked out at the countryside spinning by and reflected that he'd come a long, long way in the decade since he'd ridden out to California on an uncomfortable coach seat, eating peanut butter sandwiches to stay alive.

In New York City he was greeted at Grand Central by a mob of representatives from the local Howard Stanton Fan Club, alerted to his arrival by the studio's publicity department. The whole cluster was made up of girls. Several of them carried "Welcome, Howard!" signs printed in big, bright red letters. Howard signed many autographs and was unexpectedly and simultaneously kissed on each cheek by two especially eager fans closing in on him, an event duly recorded by the photographers on hand.

Two Regency publicity men drove him to the Waldorf and got him settled in his suite. The same two delivered him to the *Bremen* the next day. Howard's cabin, its dark decor not much relieved by the shining chrome of its modern furniture, was the biggest and best on the ship, he was informed by one of the publicity men. It was occupied more often by royalty and ambassadors than by movie stars.

Several reporters had shown up, and they asked him questions and departed, leaving him to drink champagne with the publicity men in his cabin. It was sad that his farewell should be attended only by strangers.

When the ship docked in Hamburg about a week later, Howard was shocked and disappointed to find Adrienne instead of Leni waiting for him.

"Leni sends her regrets, but she's been invited to one of the Fuehrer's banquets this evening. It would be impossible to refuse this great honor, of course." Adrienne smiled dryly. "Leni was sure you'd understand."

No, he didn't understand, and he was as furious as he was disappointed, but he didn't intend to let Adrienne know that. How he hated her! And how he dreaded flying to Berlin with her!

She plainly felt the same way. "We can sit in silence on this journey if you prefer," she said as they took off, "but I think we ought to set things straight first. We don't have to make any pretense of friendliness. It's been perfectly evident to me from the beginning that you don't like me. That doesn't bother me in the least. You're her husband, but I'm her friend. That's a good deal more important."

He looked squarely at her. "When we get back to the States, you're out."

She laughed. "I don't think so."

"You'll find out."

"It will be interesting to see who finds out what. But I don't intend returning to the States, in any event."

"I don't care where you go as long as it isn't with us. It's ridiculous the influence Leni's allowed you to have on her. She's a star and you're nothing."

"You're just too dense to understand anything. You're a movie star, and that's all you are, and that's not much. She's a movie star, too, but with a rich mind and a richer heart, and that's the difference between you and her. She's opened my eyes to what life is about."

"What in hell are you talking about?"

She smiled grimly. "Knowing what life is about is beyond you.

140

You're made of tissue paper. Someday somebody's going to crumple you and throw you away. Maybe not long from now."

"What have you done to her?" he said angrily.

"*I* haven't done anything to her. Coming home to the Fatherland has done it. Why do you think she's stayed on and on? She can't bear to leave, and I don't blame her. Think what it was like for her over there. A foreign country. A country of slums and dust bowls and goldfish swallowers and despair, a country in decline as surely as the Roman empire was two thousand years ago. Here, everything is living and growing. There's excitement in the air. Germany is *doing* something."

"You sound like Hitler," he said in disgust.

"You don't know what Hitler really says. You only know what you think he says, the twisted versions that reach you at home."

"There's no use going on with this. We hate each other too much."

"Yes, don't we?" she said blandly. "But aren't you glad we finally put it into words? It's like having an enema. I feel absolutely purged."

He tried to ignore her presence for the rest of the trip, but was only more aware of her. In Berlin he faced further disappointment. Leni had already left for the banquet.

"But you can wait awhile longer, can't you?" Adrienne said acidly. "You've waited such a long time now."

She disappeared somewhere to the back of the huge apartment, and a plump maid who spoke a little English showed him to a small room furnished in the same ultra-modern style of sharply angled pieces as the living room. A butler unpacked for him while the maid took him to a stark dining room lined with glass doors opening onto a balcony beyond which the city glittered. He sat in a cubistic chair at a glass-topped table and ate sauerbraten in the sheen of light from a dozen candles.

Afterward he sat on the long black couch in the living room and waited, looking around at the cold, formal decor and thinking that he could never get used to this place of blacks and grays and whites in a million years. Was this Leni's idea of the right background for a home—a world without color, the shadowed world of the black-and-white cinema? The thought made him shiver. How little he knew her, really.

He waited for hours in the soundless, dead apartment, and then there was the click of a lock. He was across the white rug and into the foyer before she'd closed the door behind her. She stood there in a black evening gown and a black and gold wrap, her blond hair brushing her shoulders, her eyes gleaming, her lips parted in the beginning of a smile. He said nothing. He pressed himself to her, pushing her against the door, which thudded shut behind her. His eyes looked into hers so closely that his vision blurred. He closed his eyes as he kissed her. It was as if the last time had been only a moment ago.

Leni's bedroom was even more a shrine to some surrealistic world of the future than was the rest of the apartment. Except for the floor, which was a glistening ebony, relieved here and there by small white rugs, it was all white. One wall, against which was placed a large dressing table, was simply an enormous mirror. Their nude bodies on the great low bed, which could have accommodated half a dozen lovers, were reflected dimly in it, for only one candle burned on a table near the wall of glass doors, covered by chiffon draperies, that opened to the balcony.

Leni lay with her hair flowing out on the satin-covered pillow, her eyes almost closed, as if she were ready to sink into sleep, one hand on a breast, the other at her side. Howard lay beside her, looking at her. When he raised himself and kissed the nipple of her free breast, she moaned. She was ready again, and so was he. It was the third time tonight.

An hour later, as daylight crept into the room, she said that they must sleep, and since she couldn't rest well with him, he went to the room where his things had been unpacked earlier. He lay down, but he didn't sleep. He was too overwhelmed by the excitement of the night.

He found, during the next few days, that when he was with Leni, the doubts and worries that had been pressing him vanished, displaced by a buoyant feeling of certainty that it would all turn out well. But when she was gone—as she often was, for she was involved in endless activities—the doubts and worries returned.

He was apprehensive about having it out with Leni about Adrienne. He supposed Adrienne had told Leni about the bitter flight to Berlin from Hamburg, although she'd said nothing about it. The unpleasant situation had to be discussed, and he knew that Leni would want to avoid it as long as she could. But he'd made up his mind that Adrienne must be dismissed.

Leni arranged for them to have lunch with Gurtner a few days after Howard's arrival. The director smoked cigarettes in a holder and talked arrogantly about the future of the German motion picture industry while a string orchestra played the waltzes of Johann Strauss in the background. It seemed that German moviemaking, too long suppressed during the grim years of denial following the World War, was enjoying a brilliant renascence under the Nazi regime, with the blessings and help of the minister of propaganda and national en-

142

lightenment, Joseph Goebbels, and would lead the world in artistic achievement in the years ahead.

"You people in Hollywood do not make pictures, you make pastiches," Gurtner said, looking coldly at Howard as if daring him to take a contrary view. Howard sat in angry silence, hating it that Leni was still in the thrall of this detestable man. "In Germany the director is supreme," Gurtner went on. "What he decides is the way the picture is made. It is the only way it can be done to produce a work of art."

It seemed clear to Howard that Gurtner didn't intend to return to Hollywood. His continuing dissatisfaction with the series of revised scripts for Leni's next picture was only a sham. Howard felt almost certain that any pictures the director made in the future would be produced in Germany for the benefit of Goebbels, Hitler, and the Fatherland.

The Fatherland. It seemed to mean so much here. The spirit of national unity was everywhere, and Howard was chilled by the film Leni had screened for him the day they were guests of a studio in Berlin. The picture was a review of the last Nazi Party gathering at Nuremberg. It was a frightening distillation of hysteria, a hundred thousand dedicated madmen performing in choreographed lunacy.

But the spirit of the film was in the life around them, in the aggressive way the people walked and talked, in the robust joy taken in the Party parades, such as the huge one Howard and Leni watched in which thousands of men marched down the Unter den Linden to the Chancellery, where the Fuehrer reviewed his followers.

They viewed that celebration the morning of the day they drove to Bavaria, a land of glistening lakes and combed forests, so that Howard could meet Leni's mother. The widow was as unlike Leni as it was possible to be. Stiff and spartan, she kept her neat little house with its ceramic Dutch stove in the same style she had before her daughter had become famous.

They stayed but one night there, and when they started back through the verdant hills toward the new autobahn that would take them to Berlin, Leni seemed solemn, as if she were sorry she still felt a compulsion to return home occasionally and be reminded of how simple her life had once been.

Back in Berlin, Howard brought up the issue that had to be faced. "We've got to talk about making arrangements to go home."

"But I am home."

He looked at her, and the truth he'd been looking for, the truth that had been building, finally emerged with utmost clarity. They were strangers. He'd thought that seeing her again would reaffirm their love, would make the future secure for them, but it hadn't. He'd been wrong about that and wrong about the way he felt about her. He'd been wrong about so much.

"You didn't intend ever to go back," he said.

She shook her head.

"Yet you seemed glad to see me. You wanted me to make love to you."

She nodded. "I think I will always want you to make love to me."

"But you don't love me."

"And you do not love me."

It was true that he didn't. Not anymore.

"Did you ever love me, Leni?"

"For a while. Does anyone love anyone for more than a while?"

"I think so."

"You love someone else now?"

"Yes."

She nodded. "That is good. We will both be happy. It is good that you came here. Everything is clear between us now. I am going to make pictures here. I am needed here more than I am there."

"You mean Hitler and Gurtner want you to make pictures here, and that's why you're going to do it."

"I am going to do it because I want to do it."

"Yes, you wouldn't do anything you didn't want to do," he said. "Is there anything more?"

"Yes, there is something more. I want you to know it all." She rose and moved across the room, calling toward the back of the apartment. "Adrienne!" She stood waiting at the door, statuesque, motionless, the play of light working its most dramatic effect on her. It was as if she were posing for a still on the set. She was more beautiful than he'd ever seen her before, and even more remote.

Adrienne came from the back, her eyes expectant. She must have guessed that the climax was here, for her face was radiant.

"I want you to know it all," Leni said again, smiling over at Howard, then clasped Adrienne to her. They kissed fully and deeply on the mouth while Howard watched. He thought that this wasn't really a surprise at all. Inside, he must have known the truth for a long time.

He rose and left the room. He couldn't wait to get out of there.

24

It was nine o'clock on Friday evening, and it was still so hot that little beads of perspiration stood on Tracy Gordon's brow. There hadn't been a day since early in July when the temperature hadn't hit at least eighty in the small Georgia town of Abbottsville where Tracy lived with her widowed mother in a big frame house. Tracy's mother said it had been the hottest summer she could remember for a long time.

The bathroom door was locked, and Tracy stood naked before the mirror examining her developing breasts, as she usually did every night before she went to bed. Her breasts had been growing larger over the last few months, and it alarmed her that she was maturing faster than most girls of twelve. Her best friend, Clara Cox, was still absolutely flat. Clara said that someday Tracy would have bigger breasts than most girls were blessed with, and wasn't that wonderful? Tracy didn't know whether it was or not.

So far, her mother hadn't said anything about the developing mounds of flesh, and she probably wouldn't. It seemed difficult for her to talk about the body except in terms of how to keep it in good health. Clara's mother was just the opposite. She'd already talked to Clara about important private matters, including menstruation, because she felt those were things you should know when you were twelve. Tracy was grateful that Clara promptly passed on to her important information like that.

Tracy brushed her dark brown hair, which was parted in the middle, cut to fall in a bob on her shoulders, and set off with bangs across her brow. She put down the hairbrush and looked at her face. Her eyes were an unusual color that her mother called golden but others sometimes called amber. Her nose was straight and just the right length to complement her full mouth and well-arched brows. It was said that she was a beautiful child and would be a beautiful woman. She wondered if it was true.

Tracy went to her room and put on her white nightgown and was in bed when her mother stopped to say good night. Her mother put the light out, closed the door, and went on to the bathroom. Tracy stayed in bed for a few moments longer, then slipped out and went to the window, looking down at the terraced garden basking in the moonlight. Her father had built the terraces for the garden two years before he died, part of his successful efforts to make their yard the most beautiful on the block. He had also put in high privet hedges in back and on both sides, shutting off the properties of neighbors like forbidden secrets. But it was the trees that Tracy's father had been proudest of—two elms, three sugar maples, and two weeping willows, all of them big.

The flower beds in the garden, carefully planted and tended by Tracy's mother, looked faded and sparse, but that was to be expected at this time of the year. Tracy wondered if a vision would appear among the hollyhocks. Occasionally, after her father died, she would look down there and think she saw him standing among the flowers, looking up at her window in the dusk. She knew it was her imagination and not a ghost, so she said nothing to her mother about it. But the vision of her father hadn't appeared down there for a long time, and it didn't now.

Tracy heard her mother come out of the bathroom, go to her room, and close the door. She waited for a few minutes until she was sure her mother was in bed, then retrieved the copy of *Photoplay* from under her mattress. She turned on her bedside lamp, got into bed, and turned to page six, where the reviews of the new movies appeared. There was a photograph of Howard Stanton and the new star Georgina Fox embracing. He was wearing white seaman's pants and was barefooted and bare-chested. His skin was dark, obviously from a very deep tan. She was wearing a pareu, and her skin was much lighter than Howard Stanton's, although she was supposed to be a native. They were embracing against the trunk of a big palm tree, with thick tropical vegetation around them. Below the picture the caption stated that this was a scene from Regency Pictures' new Technicolor drama, *The Great Typhoon*.

Tracy looked at the photograph again, thinking, as she often had in the past, that Howard Stanton reminded her of her father.

She returned the magazine to its hiding place and put the light out. She closed her eyes, but she didn't sleep for a while. In her mind she kept seeing a picture of Howard Stanton, bare-chested as he was in the magazine photo. He was smiling at her and holding out his hand.

Tracy disliked Saturday mornings as much as she liked Saturday afternoons. The mornings were full of work. There was the washing to do, and after that the dusting, the sweeping, and the ironing; and after that, if there was still time left before noon, there was some special job,

146

such as beating the dust out of the small carpets with the rug beater. Tracy's mother kept reminding her that someday she would be a housewife and she would have to be ready to do a good job of it.

During lunch her mother said again, as she often did just before Tracy was due to have her weekly visit to the Golden Theater, that she couldn't understand what Tracy saw in the movies. Helen Gordon hadn't been to a movie in years. On the rare occasions when she went, it was to see a religious movie like *Sign of the Cross*.

"Give me a good book anytime," she said.

After lunch Clara came by, and she and Tracy walked to the theater. Tracy felt a stir of excitement at the sight of the Golden Theater's marquee announcing "Howard Stanton in THE GREAT TYPHOON in Technicolor."

They paid their dime admissions and went inside, taking seats halfway down the auditorium. "This is a dumb theater," Clara observed, looking around with contempt at the plain gray walls. "I'd like to go to Loew's in Atlanta. They say it's got a ceiling that looks like a real sky, with clouds moving across it."

"I'd like to see that, too."

"I wonder what it's like to go to a movie with a boy?" Clara asked.

"I don't think I'd like it. Especially if he wanted to neck."

Clara snickered. "You won't get a chance to, anyway. Your mother will *never* let you go out with a boy."

"Yes, she will," Tracy said uncertainly, and was glad the show started so that she didn't have to say anything more about it. First there was a Flash Gordon serial chapter, then a Western picture. Then *The Great Typhoon* began breathtakingly with a wonderful white sailing ship cutting through the green sea. Howard Stanton was at the helm in sea captain's garb, looking through binoculars. The camera stayed on him all the time the titles were unfolding, and Tracy thought that was a wonderful way to open the picture.

She was spellbound for the next hour and a half, and she was so electrified during the typhoon that wrecked Howard Stanton's ship and tossed him ashore on an island that she gripped the arms of her seat all through it. Halfway through the picture, when he kissed Georgina Fox for the first time, she felt a peculiar warmth travel through her. It was as if he were kissing her, as he did in her dreams.

She was a little surprised at the ending. She'd expected Howard to stay on the island with Georgina for the rest of his life. But he sailed off in the rescue ship to return to his wife on the mainland. Still, Tracy could tell from the wistful look on his face as he watched the island recede from view—with the forlorn Georgina shrinking in the distance as she faded from his vision and from his life—that he wasn't leaving

147

her because he wanted to but because it was the moral thing to do.

The program was over, and so was Saturday afternoon, and though Tracy would have dearly loved seeing *The Great Typhoon* over again, there was no possibility of it, because it wouldn't be starting again for another hour and a half. Still, she was glad to have seen it even this once. She considered it one of the best Howard Stanton pictures she'd seen yet.

"It was good," Clara admitted outside, "but I didn't like the ending. He discovered he loved Georgina Fox more than he did his wife, so he should have stayed with her." Clara giggled. "Well, he *did* in real life. I'll bet they have a hot time in bed together, don't you?"

"Oh, Clara," Tracy said, "don't talk like that."

"Why not? We're friends, aren't we?"

"But we don't have to talk about things like that all the time."

"Tracy, you're so funny," Clara said. "You're never going to grow up if you keep on like this."

Church service seemed even longer than usual the next morning because it was so humid and hot. Tracy was so uncomfortable that she kept squirming in her seat in the pew until her mother gave her a sidelong look of disapproval. Her mother was probably oblivious to the heat herself, for this was her hour of joy. As she'd often said, there were no moments in life better for her than those she spent in God's house.

After the service they walked home. They always walked to and from church, because it was only six blocks. But they would have to drive to the cemetery, of course, since it was on the other side of town. Tracy's mother usually took lilies to the cemetery. She chose a dozen today because it was a day for special commemoration. John Tracy Gordon had died exactly five years ago.

At the cemetery, they drove to the Gordon plot, purchased by Tracy's great-grandfather back in 1890. Tracy's mother knelt and arranged the lilies in the flower container in front of John Tracy Gordon's headstone. When she was finished, she remained kneeling for a while. Tracy supposed she was crying to herself and praying. Tracy felt awkward standing there looking down at the headstone when her mother was kneeling reverently, and she wondered if she should kneel too, but her mother rose before she could make up her mind. Her mother took her handkerchief out of her purse and dabbed at her eyes.

"Your father was the finest man who ever lived," she said. "Someday, when you're eighteen or nineteen, a fine man like him will come along for you, too, Tracy. I'm as sure of that as I'm sure there's a

148

benevolent God looking after us. You're going to have a fine man for your husband, and loving him will be the greatest happiness you'll ever know."

Tracy's mother had said this before, and Tracy hoped with all her heart that it would be so. Her biggest dream was that a man like her father would come along for her someday.

25

It was snowing the morning of the first day of December, 1939, when Michael Baines was shattered out of his sleep by the unholy ring of his alarm clock at five-thirty. He got right out of bed and looked briefly at the sweep of campus stretching before his window. The snow was beautiful but deep. He would have to wear his galoshes to work.

He left the dormitory a few minutes later and started across the campus toward the commissary, where he worked every weekday morning from six to eight, unloading food and storing it and checking inventory lists. He liked his Saturday job of selling men's clothes at the Varsity Shop much better, but he couldn't quit the commissary job, because he needed the extra money to help him carry through his plan to leave college and go to New York.

After work he went to his American lit class and then walked down to the fraternity house. He hadn't been there since last week's chapter meeting, and he felt a little guilty about it, but the truth was that he was very busy with his jobs, his classwork and studies, and his involvement in the play production of the speech and drama department. A greater truth was that he simply didn't like fraternity life and was sorry he'd pledged in the first place.

Most of his fraternity brothers were off at classes, but unfortunately the fraternity president, Floyd Vinson, was lounging in the living room. He immediately collared Mike for another of those unctuous counseling sessions in his matchbox of an office. He suggested as he had before that Mike move out of the dormitory and into the fraternity house, which made Mike smile vaguely, as it had the last time. Then Floyd told Mike how proud the brothers were of him because of his

149

standing on the swimming team and, even more so, because of his continued scholastic excellence.

Mike smiled and nodded, but he was annoyed. The truth was that the fraternity didn't want him as a member because he was Mike Baines, nice guy, but because he was a champion swimmer and an "A" student, the only really good student they'd had in years.

"And that Laurie Butler!" Floyd was saying, having gotten around to the subject of the girl Mike was most seen with on campus. "That babe's got everything. Sure hope you're planning to bring her to the Christmas party."

"Maybe," Mike said, seeing no point in telling Floyd at this point that he didn't even intend to go to the Christmas party. As for Laurie, he knew why Floyd thought she was so wonderful—because she was a member of the most important sorority on campus, was stacked, and had a rich father. Mike himself was finding her an increasing problem.

Mike got out as soon as he could, saying he had a class. Time dragged after that until four o'clock, when he had play rehearsal, the most important part of his day. When he entered the auditorium and noted Hadley's hostile eyes, he knew the director would be giving them a hard time. In his classes, in his function as an instructor of speech and drama, Hadley was usually relatively calm. When he was directing a student production, it was often another matter. Today he kept interrupting the rehearsal to berate various cast members for poor interpretation of their lines, and his irritation built to the point where he ended the rehearsal abruptly a half hour before schedule because he said he couldn't stand watching them make fools of themselves another minute. With the cowed cast assembled around him, he reminded them that this play went on the boards right after Christmas vacation, but he wouldn't hesitate to replace the whole cast and start over if they didn't start acting less like amateurs and more like professionals.

Mike knew he would do nothing of the kind. Hadley's terror attacks on students were mostly just a lot of noise. As the company broke after today's peremptory dismissal and Mike turned to go, Hadley followed quickly, barring his escape.

"Come by and have supper with me," Hadley said.

"I can't. I've got to study."

"You can study later," Hadley said. "I'll be waiting for you."

Hadley's tone was firm, and there was nothing Mike could do but say he'd be there. By the time six o'clock rolled around and it was time to go, he wasn't as reluctant as he had been. Hadley was the only person on campus he could talk to freely about certain matters.

Hadley lived a few blocks from the campus on the second floor of an

150

old Victorian house loaded with gingerbread decoration. Mike was grateful that the entrance to Hadley's apartment was by means of an outside flight of stairs in back. It meant there was little danger of anyone's ever seeing him go there.

Hadley was dressed in brown corduroy pants, loafers, and a handsome white wool sweater. Hadley always looked far younger and different here than he did in his classes, where he wore dark, conservative suits. Mike supposed that Hadley wore his youthful clothes on his excursions to the city on certain weekends to visit fairy bars.

They sat down facing each other in Hadley's leather chairs, positioned near a large filled bookcase that rose from the floor to the ceiling. Hadley's library contained many books on the theater and other arts, and volume after volume of plays.

"I want you to know that you're doing all right in your part even if the rest of them are crummy," Hadley said.

"Thanks," Mike said.

"You'll always do all right," Hadley went on. "You might even be good sometime. You know your limitations, and that's a good sign, because it's a sickness of the young to think they're good when they're not. I think you'll get somewhere eventually, Mike. Not just from talent. A lot of people have talent. I think you'll have luck, too. It's just a feeling."

Hadley looked pensive. He picked up his glass of wine and took a swallow, although Mike left his untouched. He knew what Hadley was leading up to, with wine, supper, and talk. It was always the same.

Hadley reminisced for a few minutes about the time he'd spent in New York City in 1925 trying to find a career for himself in the theater, and Mike wondered whether he ought to tell Hadley what had been on his mind lately, but something held him back from saying anything, and then Hadley shifted suddenly to a new subject and asked Mike if he'd seen Timothy Briggs' new picture.

"Yes, I saw it," Mike said. "I thought I should, since it got such good reviews." He didn't want Hadley thinking that he went to just any picture, for Hadley spoke disparagingly of the movies, saying they were fashioned to fit the low mentality of the masses, whereas the theater was directed toward a more selective audience with much greater perception.

"It was good," Hadley said surprisingly.

"I thought so, too," Mike said.

"Briggs gave a good performance. He's queer, you know."

Mike felt uncomfortable and didn't answer. Hadley rose, filled his glass with wine again, and sat back down.

"I met a guy at a bar in the city who'd met and carried on with Briggs out in Hollywood," Hadley went on. "But even if I hadn't been told he was queer, I would have known anyway. Just seeing him on the screen, I could tell, although most people couldn't, of course. The conception most people have of twilight men is that they lisp, wear makeup, and roll their hips when they walk. Well, let them think that. It makes it easier for people like Briggs and me to get away with being what we are."

"But he's married and has kids," Mike said. "I've read about him."

"A lot of queers are married, especially in Hollywood."

Hadley decided it was time to get supper. He insisted that Mike sit in the cramped kitchen while he prepared it. It always seemed strange to see Hadley cooking, for he was so masculine-looking. He talked continuously while he cooked, mostly about what he'd read in *Theatre Arts* about the current theatrical season in New York.

They sat down and ate, and afterward Hadley quickly finished the remaining wine. He seemed to have to be a little drunk before he could get to the inevitable. He got to it now. He pointed toward the small bedroom that opened off his living room.

"No, I don't think I ought to," Mike said. "The real reason I came here tonight was to tell you I can't let you do that to me again."

"Don't be stupid," Hadley said. "You're hard already. Look at that big bulge."

Hadley advanced to him and pressed his hand on Mike's crotch. But he didn't try to kiss him. He hadn't tried that since the second or third time, for Mike had kept turning his face away. Mike hesitated now, then decided to allow himself to be drawn into the bedroom to avoid a scene. But this was to be absolutely the last time.

Hadley commanded him to undress as usual, and watched him while he stripped. Hadley never undressed himself. When Mike was naked, he lay down on his back on the bed with his head on the two pillows Hadley had prepared for him. He drew his knees up and spread his legs and Hadley knelt between them.

Mike was very hot and very hard, and knew he would come quickly and profusely. He watched in fascination as Hadley's face came to his groin like a moth drawn to candlelight. Hadley groaned and his lips and tongue moved. He kissed Mike's penis and testicles and drew his tongue over them and got them very wet, and Mike was ready to come even before Hadley took his penis into his mouth. When he did, he consumed it right down to the base, although Mike couldn't understand how he could take into his mouth something that was bigger than his mouth without choking on it.

Up and down Hadley went, with tremendous suction, and as usual

152

Mike felt an immediate, very intense sensation from it, a much sharper response than he had ever experienced with a girl. Hadley hardly made a dozen strokes up and down the shaft before Mike heaved upward and poured his semen into Hadley's mouth. Hadley clung on and swallowed it all without choking, and then would not let go. He never wanted to let go, and Mike hated that, for the moment he came, Mike was horribly depressed, and usually wondered, as he did now, why in hell he had ever allowed Hadley to touch him in the first place. He looked down at the top of Hadley's head, wishing he would let go. But he knew Hadley would hold on for dear life until Mike's penis, warmed and urged by the anxious mouth, came up again.

It did, and Hadley worked on it hungrily, up and down, consuming it voraciously, letting it out of his mouth only once or twice while he licked the shaft and testicles. When he sensed that Mike was building up to a climax again, he made the strokes ferocious and rapid. Mike groaned as he came this time. He didn't come as much as he had a few minutes ago, but he came enough to make him even more depressed than he had been before.

Hadley finally let go of Mike's impassive organ and sat up.

"I've got to go," Mike said, wanting to get out of there as soon as possible. "I've got a lot of studying to do."

Surprisingly, Hadley didn't offer any argument. He watched as Mike dressed.

"You're the first student I've ever been involved with this way," Hadley said. "I was always afraid of it before. But there isn't anything to be afraid of. You wouldn't tell, any more than I would. You'd be ruined, too."

"Of course I wouldn't tell," Mike said coldly, "and we're not *involved.*"

"I just wish you were a little older, Mike. Maybe you would understand better. I could love you if you were older and could understand. Maybe I *do* love you—"

"For crying out loud, don't say that!" Mike cut in anxiously.

Hadley smiled sourly. "You're afraid of finding yourself, aren't you, Mike?"

"I know what you're thinking! But you're wrong! I'm not a fairy!"

"You just simply don't understand yourself, Mike," Hadley said.

Mike left immediately. It was snowing again, and the night was clean and beautiful, but he was hardly aware of it. He was full of shame and rage, and he felt dirty.

Mike came out of the Varsity Shop shortly after six, finished with his Saturday job for the week. He crossed the square toward the beaming

153

marquee of the theater, which announced that Howard Stanton and Georgina Fox were appearing in *The Cavaliers*. Mike looked forward to seeing it. It was the third co-starring picture for the couple in the last few years.

An article about them in a recent issue of *Silver Screen* quoted the Stantons as looking forward to making many more pictures together. The piece had called them one of the movie colony's happiest couples. There had been pictures of them together on Malibu Beach and entertaining other Hollywood stars at their home in Beverly Hills.

Mike still read every story about Howard Stanton he could find. The star's success made his own dream seem more possible to fulfill. Howard Stanton had faced terrific odds when he'd first gone to Hollywood in the late nineteen twenties, but look where he was now. At twenty-nine, only ten years older than Mike, he was one of the big ten at the box office! Mike wondered where *he* would be ten years from now. Where Howard Stanton was, he hoped.

Mike was thrilled with *The Cavaliers*. When it bounced to its end two hours later, after Howard Stanton cut down the villain in a tremendous sword fight up and down a huge staircase, Mike walked out of the theater into the frigid night, pulling his scarf tightly around his neck as he started down the long main street of the village toward the dormitory. It was a bright night, with a full moon glowing down on the snow. The big old trees arching over the long street in their winter nudity made an eerie vista.

The sophomore men's dormitory was remote, set back from the main street on the border of a woodland. The lobby was deserted, as were the lounge rooms that opened off it. Most of the men were out on dates. Saturday night was the biggest dating night of the week.

There was an urgent message in his box to call Laurie Butler. Mike hesitated at the phone booth, then tossed the message away and headed upstairs. Did Laurie Butler think she owned him? If she asked about the message, he'd say he never got it.

But he had been in his room only a few minutes when the room phone buzzed and the switchboard operator told him that Laurie was waiting downstairs to see him. He was surprised that she would humble herself to call on a guy. Mike knew how embarrassed she must be about it.

He put on his coat and went downstairs where she was waiting in the lobby—pretty, expensive-looking, and wearing a pained expression. They went out to her car, a blue 1938 Pontiac convertible coupe. She was one of the few students who'd been given a permit to have a car. Her father was an important alumnus who contributed handsomely to the college every year, so Laurie was given privileges others weren't.

154

But with all her beauty, money, and popularity, she still wasn't happy.

"I love you, Mike," she said as she headed the car toward the main street. "That's all there is to it."

"You just think you love me," he said firmly. "Oh, for God's sake, Laurie, I don't want to sound corny, but the truth *is* corny. We're worlds apart. That's all there is to it."

"It's not true," she said as she turned the car onto the main street and headed out of town. "Mike, you can't imagine how many dates I turn down—"

"I don't want you to turn them down," he cut in.

"But I don't want to see anyone but you. It's all I think about. Mike, I can't stand this. I've never been unhappy like this before."

"You'll get over it," Mike said. "People do. We really ought to stop seeing each other."

"No," she said. "I couldn't stand that."

"You could stand it better than you can stand this, apparently. Laurie, look. I'm not interested in getting married. I'm not even interested in getting pinned. I just want to be free. Do you understand?"

But how could he expect her to understand? She thought she had the world to offer him because her father would make the guy she married an executive in his business. But Mike had other plans. He hadn't dreamed she would fall in love with him. He should never have taken her to the woods last spring. She'd been running after him ever since.

"Turn around," he said. "Take me back to the dorm."

"No. We're going to Ryan's."

He couldn't stop her. When he tried to, she speeded up, and they slipped from side to side on the icy road and almost went into a spin. In her emotional state, she would rather wreck them, perhaps kill them, than turn back. He said nothing more until they turned into the little park where a man named Ryan had six cabins where he supposedly put up tourists stopping overnight on their travels. More often, the cabins were occupied by couples who used them for an hour or so of sex and then got out, making room for other couples with the same thing in mind.

Mike reluctantly paid the two dollars in the grim little office and then unlocked the shabby little cabin they were assigned. The electric heater took a little of the chill off the place, but it was still uncomfortable. Laurie undressed quickly and lay down nude on the lumpy bed to wait for him. She had her knees up in the air and her legs spread, and it occurred to him that she was in the same position he'd been in earlier this week on Hadley's bed.

When he was undressed he moved to the bed and looked down at her, wishing, despite the desire that had taken him over, that he was anywhere but here.

She extended her hands toward him and said pleadingly, "For God's sake, make love to me before I die!"

Laurie dropped him at the dormitory just in time to get herself back to her sorority house before the women's curfew. Mike went up to his room and sat down at his desk, regretting that he'd ever gotten involved with Laurie, determined that he would never get caught in a similar trap again.

If all girls were like Marianne Sellers, the world would be a better place, he thought. Marianne was the best friend he'd had in high school. Over her parents' strong protests, she'd carried through on her determination to move to New York City after graduation. Of course, she hadn't found a place for herself in the theater yet, even after more than a year in New York, but Mike was certain she would make it. She was intelligent and beautiful, and she could act rings around the girls Mike had been performing with in plays here on campus.

Mike was counting the days until he would see Marianne again. She was going home to Grove Center for Christmas and so was he. He was certain she would be as excited about his secret plans as he was.

Mike was getting nervous. He'd been home for three days, and he was finding it difficult to act normal around his parents. He found his mother looking inquiringly at him at times, as if she knew there was something special on his mind and wondered what it was. He wished he could tell her, but he'd never been able to approach her easily, and he certainly couldn't about this.

His father had no questions in his eyes, but he kept getting onto the subject of Mike's college work, saying he was glad Mike was getting good grades because it was a financial sacrifice to send him to college in these hard times, when they weren't even up to eighty cents an hour yet at the machine shop in spite of the union's efforts.

Still, his father asserted two evenings before Christmas, it would all be worth it when Mike was an accountant one of these days. He had arrived home several hours after supper was over, having been in a saloon with some fellow workers from the machine shop since quitting time. He'd been "having some holiday cheer," as he put it to Mike's mother, whose beautiful inflexible face refused to show her resentment, though her blue-green eyes did. As he often did when he was drunk, Mike's father talked a lot that evening about his hope that Mike would someday be a certified public accountant.

156

Mike could hardly stand it. It all seemed so bizarre—the Christmas tree in the corner loaded with tinsel and ornaments, the lighted wreaths in the windows, the table with the punch and cookies awaiting visiting carolers, his mother looking ethereal in the candlelight, and his red-faced father ranting about a rosy business future for him.

But it was finally over, and at least Mike had something to look forward to tomorrow, for Marianne was due in from New York on the noon train.

Mike waited patiently until late in the day before calling at the Sellers house, not wanting to appear too pushy to Marianne's parents. As it was, he had a hard time getting her out of the house. Embarrassingly, her parents were after him to try to pressure Marianne into coming home from New York for good.

"It's just fine, really fine, that you're going to college to make something of yourself, Mike," Mr. Sellers bombasted, "and we hope you'll be able to talk some sense into Marianne. It isn't too late for her to give up that foolish venture in New York and go to college herself."

Marianne was cringing when they finally got out and started for the drugstore where they'd had many a "date" together back in high school.

"They're so stuffy!" she said. "If they keep on that way, I may just never come home again!"

But her mood changed when they were seated with their chocolate sundaes and Mike told her about his secret plans.

"Oh, Mike, it will be wonderful to have you in New York!"

She told him that by the time he arrived, she and a girl named Edna, a neighbor of hers at the YWCA, would be settled in a railroad flat on West Fourth Street in Greenwich Village, which they were moving into right after the first of the year. A railroad flat, she explained, was an apartment that ran straight back like a railroad track, with one room opening into the next one all the way through.

"Edna and I will make room for you until you get settled in your own place, Mike."

"That would be swell, Marianne," Mike said, delighted at her offer.

Marianne reported on the progress she was making in her career. She had to work as a file clerk in an office to meet her living costs, but she'd joined an acting class and was learning something new every day, and someday she would be on the Broadway boards doing exactly what she wanted with her life.

"And so will you, Mike! We're both going to get what we want. We *must* get it, and I know we will."

Mike went back to college after Christmas vacation and carried on

157

his life there much as usual, even though he would be walking out on it forever at the end of January, when the semester ended.

The play opened the second week in January, after a final harrowing rehearsal under Hadley's relentless direction, and got a good response from the students in its two performances in the main auditorium. Many students commented to Mike that he was the best one in the play, but Hadley said nothing about his performance. Hadley was disturbed because Mike kept giving him excuses when he asked him to drop by.

To Mike's surprise, he heard nothing from Laurie. Apparently she'd done some heavy thinking about the situation over Christmas vacation and had decided to spare herself further pain by simply keeping away from him.

Although there wasn't the least hope they would understand his reasons or be sympathetic to them, he wrote a letter to his parents explaining why he was giving up college, and put it aside for mailing after he was in New York.

He took his final examinations the last week and was certain he made top grades on all of them, although it made no difference now. On the last day, he had Railway Express pick up his small trunk, packed with just about everything he owned, and sent it off to Marianne at the address in New York City she'd sent him last week, along with a letter saying that she and Edna were well settled in the flat and were looking forward to having him stay with them. Then he addressed a letter to the college registrar, informing him that he was withdrawing formally from school.

He walked out into the gray, chilling day with his suitcase. He waited for twenty minutes at the Greyhound stop. Finally the bus arrived and he got in. He was on his way to New York.

26

Mike figured his time carefully. The new Howard Stanton–Denise Carroll co-starring comedy, *Love Me Later,* was playing at the Regency Grand. If he went to see it now, he would get in for early afternoon prices and save a quarter, and in addition he would have time for a bite at the Automat before he was due at class.

The theater was crowded because it was Decoration Day, and many firms had given their employees a holiday, including the firm of Rhodes, McCalley, and Whitley on Wall Street, where Mike was employed, having been promoted recently from mail boy to head of the mail room after only three months of efficient service.

He waited with other ticket holders in the great lobby, not minding the wait in the midst of such luxury. The Regency Grand's reputation for being even more splendid than the Roxy was well earned. The carpeting was so thick that Mike's feet actually sank into it. Above him, a giant chandelier made of thousands of pieces of glittering crystal extended from a gold-leafed ceiling, and large oil paintings in gold frames stared from distant marble walls. In the center of the lobby an ornate fountain cascaded water made iridescent by colored lights.

In a little while, the crowd was moved upstairs to the lavish hall of the loges with its ornate mirrors, marble busts, and rows of portraits of Regency stars. Mike noticed, as they were halted briefly near an entrance to the auditorium, that Howard Stanton's portrait was next to that of his wife, Georgina Fox.

As Mike left the theater two hours later, he thought about the picture. It was the second comedy Howard Stanton and Denise Carroll had made together in recent years. It surprised Mike that Howard Stanton was pretty good at comedy. Most romantic stars weren't. Still, Mike considered how he himself would have done the role, and thought he would have been better.

As for the picture itself, it was briskly entertaining, proving again that Regency Pictures had its finger on the pulse of public taste. But Marianne would have hated it, Mike realized. Marianne had become so blinded by what she called "the greatness of the theater and the shallowness of the movies" that she refused to see merit in any picture.

Mike no longer saw Marianne. During the two months he'd lived with her and Edna in the railroad flat, he'd learned that she could be jealous and spiteful. He'd never expected that from her. But of course he'd never expected to become involved with Edna the way he had, either.

The Times Tower lay ahead. Mike looked up at the news flashing around the sign on top of the triangularly shaped building that identified Times Square unfailingly to the whole world. The news flash said, "Winston Churchill declares that England will fight on." That took guts, Mike thought, considering the way Hitler had rolled right over Holland, Belgium, and France, and had driven the British back to their own island.

Mike had a sandwich at the Automat, then walked across Fortieth Street to Ninth Avenue, where Konstantin Fedotov's studio occupied the musty top floor of an old building. This evening eight students of the class were performing a scene from Chekhov's *The Sea Gull* under the principles of Fedotov's school of acting, which the Russian modestly kept reminding them was not his but Stanislavski's. The most important point in this approach was that you didn't merely "play" a part; you "became" the character you were interpreting.

So Mike wasn't Michael Baines as he performed but a Russian named Trigorin, and this wasn't a studio in New York City in 1940 but a Russian seashore in 1890. And this wasn't rehearsing; it was "being." This time, as before, Mike found it hard to lose his real identity, but he was getting better at it. The Stanislavski method seemed to him the most valid approach of any to creating a role.

The scene didn't go badly, but it wasn't perfect, either, and Fedotov offered detailed criticism. The old Russian knew what he was talking about. He'd served an illustrious tenure with the Moscow Art Theater before the Russian Revolution.

As usual, Mike felt stimulated by the instruction, and he wished Fedotov would invite him to stick around for some extra talk about the theater and acting, as he sometimes did; but this time he didn't. When Mike went downstairs and out into the street, Al caught up with him. Of the other members of the class, Mike liked Al the least. He had an uncomfortable feeling that Al was queer and wanted to make him.

"Hey, Mike," Al said with a wet smile, "how would you like to make fifty bucks?"

"What would I have to do, dive off the Brooklyn Bridge?"

"No, just act in a movie." Al laughed conspiratorially. "In a blue movie, that is."

Mike looked at him blankly.

"You know, a smoker," Al said. "A sex movie. All you have to do is screw a broad before a camera and you make fifty bucks."

"Oh, is that all?" said Mike. "And have your face plastered all over the world in a dirty movie. Fine. Terrific."

"They photograph you in a mask so your face doesn't show."

"If that's so, why don't you 'act' in it yourself?"

Al's face colored a bit. "I'm just the go-between for the guy who makes the movies. I line up the actors for him."

"What's to stop you from being in them yourself, if the money is so good?" Mike asked insistently, wondering if Al would admit he was queer and couldn't lay a girl if his life depended on it.

"Because I'm skinny. I don't look good undressed the way you do."

"How do you know what I look like undressed?"

Al's color heightened. "You can tell you've got a good build. You don't have to have your clothes off to know something like that."

"Nothing doing," Mike said. "I could use the fifty bucks, but I've got to draw the line somewhere."

"Well, if you change your mind, let me know," Al said.

They parted, and Mike took the subway down from Times Square to the Village. He was unpleasantly surprised when he came out of the station just as Marianne was entering. They stopped and stared awkwardly at each other. Mike was pained to see her. He was sure she was equally pained to see him.

Still, they should really talk about what had happened. The ugly memory of it was still fresh, though it had been six weeks since Marianne had screamed at Mike and Edna to move out of the apartment within the hour.

"Look, Marianne," Mike said, "why don't we have a cup of coffee together and try to look at things reasonably?"

"There's nothing to discuss," Marianne said icily. "I thought you and Edna were my friends—"

"That's just it. We *are*. We feel awful about what happened."

"You should," Marianne continued in her frigid tone. "I let you stay with me and Edna as a favor until you could get established in New York, and what did the two of you do the minute I turned my back? You carried on like alley cats. Oh, it was a pretty sight, walking in and finding the two of you like *that*."

He flushed at the remembrance. Marianne had come in unexpectedly while he and Edna were making love in the bed she shared with Edna. "In *my* bed, even!" she'd screamed, as if that were what outraged her most about it. He and Edna had gone to a hotel, and the next day he'd found Edna a room in a boardinghouse and himself the dingy one-room apartment he occupied in an old building on MacDougal Street.

"I'm sorry," he said.

"Is that all you can say?" Marianne laughed bitterly. "Well, that certainly isn't enough. I don't ever want to see you or Edna again."

As she swept down the subway steps, Mike looked after her helplessly. He really didn't see why she was so outraged over his sexual relationship with Edna unless she was sexually interested in him herself. Yet she'd never seemed so. She'd seemed to take the same pride as he had in their relationship as close friends with mutual career interests.

It was confusing, and he didn't pretend to understand it. But he wished that he and Marianne were still friends and that he'd never met Edna. He'd been irresistibly attracted to Edna because of her ripe but innocent beauty. When he'd found out their first time together that she was a virgin, an extra dimension of excitement had been added. The excitement had dimmed considerably in the last few weeks, and the last

161

time he and Edna had been to bed together was three weeks ago. He'd been thinking that it would be best for them to end their affair. Their relationship had seemed so degraded after Marianne's outburst that there was no longer any joy in it, so why go on?

A few minutes later he entered the smelly, claustrophobic hallway of his building and walked up two flights of narrow stairs to the third floor, where his boxlike apartment looked out on a cheerless scene of fire escapes and grimy walls. He sat down wearily and thought about writing a long overdue letter to his parents. His letters to them were as difficult and infrequent as theirs to him. He'd been in New York four months now, but they still weren't reconciled to what he'd done and insisted that he must give it up and return to college. In every letter he wrote them he had to repeat firmly that his decision to seek an acting career was one he wasn't changing his mind about.

His bell rang a few minutes later. He hesitated about answering, because it couldn't be anyone but Edna.

It was, and she looked pale and strained. "Thank God you're here now," she said shakily. "I don't know how many times I've rung your bell. I thought I'd go crazy if I had to walk around that block just once more waiting for you to come home."

"I was at class," he said, and frowned as she sank down on one of his dilapidated wooden chairs. "Edna, what's wrong?"

"I'm pregnant."

He stared at her, not wanting to believe he'd heard what she'd said. He frowned. She looked at him, her eyes defensive.

"It's yours, Mike, if that's what you're thinking."

It wasn't what he was thinking. He was thinking that he should have insisted that they take precautions every time instead of relying on that crazy rhythm method. But she hadn't wanted him to wear a rubber, and now he was going to have to marry her because of it.

As if she'd read his thoughts, she said, "You're afraid you'll have to marry me, aren't you?" She paused and swallowed before she went on. "Well, you won't have to, because I want to have an abortion."

She stopped and looked questioningly at him, as if she expected him to try to argue her out of it. He had no intention of doing that. He knew an abortion was dangerous, but he didn't want to think about that. He just wanted out of this mess.

"It would be silly for us to try marriage," Edna went on. "We both want careers in the theater. We can't afford to have a baby."

He certainly didn't intend to dispute that. "How far along is it?"

"About three months. I wasn't really worried when I missed my first period, because I'm irregular. But when I missed the second one, I had

162

to face it. Still, it was a while before I could force myself to see a doctor. He confirmed it a week ago."

"And you're just now getting around to telling me?"

"I didn't want to tell you until I had a solution. I've become friendly with a girl at the boardinghouse. I had a feeling something like this had happened to her, and it did, just last year. She can steer us to someone who will do the operation."

Operation. She made it sound as though she were having her appendix removed. Maybe she had to think of it that way so she wouldn't be overwhelmed by the terrible truth of what she was really doing. Or what *they* were doing. They were taking a life they'd started together. Their sin was even greater than the abortionist's. Mike tried to push the thought away, but it clung on.

"It will cost a hundred and twenty-five dollars," Edna said.

He whistled, staggered at the cost. How could he ever get that much money together? It was five weeks' pay. He'd been saving three dollars a week for quite a while, but so far he had only twenty-four dollars saved.

"I've got fifty dollars, Mike. It's my graduation money from my relatives. I was supposed to buy luggage with it, but I never did. It's a good thing, isn't it?"

But they needed fifty dollars more, and they needed it fast. Then Mike thought of Al's proposition.

"I'll get the rest of the money," Mike said.

"It will have to be quick," Edna said. "I'm going to be showing soon, and you know I can't keep my mother from coming down here for her regular monthly visit, and I won't be able to hide it from her."

"It will be soon," he said grimly.

27

It was a sinister night, intermittently drizzling and pouring, and Mike sweated under his raincoat. He stood next to a cigar store Indian under an awning on West Seventieth Street and Broadway and waited for Al, who was already ten minutes late. He was worried that Al might not show up, that the deal might be off. But Al arrived a few minutes later, grinning salaciously, and put his hand briefly on Mike's arm as he steered him out into the rain. It was all Mike could do to restrain himself from shaking Al off, but he couldn't afford to offend him at this point.

Mike chatted emptily, trying to keep his courage up as Al led him into an old building nearby, then up four flights to a dusty loft that served as a studio. A seedy-looking man with hard eyes answered the door, and he fit Mike's preconceived notion of what a producer of blue movies would look like. Al introduced him simply as Hugo.

"Let me see you without your shirt on," Hugo said.

Mike looked at Al, frowning. Al said, "Hugo just wants to confirm that you've got a good build, Mike. He doesn't want anybody in his movies but good-looking guys with good builds and beautiful broads with beautiful figures."

"That's why I pay top fees," Hugo said proudly.

Mike doffed his raincoat, then unbuttoned his shirt and removed it and his undershirt.

"Okay," Hugo said. "You're fine above. Now let's see below. Pull it out and show me."

Mike hesitated, feeling his face burn.

"Look, don't get cagey," Hugo said impatiently. "Either you've got what I need or you don't. If you don't, then I've got to get someone else quick."

His face still burning, Mike unbuttoned his fly and took out his penis. It seemed to him that it had shrunk below its normal size from the fear and disgust that were crawling through him, but it satisfied Hugo.

"Okay, come in and meet your co-star," Hugo said.

They went from the dim foyer into the large room that served as a studio. The dirty skylight above was beaded with raindrops. The floor was littered. At one end was a makeshift set representing a living room and a bedroom, with a thin wall between them. A sixteen-millimeter camera was set up on a tripod. Various floodlights connected to outlets by a tangle of wires surrounded the set, although none was turned on. A floor lamp with a fringed shade glowed feebly on a blond girl sitting on a couch in the living room part of the set. She was remarkably pretty, and her name was Sally. Mike shook her hand and smiled at her, wondering what her role in life was. He doubted that either of them would learn much about the other except the details of their anatomy.

Hugo explained the story of the movie. Mike was a magazine

164

salesman, and he had come to sell magazines to Sally, but instead they would go to bed.

"The introduction is short and sweet," Hugo stressed. "The point is to get stripped and start screwing as soon as possible after we start. Customers don't like pictures that waste too much time on preliminaries."

Hugo said that he would be moving the camera a lot to get shots from various angles during the sexual encounter, so they should be prepared to stop and start whenever he said so.

"What about a mask?" Mike asked as Hugo looked at his watch and said they had to get going.

"No mask. Don't worry about it. I shoot it so the faces don't show."

Mike didn't believe that, but there was nothing he could do about it.

Hugo went over and turned on the floodlights. The set glared under them. Mike was handed a battered briefcase containing copies of magazines and was instructed to put on his raincoat and wait beyond the door that opened into the set. Soon he heard the camera start whirring.

"All right, knock on the door, and Sally will answer it," Hugo said from the other side.

Mike knocked on the door, and Sally opened it with a smile. He stepped inside, removed his raincoat, sat on the couch with her, and showed her the magazines. Sweat started trickling down his forehead, past his ears, toward his neck. But apparently it didn't show much. Hugo said nothing about it.

Instead, he said, "Okay, start feeling her up."

Mike managed to do as instructed, with a somewhat shaking hand. He also managed to undress Sally bit by bit, while Hugo urged him to speed it up. And somehow, when he and Sally were naked on the bed, he was hard and able to penetrate her, although the last thing he felt was desire. "Don't drop your load," Hugo cautioned, but it wasn't necessary. In these circumstances, he couldn't have come in a year of trying. There was only one good thing about it. The lights were so bright that he couldn't see Al's face out there, although he could see Hugo's as he moved in with the camera and held it on them like an omnivorous eye.

It was endless. Hugo kept stopping the camera and directing them to reposition themselves, or to do something different.

"It's hard to photograph the sex organs in action so you can see them right," he announced as if he were addressing a class on the subject. "You've got to have a steady change of angles and range or the viewers get bored."

Finally it was over. But then Mike learned to his anger that it wasn't

165

over for him yet, just for Sally. Two other girls had been let into the studio while the shooting had progressed. Another picture was to be made now, with Mike servicing the two girls in the same bed at the same time.

"And the girls will be doing it with each other, too," Hugo added.

"But you said just one picture!" Mike said in rage to Al, although he couldn't remember exactly how Al had put the proposition.

"No, I didn't, honest!" Al said, shrinking back. "Gosh, you don't think you get that much dough for just one picture, do you?"

"Hey, what gives with you?" Hugo said angrily. "We haven't got all night. If you don't want to make this picture, there are plenty of others who do. We can have one here in ten minutes. But if you walk out, not a dime."

"Why, you bastard," Mike said, clutching Hugo by the collar and drawing him closer. "I ought to knock the hell out of you."

"Let me go!" Hugo sputtered. "Or I'll have your ass for this!"

"I'll let you go all right!" Mike said. "Just long enough to go downstairs and get the police."

Hugo laughed contemptuously. "You just do that, pretty boy, and we'll get the chance to spend the night in the Tombs together. And you can count on a nice long jail sentence. It's just as much against the law to be in these pictures as it is to produce them."

The thought terrified Mike. If he got into trouble like that, he would never be able to continue with his career.

He made his decision. His image was irrevocably recorded on one long reel of sixteen-millimeter film in an act of sin, so it might as well be recorded on another one as well. He had to have the fifty dollars!

He didn't even learn the names of the two girls he was photographed in bed with a few minutes later. But neither of them was nearly so pretty as Sally, who had vanished from the studio. They were avid performers and were all over Mike and each other in every way they could manage. Mike hated it. Again the filming was endless, with much repositioning for different camera angles. The girls were laughing and obviously enjoying themselves. What pleasure Mike showed was pure acting, forced by Hugo's occasional barked demands. "You're getting screwed, not going to a funeral, so look like it, damn it!"

It was finally over. As Mike dressed, he had a new fear. Suppose Hugo didn't want to pay him until he'd developed the film and was sure everything had come out all right?

But Hugo didn't try to shuffle him off. He handed him two very worn and wrinkled twenty-dollar bills and one very worn and wrinkled ten-dollar bill. Dirty money for a dirty job.

166

"You were a good stud," Hugo said with a smile, apparently willing to forget the antagonism that had sprung up between them an hour ago. "Maybe I can use you again sometime."

"Not on your life!" Mike said coldly. He threw a look of scorn at Al, who had obviously been waiting around so he could leave with him, and then he turned and walked out alone. He hurried down the stairs into the night. He kept taking deep breaths of air as he walked away, as if that would somehow expel the foulness from him.

A much worse night came less than a week later. It couldn't be postponed. The arrangements had been made, and they couldn't be changed. Besides, Edna's mother was due for a visit in a few days, and Edna had to be fully recovered by then.

"I hate what I've done to you," Mike said quietly as they walked across town toward the rendezvous.

"It's just as much my fault as yours," Edna said. "It just happened, that's all."

He wondered if she felt as he did now—that he never wanted to touch his body to another as long as he lived. He'd felt that way particularly since the night he'd made the movies.

They walked more slowly, for they were approaching the rendezvous point on Avenue B twenty minutes before they were supposed to be there. The directions had been explicit. A man would meet them at the mailbox on the corner at Thirteenth Street exactly at eight, and he would be wearing a straw hat and a white suit and brown and white shoes.

He showed up at the mailbox right on time. He had an olive complexion and heavily brilliantined hair parted in the middle and laid flat to his head. He looked sinister in spite of his dapper outfit. He looked like what he was—the go-between who was to take them to the abortionist.

He looked around carefully, probably checking to make sure they hadn't brought the police with them, and then he started walking south. They followed a few yards behind him. Two blocks south he turned toward Avenue C and stopped at a building in the middle of the block. The building was completely dark. After looking both ways, the man went up the steps and through the double doors into the vestibule. They followed. There was no light in the vestibule, and only a pale smattering of light from the street seeped through the dirty windows in the doors. But there was enough light for Mike to see that there were no names on the mailboxes.

"This is an empty building," Mike said.

167

"No kidding?" the man said in a hoarse voice, giving a mocking laugh. "What'd you expect? You don't think we do this kind of job with a lot of people around to walk in on us, do you?"

Mike felt terribly uneasy. What they ought to do was turn around and walk out. But the man had opened the door into the hall, and Edna went in quickly after him, as if she were perfectly aware that Mike wanted them to back out of this now and knew that she mustn't weaken, even if he did. He followed leadenly, wondering how she could face this. She was about to risk her life, yet she was walking straight down the hall behind that two-bit thug as if she were going to a party with him.

The apartment in the rear had a lone lamp, probably brought in for the occasion, burning in the otherwise empty outer room. A gaunt, seamed woman with a rigid mouth was waiting for them. She said she was the doctor. Mike had deep doubts that she really was, but there was no way of proving it one way or another.

"The money first," she said.

"Edna," Mike said, "I think we ought to talk about this—"

"There's no point, Mike," Edna interrupted. "There's no other way."

"We haven't got all night," the man said harshly. "Fork up the dough. Whether you have the operation or not, a deal's a deal, and you pay." The man's hand crept down to his side and patted it, as if he had a weapon concealed in his pocket to back up his demands.

Mike pulled out the money and gave it to the man, who put it into his pocket.

The woman looked at Mike. "You wait here." She put her hand on Edna's arm and steered her through a doorway into the adjoining room. A light went on. A naked bulb peered down dimly from a ceiling fixture on a cot, a table, and a wooden chair.

The woman closed the door. Mike stared at it. He was aware of the man's eyes on him, glaring hostilely, warning him not to make trouble. He turned and walked over to the other side of the room, as far as he could get from the man. He was trembling, and sweat poured from his armpits and down his face even more profusely than it had a few nights before when he'd thought, in Hugo's studio, that he'd reached the bottom of the garbage heap. But he hadn't. This was it. Why didn't he go in there and stop it?

But he didn't move, and soon he knew it was too late. The woman wouldn't have wasted any time. She would be scraping away with her scalpel right now, obliterating that semblance of life he'd left inside Edna a few months earlier. He felt sick. He expected any moment to hear Edna scream. Why didn't she? Was she dead?

168

Finally the door opened. The woman came into the room, her gaunt face set. "She'll be all right," she said to Mike. "You stay in there while she rests, but get her out of here before dawn."

The woman moved toward the door leading to the hall and her escape, the man following quickly behind her.

"But what if something goes wrong?"

The woman stopped and looked back. "If she hemorrhages, call a cop, and he'll get her to a hospital."

They were gone. He went into the other room. Edna lay ashen and motionless on the cot, staring at the ceiling. She finally slept. Shortly before dawn, he wakened her. She leaned heavily on him as they left the building. There were no cabs in the neighborhood, so they walked to the bus stop and waited eternally for a bus.

The sun was beginning to beam down on the city as he helped her up the steps where she lived. She went slowly inside, looking back at him with a pale smile. He felt terribly guilty about it, but he hoped he would never have to see her again.

But he did see her, a month later. He picked her up at her boarding-house one Sunday and they had supper together in a cafeteria. They didn't say anything about their ugly experience at first. They talked about their acting classes, and Edna said she wished she could find a job better than the one she had behind the cosmetics counter at Wool-worth's.

Finally Mike said, "I can't get it out of my mind, what we did. Edna, I'm so sorry."

"So am I. I still cry a lot about it, Mike."

"Oh, God, Edna, if we could only undo it."

She smiled sadly. "It will get easier in time. But I don't think we ought to see each other anymore, do you? It just makes me want to cry."

"Oh, God, Edna, I'm so damned sorry!" he repeated.

She reached over and patted his hand. "I know you are. That's why I can bear it. And it *will* get easier in time, Mike, for both of us."

After that, they didn't see each other again.

28

Mike was lying on his bed studying the scene from Eugene O'Neill's *Strange Interlude* that they were doing in class the following evening. He'd been over and over his part, and he was certain he was going to give a better reading than any of the others. He always did. Konstantin Fedotov admitted that. The old Russian was highly critical of his student actors, so praise from him was a sure indication of progress. Mike had been a student of Fedotov for twenty months now, and the last time they'd talked privately after class, Fedotov had gone so far as to say that Mike had the potential to be a really fine actor. Mike was still glowing from it. There was no one whose opinion he valued more.

He put down the sides he was studying and looked at the peeling paint on the ceiling, wondering about his future, as he did at length several times a week. In another two months he would have been in New York for two years. His employment on Wall Street was still meager, but he'd made considerable progress in his drama study, and he was a far better actor than he had been. Still, when he stopped to consider the staggering odds against success in the theater, he couldn't help feeling discouraged. It was no wonder so many dropped out. He'd heard from his mother—who wrote more often now, but was still restrained—that Marianne Sellers had returned to Grove Center and was now employed on the loan desk in the public library. It seemed an awful comedown to Mike.

He himself didn't intend to give up, no matter how discouraged he got at times, and he decided he would get right back to work on *Strange Interlude* after he caught the news broadcast on the radio. Two minutes later he turned it off with a frown. The Japanese had bombed Pearl Harbor!

The United States would be at war tomorrow for sure, and he was twenty-one years old. They would be after him to be a soldier if the war lasted very long. God damn it!

Mike was terribly excited about the play and his part in it. It was an antiwar play and particularly timely to get on the boards right now. But it wasn't being presented on Broadway, because the playwright hadn't found a producer. He'd arranged to do the production in a church—a new idea! The director and the actors were part of the neighborhood group Mike had joined recently, but none of them were amateurs. They were all studying for the professional theater.

Mike knew he was good in his part. The play was good, but he was better than the play was, and it made him proud to think that his strong performance as a man who didn't want to go to war and who wasn't afraid to make an issue of it before the government, or even die for it, was what would keep people in their seats through both acts.

He could see how good he was from the jealousy of the other actors. The friendliness of the other cast members ebbed away by degrees from the first rehearsal to the final one, when open hostility seethed. Still, while they were acting, they all did their best, because they were all in this together, and they were troupers even if they weren't quite professionals yet.

The pastor of the church—who had donated his auditorium because of his vehemently antiwar feelings—came to the final rehearsal and kept nodding his head in agreement from the front row as the play progressed.

There was a good turnout opening night since admission was free. Most of the audience returned after intermission, and the company got two curtain calls afterward.

The next night the play went as well as it had opening night. The following night, when they did it for the last time, they had only a small audience, but they gave their best presentation. Mike felt that he'd topped his own portrayal of the two previous nights.

It was over, and they retreated to the dressing room slowly after the applause trickled out for the last time. There was to be no celebration tonight, no closing night party. They would just go their separate ways and wonder when the next chance would come to show themselves to the public.

Mike felt let down, and his face was sober as he smeared on a dab of cold cream to take off the makeup. He was a little startled when a man appeared in the mirror, a well-dressed man in a double-breasted blue suit with gray pin stripes.

"Permit me to introduce myself," he said, and handed Mike a card which read "Jason Alderman, Regency Pictures," and then gave an address on Fifth Avenue. But the address didn't register in the flood of

171

excitement that plunged through Mike. The words "Regency Pictures" were what registered.

"Please give me a ring at your earliest opportunity," Alderman said, and was gone before Mike was able to say that yes, he certainly would.

Mike walked around the crooked streets of the Village for hours that night, thinking about the surprise at the church, wondering what would come of it. The nagging fear that it might come to nothing alternated with the hope that this might be his big chance. He was far too excited to fall asleep easily when he finally went home and got to bed.

He was nervously awake at eight, anticipating making his call to Alderman at nine, when business commenced in New York offices. When he called at two minutes after nine from the hall phone downstairs, the switchboard operator at Regency Pictures told him that Alderman wasn't scheduled to come in until two o'clock that afternoon, and was there a message, please?

"Would you tell him that Michael Baines called and that I'll call him back after two?"

He hung up, feeling even more nervous than before. Two o'clock seemed impossibly far away, and suppose he couldn't get in touch with Alderman even then? Still, he couldn't take the risk of possibly missing what might be an important opportunity, so he called his employer, faked raspiness in his voice, and said that he hadn't reported in this morning because he had a strep throat that would need looking after all day.

He went back to his room and waited. The hours crept by. At one o'clock he polished his only good shoes to a high gleam and put on his only good suit just in case, as he hoped, Alderman would want to see him that day. At two minutes after two he phoned Alderman and got right through to him.

"I'm glad you called, Mike," Alderman said cheerily, as if he'd known Mike for years. "Can you come up here this afternoon? I think we should have a talk, but I ought to point out that all I can do for you right now is to give you an interview. No promises of any kind. I'll be perfectly frank. We see a lot of people. Not many make it with us."

"Don't worry, I understand; I really do," Mike said excitedly.

For the first time in his life, Mike took a taxi. It cost him fifty cents, including a dime tip, to get from the Village up to the handsome building on Fifth Avenue three blocks below Rockefeller Center where Regency Pictures' New York offices were located. The offices occupied the entire twelfth floor of the building, and Mike was let out of the elevator into a thickly carpeted foyer whose walls were hung with oil

172

paintings. A woman at the reception desk inquired about his business, checked with Alderman on the intercom, and then called for a page to lead Mike down a corridor to Alderman's office.

Jason Alderman didn't look much like the man who, in the turmoil of the previous night, had registered only slightly on Mike's mind. He seemed older and different somehow.

"As you've certainly guessed," he said with a smile, "I'm Regency Pictures' talent representative in New York City."

Mike nodded. He didn't know what to say. He hoped he didn't look as awkward as he felt.

"When I hear about people doing good work," Alderman continued, "I try to check them out. But of course I can't check out everyone, and I'm glad I was able to catch your play last night."

So was Mike! Should he say it? No. He merely smiled.

"I didn't particularly like the play," Alderman said, "but I liked your performance. You came across. By that I mean, of the six or seven persons on stage last night, I kept looking at you and listening to you much more than the others. That's why I think you might have movie potential."

Mike smiled again.

"Of course, just because you come across on stage doesn't mean you automatically would on screen," Alderman went on. "But let's talk about it. First, are you interested in the idea of acting in movies?"

Mike nodded his head vigorously. "Oh, yes!"

"I'm glad to hear that. Some stage actors aren't, or think they aren't. Some think that movie acting is an unworthy career compared with acting in the theater."

"I've been studying for the theater," Mike said, "but I've been thinking of it partly as a springboard to the movies. I've always liked the movies better than any other art form."

Alderman smiled. "So you consider the movies art? Good. A lot of people would disagree with you. Even some Hollywood people. They would say that maybe the movies were art in Griffith's heyday, but that they aren't now."

"I think they are."

Alderman continued smiling. "We'll arrange to have some pictures taken of you this afternoon, Mike. Then I'm going to write up an enthusiastic report about you and send it with the pictures to Hollywood and we'll hope for the best. You see, the next step, if there is any, depends on what they decide out there."

Alderman had warned Mike that it might be weeks before there was any news, but knowing that didn't make the waiting easier. When the news came, it would be either good or bad, nothing in between, and knowing that made the suspense even more difficult to bear. Every day after work, Mike rushed home to look in his mailbox, always with agitated heartbeat, dreading finding the letter there, fearing that it wouldn't be.

Finally, almost three weeks after his interview with Alderman, it *was* there. Mike was shaking when he tore open the envelope. It was good news! Jason Alderman's joyful message was that Mike was to be given a screen test right here in New York.

"Hooray!" Mike shouted in the hallway, with no one to hear. There was no one to tell, anyway. He wasn't sure how his parents would respond to the news, so he decided not to write them. He decided not to tell Konstantin Fedotov, either. Considering the Russian's often contemptuous remarks on the quality of movie acting in America, he would probably be against this. Anyway, much as Mike hoped the test would be a great success, suppose he flopped? If he did, the fewer who knew about it, the better.

The day of the test started badly when Mike called in to the firm to report sick and was crustily informed by his supervisor that if he continued being sick so often he could start looking for another job. Now everything was staked on what happened today, Mike thought as he apprehensively sat through the long subway trip to the Bronx, where the sound stage, a sooty brick barn of a building, was located.

The director's name was Flax, and he had a flimsy handshake and an unconcerned manner. He said they would do the test on the only set standing, a replica of a shabby office that had apparently been recently used, for there were fresh ashes in the ashtray and the lights were in place. But it was evident at once that it wouldn't matter what background the test was shot against, for there was no script.

"You'll sit behind the desk, and I'll sit at the camera and talk to you," Flax said. "You'll answer my questions and do the things I say to do."

"That doesn't sound like much of a test," Mike said.

"It's the standard test when we're doing a single," Flax said coldly. "There's just nobody around for you to test with today, kid."

Mike tried not to show on his face how much he disliked Flax for being so casual about this test and for calling him "kid."

"We'll finish off by having you read something from this," Flax said, handing Mike a book. It was *The Collected Works of Edgar Allan Poe.*

A man appeared at Flax's beckoning and did a very minor makeup

174

job on Mike's face, while Flax had an adjustment made on some of the lights peering down from the top of the set, which had no ceiling. The camera started, recorded a chalked slate stating that this was a test of Michael Baines, then centered on Mike.

"Okay, Mike," Flax said in a much warmer manner than previously, probably because he was now being recorded for the film even if he wasn't going to be seen on it. "When were you born?"

"In nineteen twenty," Mike said, and then answered other questions, telling Flax his hair was dark blond, his eyes were blue, he weighed one sixty-five, was six feet tall, and was partial to everything from murder mysteries to the classics in his reading habits, was a good swimmer, and went to the movies two or three times a week.

Then he was told to walk around the set and touch some things, to sit down and get up, to lean against the desk, open the book of Poe's works, and read from the first selection he turned to. It happened to be "The Raven," a work he was familiar with and liked. He began to read, glad that at last he was able to do something in this test to show his ability, but Flax curtly said, "Cut!" just as he finished the fourth line.

"Okay, that was good!" Flax said, already up from his chair at the camera.

"But it wasn't good!" Mike protested. "I didn't get a chance to show what I can do."

"Look, kid, you aren't testing for a role, you're testing for a contract, and believe me, this is the way it's done."

Mike didn't believe this was the way it would be done in Hollywood, but of course they weren't in Hollywood. Besides, what could he say? He left the building feeling leaden, hoping his chances weren't ruined.

The next day, during lunch hour, Mike called Jason Alderman to say the piece he'd carefully prepared during a long night of virtually sleepless tossing.

"It isn't that I don't appreciate the opportunity to test, but the way it was done, anybody seeing it will think I haven't got talent for doing anything but being a ninny."

"You're wrong, Mike. The test may have seemed stupid to you, but it will answer that all-important question of whether you come across on screen or not. That's the only thing the decision-makers in Hollywood want to know about you at this point."

Mike was still doubtful, and when the weeks dragged by without his hearing anything from Alderman, he was beginning to think he never would. But one bright morning almost a month after the test, Alderman called him at the firm, said cheerfully, "It's good news," and asked Mike to come see him right away. Mike walked into his supervisor's office and told him with the greatest of pleasure that he was quitting immediately. He whistled as he walked out while the supervisor was in mid-spiel about Mike's lack of consideration in not giving notice. All Mike could think of was that Alderman had said it was good news. That could only mean that they liked the test and were going to give him a contract!

But it wasn't quite that. They were just going to pay his expenses to Hollywood, where the final decision would be made by the two men at Regency Pictures who had the final say on everything—Augustus Dalton, the studio head, and Alexander Renfew, the production chief.

"It's all right, Mike," Alderman said with a smile. "I'd almost bet my last dollar you're going to go over big with them."

Mike went home and packed what little there was to pack, and that evening he went to tell Konstantin Fedotov what he was going to do. Fedotov was surprised at what had happened. He wished Mike well, but he was obviously not enthusiastic about the venture. As Mike left him, he said there would always be a place for Mike in his class in case it didn't work out for him in Hollywood.

But it must work out for him! Mike thought as he locked his apartment for the last time the next morning and went softly down the stairs with his suitcase.

29

I love California! Mike kept telling himself. Lots of blue sky, lots of bright sunshine, lots of palm trees, and lots of healthy people. And look what dividends you got from living out here! A few miles' drive and you were at the ocean. And if you weren't in the mood for the ocean, you could turn around and head the other way, toward the mountains or the desert.

Mike liked it and yet didn't like it, although he wrote his parents that he did. They were flabbergasted to learn that he was in Hollywood and had a contract. He hoped they were ashamed over their past attitude.

176

He didn't tell them he'd been uncertain at first that he would get a contract.

He'd thought, during his first interview with Dalton and Renfew, that they didn't like him. Two terrible weeks of waiting were forced on him before they rendered a favorable decision. Then he was called in to sign the contract. The various provisions were explained to him carefully by a man from the studio's legal department, since he had no agent yet to represent him. He was to get a hundred dollars a week for the first year, although it could be increased at six months if the studio saw fit, and then he would get increases every year if his options were picked up. The contract was for seven years, but the studio could drop him any time a yearly option came up. Also, contracts were invariably renegotiated if the player became a star, which, the lawyer explained dryly, happened in about one out of five hundred cases. The morals clause was emphasized. Any sexual shenanigans that came to light and caused the studio embarrassment would cause him to be dropped like a hot potato.

It was compulsory that he attend the studio's acting school, and he thought that was ridiculous. He'd long ago advanced beyond the elements of acting taught there. The acting coach recognized this and asked him, in a private moment, simply to bear with her, telling him that he would eventually get more out of this than mere affirmation that he already knew how to talk, walk, and sit well. Her name was Mrs. Hetman, and he'd recognized her aging but familiar face immediately. She'd played character parts in pictures for years. She admitted she went back to the early twenties, when she'd worked for Irving Thalberg in the pristine years at Universal Pictures.

She was right. He was soon getting something out of the classes that all new contract players were required to take three hours a day when they weren't involved in picture production, for screen acting technique was far different from stage acting technique.

"Always remember," said Mrs. Hetman, "that screen acting is a matter of intimacy with the camera and with your ultimate audience in the motion picture theater, for the camera records ruthlessly what it catches. That's why a poor actor will seem poorer on screen than on stage. His poorness is enlarged by the camera and passed on to the audience in giant size."

Mrs. Hetman also pointed out that it was difficult to develop and sustain a character in screen acting "because shooting is done in spurts and seldom in sequence. In a typical day you'll be before the cameras ten or fifteen minutes, and the rest of your time will be spent waiting or preparing or repeating. It's not glamorous in the way movie magazines lead fans to believe it is." She smiled. "It's simply the most exciting thing you could do with your lives, that's all."

There were six others in the current class, three of them men whom Mike didn't think would offer serious competition. He was impressed with all three of the girls, but the truly outstanding one was Mona Gaillard. Her name had been chosen for her by the studio, she told the class when she recited a short autobiography, as they all had to do on joining the class. She also told them that she was a dancer, although it was to be some time before Mike was to know that she was such an extraordinary one that she was dubbed "a dream in motion" by the publicity department.

Mike was mesmerized by her beauty and magnetism. In the circumstances of the class, it wasn't possible to be sure if she was intelligent as well, but she gave the impression she was. He doubted that there was a more beautiful woman in Hollywood, and she was assuredly a woman, not just a girl, even though she was, as she told them, only twenty years old. In his mind, Mike tried to work up suitable descriptions for her beauty, but they were hopelessly inadequate. To him she was the most beautiful woman he'd ever seen.

He thought about her more and more, and wished he had a car so he could ask her out. But a car wouldn't have helped. In the recital of her autobiography, she'd forgotten to reveal that she was married. Mike saw her husband pick her up at the studio one afternoon. He was twice her age. And Mike hated him at first sight.

Shortly after he signed his Regency Pictures contract, Mike found a room with an outside entrance in a widow's house not far from the studio. But he was more at home on the studio streets than he was in his room. He was told that the front and back lots covered two hundred and fifty acres, and he walked over most of them in his first few weeks at the studio.

He tried not to miss anything. Looking boldly casual, as if he were on official business, he wandered in and out of such exotic places as the armory, where they were at the moment making swords for a new swashbuckler; and the costume warehouse, where he found thousands of costumes from all periods; and the miniature shop, where they were currently constructing miniature battleships and cruisers to fight battles in the studio tank for a projected war picture.

He even walked through the writers' building one day. An open door revealed the typical writer's office as a simple affair, furnished only with a desk, a typewriter, a couple of chairs, and a file cabinet. It was a far cry from the sumptuous offices occupied by the top executives in the administration building, which Mike knew from having been in Dalton's kingly quarters when he'd been interviewed and awarded his contract.

The back lot was of endless fascination for Mike, with its jungle, its large "sea" with half an ocean liner and a full-scale sailing ship moored at its wharves, its medieval castles and Renaissance palace and French village and New York City streets, one of which was a turn-of-the-century model, the other, complete with subway kiosks, strictly up-to-date. And there was a Western street whose face was lifted slightly for each new B Western shot there, and far in the back was the lonely battleground that had served for *The Young Soldier,* Howard Stanton's first starring picture, which Mike had seen more than a decade ago.

But there was nothing that fascinated him more than the sound stages. He could never enter one where the red light was on, indicating that shooting was in progress, but he entered many where preparations for shooting were going on, and no one ever questioned him, for his face wasn't known yet, and he might easily be taken for someone on the crew. So he would walk through the cavernous stages from set to set, and wonder at the miles of thick cables that powered the giant lights hovering over and around the sets and being continually shifted by the crews of grips under the direction of their barking supervisors.

He would listen while the cameraman instructed his camera operators and the assistant directors placed the stand-ins where the stars would be once the scene was started, so the lights could be adjusted and changed; and above on the catwalks the crew would change the lights as they were directed.

And then he would go on to another set on another stage, where construction was just beginning. Huge doors would be standing open at one end of the stage, and vans would be disgorging pieces of furniture that were to be moved down and placed by set decorators exactly where they belonged according to a plan in the hands of a supervisor.

People, people, everywhere. The studio was a small city in itself, and it took hundreds of persons to make it work. It was all endlessly interesting to Mike, even after he'd been at Regency Pictures for months. He never tired of the strange sights. He would still turn his head for a second look when he passed a procession of colorfully costumed extras on their way to a sound stage, such as the day he saw Indians in war paint, a couple of circus clowns, and an elephant led by a maharajah with a sapphire in his turban, all walking together.

That was the day there was a message waiting for him when he reported to the acting school. It was from Renfew's office, asking him to report there. It must mean, thought Mike hopefully, that he was to get a picture.

"What you need first of all," Alexander Renfew said before he sent Mike over to Enrico Sangenelli's office, "is experience before the camera. We liked your test well enough to sign you, and we like the reports we've had on you from the school, but the fact remains that you've got to get going on film, and this is a good way."

Or was it? Mike wondered as he left Renfew's office and headed for Sangenelli's office, which wasn't in the producers' and directors' building but in a small office building serving the back lot. On the way over, Mike's reflections on the question took a dozen different turns. It got down to two main points. Yes, you had to start somewhere. But you could stay where you started, too. Some people never got above the first rung of the ladder. They got typed for a particular kind of picture. He didn't want to be typed as a cowboy in B Westerns—and singing Westerns at that!

He was quite depressed by the time he reached the ordinary boxlike building that housed Sangenelli's office. Mike supposed that Sangenelli, who produced Regency's B Westerns, had been put there principally because his pictures were filmed for the most part on the back lot, although some scenes were made on the studio's ranch in the San Fernando Valley. Sangenelli's office, like the building in general, was a very poor sister in size and decor to those in the elaborate structure at the front of the lot where the producers and directors of A productions were quartered. Sangenelli himself was a wisp of a man who looked even smaller scaled behind a desk heaped with papers and folders.

It seemed incredible that this little man could be the producer of action pictures. Still, if he looked like a pipsqueak, he spoke like a Trojan in a deep basso profundo voice that slapped Mike with its aggressiveness. Sangenelli waved a large cigar in the air to emphasize his points.

"Here," he said, throwing a folder at Mike, "is a script. Take it home and look it over. Can you ride? Horses, I mean."

"No."

Sangenelli shook his head. "Another one who can't ride. Danny Evans can't ride very well, either, but at least he can sit on a horse without falling off. Why does Renfew send me guys who can't ride?"

"Maybe I could learn," said Mike.

"In three days? Production starts Monday."

Furthermore, it was a two-week production schedule. All B pictures were on tight schedules and even tighter budgets. Mike went home and looked over the script, which was full of action and light on dialogue. The story seemed silly to him, but he was determined to do as good a job as he could, even though his role as sidekick to Danny Evans, a standard role in the series, seemed incredibly corny.

On Monday, with his few bits of dialogue for the whole picture thoroughly memorized, he arrived at the studio at six A.M., three hours before production was due to start; and when he was still standing around two hours later, he felt embarrassed at his eagerness. People only reported in at six if elaborate makeup jobs were required before they faced the camera. Still, a lot happened in the last hour. He was fitted into a costume provided by the wardrobe man and introduced to Danny Evans and Cathy Younger, who would sing a couple of duets in the course of the picture, the story of which concerned Danny's saving Cathy's widowed mother's ranch from depredation by a gang of crooks who figured there might be some veins of gold running through it.

"I feel guilty because I can't ride well and I can't shoot," Danny confessed to Mike that first day as they ate lunch from the buffet provided on a commissary truck serving companies shooting on the back lot. "It's a cheat on the kids."

"It isn't a cheat at all," Cathy said. "You're a man kids can look up to. That's what matters."

Danny smiled. "Cathy's good at consoling me. And she's the only girl I've ever felt comfortable acting with. If you can call what we do acting."

"The audience it's directed to believes in it," Mike said. "That's what's important."

"I'm glad you don't look down on us, Mike," Danny said. "The last guy they sent in to give him experience before the camera couldn't hide his contempt. It came across in the rushes, and they took him off the picture."

"That won't happen to me," Mike said.

The first day of shooting was concentrated on scenes taking place on the dusty Western street, a permanent set representing a frontier town. Mike's inexperience with horses revealed itself when the scene came up where he and Danny were to ride into town and dismount at the sheriff's office.

"Hey," Danny said with a laugh as they prepared for it. "You mount from the left, not from the right, Mike."

"Ye gods!" said the assistant director, a nervous type. "You mean you've never been on a horse before?"

In the next ten minutes Mike received some rapid instruction on mounting and sitting a horse. Fortunately the scene showed them coming in at a walk. He got through it.

The afternoon was devoted largely to a gunfight that was one of the major climaxes toward the end of the picture. Mike spent most of the scene squatted behind a barrel, pretending to pump his six-shooter at the desperadoes across and down the street.

The next morning he reported in early again, but this time he didn't stand around waiting. Two hours were spent teaching him to look authoritative in the saddle.

"You look as though you were born on a horse," beamed Danny after their first scene that day.

Production moved quickly. A scene was rehearsed, shot from a few setups, and then the company moved on to another scene. Mike wished it was possible for him to see the rushes. He was doing the best job he could with his lines and his bits of business, being especially careful to make his physical movements authoritative, the natural movements of a man of action, but he couldn't be sure how effective he was.

The director reassured him one day. "You're doing okay. Maybe you don't know this, but Renfew was here yesterday watching you do a scene."

"He was? Why didn't you tell me?"

"Renfew doesn't like it known when he's around. It makes actors self-conscious. It's even worse when Dalton is on the set. Anyway, they must have something in mind for you. Renfew doesn't drop around to B sets for nothing, you know."

Mike was enormously excited at hearing that and kept wondering what Renfew's plan for him was. He was glad he was doing as well as he could in his part. Renfew would respect that.

Mike took even more interest in the production after that. He was on the set even when he didn't have to be, for he didn't want to miss anything that went into the making of a picture. He even went to the music recording stage with Danny, Cathy, and the quartet known as the Frontiersmen and listened while they recorded the songs for the picture. Two days later the songs were played back while the group mouthed the words before the camera. These were the final shots in the picture. Mike was sorry it was over. It had been a fine experience.

Mike thought as much about sex in Hollywood as he had in New York, but he didn't participate in it quite so often. New York was a big place where anonymous sex was readily available, and that was the safest kind emotionally. Hollywood was a small place where you kept running into the same people again and again, and sexual involvement could easily lead to more complex relationships.

His experience with Edna two years before had soured him on any sex at all for quite a while, but inevitably he had gotten back into it, always seeking impersonal encounters where there was little risk of an emotional aftermath. In Hollywood there was more risk of consequences, and he was watching that, but he was quite aware that he would have welcomed it with Mona Gaillard if it were possible. He kept thinking about her. He wanted her, but there was no chance of getting her. She was married, and she wasn't wanton, even though she looked as if she might be. He'd decided that not from knowing her—because he hadn't spoken with her much—but just from observing her at school. Whatever else she was or wasn't, she was certainly tantalizing. He supposed it was just as well that she wasn't available to him. He wanted nothing and no one standing in the way of his career, and he had a fear that love or some other kind of compulsive attachment might somehow abort his progress.

He met Mona on a studio street the day after he finished the picture with Danny Evans. She was wearing a jersey sweater and shorts, and he saw that her legs were as nearly perfect as the rest of her. Her sweater came up to her neck, hiding the cleavage of her breasts, but its tightness accentuated their fullness. She was smiling ecstatically. She'd just come from the set, she said, and was on her way to the commissary. Was he interested in lunch?

He'd just had lunch, but he didn't mention that, and he accompanied her to the commissary. She talked brightly. She'd been suddenly called out of the acting school almost two weeks ago, just about the time Mike had started the singing Western, to be tested for a role in Georgina Fox's new picture.

"I'm playing the 'other' woman," she said as she toyed with her salad of cottage cheese and pineapple slices. "I've already done two scenes."

"I'll bet you're good," he said.

"I hope so."

At first he'd wanted her to be interested enough in him and what he was doing to ask about the picture he'd just finished. Now he didn't. She was in an A production and he'd just made a B, and there was all the difference in the world. He even felt a little ashamed about it, although he knew he shouldn't.

"Georgina Fox is a marvelous actress," Mona said, "but she's no competition for my type."

183

"No, I don't suppose so," he said cautiously.

"Denise Carroll is my only real competition at the top, and I intend to topple her."

"You don't make any bones about it, do you?"

"Why should I? I'm going to do it."

"I wish you luck," Mike said, "but Denise Carroll seems firmly entrenched as the top female star of this studio."

"But she's in her late thirties and I'm only twenty. That's one good reason why I'm going to be the top female star here next year instead of her. Another is that I've got a good deal more to offer."

He'd always been rather awed by the enormity of his own ambition, but it paled when compared to hers.

"When a new star rises, one has to fall," she went on. "Isn't that a rule? Like the square of the hypotenuse is equal to the sum of the other two sides or something?"

"You don't want just a piece of the world for yourself, do you? You want the whole world."

Her eyes brightened. "That's exactly what I want."

Mike was assigned to do another picture with Danny Evans three weeks after he'd finished the first one. Though he expressed appreciation for being given another picture so quickly, he went into it with uncertainty, wondering if Renfew hadn't liked what he'd seen the day he'd watched him on the set and had decided that Mike's career should end on the back lot; that the only audience who should ever see him were the kids who went to see the Danny Evans series.

Danny sensed how he felt. "You're slated for other things, Mike. They're just using you with us again because they figure you might as well be getting experience while they're finding a role in an A picture for you. You'll soon learn that Regency Pictures is ninety percent business-conscious and ten percent art-conscious. They're paying you for forty weeks of the year, so they want you to work as many of those weeks as you can."

Mike was still skeptical, but he went wholeheartedly to work to make something of his part in the new picture anyway. The role was similar to the one he'd played in the first picture, just as the picture as a whole was similar to the last picture and to all other pictures in the Danny Evans series. As Danny said, the formula for his pictures was basic. Danny always had to face a set of obstacles and a villain or so, and he won over them with the help of Whitey, his Palomino; his sidekick—in this case, Mike; and the Frontiersmen. Cathy's presence

184

allowed Danny to rescue her from terrible fates when he wasn't busy dueting with her.

Mike was soon doing a better job in this picture than he had in the first one. He rode better and moved better and said his lines more convincingly.

The trouble was, he could probably have done even better if Mona Gaillard had been less in his thoughts. He couldn't deny to himself that he wanted her. He just hoped he wouldn't fall in love with her. He didn't want to love someone and not be able to control it. He didn't want to love Mona Gaillard or anyone else until he was ready for it, and that wouldn't be for a long, long time.

30

Mike approached his appointment with Renfew uneasily. It seemed improbable that the studio production chief would be calling him to his office to say that he'd been assigned to a third Danny Evans singing Western, but Mike was filled with dread that it might be exactly that.

But Renfew had something different in mind. "We want you to test for a role in Howard Stanton's next picture. We liked the job you did with Danny Evans. You put yourself wholly into both pictures, whether you thought they were idiotic or not."

"I did the best I could."

Renfew nodded. "We ran some reels from both Evans pictures for Howard Stanton, and he's asked for you for his next picture if the test works out. As a matter of fact, he's agreed to do the test with you. It's unusual for a star to agree to test with a newcomer, you know."

"Yes," Mike said excitedly. "I really appreciate that."

Mike met Howard Stanton and John Edsel, the director, the next day, and they discussed the picture in Renfew's office. It was to be a big Technicolor production about the submarine service called *Submarine Attack*. For Mike's benefit, Edsel outlined the story, explaining that the script called for a submarine crew to be ordered to sea on a special mission to free American scientists and military leaders imprisoned on a Japanese-held island. They were to blow up the island as they left.

"Howard commands the sub, and you, Michael, if your test works out, are assigned to the sub as his executive officer. In the meantime, you've unknowingly fallen in love with Howard's girl, which establishes the conflict. The girl's role isn't cast yet—we're deciding on it this week." Edsel smiled at Mike. "I'm afraid Howard keeps the girl in the end."

"That's okay with me," Mike said cheerfully. "If I can get the role, I don't care whether I get the girl."

The test was shot on the back lot, where a section from the submarine base at New London, Connecticut, had been re-created for the picture. Models of submarines rested in slips in the tank. Mike was provided with the handsome blue uniform of a United States naval officer, and he was surprised at how much older and more dignified he looked in it.

The test was the scene from the picture where he reported to Howard as his new executive officer. As the camera rolled, focused on Howard as he stood on board the ship, Mike felt self-conscious as he walked into camera range, hoping he would get the salute and the other business right. They'd rehearsed only once.

But he must have done well, because Renfew called him to his office three days later and told him he had the role. When he reported the next day for wardrobe fittings, Howard Stanton was there, too, and told him it had just been decided that Mona Gaillard was to be cast in the picture. Mike was filled with a feeling he couldn't describe. Perhaps it was anxiety.

This picture, Howard said, had to adhere to a very strict production schedule, because he was due to start his next picture in December and the one after that in March. It was hoped that he would be able to complete still another one before he went into the service. The studio wanted to have several of his pictures on hand for periodic release in case the war lasted a couple more years.

"What about you?" Howard asked. "What's your draft status?"

"I haven't heard anything yet," Mike said uneasily, not adding that he dreaded the day he did. It was one thing for Howard Stanton to go off to war, for he was an established star, and he could come back afterward and pick up where he'd left off. But Michael Baines would go off to war virtually unknown and would perhaps lose the one chance he had to get somewhere in this business, for who knew if he could start over when he came back?

Mike hated the thought of it. He didn't want to go to war. He only

186

wanted to make pictures and become as big a star as Howard Stanton. Or bigger.

It seemed an especially ambitious goal, for Howard Stanton was certainly big. But regardless of the dash and verve that Howard Stanton brought to his roles and the authority he commanded in his scenes, he wasn't a very good actor, in Mike's view. Howard Stanton was popular with the public because of his outstanding physical attractiveness and the magnetism he brought to the screen, but Mike was sure he could out-act him. And he was only starting. With the right chances, Mike would bring to the screen the same qualities Regency's current top male star did plus superior performances.

Mike was aware that his desire to steal Howard Stanton's thunder was an ungrateful attitude in view of the fact that Stanton had asked for him in this picture. But everybody wanted to be top dog. Just a few weeks earlier, Mona had told him she was going to topple Denise Carroll from her perch one of these days. It would be ironic if he did the same thing to Howard Stanton, wouldn't it?

But he didn't intend to risk anything by being too pushy at this point. If he tried to outperform Stanton in this picture, the star might see that he didn't get any future chances. So he got off to a careful start by not overdoing it in the preproduction script readings in Edsel's office.

Mona wasn't in on these readings because she was finishing her role in Georgina Fox's picture.

"Dalton must have big plans for her," Howard observed to Mike the first day he asked him to lunch with him at the commissary. "She's coming onto *Submarine Attack* after production begins and without testing for the role."

"She's something, all right," Mike said, feeling a tinge of jealousy. "We were in the acting school together for a while. She's got a stunning face, a stunning body, and a stunning personality. And she's got one thing on her mind. Career."

"That's hardly a sin here, Mike. What have you got on your mind?"

Mike laughed. "Career."

That day they were joined at their table by Timothy Briggs, and Mike was immediately taken with the star's warm manner. Following the Hollywood dictum that the best way to get off on the right foot with a star was to compliment him, Mike told Tim he'd thoroughly enjoyed his last picture, thought it was his best performance to date, and had been surprised when the picture and Tim hadn't been nominated for Academy Awards.

Tim smiled. "The trouble is, the picture earned prestige, but it didn't make money, and since it didn't get an Oscar, there probably won't be any more chances for me to do anything as good again." He shrugged. "That's the way it goes in Hollywood."

Howard had to cut his lunch short because he had a meeting scheduled with Renfew. Mike stayed at Tim's urging to have an extra cup of coffee with him.

"I want to wish you luck," Tim said. "You're getting a great start. There's no one better to work with than Howard."

"I consider myself very lucky to be on a picture with him."

"He'll be coming out to my ranch some Sunday soon. Why don't you come along? It would give us a chance to get better acquainted."

"That would be great," Mike said, thinking that it wouldn't hurt to know Briggs better. He ranked considerably below Howard Stanton in star stature, but he was important nevertheless. Maybe if Briggs liked Mike, he'd ask for him in one of his pictures, as Howard Stanton had.

It had originally been intended to make *Submarine Attack* partly on location in New London, Connecticut, but that plan had been abandoned when Howard's tight schedule had been laid out. A second unit had been dispatched to New London and had come back with reels of background scenes of the submarine base that would be used for process shots. The re-creation of a part of the base on the back lot, where Mike's test had been shot, would lend further authenticity. The picture was to be shot largely on stage three and on the edge of and in the back lot tank, with underwater scenes of the miniature sub to be photographed through windows on the sides of the indoor tank.

Because of Edsel's careful preproduction preparation, the picture was already a day and a half ahead of schedule by Saturday of the third week of production. From Mike's viewpoint, it was coming to an end entirely too fast. Half of his scenes were already in the can.

The next day Mike accompanied Howard out to the San Fernando Valley at Timothy Briggs' invitation to visit him at his ranch. Howard was driving a sleek Lincoln Continental convertible with fine leather seats, and Mike told himself that he would have a car like this in a couple of years if things continued to go right.

On the way, Howard observed, "I think Mona is going to be big."

"Yes," Mike said tautly. It disturbed him that Mona might turn out to be bigger than he would, although he knew it was ridiculous to think that way. He wasn't competing with Mona for his place in the sun. He was competing with Howard Stanton and Timothy Briggs for it.

"She takes over the scenes she's in," Howard went on. "You leave the projection room thinking about her and you're still thinking about her two hours later. That's what makes a star."

Mike agreed with Howard, but said nothing.

"She's a natural," Howard continued. "I don't suppose she's had much formal acting training, but she doesn't need it. Someone said she was a dancer. I can believe it. She moves like one. And talks like a vamp. No, that isn't right. 'Vamp' applies to a type of lady we had in the twenties. She doesn't seem to fit any particular type we have on screen today. Maybe she's a new type."

Mike was disturbed about Howard's apparent interest in Mona, and wondered if the star involved himself in extramarital affairs when the opportunity presented itself. He hoped it wouldn't present itself with Mona.

They were greeted warmly at the Briggs ranch. Mike immediately liked Tim's wife, Phyllis, and their toddlers, Leonard and Timothy, Junior, both miniature models of Tim. But he soon had a feeling that Phyllis wasn't really happy as the wife of a movie star. During lunch she talked so much about their former life in their hometown in Nebraska that Mike got the impression she wished they were back there.

The men spent the afternoon together riding horses over the ranch and shooting rifles at targets set up near the stables. After his experience in the singing Westerns, Mike wasn't quite the amateur he might have been on the chestnut from Tim's stable, but he was a complete novice with a rifle and envied Howard and Tim their skill in knocking off bull's eyes.

"You make a few return trips out here," Tim said to Mike when Howard was temporarily out of earshot, "and I'll teach you to be a champion rider and crack huntsman in no time."

"Sure, that would be great," Mike said after a moment, though the idea made him uneasy. He realized that he could have misinterpreted, but the look in Tim's eyes and his quizzical smile seemed to have a quality of longing to them. Mike had never forgotten Hadley's remark that Timothy Briggs, ostensibly a normal family man, was really a homosexual.

Still, Mike accepted the invitation of Tim and Phyllis to spend the night. Howard went back into town. In the morning, Tim started to drive Mike back to Hollywood, but they were hardly out of view of the ranch when he asked Mike if he would like to take a plane ride.

"Sure," Mike said, although he wasn't really certain that he liked the idea.

"I didn't mention it at home because Phyl worries when she knows I'm up. Actually, you're safer in my plane than you are in my car, but Phyl has an idea that it's dangerous. Flying thrills me like nothing else does! If I didn't have family obligations, I'd join the Army Air Corps."

At the airport, Mike looked admiringly at the trim monoplane. Once inside, he felt a little peculiar as they started down the runway and the moment approached when he would be off the ground for the first time in his life. But they were up before he knew they'd left the ground, and he silently sighed his relief that nothing terrible had happened.

They were over Malibu in no time, and Tim flew lower so he could point out Howard's beach house to him. Then they flew out over the ocean. Mike got a little nervous as he looked back and saw the land rapidly receding, but he said nothing.

"Sometimes," Tim said, "I feel just like flying on and on to see if I can reach the horizon."

Mike wondered if that meant that Tim sometimes felt confined by family life, that basically he wanted to be free.

Finally they turned back. "I'll tell you a secret," Tim said as the shoreline appeared below and they headed for the airport. "I feel better up here than I do anywhere else. I feel free; I feel that I'm genuinely myself. I don't feel that way about myself anywhere else. That probably doesn't make sense to you, but maybe you'll understand it better after you've known me for a while."

Mike looked cautiously at Tim. He didn't know what to say. Tim smiled. "You'll understand sometime, Mike. Friends understand each other, and we're going to be friends. I can tell, can't you?"

"I hope so," Mike said, and quickly turned his face away. He felt awkward and embarrassed.

Mike kissed Mona seventeen times that day before they got it right and had a good take. Edsel almost became impatient, because Mike was stiff as a board and couldn't make himself look as if he were forcing a kiss on Mona.

"Don't treat her like a Dresden doll," Edsel said. "You're supposed to be desperate, Mike."

He *was* desperate. Touching her had made him more nervous than he'd ever been in his life. None of his scenes with her had worked out as well as they should, but this one was the worst. He hated it that he wanted her so much. He knew that he would have a hard-on if he weren't so nervous, because he'd never been so affected by touching anyone as he was from touching her.

They finally got a good take and broke for the day. Mona looked at him peculiarly as she walked away, and he wondered if she was beginning to sense how he felt. He hoped not. He would get over this

190

before it went too far, and there was no reason why she or anyone else should ever know about it.

But inside, he didn't really feel confident.

That evening, instead of going to bed early as usual so he would be fresh for tomorrow's scenes, Mike went to a neighborhood tavern to try to take his mind off Mona with a few beers. He sat down beside a very pretty red-haired girl who, unsurprisingly, said she was in Hollywood trying to break into pictures.

Also unsurprisingly, she went back to his room with him a little while later, where he was almost brutal to her in bed. "There!" he cried, lunging so deeply into her as he neared his climax that it seemed as if he would tear her apart. "How do you like that, baby? Right into the pit of you!"

She gasped in pain, and he was ashamed of hurting her and ashamed, too, because he didn't really want this girl but wished that it were Mona lying under him. Yes, it was Mona he really wanted to take revenge on, wanted to hurt. He ground his teeth together as he came, wishing he didn't want Mona so much.

"I'm sorry," he said to the girl as he slipped out of her, regretful for punishing a stranger for his own misery.

But she smiled and said, "It was wonderful, just wonderful!"

Mike looked at himself in the mirror for a long time, happy about the way the costume looked and fitted. He picked up the ray gun and smiled at the image of himself holding it. He'd borrowed the costume from the wardrobe department. It had been made for a Buck Rogers serial the studio had contemplated in the early thirties and had never made.

He put on the eye-mask and waited. In a few minutes Tim and Phyllis showed up in their station wagon. They were dressed as Pierrot and Pierrette.

"This will be a real experience for you, Mike," Tim said as they drove off. "Your first Hollywood party."

"And certainly not an ordinary Hollywood party," Phyllis said.

"Howard and Georgina have at least one big smasher a year, and a lot of little ones," Tim said. "I don't think Howard goes much for this big stuff, or for parties at all, for that matter, but Georgina does."

"Tim and I don't care much for big parties ourselves," Phyllis said, "but Howard and Georgina are such wonderful people that we wouldn't miss this for the world. And the costumes are certain to be marvelous."

A battery of spotlights flooded the entrance of the Stantons' mansion

191

as they drove up from the long driveway and relinquished their vehicle to an attendant. The enormous carved front door stood open. Just inside, Howard, dressed as a matador in a blue and silver suit of lights, and Georgina, garbed in a scarlet gypsy's costume, were receiving their guests.

Mike soon took off his mask when he saw that almost everyone had unmasked. The object was to be identified, not cloaked in mystery. The costumes were lavish and as varied in type as the guests themselves, with the men dressed as everything from pirates to Egyptian pharaohs, the women from harem dancing girls to French queens.

There was much merriment inside and out, for the party extended out to a garden, where a marquee had been erected and circus people were performing. Mike was soon separated from Tim and Phyllis and felt uneasy when a look around confirmed that he was one of the few unestablished persons present. Even fortified with the champagne that kept appearing, borne by caterers dressed as eighteenth-century footmen, he didn't feel like pushing in anywhere and introducing himself, although he recognized that he was missing a perfect chance to make good contacts. He supposed he would regret later that he hadn't seized the opportunity to meet Tyrone Power, Marion Davies, Errol Flynn, and some of the other luminaries who were here tonight.

But he was soon occupied with other thoughts when he entered the huge living room and saw Mona. She was dressed in a revealing costume composed of a heavily jeweled gold lamé bra and, below her bare midriff, an equally heavily jeweled girdle from which flowed chiffon pieces that allowed a muted but excellent view of her perfect legs. Her luxuriant titian hair, hanging down her back, was crowned by a jeweled circlet from one side of which, flowing down over the right side of her face, hung several pieces of chiffon of the same varied pastel colors as the larger pieces flowing from the girdle. It occurred to Mike that she was made up as Salome. He wondered if she intended to dance for them and discard her delicately hued veils one by one.

Her husband was at her elbow. He was a manufacturer of engine pistons, it was said. It seemed strange to Mike that Mona would be married to someone so foreign to the Hollywood world. He looked humorless, but he was good-looking in a mature way. Mike guessed him to be forty-five, old enough to be Mona's father. An unwanted vision crowded into his mind of the two of them in bed together.

A middle-aged woman, bright-eyed with too much champagne, tugged at his arm suddenly. "Come dance with me, handsome."

She pulled him into a room where the carpeting had been removed and a small orchestra was playing a rhumba. The woman danced close to him, jabbing his chest with her large breasts, although the rhumba called for dancing apart.

The woman smiled. "I know something I'd rather be doing with you than the rhumba, you beautiful hunk of man."

He ignored her remark and lost her a minute later when they got involved in a conga line. As the line reached the French doors that led out into one of the gardens, he simply slipped out of it and went outside. He didn't want to know who the woman was who'd tried to seduce him. She was probably the wife of someone important, and he didn't want her getting him into trouble.

He walked around in the garden for a while, then went back into the house to find Mona. His feeling for her was irresistible, he finally had to admit to himself. He loved her. He loved her and wanted her and couldn't have her.

He found her in the room where the dancing was going on. She was dancing with a man as graceful as she. Mike envied the man, wishing he could dance as well as he did, wishing he had the nerve to ask Mona to dance, wondering why she wasn't dancing with her husband, wondering where her husband was.

Mona's partner bent her back in a dip as the dance ended. She came up laughing and saw Mike.

"Oh, Mike, I didn't know you were here!"

She came forward smiling while he tried to suppress his irritation that it hadn't occurred to her that it was just as logical that he would be invited to this party as she.

"Aren't you going to ask me to dance?" she asked.

He didn't want to dance with her. He was no good on the dance floor. He told her that he'd promised to have a drink with someone in the other room and walked off, a little resentful that she didn't seem to care in the least. She went blithely into a tango with the man she'd been dancing with a minute before.

"It's been a great party," he told Howard and Georgina sometime later, when Tim and Phyllis were finally ready to go. In the car he repeated that it had been a great party, and Tim and Phyllis said they thought it had been, too. Mike was glad they didn't know how he'd hated it.

31

In less than an hour it would be dawn. The house was quiet, although the caterers and the servants were still cleaning up downstairs. Howard, in a silk robe, sat in a chair in Georgina's bedroom, watching her at her dressing table brushing her lustrous dark hair.

"I think we can score another triumph for you tonight as one of Hollywood's top hostesses," Howard said.

"It was a good party," she said a little defensively. "People enjoyed themselves. We may not have a chance to do much more of this as we get deeper into the war."

"I can take it or leave it," Howard said.

"But you'd rather leave it, I know. That's always surprised me a little, Howard, since you attach such importance to being a star. What we did tonight was act like stars."

She put down her hairbrush and turned on the bench to look at him.

"What's happened to us, Howard? Have we used up our dreams already?"

"What do you mean?"

"Only a few years ago there were three things of overwhelming importance to me—being a good actress, being a star, and being a good wife. I've succeeded with the first two, but they don't seem so important to me anymore. I don't think I'm succeeding very well as a wife, and that is important."

"You're a good wife, Georgina."

She turned back to the mirror and looked at herself. "Sometimes I don't think you understand me very well, Howard. But why should you? I don't understand myself very well."

"Most of us don't understand ourselves very well."

She went back to her brushing, and there was silence between them for a long minute or two. Then she put down her brush again and caught Howard's eyes in the mirror. "Mona and Mike are just starting out. I wonder if they have the same dreams we had in the beginning."

He frowned, wondering why she'd brought that up. He felt uncomfortable about the trend of this conversation.

"I suppose they do," she went on, answering for him. "They probably want to be big stars as much as we did. Mona will certainly make it. I have to admit I found working with her a little frightening. She consumes the screen with her presence. And of course she's ravishing. She's going to eat men alive, off screen and on." She paused. "Like Leni Liebhaber."

She was still holding onto his eyes in the mirror. He looked back at her, off guard. He didn't know what to say.

"We never talk about her," Georgina went on. "I wonder why."

"Because there's no reason to. That's all in the past."

"Oh, it's not so long ago, Howard, and I know you think about her a lot."

"Not a lot. But some. Naturally I wonder what's happening to her in Germany. After all, we were married—" He stopped.

"Yes, you were married," Georgina continued, holding on determinedly to his eyes in the mirror. "And you loved her terribly."

"I loved her." He met her eyes firmly. "And I love you."

"But differently."

"Of course differently. You're two different persons. Georgina, why are we talking like this?"

"Don't you think important things eventually *have* to be talked about, no matter how much they've been avoided?"

"I wasn't aware that we avoided talking about this," he said. "And it's no longer important that I once loved Leni. It has nothing to do with now or with you or me."

"I'm not so sure about that, Howard, but I'm glad that something has finally been said about it anyway."

"So am I, if you feel it's important. But I hope you're looking at it honestly."

"I think I am. But how about you? Most of us are good at lying to ourselves when it's to our advantage." She suddenly turned her eyes from his and resumed brushing her hair. "But we were talking about Mona, weren't we? Tell me what you think of her."

"I think she's beautiful," he said uneasily. "I also like working with her. She's very professional."

"Would you like to go to bed with her?"

"I've never thought about it," he said, although it wasn't true, and he had to force himself to meet her gaze.

"Aren't you going to ask me if I'd like to go to bed with Mike?"

He tried to conceal his surprise. "I wasn't going to, but I will. Would you?"

"He's certainly striking. He's probably magnificent in bed." She paused. "He strikes me as having strong star quality, like Mona. Aren't you a little afraid of him?"

"Of course. But if it weren't he, it would be someone else." He rose and went to her, standing behind her, looking at her in the mirror. "You dropped the subject of going to bed with Mike quickly enough."

"Yes. I proved my point. I think you were upset at the idea of it."

"You're right, I was." He reached down and took her hand and pulled her up, turning her to face him. "I'm the one who's taking you to bed—right now."

She leaned against him, pressing up to him. "Sometimes I wish we didn't have to worry about anything but loving each other, Howard. Sometimes I wish the rest weren't important at all."

He didn't intend to let her talk about whatever that meant. He took her to bed and made love to her, and there were moments during their embraces when he was reminded of their first time together, when he'd taken her virginity under a palm tree in Samoa. Her response to him then had been a blend of tenderness, trust, and abandonment. It still was, but with diminished excitement. Still, that was to be expected. He felt the same way. Desire for her remained a craving in him, but it wasn't so strong as it had been in the beginning.

She went to sleep almost as soon as they had finished, unquestionably exhausted from the party and emotionally drained from their talk. He was drained himself, but he couldn't sleep. He put on his robe and went downstairs. He walked out to the swimming pool and stared into the water, rosy with dawn's light, while he tried to sort out his thoughts.

Georgina had struck an unwilling chord in him tonight when she'd brought up Leni. It was true that he still thought about her and wondered about her more than he wanted to, and obviously Georgina resented that. He couldn't blame her. He resented it himself that Leni still seemed to have an emotional hold on him. He should hate her for what she'd done to him. That last scene between them, when she'd kissed Adrienne in a final terrible taunt, was locked in his mind in grotesque clarity.

He should hate her for what she'd done to him, but did he?

He didn't want to think about her anymore. He went back upstairs and stopped outside Georgina's door, wanting to waken her to talk about what still needed to be talked about—about what they'd been leading up to an hour ago but hadn't confronted. They needed to talk about the way their marriage seemed to be slipping away from them.

But he didn't go in to Georgina. He was afraid to talk about it, and he thought she was, too. As he went to his room he felt overwhelmingly alone.

Mike couldn't get Mona off his mind. The terrible thing about it was that he'd acknowledged to himself how he felt about her, yet he still could do nothing about it. He rejected the idea of confessing his feelings to her, because he was afraid of how she would react. He couldn't bear the idea that she might laugh it off. He supposed he could discuss it with Howard or Tim, and perhaps receive good advice from them, but he couldn't bring himself to do it. He could only hope that one day he would wake up and discover he didn't love Mona after all.

He felt better the day Renfew told him he would be tested for the second lead in the next Howard Stanton picture, which would start production in just a couple of months. They'd all liked Mike's work in the last picture, and Howard had asked for him again. He was definitely going somewhere now!

Then one evening to his surprise Tim phoned. He said he was going to a small party at the Garden of Allah on Sunset Boulevard and wondered if Mike would be interested in coming along. Mike hesitated, then said yes, since he'd always wanted to see the place.

It turned out to be much as Mike expected, a dozen or so buildings in Spanish style called "villas" grouped around a swimming pool in tropically landscaped grounds. The party was in one of the smaller villas occupied by a screenwriter. There were only two other guests besides Tim and Mike, another screenwriter and a director. Mike immediately felt uncomfortable and suspicious because there were no women present, and almost expected the host, who was rather effeminate, to press his hand when he gave him a drink.

But nothing overtly out of order was done or said in the hour that he and Tim remained there, although Mike was stiffly expectant through most of it. He was glad when Tim begged them off early with the excuse that he had a long drive home to the Valley ahead of him.

Tim was quiet as he drove Mike home. When they arrived, he asked if he might come in for a few minutes.

"Well," said Mike, and hesitated. He wasn't really surprised when Tim suddenly moved over and tried to put an arm around his shoulder. "Don't!" Mike cried, wrenching Tim's arm away and pushing him aside.

"I can't help it, Mike. I can't hold back any longer how I feel about you."

Mike opened the door to get out. "I'm going to forget this happened. You'd better go home and forget it, too."

"You can't forget it, and neither can I."

197

"Yes, we can! We've both had too much to drink this evening."

"We can't leave it like this. It's been building up in me for so long! I've been waiting for you for years, and I'm not going to let you get away."

"Cut that talk, Tim!" Mike was out of the car. "Go home!"

Tim called after him. "Mike, please!"

But he didn't turn back to answer Tim's pleas. He walked quickly around to the back of the house, went inside, and bolted the door, determined not to open it to Tim even if he came back and pounded on it all night.

But Tim didn't come, and Mike lay on his bed and regretted what had happened. This would cost him his growing friendship with Tim, and that was too bad. Tim might have helped him get good roles in his pictures, but now he certainly wouldn't.

Before he went to sleep, Mike had begun to feel that maybe he should have responded favorably to Tim's overtures. Maybe, he thought in confusion, he even wanted to.

But his confusion and anxiety over the situation with Tim were forced into the background the next day when Mike received his Greetings from the President of the United States.

In another few days there was no question about his immediate future when he passed his physical examination for induction.

He kept a fixed and unnatural smile and tried to act nonchalant at the studio as he made his farewells. But he felt terrible. He wasn't patriotic and he didn't want to risk his life. He just wanted to make pictures and become a movie star. And now it might all be ruined.

Dalton and Renfew didn't think it would, or if they did, they didn't indicate it. They regretted that Mike was being drafted before he could undertake his role in the next Howard Stanton picture, of course, but he would be back in a year or so, all the better for his experience; and they were so pleased with his work that they weren't going to suspend his contract while he was in the service but were going to put that hundred dollars a week in the bank for him.

That was nice, wasn't it? Mike thought. He would be getting fifty dollars a month from the government for serving as cannon fodder and four hundred dollars a month from the studio for doing nothing for them at all.

Howard took him to lunch at the Brown Derby his last day in town. That evening he called his parents and told them in as cheerful a voice as he could muster that he didn't expect the Army to be bad at all. Then he packed the small bag he would take along when he reported to the draft board the next day to be herded off with the others in the bus to the Army reception center.

198

He lay down on his bed, feeling sick and hollow and empty, and he thought of Mona. He wasn't certain that Mona even knew he was being drafted. And even if she did know, she wouldn't care.

There was a knock on the door. It was Tim. He'd driven all the way in from the Valley to say good-by and to wish Mike all the luck in the world.

"I didn't want you going away resenting me if I could help it," Tim said.

"I wouldn't," Mike said. "I'm glad you've come."

"And now that I'm here I can't say what I intended to say—that we should forget it happened, as you said we should. You just don't understand how I feel, Mike. I think about you all the time. Please, Mike. Don't push me away this time. Just close your eyes and lie back. You won't have to do a thing."

Mike looked at Tim thoughtfully. Then he turned and went to the bed and lay down on it. He even extended his hands to Tim as he approached.

32

Mike didn't like the Army, but it turned out that he didn't dislike it as much as he'd thought he would. He'd hoped they would decide at the reception center that since he was an actor, he should be assigned to a special services unit. They decided instead to put him in the field artillery.

But that was better than getting stuck in the infantry, he and the others agreed on the long, boring train ride to Georgia, where they were delivered to a flat and sandy camp, a wasteland of monotony, with one area of white clapboard barracks after another. They'd been sent here for thirteen weeks of basic training, after which, they were informed, they would probably be shipped overseas to do their stuff.

Mike soon proved that he was a good soldier. Early in basic, he was appointed an acting corporal in his howitzer section and would now be responsible, under the section sergeant, for supervising the seven-man crew that operated their big cannons.

He reported all this to Regency Pictures' publicity department as requested, but he doubted that it would go out in their releases to movie magazines and newspapers. His name couldn't be very well known yet. The Danny Evans pictures had probably been released by now, but they certainly wouldn't have established him. And as Howard had mentioned in a recent note wishing him luck in the Army, *Submarine Attack* was still being edited, scored, and put into finished form, which together usually took several months for an A production.

He didn't report to the publicity department that the battery commander had told him he might later be recommended for officer candidate school in view of his apparent ability to lead and his high intelligence test score. Mike thanked the captain and saluted smartly as he withdrew, but he felt depressed. He wasn't at all certain he would make a good officer or that he wanted to be one. Although the studio might like it if one of its upcoming actors, a future star, was an officer in a combat unit, when so many Hollywood people were ending up in technical positions in the service that it was almost embarrassing.

Combat. He hated to think of it, but there was certainly the possibility that he would be at the front somewhere in a few months. Would he survive? Would he be able to finish what he'd started in life? The unanswerable questions were frightening.

There was nothing to be done about it. Tim had arrived. Mike was called to battalion headquarters right after retreat to accept a phone call from the outside world, and Tim was on the other end of the line. Not in California, but here. Twelve miles away, in town, checked in at the hotel and waiting. Tim said he'd had a hell of a time getting there. He'd been bumped from his flight in Houston because he had no priority, and he might have been stuck there forever if someone hadn't forfeited a reservation on another flight, thereby giving him a precious seat to Atlanta. Then there'd been the endless bus ride, but that didn't matter, for he was here, and could Mike come to town right now?

Mike managed to get a pass, but he went to town reluctantly. He didn't want to see Tim, who was obviously here because he thought what had happened between them the night before Mike had left for the Army had a future. Mike had to make it plain that it didn't. The extra dimension that had been added to their relationship that night didn't belong in it. Tim had taken advantage of Mike when he was in a depressed state.

Mike knocked reluctantly on Tim's hotel room door, hoping Tim wouldn't embarrass him by trying to embrace and kiss him right away. But he didn't. He only clung to Mike's hand and said how glad he was to see him.

"It seems so long," Tim said in a strained voice, on the verge of tears.

200

He didn't get right to the point as Mike had expected. They sat together on old overstuffed chairs in the rather seedy room with a bottle of bourbon on a low table between them. Tim began by telling Mike what was going on at the studio. It seemed that Regency Pictures had more productions planned for 1943 than ever before, because 1942 had proved the biggest year of all at the box office.

And, Tim went on, Howard was leaving for the service soon. He wouldn't be able to leave the backlog of four pictures the studio had hoped for—just *Submarine Attack* and another war picture he was finishing up now—because he was going into the Navy sooner than he and the studio had planned. He'd been given a direct appointment as a lieutenant senior grade and he was going to be involved in the Navy's public relations program.

That was a sinecure for you! Mike thought. Howard would be nice and safe in something like that, and would finish the war alive and in one piece, while there was certainly a chance that Mike wouldn't.

Tim told him he'd tried to enlist.

"But why?" asked Mike. "What about Phyllis and the kids?"

"I thought I had to try, Mike. But no go. I've got a heart murmur. Nothing serious, they say. But enough to keep me out."

Didn't he know how lucky he was? What was the matter with him—trying to enlist!

Denise Carroll's death from an accidental overdose of sleeping pills had been a tragic surprise, Tim said. They still weren't over the shock of it at the studio. More than three thousand persons had shown up at the church for her funeral services, and most of them had been forced to stand outside in the rain and listen to the services over a loudspeaker.

"The studio had three properties lined up for her to do," Tim said, and it occurred again to Mike, as it had when Denise Carroll's death had been announced the previous month, that Mona might be given those roles. It was grim irony. Mona had said she would take over Denise Carroll's spot someday, and now she had, much sooner than she could possibly have dreamed.

"Tim, why did you come here?" Mike finally brought himself to say.

"You didn't answer my letters. I had to come. You can't just let something like what happened between us hang in midair."

"As far as I was concerned, nothing was left hanging. What happened that night shouldn't have. I just wanted to forget it. I hoped you would, too."

"Forget it? I wouldn't forget something that important to me for a single moment!"

Tim reached across for Mike's hand, but Mike pulled it away. He sat rigidly. Tim's hand retreated.

"I understand," he said. "It takes a while to get used to it. But don't think I'll let you go after finally finding in you what I've been looking for all my life."

"Don't say things like that!"

"I've got to. This is too important to me. It's important to you, too, Mike. You just don't know it yet."

"What I know is that I wasn't myself the night we were together."

"You were much more yourself than you are now."

"Don't try to be a psychologist, Tim. Just face it that what happened that night isn't ever going to happen again. Just go home."

"Go home? But I *love* you. That's why I'm here, Mike."

Mike rose, red-faced and furious. "Stop it right now! I won't listen to any more of this shit!"

Tim rose, too. "Mike, I won't let you throw this away—"

"I can't throw away something that doesn't exist!" Mike said hotly.

Tim stepped forward, extending a hand.

"Stay back or I'll knock you back! I mean that."

Tim stopped. His face twisted with hurt. Mike hoped he wasn't going to cry.

"Go home, Tim. Go home to your wife and kids."

As he turned and went out the door, he thought he heard Tim start to cry, but he didn't go back to find out.

The painful scene stayed with him a long time, but, looking at it in retrospect, he doubted that anything would have been gained from trying to be subtle. That would only have encouraged Tim. Mike regretted losing Tim's friendship, but for them to have any relationship at all in the future was impossible now. He supposed Tim was bitter, and he was sorry about that, but he wanted only to forget it.

Submarine Attack suddenly appeared at one of the post theaters two months later when he was almost at the end of basic training. Mike went to see it with a certain amount of trepidation but emerged highly pleased with himself and the picture. It was an exciting movie, beautifully produced and mounted, and so authentic-looking that no one would have guessed that many of the scenes had been done with miniatures. But what was important was that he was good. He came across. He was sure of it.

A number of men in the battery went to see the picture and told him he was good in it. They seemed to regard him with a certain amount of awe now. The word had spread before that he was a movie actor, but they hadn't taken it very seriously or given it much thought. Now they did.

And then one morning Mike received his orders to report the following week to the field artillery officer candidate school at Fort Sill, Oklahoma.

Mike was a new second lieutenant. He'd come through the officer's training course with flying colors, although it had taken hard work and study, and now he was authorized to wear shining yellow bars on his epaulets and qualified to lead men into battle.

What he wanted to be doing was making movies for Regency Pictures, not leading men into battle, but there was no choice. He was reassigned to his old outfit in Georgia because they'd asked for him. It made him a little uncomfortable to return to them as an officer, but both he and the men adjusted quickly to the idea of a changed relationship between them.

Soon after Mike rejoined the battalion, they found themselves under orders to begin preparations for overseas movement, with the probability that they would be shipped to a port of embarkation in a few more weeks.

Mike had some depressing drinks alone at the officers' club thinking of that. This war was stretching out far longer than he'd hoped, and he was sure there were still many invasions and battles to be faced in both Europe and the Pacific before it ended. He wasn't certain which disturbed him more—that he might be killed in battle or that he might not be able to pick up his movie career again if the war went on too long.

When Mona's new picture arrived at one of the post theaters the following week, Mike looked forward to it with mixed feelings. He was glad Mona was appearing in her first starring role so quickly, but it was a cutting reminder that if he hadn't been drafted he might be in a similar position today.

But his envy and resentment subsided when he looked at the color poster of a stunning, radiant Mona Gaillard out front beckoning patrons into the theater. He had the uncanny feeling that she was smiling specifically at him as he stared hypnotized at the poster for minutes before he went inside.

The picture was called *Dream World,* and it occurred to Mike as he sat watching Mona, and loving her, that *Dream Girl* would have been a better title, for that was exactly what she was. He couldn't help envying her because she was already a star and he wasn't, but there was no denying that she deserved her stardom and would have reached it anyway, even if the gap left by Denise Carroll's death hadn't helped to hurry it along. Mona was a ravishing and vital woman, a goddess, but

203

paradoxically not so remote that an ordinary man might not at least dream that she was obtainable. That sort of quality made big stars. Besides, she was a fine performer. She was especially good in the musical numbers in this picture. She was one of the best dancers Mike had ever seen.

Mike sat through the picture twice, and when he left the theater, he walked around thinking of Mona. He felt lonelier than he had for a long, long time.

33

Tracy Gordon had been attending Abbottsville High School for over two years and still hated it. What bothered her most about it was the unwanted attention she got in the halls from the boys. They whistled at her and muttered racy remarks about her behind their hands. Some even went so far as to pinch her on the behind. She felt like slapping them for that, but she never did. She only hurried away red-faced, as if it were *her* shame, not theirs.

Now that she was sixteen, her mother permitted her to go out with boys on special occasions, such as school dances, if she had met and approved of the boy in question or knew his parents from church. But Tracy seldom accepted a boy's invitation, for she didn't like the school dances. She preferred to dance with an imaginary partner in her room than with the boys at school. She always listened to the radio in her room on Tuesday, Wednesday, and Thursday evenings when the Chesterfield show was on, dancing in her bare feet to the music of Harry James' orchestra, holding her bed pillow against her as her partner.

She realized that people would think it odd if they knew she preferred to dance with dream partners in her room rather than the flesh-and-blood boys in her class, some of whom were very good dancers and especially good at jitterbugging. But she didn't feel comfortable being so physically close to boys.

She also realized that her classmates thought it strange that she didn't like to do most of the things they did. She didn't enjoy baseball, football, or basketball games, and she lacked school spirit. That was especially noted when she declined to try out for cheerleading when asked, although it was generally conceded, even by those girls most jealous of her, that she would make a fabulous-looking team booster.

But cheerleading called for loudness and boldness, and Tracy didn't know how to be loud and bold. She'd always been shy, and she didn't know how to be any different. But to her classmates she was just a prude and a loner, though none of them understood why. Tracy didn't understand why herself.

Tracy still went to the movies every week, but now she went by herself instead of with Clara. They were still friends, but they weren't nearly so close as they had been. Clara's life was centered on boys, so they had little in common anymore.

One Friday evening in December, Tracy prepared for a trip to the movies. She put on a sweater, skirt, and saddle shoes and checked herself carefully in the mirror before going downstairs. Her mother was sitting in the rosewood rocker, working on an afghan she was crocheting.

"I'll be going now, Mama. I'll be back around eleven. It's a double feature, you know."

"I just don't know why you go to so many movies, Tracy. I really can't understand what you see in them. It's always seemed like living in dreams to me."

"That's what it is, Mama."

"You have a happy life, don't you, Tracy? Why do you have to live in dreams?"

"Oh, Mama, I don't, really—not very much. Mostly I like the movies because they're fun to watch."

"I still don't understand it. I never liked them, even when I was young, and neither did your father."

That seemed strange. Tracy would have thought her father had been a dreamer type. But she couldn't make such an observation to her mother, so she said good-by and left the house.

When she reached the square, there were two soldiers standing on the corner waiting for the light to change. One of them whistled at her as she crossed the street and walked toward the Golden Theater on the other side. She didn't look back.

Both features were about the war, and Tracy didn't like either of them much. She seldom liked war pictures, although she'd liked the ones Howard Stanton had made before he'd gone off to war himself.

Tracy thought about him as she left the theater and walked home. He remained her favorite star, and she mentioned him often in her prayers, asking God to keep him alive through the war.

Christmas wouldn't be the same again until after the war. They certainly couldn't bake on the scale they had before because of sugar rationing, and the former abundance of Christmas cookies and cakes produced at the Gordon house had diminished greatly last year and would amount to practically nothing this Christmas of 1943. But there would be a small turkey, and Tracy's mother said they should give thanks for that. As Tracy and her mother walked to church for the Christmas Eve service, her mother pointed out that they did indeed have a great deal to be thankful for in spite of wartime shortages and inconveniences.

At the service they saw Reverend Gaylord's son Jefferson among the congregation. He nodded at them, and Tracy's mother smiled back. She thought it was wonderful that Jefferson was studying at a seminary and was soon to be the third Gaylord to become a Baptist minister. Tracy had seen him off and on at services in the last few years when he'd come home from the seminary on visits. He was tall and pale, and Tracy had found it awkward talking to him on the occasions he'd sought out her and her mother for a few words. Tonight it was much worse. Somehow Tracy found herself with her mother, Jefferson Gaylord, and Reverend Gaylord in the church anteroom after the service, and it ended up with Tracy's mother inviting Jefferson Gaylord to call the evening after Christmas.

"Why did you do that, Mama?" Tracy asked as they walked home. "I feel funny around him." She almost said she didn't like him, either.

"Why, I'm surprised at you, Tracy. Why should you feel that way? Jefferson Gaylord is one of the loveliest young men you'll ever be privileged to know. Such beautiful manners. And so well educated. Reverend Gaylord tells me he's an honor student at the seminary."

"That makes it all the harder for me to talk to him. And, Mama, he's so much older than I am."

"Stop exaggerating. He's only five years older than you. Besides, you're just going to have to learn to talk better with older people, Tracy. Especially with men. It happens more often than not that the man is older, maybe even considerably older, than the woman he marries."

It struck Tracy then that perhaps an idea had come to her mother that Jefferson Gaylord, soon to become a minister of the Baptist Church, might be that perfect love that would come into Tracy's life one of these days. No, no, no, thought Tracy, and worried about it that night and all day Christmas and the day after. She kept hoping right up to the last that Jefferson Gaylord would get a bad cold suddenly and not be able to call. But he showed up at exactly seven the evening after Christmas in a black suit that would have been perfectly appropriate for the pulpit if he'd worn a clerical collar with it. Instead he wore a white shirt with a regular collar, set off by a solid black knit tie.

The three of them sat stiffly in the front parlor while he outlined his plans for the future in response to polite inquiries from Tracy's mother. Tracy had little doubt that her mother already knew his plans. She supposed that Reverend Gaylord had talked to her about his son.

But Mrs. Gordon listened with a raptness equal to Tracy's boredom while Jefferson Gaylord told her that he hoped to go into military service as a chaplain after ordination in June. Then, after the war, he expected to go into the church's missionary service.

"There's nothing more important than the missionary service," Tracy's mother said, her eyes lighting up. "I've always thought that. Tell me, do you have a country in mind where you'd like to serve?"

"Africa," he said, and looked at Tracy. "Africa is a very beautiful country, you know. It isn't just mosquitoes and snakes."

He was obviously waiting for Tracy to say something. "I'm sure it's very beautiful, the jungles and everything," she said after a moment.

Jefferson turned back to her mother. "I wonder if you would mind if I took Tracy out for an hour or so this evening, Mrs. Gordon? You know, I've been away so much the last few years, it would be nice just to look around our beautiful little town for a while."

"Why, of course I wouldn't mind," Tracy's mother said, turning to her. "Go get your coat, dear."

Tracy went reluctantly, and then had to endure Jefferson Gaylord helping her into it. When they went outside, she found that he had his father's car, a black sedan. He took her elbow to help her in as she stepped up on the running board, although she didn't need help. As he started the car, he remarked that the rationing board had recently granted his father a C gasoline sticker to replace his B sticker because he needed more gasoline to visit the sick.

"I don't think we'll hurt the war effort by using a gallon or so for a little pleasure driving this evening," he said. "After all, this is a special occasion. What would you like to do?"

She hesitated, then said, "Go to the movies."

"Oh, I'd rather not do that. It would take all evening. Wouldn't you just rather talk and get to know each other better?"

There was nothing she wanted less than to get to know him better. She frowned and didn't answer.

"I think we ought to take a ride out into the country," he said.

"Why?" she asked quickly, feeling uncomfortable about it, thinking of all the talking she'd be expected to do on the way out and back. "It's too dark to see much."

"It would be nice to drive out anyway," he insisted.

He drove them out of town to a road winding through the hills. The area, thick with pines, was quite pretty by day, but, as Tracy had expected, there was nothing to be seen at this time of night. Jefferson Gaylord had lapsed into silence, and at first Tracy had been glad about it, but when it continued, it made her nervous.

Finally he spoke, saying, "I've watched you get prettier and prettier over the years, Tracy, and I expect you're now the very prettiest girl I've ever seen anywhere in my whole life, and that includes Columbia, South Carolina, where I've seen many pretty girls in the walks I've taken around town with my friends at the seminary."

Tracy went rigid. She wished she could be anywhere but here. She was both embarrassed and angry. She didn't want Jefferson Gaylord telling her she was pretty. She didn't like him.

"You probably think," he continued, "that I didn't notice you when you were a child. But I did. I used to see you in church with your mother, and I remember thinking how pretty you were even then, when you were ten or eleven. I've seen you only occasionally since I went away to the seminary, but each time I have, you've been prettier than the time before."

Stop it! she screamed inside herself. When he suddenly slowed the car, she thought of opening the door and jumping out. But he slowed only long enough to turn off the main road into a smaller one.

She forced herself to turn and look at him. "Where are you going?" she asked, alarm rising in her.

"Don't you know?" He turned briefly and smiled, then looked back at the narrow road unfolding ahead. "Don't try to fool me. I'll bet boys have taken you to the grove plenty of times."

"No, they haven't. I've never been there."

"That's hard to believe, Tracy. The kids with cars used to go to the grove to pet when I was in high school, and I know it hasn't changed. There may not be so much of it nowadays, because of gas rationing, but it still goes on."

"I've never been there," she said insistently, "and I don't want to go now."

"We're already there," he announced and turned off the road toward a cluster of pines. He entered the grove between two trees barely wide enough to admit the car. Inside, there was an open space surrounded by trees. There were no other cars there. "I didn't think there'd be anyone here the night after Christmas," he said.

He pulled the car around to the far side and stopped. He turned off the lights and the engine. Tracy's mind was racing, but she didn't know what to say or do. It was hard for her to believe this was happening. But

208

the reality of his hand covering hers on her thigh reminded her quickly that it was. His hand was clammy. She tried to wrench her own out from under it, but he held her tightly, pressing so hard that it hurt.

"Please!"

"Relax." His left hand kept pressing hers, and his free arm came around her shoulder. "You're stiff as a board. If you'll relax, you'll find this is the nicest thing that's ever happened to either of us."

"Take me home!"

"Stop playing Miss Innocence. I'm going to kiss you."

She turned her face away, but he used his free hand around her shoulder to push her head around till she faced him. "Don't," she breathed as his face came to hers. His lips seemed dry and brittle as they pressed against hers. He pressed and pressed before his lips finally left hers.

She took a gasping breath. She'd hated his kiss. But it was only the beginning. "Don't," she said again as his hand left hers and reached under her coat and dress, pushing between her thighs up to her pants. "Don't, don't, don't," she kept saying, pushing uselessly against him with her free hand. But he wasn't hearing her. His forehead was shiny with sweat and his eyes were glazed.

"Oh, my God!" he said as his fingers crept under the elastic of her pants to the place between her legs. "Oh, my God, oh, my God!"

His hand stayed there, unmoving for a little while. She was so stiff with shock that she felt she had stopped breathing. The hand moved. The fingers moved along the flesh protecting the entrance. She felt them probe. They wanted in. When they went in, she would scream; somehow she would scream.

But they didn't go in. The hand squirmed out from under her pants. It emerged and went to his pants, fumbled with buttons, and out came a white tube of flesh. "Feel it!" he commanded, and when her hand remained resolutely still, he picked it up and forced it around the tube, holding it prisoner there.

He sighed. "We'll do it in the back seat. I'll take it out when I feel I'm going to come. I don't want to get you into trouble."

Somehow she wrenched loose. Somehow she managed to get the door open and jump out before he could grab her. She staggered into the trees. The darkness was terrifying, but no worse than what he wanted to do to her. Soon she stopped, sagging breathlessly against a tree, listening to him call.

"Tracy, please!"

Please! She'd said, "please," too, and it hadn't done any good. She'd said, "Don't," too, and that hadn't done any good, either.

"Tracy, Tracy!"

209

The voice was louder, more anxious, but it was moving away from her. He'd misjudged. If she just stayed still and didn't make a sound, he wouldn't find her in these trees all night. She thought about what would happen. If she wasn't home by nine-thirty, her mother would be alarmed. At ten she would call Reverend Gaylord, and he would call the police. When the local police didn't find them, they would contact the county and state police. But nobody would think to look for the pious son of Reverend Gaylord and his companion in this grove of pines known as petters' paradise.

The thought of the trouble Jefferson Gaylord would be in was satisfying only until Tracy considered the trouble she would be in. The scandal would be broadcast all over town in no time. Her mother would feel disgraced, even though none of it was Tracy's fault. The story would be distorted, and at school they would talk about it behind their hands, laughing about it, glad that the prim and proper Tracy Gordon had groveled in the dirt, unwillingly or not.

"Tracy, Tracy, where are you?" His voice, hoarse with his fear, boomed through the night. "Come out, come out! *Please!* I promise I won't touch you."

Silence. He'd stopped moving around. She supposed he was listening for a sound of her. But he would hear nothing. Not even her breathing.

"I promise, as God is my witness!"

She hesitated even then. But she decided that he would be afraid not to keep a promise like that. She started out and saw light. He'd turned on the headlights and was standing in their glare when she reached the boundary of trees surrounding the clearing. She stopped there, ready to run back into the trees and hide again if necessary.

With the headlights behind him, she couldn't see his face, just the silhouette of his tall, spare body. But she could see that he was shaking.

"Come out—please come out," he pleaded as she hesitated at the trees.

"Remember, you promised as God is your witness—"

"I won't touch you, I won't, I won't." His voice choked. It sounded as if he were crying.

She came into the clearing then and walked up to the car, opened the door to the back seat, and got in. He got in behind the wheel and turned for a moment, and she saw that he *was* crying. He tried to say something, but it didn't come out. He turned and started the car. He drove them out to the road. They were halfway back to town before he had control enough to speak.

"I don't know what got into me. I've never done that before." He took a deep breath. "You could ruin my future."

210

"I'm not going to tell," she said. "Just keep away from me, that's all."

"Your mother will wonder if I don't ask to see you again. So will my father."

"They don't have to know anything about it."

He began to cry again. She supposed it was from his shock of discovering he had the devil in him. It seemed unbelievable that a minister's son would have the devil in him, but Jefferson Gaylord did.

When they reached the house, he insisted on taking Tracy inside, though she knew her mother would see at once that something was wrong.

It was an awkward scene. Jefferson Gaylord stood there with his tear-reddened eyes and forced smile and thanked Tracy's mother for everything, saying this was one of the nicest evenings of his life, saying he would be thinking how nice it was when he was back studying at the seminary, saying he hoped they would let him call again sometime.

"What happened?" Tracy's mother asked her the instant the door closed behind him.

"Nothing," Tracy said.

"Tracy, I never thought I'd see the day my daughter would lie to me. But I know you are. It makes me want to cry."

"I'm not lying. Nothing happened." It wasn't a lie. Nothing *had* happened.

"Oh, Tracy, you disappoint me terribly." Her mother turned her eyes away. "When you're ready to tell me about it, I'll be ready to listen."

But Tracy knew that she and her mother would never talk about it.

Once in bed, Tracy couldn't get to sleep. She kept thinking of Jefferson Gaylord forcing her hand around his hard organ, turned toward her with that rigid pole of white flesh sticking out from him.

It was grotesque, ugly. She didn't *ever* want an ugly pole of flesh like that inside her, battering at her.

It was a long time before she went to sleep.

34

Howard went to the window and looked out into the London street, especially at the stone building across the way, whose every detail of ornamentation was locked permanently into his memory, so often had his restlessness caused him to stare out into this scene during the last three months. The building's walls glistened with drizzle. The day was dying. Howard closed the blackout shutters and went back to his desk, which, together with a chair and a small couch, occupied much of the space of his small office, a room never meant for its current use. Until a few months ago, when the building had been taken over for naval use, it had been a private residence in somewhat decaying state. Now its hive of rooms served personnel of various Anglo-American naval operations that didn't seem to fit into the scheme of things anywhere else.

Howard sometimes wondered if he and Jebley served any good purpose at all. Jebley kept insisting that their work was vital, but Howard felt that the officer was just trying desperately to feel important. Jebley was no more knowledgeable about their public relations task than Howard, having come to the assignment equally lacking in experience. Jebley was a former gunnery officer who was over-age in grade and, like Howard, couldn't be suitably assigned to a ship, so he'd been put here.

Howard reread the notes on his desk. They represented the work of the last several days, during which he'd contacted various offices about arrangements for an important meeting of certain high-ranking British and American naval officers the following week. These men would decide in general how publicity after the fact about their joint efforts in the forthcoming invasion, whenever that might be, would be handled.

He put his desk in order and stepped over to Jebley's office. The naval commander was sitting erect behind a neat pile of papers on his desk.

"I thought I'd leave early, unless you have something more you want to see me about today, sir," Howard said.

"Oh, I doubt there'll be anything more, unless the invasion suddenly starts." Jebley smiled wryly. "Not a very good joke, but the invasion is just about all most of us think about nowadays, isn't it?"

Howard nodded. "It's got to come soon."

"It's got to come this summer, I'd think. Of course, everybody thought it would come *last* summer, and it didn't. But I don't think the Russians will stand for much more delay."

"The sooner it comes, the sooner we can all go home." Howard looked at his watch, then back at Jebley. "If it's all right with you, I'll run along now."

Jebley smiled. "Heavy date?"

"No." Howard looked him straight in the eyes. "Something else." This time it was true. "Good night, sir."

Howard walked out. In the hall he saw Penelope, trim in her dark blue uniform, coming toward him from the office where she worked in a unit that had a combined British and American staff. Two British officers walked slightly behind her, so Howard could do nothing but give her a barely perceptible nod as they met and passed. He never thought much about his guilt when he was with her, but he did at moments like this, when they met and couldn't openly acknowledge each other.

He walked out into the murk. It was such a gray and dismal city, and he wondered sometimes if any sunshine would leak through even when summer came. The city had dissolved into night, although it was barely six o'clock. In Hollywood this time of day was considered late afternoon.

He walked the few blocks to Regency Pictures' London office. The manager, a man named Canfield who was too old to qualify for war duty except as a reserve air raid warden, waited with a projectionist. They went immediately to a small screening room.

"I'm sorry to put you to so much trouble," Howard said as they sat down and faced the rather small screen.

"No trouble whatever," Canfield said cheerfully, in the usual polite British tone. "The government was quite willing to lend the film. I've already had a look at it. I'm afraid Goebbels' influence is all too obvious. Of course, the Jerries swallow it whole. They're an extremely unsubtle people."

Canfield smiled uncertainly at Howard, as if it had just occurred to him that perhaps he'd overstepped, considering the importance that Leni Liebhaber had played in Howard's life. Perhaps Canfield wondered if Howard was still in love with his ex-wife, if that was why he'd asked to see this film.

Howard didn't care what Canfield wondered. He wasn't even sure himself why he wanted to see the picture. But he'd asked Canfield to arrange to borrow it after he'd learned that one of Leni's recent pictures had found its way to England through Switzerland.

The picture started. German titles drifted by, accompanied by heavy Wagnerian-type music, and then the story opened with a close-up of Leni looking through a mist-shrouded window, a typical beautifully composed Karl Gurtner shot. Howard wasn't surprised that Leni looked as lovely as ever.

Although he could hardly understand a word of the German dialogue, he soon knew what the story was about. Leni was a spy, gathering vital information for the Fuehrer in some unidentified country that might have been the United States. Then the scene shifted back to Germany, and the film thumped with jackbooted soldiers marching to heavy military music while crowds cheered. Presumably the picture had been made recently, but there was no sign of the devastation the Germans had been suffering from Allied bombings.

Leni's performance was full of vitality, but there was something wrong about her eyes, and Howard wondered if it was fear he saw there. Certainly by now her enthusiasm for Hitler would have been dissipated by the truth. She was a smart woman, and no matter what Goebbels or Hitler told her, by now she must be aware that the end couldn't be far away and that it would be disastrous. How often she must ask herself what was to happen to her.

He wondered himself as he walked out of the place. He still thought about her often, and worried about her ultimate fate in the war, although he told himself she didn't deserve his concern. He wondered if she would come back to the States when the war was over. As eager as she'd been to go back to Germany a few years ago, he would bet a good deal that she would be as glad to return to America now. If she did, how would he feel about facing her again?

He didn't want to think about that. He hurried to his quarters to change his uniform before meeting Mike.

Mike was waiting at the bar of the Underground Club. He'd learned from the bartender that the club's name came from its proximity to an underground entrance nearby where customers had fled when Nazi bombers had come over during the Battle of Britain. The club was expensive-looking. It occupied the ground floor of a former mansion and retained the original damasked walls and marquetry floors.

Mike gazed out at the dozen couples dancing dreamily on a small dance floor to "Body and Soul," played by a small but good band. The men were all officers, mostly American, and the women, except for a WAC lieutenant, were all well-dressed British civilians.

214

Mike wondered how often Howard came here. It wouldn't be bad to sit out the war in a place like London and frequent places like this. Howard had certainly had it lucky in the service. He'd been directly commissioned a naval lieutenant, had done a tour in New York City for about six months, and then had been shipped to London a few months ago. He'd found out through the studio that Mike was in England, had traced him to the camp in the south where Mike's unit had been training for the invasion for the last six months, and had asked him to come up to London to see him. So here he was, on undoubtedly his last leave for a long time to come, and it was disturbing to see how well Howard Stanton lived when it was plain that Michael Baines was going to be living in foxholes all too soon.

Howard arrived at that moment. He looked wonderful. But it was Howard who said that Mike looked wonderful as they shook hands and smiled at each other. They were shown to a table and waited on royally, and Mike was aware that many eyes were on them. But Howard was the center of attraction, not him. Howard was a great movie star, and he wasn't.

He felt stiff and awkward as they filled each other in on their activities since their farewell luncheon at the Brown Derby almost a year and a half earlier, just before Mike had gone into the Army.

Then Howard suddenly brought up the subject of Tim.

"I'm very worried about him. He was never a drinker, but he is now. It got so bad that Phyllis wrote me about it, asking for advice. I wrote Tim and told him that the word was out on his drinking and he'd better get himself straight or he'd be in trouble, but I'm not sure I said it properly or that it will do any good. He's changed a lot. I noticed it particularly the last couple of months before I was called up."

Howard was looking at Mike with a frown, and Mike wondered if Tim had said anything to him about their brief and regrettable relationship and the traumatic way it had ended. Mike found the thought humiliating. He looked down at the table, away from Howard's eyes. Another disagreeable thought struck him—that Tim's drinking might be from unhappiness over Mike's rejection of him.

He forced himself to look at Howard again. "That's too bad."

"Yes. Drinking and whatever unhappiness is causing it won't help his heart murmur. On top of it, he's getting himself in trouble with the studio. He turned down a good role recently. Phyllis thinks he did it just to throw his weight around. It's true that Hollywood is short on established leading men because of the war, but Regency Pictures won't hesitate to suspend him if he goes too far."

Mike balled his fist. "That damned fool! Doesn't he know how lucky

215

he is to be able to *make* pictures? I wish I had his chance. I don't want to be in this damned war. I don't think you want to be, either, even if you *are* in a soft position with practically no danger of being killed—" He stopped. He hadn't expected to go that far. It had just burst out of him.

"You're absolutely right," Howard said after a moment. "Go on, Mike. Why do you think I joined the Navy? Do you think it was to save my public face because so many other stars have gone into the service?" He waited for Mike to answer. When he didn't, Howard continued, "I suppose that *was* the real reason. But I also expected to contribute something, which I haven't. I'm not proud of that. But I can't reverse my situation, any more than you can reverse yours. You're a combat officer and I'm not. It's as simple as that."

"I'm sorry, Howard. You're right. I feel like a fool."

"Don't be sorry for being honest, Mike. I think I'd feel the same way if I were in your shoes."

But Mike doubted that he really would. And though there were no more disagreeable moments during their several hours together that evening, Mike didn't feel at ease during any of it, and he didn't think Howard did either.

There was a letter from Georgina, the first in weeks, with no explanation or apology for the gap since the last one. She didn't have much to say, either. She talked about finishing her current picture, her work at the Hollywood canteen, and her projected USO tour to the Pacific with several other stars.

Howard reread the letter, looking for hidden meanings, but he didn't find any. Still, the letter had all the elements of one written out of duty, not love—much the same as his letters to her had been lately.

Actually, her letter was that of a stranger. Time, distance, and the war had made them married strangers, Howard reflected as he dressed to go to Penelope's.

But of course it was more complex than that. Georgina had changed a great deal in the last couple of years, but instead of understanding her better, he'd understood her less. They hadn't talked enough about it, he realized, and now they couldn't. The emptiness in their letters screamed of the things that needed to be said.

He set off for Penelope's, wondering if his affair with her would ever have happened if his estrangement from Georgina hadn't begun long ago. Yes, he thought, it probably would have.

He reached the building where Pen lived and walked up the creaking stairway four flights to her flat. She opened the door at once, before his hand was off the buzzer, and he stepped in and kissed her. Her hair was unknotted and lay loosely down her back in rich brown strands, and he caught it in his hand as he kissed her deeply.

Finally he let her go, and she stepped back a bit and smiled. "Time for that later. I've got to see to the stove. We're having kidney pie. I would imagine you've probably never had that, have you? It's not exactly an American dish."

"No, I haven't," he said, sitting down in her one armchair, a comfortable affair with a footstool, both pieces covered in worn chintz. Her furniture had been lost in the bombing of her first flat, a casualty of the Battle of Britain, and she'd had to furnish this small place—a tiny parlor, bedroom, bathroom, and kitchenette—with whatever she could beg or borrow. "Wartime pastiche" was the way she cheerfully described the decor, and Howard marveled that she'd managed to make such a warm, inviting place with only these miserable pieces to furnish it.

Penelope Ashcroft. A lovely name for a lovely woman. She was fragile-looking, with delicate facial structure and a slenderness verging on thinness, and with dreamy, misty-green eyes. She looked fragile even in the mannish uniform and severe hairdo she affected at headquarters, but her looks belied her strong will and strength, her courage, her capacity for sacrifice.

She hummed "The Lambeth Walk" in the kitchenette as she worked. Howard looked over at the photograph of her husband sitting on the end table beside the daybed. The man smiled out from a friendly, open face, full of character. He was a Spitfire pilot, and he'd been shot down in the Battle of Britain not a week after their flat had been destroyed in a bombing. Pen seldom talked about him, but there was no doubt that she still thought about him a great deal, even though it was now three years since his death.

She came in with two covered dishes which she set on the small table beside the window. The blackout curtains were drawn, but there was a breeze, and the curtains were blowing in a little. Damp though it was, it was almost comfortable this evening.

They sat down to eat. "This is delicious," he said as he tasted the pie.

"You can't possibly mean that," she said with a laugh. "It seems all right to me because I've been used to this kind of cooking all my life. The fact is, we British are dreary, unimaginative cooks, and we dine not so much for pleasure as from necessity."

"It's still delicious," he insisted.

"You're just saying that because you like me."

"Well, I should say I *do* like you, Pen. In fact, I can't remember anybody in my life I've liked better—"

"Howard, please." She was suddenly solemn. "Let's not talk about it. Let's just accept this for what it is and not try to make more of it than that. Otherwise, we couldn't go on with it with any degree of comfort, could we?"

He'd been ready to speak, had been ready to say what needed to be said, but she'd cut him off at the crucial moment again. Perhaps she was right. Perhaps it shouldn't be talked about at all.

A couple of hours later, they got ready to make love. The bed occupied virtually the whole bedroom, so they undressed as usual in the parlor, leaving their clothes folded neatly on the daybed. They embraced standing up, his hardness pressing against her stomach, before they went into the bedroom. She opened the blackout curtains there, since they always made love in darkness, and the moonlight that managed to find its way through the mist shone on her beautiful body. He kissed her breasts again and again. She had small but ripe breasts. Delicate as she looked, she was as sexual as Leni. He knew it wasn't right to make comparisons, but he made them nevertheless.

Their tongues worked in each other's mouths, and then he tongued her down her body the way she liked. She moaned ecstatically as his tongue worked lower and lower. He went clear down her left leg to her foot and then up her right leg to her nest. He pressed his face against her there as she moaned her rapture. He pushed her legs apart and worked his tongue into the folds of flesh. He moved up to her clitoris and took it between his lips and sucked gently on it until her body shuddered and she came.

He kept his face pressed to her nest for a long time while she lay as still as he was. Then he moved up on her until his face was against hers and they kissed hungrily. Her nails dug into his back as she tried to pull him even closer to her than he was, and it hurt, but he didn't mind. He went into her and made one long deep stroke after another. She moaned and sighed and came again just as he was building to his own climax.

He stopped then and remained unmoving inside her, not wanting to come this fast, even though they would surely do it more than once tonight. They always woke up once or twice in the night to do it, and in the morning they did it again before breakfast, and sometimes after breakfast they did it again if there was enough time left before they had to report to their offices.

Yes, she was extremely sexual. She would go all night if he was up to it. As it was, she had three or four orgasms to his one. Her body and her

218

emotions were greedy for sex. Still, she had to have the right person to let herself go this way. She'd told him that until he'd come along, there'd been no one in her bed in the three years since her husband's death. He believed her. She was incapable of lying.

He started again, building up with the long thrusts she liked. He quickened the strokes until he was unable to stop. His climax towered in him. She was crying out, coming again herself.

They lay locked together for a while as his spasms subsided, and then he moved gently off her and lay back, relieved of one tension but now filled with another. It was always at this time, when they'd just finished, that he felt his guilt the most. He was injuring not only Georgina but Pen too. He had never expected it to go this far. But it was running away from them.

"I can tell you're worrying again," she said softly.

"I'm afraid I can't help it."

"There won't be any consequences from this, Howard, because we're not going to allow any. Let's not ruin what we have by worrying about tomorrow and the next day. These are our moments, and we deserve them. Let's keep them until we have to give them up. Someday we'll have to say good-by, so we'll say it. I'll expect it, and I'll be ready for it when it has to happen."

He didn't believe she would be. He believed that she was in love with him even if she didn't say so, even if she'd gone into this determined not to hurt herself.

He'd thought so much about it. He thought about it more now. He didn't go to sleep for hours.

Adrienne had dated the letter the sixth of February, 1944, but it didn't reach Howard until early in May. It had been smuggled out of Germany into Switzerland and then had been forwarded by the United States Embassy in Geneva to Regency Pictures in Hollywood, where Adrienne, naturally unaware that Howard was now in England, had addressed it. The studio had forwarded it, together with other correspondence, and it had obviously come by ship, for the studio letters were dated the second week of April.

Howard opened Adrienne's letter with a feeling of trepidation. Nothing good could be coming from her. She hated him too much. He started reading and was subjected to three paragraphs of rationalization about how good life was in Germany. Adrienne had changed her mind about nothing. Germany's destiny was still to rule the world, and the war would soon take a turn. She had faith, and of course Leni did, too.

It was the fourth paragraph that made his pulse jump.

219

Your son is now four years old and very handsome. He has more of your features than Leni's, but I am happy to say that he has Leni's soul. You didn't know about him, did you? We decided not to tell you. What good would it have done? But now I've come to think that you should be told what you're missing. Incidentally, there's no doubt that he is your son. He was born nine months from the time you were in Berlin, and no matter how cruelly you may think of Leni, you are the only man she's been to bed with in the last ten years. We named the boy Ernst Liebhaber and we are raising him as our son . . .

Oh, God, the perverted bitch!

Howard bowed his head, and the tears came. It was minutes before he was in control of himself.

He read the letter again, and two questions came to mind. Was the letter exclusively Adrienne's idea, written without Leni's knowledge with the express purpose of filling him with despair? Or had Leni made Adrienne write it to let Howard know about his son, hoping that he would come after the boy—and her—when Germany collapsed?

He took the letter to Pen and watched her go pale as she read it. She looked at him with saddened eyes when she'd finished. "How terrible for you to find out this way!"

"Somehow I'm going to get my son," he said, "and he's going to have the kind of father he should have, the kind I didn't have. Mine was always a hostile stranger to me. It's going to be different between me and my son."

"Of course it is," Pen said quietly.

35

Mike's battalion was informed early on the morning of the seventh of June that the invasion had started the day before. Early reports indicated that it would be a sustained success, although the Germans were naturally using every possible resource in their efforts to hurl the Allies back into the channel.

Mike heard disappointment expressed here and there that the battalion hadn't been included among the invading forces, but he doubted the sincerity of those expressing it. Nobody wanted to die, and it was simple logic that the longer you stayed out of combat, the better your chances were to survive.

As it was, they went into France soon enough. The corps was alerted in the middle of July and put ashore in Normandy early in August. Then there was a week of getting organized in an incredibly soggy reception center before they were sent to the front.

They went into action almost immediately after entering the combat area, opening fire with their howitzers on a German headquarters in a rural schoolhouse miles away. Soon the headquarters was no more, the surviving Germans had fled, and the battalion moved up to shell an enemy infantry regiment fleeing north. German eighty-eights zeroed in on them and knocked out two howitzers in Mike's battery, killing six men at the same time.

Two days later it was worse when they were suddenly under attack by a panzer unit after being told that the Germans had no tanks left in the area. The battalion would have been pulverized if the Air Force hadn't swooped in and wiped out the panzers.

After six weeks of combat, the battalion liberated a village the infantry had bypassed, and then was sent to rest on the grounds of the village château. It was there that Mike heard the staggering news that Tim had committed suicide by plunging his plane into the Pacific.

He didn't know the full story until Howard's letter reached him two weeks later. It seemed that the newspapers had conjectured that Timothy Briggs' suicide had been motivated by dejection over his wife's leaving him, disagreements he'd been having with his studio, and depression from being rejected for military service.

Dalton had written Howard the details that the studio had managed to keep from the papers. It seemed that months back Tim had been tossed into jail for trying to pick up young men in Pershing Square, and the studio had bailed him out and put him back to work on his current picture only on the understanding that it would tolerate no further bad publicity.

It seemed that Phyllis had taken the children and gone to her parents at that point, and Tim had gone from bad to worse. Recently he'd been arrested again, this time in a compromising situation with a boy of sixteen in the back of his car. The night of that arrest, Dalton had decided to carry through the studio's previous threat to invoke the morals clause and cancel Tim's contract, even though his uncompleted new picture would have to be shelved at considerable loss.

But Tim had never learned of Dalton's intent. The day after his arrest, when he was released from jail on bail pending trial, he took his plane up and crash-dived it into the ocean.

Mike kept wondering if in a way he had murdered Tim by ending it

221

between them in that hotel room in Georgia. For a long time, he couldn't get it out of his mind.

Howard didn't tell Mike about the other letter he received just before Dalton's. That one was from Georgina, and she revealed that she was in love with an Air Force officer she'd met on her USO tour in the Pacific.

I think it would have happened even if things hadn't begun to go wrong between you and me long before you left for the service, Howard. We talked around it, not about it, and the gap between us kept widening. Our love was slipping away from us, and we both knew it, but we didn't talk about it because we didn't want it to happen. We were cowards. When you don't talk things out, you don't avoid the inevitable—you assure it. And that's what happened to us. But even if we'd talked, I don't think the end would have been any different.

Georgina went on to say that the officer she was in love with had been reassigned to the States near Los Angeles shortly after she'd returned home from her tour, and she'd been seeing him steadily in the months since. She was certain about how she felt, and she wanted to start divorce proceedings. In civilian life the officer was a businessman in Chicago. After the war, when he returned there, Georgina intended to give up her movie career and go along as his wife.

On the way to Pen's, Howard thought of that time not so many years earlier when being an actress and a movie star had been of primary importance to Georgina. How she'd changed!

"This is certainly a surprise," Pen said when he told her.

Yes, it would be. Pen knew nothing of the empty letters that had passed between him and Georgina since the war had separated them. She knew nothing of the deterioration in their relationship either before or after that. Pen had justifiably assumed that Howard would be returning to Georgina after the war, and had accepted her affair with him on the basis that it would end when the war did.

He could tell from the light of hope in her eyes what she was thinking. Georgina's letter had freed him, and when their divorce was final he could marry her—if he wanted to.

He wasn't ready to talk about that or think about it, and he turned his eyes away from Pen's, wishing now that he hadn't come straight here with the news.

"Well, of course," Pen said after a moment, "it will take time for you to sort things out."

He looked back at her, smiling gratefully. Her tone showed that she understood how difficult this was for him, that she wasn't going to rush him, even though her own future was at stake. How like her!

222

He returned to his quarters. He needed to be alone, to think. He looked a long time at the photograph of Georgina he kept on his bureau. He'd loved her very much, and maybe he still did in a way, but he had to admit that he felt relieved that Georgina had ended the illusion that they might start afresh after the war.

He sat down at his desk and wrote a letter to her, saying that he understood her feelings, that they reflected his, that he would support her in the divorce proceedings.

He took out the photograph of Leni that he kept in his desk. It was a typical glamorous studio shot. Looking at her, smiling seductively in a dazzling beaded evening gown, he found it hard to picture her as a mother. The mother of his son!

He tried to visualize the boy, as he had many times before. What did he look like? Adrienne had written that he resembled Howard more than Leni. Was he a happy child? Was Leni giving him the kind of affection he himself had never gotten from her? What kind of life did the child have in Berlin?

He returned Leni's photograph to the desk drawer. She had come into his life and left it, and now Georgina was leaving it. He had loved both of them, and he loved Pen now. Or did he? After what had happened with Leni and Georgina, how could he believe in the permanence of any relationship? And how could he ask Pen to marry him when his life was so unsettled, particularly in regard to his son?

He got up from his desk. He decided to go to the Underground Club and have a drink. Maybe several.

The building was silent. No one worked late, now that the war in Europe had ended. Jebley had been gone for hours, but Howard still sat at his desk. Twilight sifted into the room, but he didn't move to turn on a light. He stared at the two pieces of paper before him. One, which had arrived early this morning, ordered him back to the States for reassignment. The other, which had arrived late in the afternoon, was the answer to the inquiry he'd made right after V-E day.

The answer had been almost a month in coming, but it was a very definite one. Leni, Adrienne, and the boy had been killed in their apartment in Berlin in one of the final air raids of the war. There could be no mistake about it. The Germans kept very accurate records.

Howard finally rose and went to the window. Lights gleamed in the building across the way. People walked by on the sidewalk and cars passed in the street. Life was going on in its normal way out there, but Howard felt as if it had ended for him. The awful finality of death had forced the truth on him with full clarity. He'd told Leni he no longer loved her when they'd parted. But now he had to admit that he had continued to love her even while he'd loved and been married to Georgina—and he had always harbored a secret hope that she would come back to him someday.

But of course now she never would, and he would never see her again. And he would never know their son, either—the son that had been the only tangible evidence of his and Leni's love.

He cried quietly at the window a long time. Then he returned to his desk and picked up the phone to call Pen. He was going to see her and ask her to marry him tonight. She was his only hope for happiness now.

In the taxi on the way over to her place he kept telling himself how lucky he was. He was lucky that Pen loved him. He was lucky that he had survived the war. And he was lucky because Regency Pictures was waiting for him to come home and make movies. Oh, God, he was lucky!

But it didn't begin to make up for his loss.

36

Early in June of 1945 Tracy Gordon graduated from high school without definite prospects. A couple of weeks later, there was a surprise letter from her cousin Hazel inviting Tracy to visit her and her husband in New York City right away. It seemed that Fred had been discharged from the Army after months of hospitalization for wounds he'd suffered in the Battle of the Bulge in December. A month ago Hazel had found them an apartment in Greenwich Village, a real miracle, considering the awful housing shortage in the city.

"Come and plan to stay at least a month," Hazel urged.

Hazel had promised a couple of years ago that she and Fred would invite Tracy to visit them if they settled in New York City sometime. And now here was the invitation, and Tracy was both frightened and excited at the prospect of it.

But Tracy's mother didn't think it was a good idea at all. "I'd worry about you all the time you were gone, Tracy."

"What would there be to worry about?" Tracy argued. "I'd be with

224

Hazel and her husband. You don't think they'd let anything happen to me, do you?" Tracy added that she'd hardly ever been outside Abbottsville and that she wanted to see something of the world.

"The world's just fine, right here," Tracy's mother insisted, but Tracy kept arguing, and finally her mother agreed to let her go. Two days later, after a long distance call to Hazel, the arrangements were made, and on the following day Tracy was on the train headed for New York. She was sad and lonely for the first two hours of the trip, but then she shook off her loneliness and settled back to dream of the excitement she hoped to find in New York.

It was the hottest July New York City had seen for many years, the newspapers kept saying, although Tracy didn't think it was any hotter than in Abbottsville, Georgia. Anyway, she really didn't mind the heat or anything else about New York. At first she was a little afraid of the surging crowds, but then she began to get used to them. It amazed her that with all these people around, no one seemed to pay any attention to anyone else. She liked the idea; a person could have a really private life here.

When Tracy's mother had said that she could visit with Hazel and Fred, a month had seemed a long time, but now it was slipping away like the wind. Tracy had decided the first week that she wanted to get a job and stay in New York, but so far she hadn't had the courage even to hint at such a thing in her letters home.

Hazel told Tracy that she would have no problem finding a job, and that she could stay with her and Fred as long as she liked. Of course, the conditions were not exactly ideal. The apartment was small; the one tiny bedroom was consumed almost entirely by the double bed Hazel and Fred occupied, so Tracy slept on the studio couch in the living room and kept her clothes in the hall closet.

But maybe, she thought, after she got a job she would live in a women's hotel, as Hazel had done until Fred had been discharged from the Army. Hazel had come to New York City shortly after she and Fred were married last year, soon after Fred was sent overseas, and had been working in the New York branch of the Office of Price Administration ever since. She thought she might even help Tracy to get on there, as a file clerk perhaps.

"Of course," Hazel said, "what you should really be is a model."

"Amen," Fred said.

"That's crazy," Tracy said.

"What's crazy is that I'm not more jealous of you than I am," Hazel said. "There's no prettier girl in this city right now than you are, Tracy

Gordon, and what's more, in a few years you're not just going to be pretty, you're going to be beautiful. There's a difference, you know. Girls are pretty. Women are beautiful."

Yes, Tracy knew. But she still thought it was crazy. Sometimes, in spite of the way people looked at her, no matter what anyone said, she didn't consider herself even very pretty.

The first time Tracy encountered Harlan Dobbs, she thought he was trying to pick her up. It happened as she hurried home from the delicatessen one day with some things for supper. She'd observed this man before, standing in a well leading to a basement apartment, looking out over the street, sometimes holding an expensive-looking camera. He was tall and thin, with kind eyes and a graying Van Dyke beard.

He looked anything but sinister until he suddenly appeared before her that day, saying something about wanting to talk to her. She didn't give him the chance. She bolted around him, ran the few more steps to the house down the street where Hazel and Fred lived, bounded up the stairs to their apartment, and locked herself in. She expected the man to follow and pound on the door, but he didn't. Instead, he stopped Fred on the street as he came home that evening, said he'd seen him around with this lovely young girl lately, and asked if he might photograph her.

Fred reported to Tracy and Hazel that Harlan Dobbs had cited impressive credits. It seemed that his photographs had appeared in *Life, Look,* and other important magazines. Right now he was collaborating with a writer on a book they'd been commissioned to do about New York during the war years. The book would be mostly pictures and captions. Dobbs wanted to photograph Tracy in a picture essay for the book about a young girl sightseeing around New York.

"Oh, I don't know," Tracy said doubtfully.

"You *must* do it!" Hazel said. "It's a perfect chance for you to get into modeling."

"But first we're going to check out this guy," Fred said. "No use taking any chances."

Tracy felt grateful. She liked Fred Henderson a lot. She thought Hazel was lucky to have a husband who was so nice and considerate. But occasionally she caught Fred looking at her with desire. Sometimes that worried her and sometimes it didn't. Sometimes she was even glad he looked at her that way.

Later, while they were doing the dishes, Hazel spoke about Fred. "He's wonderful, Tracy. It's so wonderful to love him and know that he loves me. You just can't know how it is until it happens to you. And I hope it happens to you the way it has to me."

226

Harlan Dobbs' credentials checked out scrupulously. But Fred insisted that they have him over to dinner to get to know him a little better before they agreed to the project. "And let's not be too eager," he cautioned. "You Rebels give in too easily. You think everybody has honorable intentions."

"No, we don't," Hazel said. "We're just more inclined to give the benefit of the doubt than you Yankees are."

Harlan Dobbs came to dinner the next evening, obviously aware that he was going to be looked over.

"You're concerned about this," he said to Fred and Hazel, "and I can understand it. We obviously have an innocent here." He looked at Tracy. "That's the charm and the wonder of it. The first time I saw her walk down this street, I knew I was seeing a rare paradox, an unsullied beauty." He looked back at Hazel and Fred. "If that arresting beauty combined with stark innocence comes through so strikingly to the eye, it will probably come through on film, and that's why I'd like to use this girl for my project."

"Assuming we agree to this venture," Fred said, "just what would be expected of Tracy?"

"Only to follow my instructions while I photograph her in every interesting situation and background I can think of that would be suitable to the subject. Then we'll winnow out the best, and that will be it. It will be work, but it will be worth it. I'm not going to try to seduce her. That's what really worries you, isn't it?"

Fred laughed uneasily. "The possibility has crossed our minds. This is New York, you know, where one has to be careful."

"One has to be careful anywhere," Dobbs said. "Sexual desire knows no geographical limitations. But when I'm attending to business, I'm all business. Still, if you agree to this and one of you wants to come along while we're doing the photographing, I won't object, as long as you keep quiet and don't make suggestions. If there's anything I can't accept, it's advice from amateurs on my work."

"I guess it wouldn't be necessary for one of us to come along," Hazel said.

"I suppose not," Fred said.

"Good," Dobbs said. "Then we're all agreed that we're going to go ahead on this?"

Fred and Hazel looked at Tracy, who took a breath and said, "Yes, I want to do it."

Dobbs smiled at Tracy. "I have this tremendous certainty that you're the greatest discovery I'll ever make."

A few days later, Harlan Dobbs began photographing Tracy. When he'd said he was going to photograph her in as many interesting

227

situations and backgrounds as he could think of, and added that it would be work, he wasn't exaggerating. For over a week they went out together every day, usually all day, and they went by bus and subway and sometimes by taxi, when they could get a taxi, to and from the many locations Dobbs chose from which to make the shots. And there were many, many shots taken at all locations with one or more of the several cameras Dobbs lugged along in his two big cases of equipment.

Tracy was often stiff and tired from the intensive efforts made at every location, but she didn't complain. Children complained, and she didn't want him thinking her any more a child than he already did. She almost disliked him for his frequently voiced hope that her "quality of innocence" wouldn't elude them in the final product. She wanted to wear some of Hazel's clothes for the pictures, but he wouldn't hear of it. He wanted her only in the simple dresses she'd brought from home, dresses she said made her look like a schoolchild but which he insisted made her look "classic, which is the effect I want." He also insisted that she wear rather plain flat-heeled shoes instead of the wedgies she was going to borrow from Hazel. And no lipstick. And no pompadour.

"I want you absolutely natural," he said.

He photographed her doing everything from buying souvenirs in Chinatown to riding the roller coaster at Coney Island to waving at returning troops from a West Side pier.

When he was finally finished, he said, "We've got something great in this. I know we have."

It was very hot. The radio had announced that the temperature was now ninety-one humid degrees at two in the afternoon and was expected to go to ninety-three before the day ended. Tracy was wearing nothing but a slip. She was sitting at the kitchen table trying to write to her mother. She had started the letter twice already and was beginning again. It was a difficult letter to write. She was now finishing her third week with Hazel and Fred, and her mother expected her to come home in another week.

What Tracy had to do in this letter was tell her mother that she would like to stay on in New York for a while and get a job. She also had to tell her about the photographs that were going to appear in a book, the photographs that might eventually help her to have a career as a model.

But she couldn't tell her mother *that!* Her mother would be horrified to think of her as a model. There was really no way she could tell her any of it and hope to get her approval. The moment she read the letter, she would be on the phone, shocked and hurt, demanding that Tracy take the next train home.

228

Tracy put down her fountain pen, hoping that later in the afternoon she would find a way to write the letter. She got up from the kitchen table and went into Fred and Hazel's small bedroom. She stood before the full-length mirror on the closet door, raised her slip over her head and dropped it on a chair. She looked at herself nude. She raised her arms and ran her hands slowly down her body, over her breasts and on down the sides until they met at her groin.

Finally she turned from the mirror. She felt tired. Maybe she would lie down on Fred and Hazel's bed for a while and take a nap. There was plenty of time. They wouldn't be home for hours yet.

At first she thought she was dreaming. Reality came slowly. She seemed to float out of sleep. She became aware of the heat, the closeness of the room, the prickly moisture on her brow, the dampness of her skin. She opened her eyes. Fred stood at the bottom of the bed staring at her. She didn't move. She didn't say anything. The clock on the dresser behind him said three-twenty. She wondered what he was doing home early from work. She was perfectly aware that she was nude. Yet somehow she couldn't move to cover her breasts or the area between her thighs. Her arms remained at her sides, her fingers clutching the sheet.

She saw Fred swallow. She saw the sweat trickling down from his forehead, a stream of it forking off to the corner of his mouth like a tributary of tears. She saw the bulge in his pants. She had a vision of Hazel sitting at her desk at work. "Think of Hazel!" she wanted to say to Fred, to stop him before he started, but she couldn't speak, any more than she could move.

"Think of Hazel, think of Hazel, think of Hazel!" It kept going through her mind as Fred stood there staring at her, sweating and swallowing. But she couldn't get it out. And then he leaned over the bottom of the bed toward her, his hand reaching, finding her calf, traveling up her leg, stopping inside the thigh, then moving on. She didn't make a sound, but her mind was racing. She was trembling as his fingers reached her triangle of pubic hair, found the flesh beneath, pressed gently. It was so very different from the secret moments when she had pressed herself there. There was a whole world of difference.

His hand moved away, back down her leg and off. He straightened. His eyes were glazed. He grabbed at his tie and twisted it off, then took off his shirt. Her pulse was pounding. She opened her mouth to tell him to stop. Nothing came out. She was rigid. She couldn't take her eyes off him, and she felt she was going to cry. His zipper stuck and he wrenched it apart getting out of his pants. He stood there with his penis

229

sticking out of the fly of his boxer shorts. It was a big pole of flesh, like the penis of Jefferson Gaylord. Her hand had been forced around that penis, and she had run from it. This penis would be put inside her, and she couldn't run.

She opened her mouth, and this time she said something. "No." But he didn't hear. He stared at her, transfixed, sweat running down his face. He dropped the boxer shorts and pulled off his socks. "No," she said again. Again he didn't hear. He lay down on top of her.

And then it was happening. She felt his lips everywhere. His lips on her lips and his tongue working into her mouth. His lips on the lobes of her ears, his lips on the palms of her hands, on the nipples of her breasts. His lips on the insides of her thighs, on the flesh of her vagina.

She held herself rigid through it, her hands clutching the sheet, wanting to say, "No!" Then it was too late to say no, for his penis was in her, hurting, hurting, then not hurting. And then slipping out and gone.

He lay back from her. After a few minutes he got off the bed and quickly started to dress. She pulled up the sheet to cover herself.

He turned to her. "I'm not going to tell you I hadn't thought of it before. I guess I started thinking of it the first time I ever saw you. I just couldn't help myself this time. I walked in, and there you were, and it almost seemed as if you were waiting for me."

"I wasn't!" Tracy said.

"No, of course you weren't."

He looked out to the living room, and she knew what he was thinking. Hazel would be coming soon. Hazel. That was the worst of it. What they'd done to Hazel. Tracy felt horribly ashamed.

Fred looked back at her. "I know this is hard to believe, but I love Hazel."

Yes, it was hard to believe. But she didn't say so.

"I don't think you understand what you do to men, Tracy." He paused. "We've got to decide what we're going to do. I know we can't forget it. But nothing would be gained by telling Hazel. It would just hurt her."

No, she couldn't bear the thought of telling Hazel. And it wouldn't ease their guilt. The damage was done.

"It isn't your fault at all," Fred went on. "It's mine. I couldn't resist it. But I promise you, Tracy, I'll never put a hand on you again."

She believed him. But she knew it would be very awkward to be around him and Hazel now, and there was no question of staying on with them for even a little while if she got a job. She would have to move to a women's hotel promptly.

230

Tracy was very nervous that evening, and she knew that Fred was, too, but if Hazel noticed anything unusual about them, she didn't show it. Tracy was greatly relieved when the evening was finally over and they went to their bedroom. Tracy retired to the studio couch and tried to sleep, but she lay awake for hours.

She kept reliving in her mind what had happened that afternoon. Her fingers traced the places Fred's lips had been. They probed where his penis had been. She thought and thought about it and tried to sort out her feelings. The truth was that what she'd expected all her life to be a nightmare hadn't been. Her sexual initiation had not been the ugly and humiliating experience she had dreaded.

She also realized now why she'd sometimes been glad when Fred looked at her with desire. She'd wanted what had happened today to happen. She'd regretted it immediately afterward. Now she didn't.

Tracy never wrote the letter to her mother she intended to write. Two days afterward, when she was still trying to find a way, something staggering happened. She heard the astonishing news that Regency Pictures wanted her flown to Hollywood for a screen test!

Harlan Dobbs had shown pictures he'd taken of Tracy to Regency Pictures' talent representative in New York City. The representative had immediately sent them to the Coast in the expectation that the studio head, Augustus Dalton, would react to them exactly as he had done.

Tracy took on the terrifying task of phoning her mother about it. Her mother refused to believe what she was hearing until Tracy told her the story twice, and then she angrily denied permission for Tracy to go. But Tracy found herself saying, "I must do it, Mama." This was vitally important, and she knew she was going to do it even if her mother never spoke to her again. She was different, so very different from the child her mother had known only a few weeks ago.

Tracy was sick on her first airplane flight, and she was bumped from the plane by a priority passenger at the stopover in Chicago and had to continue on to the Coast by train. She cried privately several times along the way and wished she hadn't come. She wished it even more when the Regency Pictures representative who met her at the train in Los Angeles delivered her to a drab hotel in Hollywood to wait it out.

She was taken to the studio two days later to be prepared for her test. The scene she was given to study seemed silly to her, but she knew she couldn't have done any better with a good one. What was she doing here? she kept asking herself. And why didn't she run? But she stuck on, even after the studio acting coach told her she had the most impossible accent she'd ever had to deal with. ("You are just one big slur, Tracy Gordon.") By the time they shot her test, two weeks exactly from the day she had arrived in California, she was no longer crying herself to sleep.

Two big things happened on the fifteenth day of August, 1945. Japan surrendered, ending the Second World War, and Regency Pictures decided, even though her screen test had been frightful, that they were going to try to make a screen star of Miss Tracy Gordon, formerly of Abbottsville, Georgia.

37

In the two years between August of 1945 and August of 1947, sometimes it seemed as if a lot had happened to Tracy Gordon, and sometimes it seemed as if practically nothing had.

Tracy began as a starlet and remained one for the next two years, with only a few walk-ons and bit parts to her credit. The word was soon around the lot that Mona Gaillard, Regency Pictures' reigning female star, had let Augustus Dalton know in no uncertain terms that she'd better not see this small-town upstart from Georgia getting any choice roles or there'd be hell to pay.

And of course it would have been dangerous to thwart Mona Gaillard at that point, for she was box office dynamite for Regency Pictures in the same way that Betty Grable, Rita Hayworth, and Lana Turner were for other studios in the immediate postwar years.

But the studio kept picking up Tracy's options, even if it didn't use her much in pictures. Dalton felt it wise to keep her around as a threat to Mona Gaillard. Besides, as Dalton revealed privately in a talk shortly after Howard had met Tracy, he expected something big out of Tracy Gordon one of these days when the right role and picture came along for her.

"You see her on screen and you want to go to bed with her," Dalton said. "Very few come across that strongly, and it's the biggest box office you can get."

Tracy had seen Howard Stanton and Michael Baines on the studio streets often before she met them both on stage nine in July of 1946 at the party celebrating the completion of Howard's second postwar picture, a suspense drama co-starring him with Mona Gaillard, which still didn't have a final title at that point.

"What it ought to be called is *Surprise,*" Mike told Tracy after he introduced himself. "Howard plays a murderer who gets caught and convicted. Whoever heard of that happening to an American movie hero?"

Tracy sipped on the champagne Mike had brought her from the buffet when he'd come over to introduce himself. It was the first time she'd tasted champagne, and she liked it.

"Still, I wouldn't have minded having that role myself," Mike continued. "I've been back from the war for ten months, and the one picture I've done hasn't been released. Sometimes I wonder if it ever will be. Maybe it should be shelved. I've got a strong feeling it's crummy."

Tracy took another sip of champagne and said nothing. She was thinking of a few years back when she'd seen Michael Baines as the second lead to Howard Stanton in *Submarine Attack.* And now here she was talking to him, or being talked to by him, rather, and she didn't think she liked him much.

"I've seen you around," Mike went on. "You're in the acting school, aren't you? I went through that before I went into the service. I suppose it helped me somewhat."

"I like it," Tracy said. "I've practically lost my accent, and I've learned to carry myself better. But I don't think anybody could ever teach me to act."

"That doesn't matter," Mike said with a shrug. "Movies don't require acting. What you've got to have is looks and personality, which you've obviously got plenty of, and a lot of luck on the side. On the stage, especially the New York stage, you need to be able to act. I studied for the stage, but I got a chance to come to Hollywood, and I took it." He paused and said suddenly, "I'd like to take you out."

"From the way I've seen you looking at Mona Gaillard while you've been talking to me, I think she's the one you'd like to take out."

"She's a bitch," he said after a moment of hesitation.

"She also has a husband. And something tells me you don't like that very much."

"She's a bitch," he repeated tautly. "And you didn't answer me about taking you out."

"I think you'd be disappointed. I just like to dance and go to the

233

movies, and I won't go to bed with you. Some people around here seem to think I go to bed at the drop of a hat, but I don't."

"All right. So we'll dance and go to the movies. Or go to my place and cook spaghetti. I have a neat apartment in North Hollywood. You'd like it."

"Maybe. But I don't think I'm quite ready to see it yet."

He stiffened. "You're not going to get anywhere in Hollywood being unfriendly."

He left her and moved off toward the champagne. She supposed he resented her for rebuffing him. She wasn't quite sure why she had. Why should she dislike him without giving him a chance?

But she didn't want to think about it. It was beginning to worry her that she hadn't met Howard Stanton yet. Her hope to meet him was the reason she'd been glad Dalton had invited her to this party.

Now if she were Mona Gaillard and wanted to meet someone, she would simply walk up and introduce herself. But she wasn't Mona Gaillard, movie star; she was Tracy Gordon, starlet. She'd been in California almost a year and didn't have much to show for it except a lot of cheesecake stills. One really good role in one really good picture was all she needed. It was all anyone needed. But Tracy didn't think she would ever see that role. She didn't think a lot of things would happen. She didn't dream much anymore. She was older.

But she soon found she wasn't going to leave this party disappointed after all. Dalton came by, asked her why she was standing behind a klieg light like a wallflower at a senior class dance, and said it was high time she met Howard Stanton.

"When you're ready, you'll be making pictures with him," Dalton said.

Not if Mona Gaillard had anything to say about it, Tracy thought as she walked across the stage floor with the studio head. Mona Gaillard was surrounded by men near the buffet table. She laughed as Tracy passed, and from its note of contempt, Tracy knew the laugh was directed toward her.

But she didn't care. What mattered was that she was finally meeting Howard Stanton. He shook her hand and smiled at her and presented her to his wife Penelope. He said that it was about time they met after seeing each other around the studio so often. He said other things, too, but she hardly heard them. She was thinking of the dreams she'd been having about Howard Stanton since childhood. She was thinking that here was a man she could love but could never have.

Tracy met Cliff Iwiansky when her car wouldn't start in the studio parking lot one day. She'd bought a 1941 Plymouth coupe to get her to and from the studio, but it had seen its best days long ago, Cliff cheerfully pointed out after he raised the hood and investigated. There was a connection loose on the distributor, and he reconnected it, but he said there was no guarantee it wouldn't pop loose and strand her halfway home, so he'd just better follow her in his car.

She protested that it would be an inconvenience, but he insisted it wouldn't be at all. She lived in the Hollywood hills and he lived just south of there.

She felt better about having him follow her home, but she wondered what she should do when they got there. Invite him in for a Coke? He reminded her of Fred in a way, she thought, as she looked in the rearview mirror to make sure he was still following her. A big, stocky body and very masculine. The type to fight wars and go hunting. He'd said he was a grip, and she supposed he was good at it. He would be fearless scrambling over the superstructure of the set, arranging lights and doing the other things required of grips at perilous heights.

She pulled up in front of the old Spanish building that housed her apartment, and by the time she was out of her car, he was out of his, had bounded up, and was closing her car door for her. Yes, he'd like to come in for a Coke.

Inside, while she was in the kitchenette pouring them, he asked from the living room how long she'd lived in the apartment. Not long, she said; she'd lived in the Hollywood Studio Club for about eight months before moving here. He told her, as she took the Cokes in and they sat together on the couch, that he'd had an apartment a lot like this one when he'd come to Hollywood in 1937, hoping to be a movie star. He also told her that he'd married a would-be actress two years later and they had twin boys of six.

"A lot of people who come to Hollywood end up being what they don't expect to be when they come out here. A lot of us stay on doing other things."

She nodded.

"You're going to be a star," he went on. "There are some you can just look at and know they'll make it." He smiled. "I'm glad you're not a star yet. If you were, I couldn't be here with you."

"Oh, I don't know about that."

"I do." He put his Coke down on the coffee table. He moved up against her and put his arm around her shoulder. His hand came down and caressed her breasts. "I can't help myself," he said huskily. "You know what I want to do."

A few minutes later, he lay back from her in the bed.

"It was wonderful," he said.

Yes, it was, she thought. They lay side by side, his muscular thigh

235

pressed against hers. His big hand covered hers, and his penis, though flaccid now, seemed almost as big as it had been when it was driving into her not two minutes earlier. He had big hands, big feet, and a big penis. She'd heard one of the girls at the Hollywood Studio Club observe that those were the marks of a peasant.

But he hadn't done it to her like a peasant. It hadn't been in and out and good-by. He'd kissed her all over and had stroked her skin and had made her tremble; and when she hadn't come when he had, he'd put his head between her thighs and made her come with his mouth.

"I've got to go in a minute," he said, "but I'd like to come back."

"Yes, I want you to," she said.

"I know already that I could love you. But I can't let myself, so I won't."

That was fine. She didn't want him loving her. There was only one man she wanted loving her, and that was Howard Stanton.

In the first half of 1947, three events of significance happened to Tracy Gordon. Augustus Dalton decided to lend her to United Artists for a picture, she returned to Georgia for her first visit home since she'd signed her contract, and she met Crandon Lane.

The picture came first. She was called to Dalton's office the first week of January to discuss it. She'd been to the studio head's office only once before, to sign her contract. On that occasion he'd predicted a great future for her that hadn't materialized.

She knew the one big reason for that. But Dalton claimed now, "We just haven't had the right roles come along for you, but they will, and in the meantime you can get good exposure with this picture."

It turned out that the director, Neill Yeager, had seen her in one of her bits and had convinced United Artists that she would be perfect for the leading female role. When she read the book on which the script was based, she was alarmed. She didn't think she could handle such a strong part. The woman was an alluring small-town girl who didn't let the fact that she was from the wrong side of the tracks hold her back. After involving herself in an unhappy affair with a rich man she didn't love and ruining his marriage, she left him for a stranger in town, learning only after she had fallen in love with him that he was a wanted criminal hiding out under an assumed name. When the law closed in on them, she had a chance to slip away, but she chose to go with him, and they died in an automobile crash trying to escape pursuing law officers.

When Tracy had the actual script of *Heat of Passion* in her hands, she was even more alarmed. She had a lot of dialogue. She was in more

236

scenes than anyone else. The star of the picture was Paul Matalon, who was being groomed as another Humphrey Bogart, but he didn't have nearly so much to do as she did.

"Don't worry about it," Neill Yeager told her when they met for the first time in the producer's office. "You're going to do just fine."

Just fine! What did he know about it? He was a freshman director in Hollywood, with only stage experience behind him, and he'd chosen her for the role on the basis of one little scene he'd seen her do, with six lines of dialogue, and now she was being thrown into a big role when she wasn't ready for it!

She thought it showed plainly when she stumbled through preliminary readings of the script. There was still an opportunity to replace her, and she bluntly asked Neill Yeager why he didn't.

"Because Matalon may be the star, but you're going to make this picture a hit. Don't you know what you've got? All you've got to do is walk into a scene, and you electrify it."

It sounded nice. She wanted to believe it. But she was convinced that Neill Yeager was only trying to build up her confidence.

After the first day of shooting, when there were twelve takes of the one scene she did that day, she was even more convinced of her inadequacy. She was in agony. And there was no one to talk to about it. Neill Yeager was the only one on the picture she felt any rapport with, and he was much too busy the first day of production to take any extra time with her. She went home that evening and did something she'd never done before in her life. She got out the bottle of Scotch she kept on hand for visitors, and she got drunk.

It didn't get better on succeeding days, and Tracy hated working on the picture. When she'd done her bits at Regency Pictures, she'd spent at most two or three days on the set. There were forty-five shooting days scheduled for *Heat of Passion,* with more to come if the picture couldn't be brought in on time, and Tracy had at least one scene for almost every day of production.

She tried hard. She studied her lines every evening for the next day's shooting, and she went to bed early so she would be fresh at the studio. Then she spent the tormenting hours waiting for the day to end.

Neill Yeager let her see the rushes of the first week of work to show her that she was "doing just fine," as he told her. She thought she was doing horribly. She didn't like the sound of her voice or the way she looked or her performance.

After that, she didn't look at the rushes. She just wanted the picture to be finished. She wished she'd never come to Hollywood. She

237

wished she were still a child, living in dreams and going to the movies, not knowing what making them was really like.

Cliff was the only person Tracy saw away from the studio, and she didn't see him often. Perhaps twice a week, on the best weeks, and then only for an hour at a time, at most.

She felt safe about him. No one knew about them; they were never seen together. Neither of them would tell anyone about their affair, so no one would gossip about it, and no one would get hurt.

She knew he felt guilty, cheating on his wife. He didn't talk about her or their children after the first time. Tracy didn't feel guilty about her as she had about Hazel, because she didn't know her. Sometimes, in fact, there was a certain excitement in thinking that she was having an affair with a married man.

But she realized that it wasn't really an affair because there was no emotional involvement—although she hadn't forgotten Cliff's remark that it would be easy for him to fall in love with her. He would arrive, have one of the bottles of beer she kept in the refrigerator just for him, and then they would go to bed. Usually he would take her, rest a few minutes, and then take her again in the hour he spent with her before he went home to his family.

She continued to get great physical pleasure from their meetings, for he always saw that she was fully satisfied. Once he said, "There isn't anything I wouldn't do with you," and the way he said it made her think she was the only one he wouldn't draw a line with, even his wife. The thought was exciting.

His body was exciting to her, too. It was big and powerful, and when she was in his arms she felt consumed by him. Their encounters temporarily relieved her nervous tension over the picture as well. She even stopped worrying about what her mother would think if she knew about the relationship.

But much as she liked Cliff, she doubted that she would see him if they could be free and open about it. He wasn't what she wanted. There was only one man she really wanted.

When Tracy went home to Georgia for a visit, almost two years had passed since she'd taken that fateful trip to New York City to visit Hazel and Fred. She'd written perhaps a hundred difficult letters to her mother in the meantime. She'd said twice that she was coming home for Christmas, but she hadn't gone. She'd said she was coming other times, too, and then had found excuses at the last moment.

This time there was no excuse. She flew in to Atlanta, and her mother met her at the airport.

238

At home the two studio portrait-photographs of herself she'd sent in silver frames were sitting prominently on the marble-topped Victorian table in the front parlor, but Tracy was under no illusion that this indicated approval by her mother of her Hollywood career. Tracy knew that her mother would always feel she'd been betrayed by her only child.

Tracy's mother brought up the subject the second day Tracy was home. "If you hadn't left home, you'd be married, and I'd have my first grandchild by now," she said reproachfully.

"Not necessarily, Mama," Tracy said.

"But you'll come home to stay after you get that out of your system."

"By *that,* you mean my career, I suppose."

"You'll come home to stay," her mother repeated. "You'll want to, Tracy. You'll see. There's only one real home for everybody, and it's all that's worthwhile."

"I don't believe that, Mama," she said defensively, and saw her mother turn pale. It was the first time in her life that Tracy had ever disputed anything her mother said.

The rest of the visit didn't go at all well, and Tracy returned to California three days early.

Tracy met Crandon Lane as she came out of Grauman's Chinese Theatre one evening. He was standing in the forecourt, looking down at the leg print of Betty Grable embedded in cement, and looked up as she approached.

"I think it's degrading to record yourself in cement," he commented. "But these fools can't wait to be big enough to win this kind of idiot's immortality."

"I don't see anything wrong with it," Tracy said, wondering who this good-looking and impeccably dressed man was.

"There isn't anything wrong with anything at all if you're an idiot," he went on, "as most movie stars are."

"I don't think that's fair," she said, although she didn't see why she was talking to him at all. She turned from him and walked on. He fell in beside her immediately.

"I'm sorry I offended you. Does that mean you're a movie star? I hope not. I'd hate to think I was trying to pick up a star, because that would mean all sex and no substance. As a matter of fact, I *know* you're not a movie star, for there's no escaping not knowing who the movie stars are. But you're more beautiful than most of them. Maybe all of them. We'll see whether I still think that after we've been together one or two times."

239

"We're not going to be together at all," Tracy said, bristling.

"Oh, but we must. My curiosity is sparked. I have a feeling that you're the usual stereotyped combination of beauty without brains that proliferates in these parts, yet I still want to know you."

"You're not going to, so you might as well not waste any more of our time."

They'd reached the lot where she'd parked her car. She walked toward it.

He followed. "I'm Crandon Lane. Does that mean anything to you?"

The name sounded familiar, but she said, "No." She got into her car and closed the door.

"You may drive away from me now," he said, "but you're going to see more of me. I'll find you."

She drove off, but she kept thinking of him, and then she remembered reading in one of the fan magazines that he'd won an Academy Award for a musical score a couple of years back. She didn't expect ever to see him again.

Tracy was embarrassed when the advertisement announcing the upcoming premiere of *Heat of Passion* at the Egyptian Theater appeared in the Los Angeles *Times*. It featured a picture of her in a low-cut peasant blouse that she'd objected to when she'd first seen it, because the top of the blouse fell so low on her bosom and her upper arms that it looked as if she were taking it off. The punch line beneath the picture was equally embarrassing: "This woman is the heat of passion in *Heat of Passion*."

All she could think of was how embarrassed her mother would be when the ad appeared in the paper at home in a couple of months, when *Heat of Passion* would be playing at the Golden and other small-town theaters all over America in second-run engagements.

The day after the ad appeared, Crandon Lane showed up at Tracy's apartment with a dozen red roses in each arm.

"Don't expect me to use a cliché like 'American beauties for an American beauty,' " he said as he stepped around her and inside. "And don't expect me to tell you how I got your address. We're going to get started on our relationship immediately. I wish I didn't feel I had to pursue you, since that terrible ad in the *Times* yesterday obviously means that you're determined to be a movie star, but I've had a compulsion about it ever since that evening I wanted to pick you up and you wouldn't let me. So right now, we'll begin with dinner at the best place in town—my house."

240

He lived in Beverly Hills in a big, sumptuously furnished rented house surrounded by ornate gardens. He had several servants, one of whom served lobster thermidor as they sat at opposite ends of a long table in the dining room. Crandon did most of the talking. She got the impression that music was the only thing that mattered much to him. And she had the feeling that there was a certain inevitability to this; that, like a movie, it would run on until it was finished.

A few nights later, he escorted Tracy to the premiere of *Heat of Passion*. Paul Matalon was the star of the occasion because he was the star of the picture, but Tracy was the star of most of the reviews that appeared subsequently, not for her acting ability, which admittedly wasn't great, but because of that "indefinable something" that made her the object of almost exclusive attention every moment she was on screen. The various reviewers talked about her "star quality" in different ways, but it all added up to the same thing.

At the premiere, Tracy didn't dream that such laurels were forthcoming, and she barely sat through the picture, closing her eyes and holding her hands over her ears at points where she couldn't stand looking at and listening to herself.

"I was awful, awful, awful," she said to Crandon afterward as they drove to the premiere party being held at the Mocambo.

"You weren't awful, but you weren't good. Maybe with experience, you will be. But it won't be from talent, just from work. Most movie stars don't have a shred of talent. Talent is something you can't create. It has to be in you before you can develop it. But don't despair. You're going to be a star. I wish you weren't, but you are."

"Well, thank you very much for your kind wishes."

"I told you I don't like movie stars, but even someone like me can't have everything in life exactly as he wants it, so I'm going after you anyway."

"I have an uncomfortable feeling we're going to end up hating each other," Tracy said.

"Do you think it possible that we might love each other a little before that?" he said with a smile.

She didn't say so, but she found it hard to imagine him capable of love.

Often, Tracy asked herself why she continued to see Crandon Lane. She never felt at ease with him unless she was drinking, and she found him insulting much of the time. When she told him angrily once that if he didn't stop taunting her, she would stop seeing him, he only laughed.

"Don't be absurd!" he scoffed. "How can you think that I'm insulting you when I'm only telling you the truth? You're basically an honest person. I think you want to hear the truth."

Not when it hurt, she didn't.

"Besides," he went on, "there's an antagonism between us. It creates resistance in both of us, and mutual resistance is essential to an interesting relationship."

"I don't understand you."

"I hope not. When people understand each other too well, boredom sets in."

It was true that she didn't understand him, but she began to learn about him. He was thirty-four years old; he had a haughty mother in New Hampshire whom he'd stopped communicating with; he had an ex-wife in Connecticut he was resentfully paying alimony to; he had a fine income from the family banking business at home which he'd never participated in; he'd attended Groton (whatever that was) and Dartmouth (she'd heard of that) and had studied with the greatest music masters in Europe (he rattled off names, including Stravinsky's, and thought her ignorant when she recognized none of them); he'd lived in London, Paris, and Rome (they were the only three cities in the world worth mentioning, he insisted); and he hated California (it was boring, and there was no culture outside the research rooms at the public library) and had stayed on here only because he believed he could elevate film background music.

"Or maybe I really stayed on because I knew I was going to meet you," he said one day.

"Don't tell me you believe in fate?"

He laughed. "Now that *would* be idiotic, wouldn't it? Let me put it this way. I had a feeling that something was going to happen in my life to make it better, and that feeling was particularly strong the day I stopped to look at Miss Grable's leg print. And you came strolling out of the theater at the proper psychological moment—"

"And you thought you could get me into bed. But you haven't."

"It isn't that you don't want to," he said.

"Your ego would never let you think otherwise."

"True. And my ego is always right. It tells me that you'd go to bed with me tomorrow if I asked."

"Don't ask. You'd be sorely disappointed."

But he didn't ask her to go to bed. What he asked her was to marry him. Even more surprising was how quickly she said yes.

38

Tracy Gordon was only a starlet before *Heat of Passion* was released throughout the country in September 1947, but after that she was a star.

It put Dalton in an awkward position, since Mona Gaillard was now more determined than ever to see that Tracy didn't get good roles at Regency Pictures. And Mona was in a good bargaining position because *Lisa,* her most magnetic creation to date, abetted by her electric teaming with Michael Baines, was Regency's most successful picture at the box office in years.

Dalton somehow had to appease Mona, yet still take advantage of the tremendous success Tracy was enjoying with *Heat of Passion.* The public had responded so overwhelmingly that she'd been given her first spread in *Life.* Dalton's only regret was that *Heat of Passion* had been made by United Artists, not Regency Pictures.

Tracy had continued to see Cliff while she was seeing Crandon, though not quite so often, and with growing misgivings. Cliff seemed to sense that something was different, and he wasn't surprised when she told him that she was getting married and couldn't see him anymore.

"I hate this," he said. "I don't want it to be over between you and me. I wish you loved me, not him."

She didn't know what to say. "Even if I did, what could we do about it?" she finally said. "I don't believe you'd leave your wife and children for me."

"Oh, God, I don't know what I'd do!" he said intensely.

Apparently he *had* fallen in love with her, even though he'd said in the beginning that he wouldn't let himself. But they didn't talk about it. He left abruptly, and she didn't call him back. She felt shaken. But she didn't know what she could do about it.

She had enough to handle anyway. Now that they'd decided on

marriage, Crandon wanted it done quickly. There was no question of their having a "Hollywood carnival wedding," as Crandon put it. Neither was there a question of having it in Abbottsville. Crandon would have laughed in Tracy's face if she'd suggested it.

She had a painful time phoning her mother with the news. She would have preferred writing to her, taking more time to think out the best way to say it. As it was, she blurted it out so fast that she had to repeat it. She said she was going to be married in Las Vegas tomorrow and wished her mother could be there for the wedding, but she knew it would be asking too much for her to fly out on such short notice.

Yes, it would be, her mother's silence told her.

"The reason we're getting married immediately is that I have to be back at the studio in about a month to prepare for my next picture," Tracy went on, "and Crandon wants to take me to Rome on our honeymoon. That's Rome, Italy, Mama. Don't you think that will be lovely?"

Silence again, then, "Do you love him, Tracy?"

"I wouldn't be marrying him if I didn't."

"Wouldn't you?" her mother said quietly.

The next day, as Tracy and Crandon flew to Las Vegas in a small plane, Tracy suggested that instead of going straight on to New York the following day for the flight to Rome, they make a side trip to Georgia so her mother could meet Crandon.

"Don't be ridiculous," he said. "I wouldn't dream of inflicting my mother on you. I expect the same courtesy in return."

"But you'll have to meet her sometime."

"I hope not. It's improbable that she'd like me, and I'm sure I wouldn't like her. Your mother's influence is obviously one thing that's very wrong with you."

"What would you know about it? I haven't even told you anything about her."

"Your avoidance of the subject has told me a great deal. You're quite transparent, Tracy. I've learned more about you in the last couple of months than you'd ever dream."

"Have you? I can't say the same. Sometimes I don't think I know you at all, Crandon."

"Good. Then you still have a lot to look forward to."

She looked at him thoughtfully. "It scares me a little, running off like this. Do you think we're doing the right thing?"

He smiled sarcastically. "Do you think we should have gotten permission from that pompous nabob Dalton?"

"I don't know what a nabob is, and you know I don't. I wish you wouldn't use words like that. You do it just to humiliate me."

"I do it to help you learn something, Tracy. You can't expect to grow without learning. One thing you can expect from our marriage is that you'll keep learning."

"You didn't answer me. I asked you if we're doing the right thing, running off like this."

"And I asked you if you thought we should get permission from Dalton. You don't seem to understand that stars do what they want nowadays, Tracy."

"You still don't understand what I mean. I mean, I wonder if we should wait."

"Wait? You mean to be *sure?*" He laughed. "That's very funny, Tracy. Don't you know that there is no such thing as being sure? Besides, if we were sure, we probably wouldn't do this at all."

The first thing Tracy thought when she woke the next morning was that she didn't feel married. She looked around the gaudy bedroom of the hotel suite. She could scarcely remember it from the night before.

She could scarcely remember anything at all from the night before. She had only the vaguest recollection of the wedding in the home of a justice of the peace, followed by a wedding dinner, much champagne, and blaring entertainment here in the hotel, with reporters and photographers swarming around them, and Crandon snapping at them.

She remembered Crandon undressing her and putting her to bed. She remembered little of their union, but thought that it had happened more than once, and that Crandon had slapped her. But that couldn't be so. Why would she think that? But why didn't she feel happy? And why wasn't Crandon still in bed with her, ready to take her into his arms when she wakened?

His electric razor was whirring in the bathroom. It was a long time before he finally came out. He was wearing blue silk pajamas. He looked over at her but said nothing, then went to the window and opened the draperies. Light poured in. He walked over to the bed and looked down at her thoughtfully, unsmiling. She'd pulled the sheet up around her when he'd come in from the bathroom. He pulled it down now, completely off her.

"Why cover it up? Your body is a work of art. Of course it's not a work of art *you* created. It just happened that way, so you're not to be congratulated for it."

His remark hurt her, and she frowned. "I think that's a strange way for you to start off our first day together as a married couple."

"Did you think we'd begin it with sex?" He sat down on the bed and put his hand on her thigh. "Is that what you want?"

What she wanted was for him to kiss her and tell her that he loved her and that this wasn't all a terrible mistake.

"Yes, I think that's what you want," he continued. "You're a highly sexed woman. You couldn't have shown it better than you did last night. There wasn't anything you weren't agreeable to and didn't love. But you wouldn't remember that, of course. You didn't know what was going on. You had too much champagne to know. But *I* didn't. I knew exactly what was what!"

He got up suddenly and went over to the window, standing with his back to her, talking coldly to her over his shoulder.

"Why did I think you'd be a virgin? Is there such a creature anymore?"

She found it difficult to speak. "If you'd asked me, I would have told you I wasn't one."

"How many have there been?"

"Two."

"Who?"

"What good would it do for you to know? I wouldn't want to know about the women in your life."

He turned and looked at her. "There hasn't been anyone in my life but you since we met. Can you say the same?"

"There was a married man I was seeing when I met you," she said after hesitation. "I told him a couple of weeks ago that I couldn't see him anymore."

"A couple of weeks ago. I'll bet you let him screw you right up to the last, didn't you? Not only didn't I marry a virgin, I think I married a whore."

"I'm not!" she cried.

"I'd just better not catch you proving I'm right," he said harshly.

"Oh, God, oh, God!" She turned on the bed to hide her body and her tears from him. Her marriage wasn't twenty-four hours old yet, and already she was wondering how she could possibly make it work.

Crandon had been unhappy enough about photographers hounding them in Las Vegas. He was openly angry about it when they were besieged again in New York at Idlewild International Airport while they changed planes for the flight to Italy. He finally posed with her, but sullenly.

246

"I hope that idiocy is over for a while," he said as they boarded, leaving the cluster of reporters and photographers behind.

Tracy felt ill at ease with the press, too, but acknowledged that cooperating with them at this point was prudent. Only really big stars could afford to ignore them. Their present interest in her seemed to leave no doubt that *Heat of Passion* had really established her as a star, that the public was genuinely interested in knowing about her.

To Tracy's surprise and Crandon's annoyance, then anger, she was readily recognized almost everywhere they went in Rome, too. The now-famous picture of her in the peasant blouse had made its way to Europe. It was soon evident that they couldn't even sit quietly at a sidewalk table outside the Hotel Excelsior, where they were staying, without passersby picking Tracy out and stopping for autographs.

Crandon blew up over that, and he blew up again when she said she wanted to see Howard Stanton's new picture, which had just opened at a theater near the hotel.

"I might have expected that you would come to one of the greatest cities in the world and spend your time running to movies!" he said angrily. "That's typical of a Hollywood person."

"I don't call going to one movie running to them. And if I'm a Hollywood person, what are you? You've been there a lot longer than I have."

"I've had a longer physical presence there than you have, but I'm not a Hollywood person, and I would not be a Hollywood person if I lived in that moron's paradise for twenty years. A Hollywood person has an incurable state of mind. A Hollywood person lives and breathes movies. Nothing else is important."

"I don't see anything wrong with something mattering that much."

"Tracy, there's nothing wrong in dedication if the cause is worthwhile. But Hollywood is not a worthwhile cause."

"You've stayed, Crandon. And Hollywood's done all right by you, hasn't it? You won an Academy Award."

"I've done all right by Hollywood, not the reverse, Tracy. As for the Academy Award, ask me sometime what I did with it, and why I did it. But not now. I don't think you've learned enough to understand yet." He frowned at her. "One thing in particular I hope you're going to understand sometime is that it's far more important to be Mrs. Crandon Lane than a mere Hollywood star."

He showed his moody side much more often than he had before their wedding, but there were good moments, too. One morning he roused her before dawn because he wanted her to see the sunrise from the top of the Janiculum hill. He took her there and stood with her clasped to him while the roofs of Rome turned from gray to pink to saffron beneath them. He'd said it was one of the loveliest sights she would ever see, and it was. Finally he kissed her. At that moment he seemed as unworldly as she was. At that moment she thought he loved her.

There were other times, too. He drove her out to Tivoli and took her to the ruins of Hadrian's villa, and that was half nice and half not. It hurt her because he laughed when she admitted she'd never heard of Hadrian, who had been the most enlightened of the Roman emperors, he explained, and who had re-created many wondrous buildings of the ancient world right there on those grassy acres. There was little left but an occasional wall and groves of olive trees, but it was still a beautiful and peaceful place, and he took her arm as they walked about and said he wanted to make love to her right there. They didn't, but his wanting to pleased her.

They walked arm in arm in the Roman Forum, too. She thought it just an ugly long hole in the ground when they looked down at it from the Capitoline steps, but she tried to act impressed when Crandon reminded her that the rectangular patch of dirt they walked on had been the center of the ancient world.

But then his mood changed. "You don't care," he said.

"Yes, I do," she said, her hand tightening on his arm. "I want to know."

"No, you don't," he said coldly. "You just want to be stupid. Forever."

Tracy liked Rome, even considering the periods of unhappiness she suffered there during her honeymoon, but she was glad to get home. Not that there was anything homey about Crandon's Beverly Hills mansion. He'd rented the house a year before from a deposed M-G-M producer who'd gone downhill a few miles in distance and station to Westwood Village, and he called the house a "rococo mess." Tracy would have felt more at ease in less pretentious surroundings, but Crandon said he wouldn't consider moving unless he found something that was in even more "egregious taste" than this place. He said it would be difficult to express better than this hideous house did the awfulness of Hollywood and everything the word connoted.

He had an opportunity to score a picture for Paramount almost immediately after they got back to California, but he returned from the screening with nothing but contempt for the film, saying he couldn't write music for something he didn't respect.

"I refuse to be associated with mediocrity. You'd be smart to start practicing that principle yourself. You could begin by turning down that idiotic script they've got lined up for you."

248

"But the studio would suspend me!"

Actually, she wasn't sure what Dalton would do if she suddenly showed temperament. After her surprising success in *Heat of Passion,* the studio had voluntarily renegotiated her contract with her new agent, Emory Deems—who was also Howard Stanton's and Michael Baines' agent, she discovered—and she'd leaped from three hundred dollars a week, which had seemed a lot of money to her just a few months ago, to two thousand, which seemed like a great deal of money unless she compared it with the eight thousand dollars Mona Gaillard was getting under her new contract.

In any case, she didn't think the script was idiotic, as Crandon said it was. *Love on the Loose* was an attempt to re-create the "screwball" type of comedy that had been popular in the thirties. The lines seemed bright and witty to her. What frightened her most about doing the picture was that she was to be teamed with Howard Stanton in it—a sudden turn of events, since she'd been told originally that Michael Baines would be her co-star. How could she expect to be anything but nervous, working with Howard Stanton for the first time?

The matter of delivering that bright dialogue properly also concerned her. Playing comedy required a sense of pace and finesse that she didn't have. The role she was supposed to bring to life was that of a sophisticated madcap heiress out to do in the career of a crusading editor—played by Howard Stanton—who in turn was trying to do in the political career of her multimillionaire father. It was as nearly opposite the sultry seductress she'd played in *Heat of Passion* as it was possible to get, and much more demanding. After she watched screenings of some screwball comedies made by Denise Carroll, Claudette Colbert, and Irene Dunne a decade back, and saw how capable they were in such roles, she felt even more insecure about her ability to play the part.

But the director thought otherwise, and so did Howard Stanton. When she admitted how inadequate she felt to the task ahead, Howard said he felt that way at the start of each new picture—and this was after making them for eighteen years.

"We're going to do all right together," he said. "You'll see."

Do all right together! It sounded so innocent, and from his viewpoint it was. He had no idea how she'd looked up to him all these years, how she'd wanted him, how she still did. To have revealed any of it would only have embarrassed him and made a fool of herself. But the first time he took her into his arms and kissed her for a scene, she trembled uncontrollably. Although she was sure he took that for her natural nervousness, it was much more besides that.

Still, it worked out. Howard was kind, cheerful, and considerate, and soon he was treating her like an old friend, although "friend" wasn't what she wanted to be to him. Getting to know him better confirmed that he seemed to live up to the image she'd formed of him since her childhood. Yet that was more disheartening than otherwise, for he was unattainable. And it made her marriage to Crandon seem like an even worse fraud than she'd begun to think it was. It was increasingly difficult for her to study comedy dialogue for the picture when she was simultaneously asking herself why she'd married Crandon.

In spite of it all, she and Howard played well together, and when a coach from the acting school was brought to the set to help her with her dialogue, she seemed to be doing all right. She risked looking at some of the rushes, and although she didn't think she was good, Howard said she was. So did Renfew and Dalton.

More important, the reviewers said so, too, when *Love on the Loose* was rushed into release only three months after filming was completed. But Tracy's big thrill was the tribute Howard paid to her in a radio interview with Aster Bigelow shortly after. Howard said that Tracy was just about the most natural, honest person he'd ever worked with and that she was a good actress.

Tracy rather timidly called the radio station the next day and asked if she might have a transcription of the broadcast. After she received it, she played it over and over when Crandon wasn't around. She wouldn't want her husband to know about it, any more than she would want him to know that she kept scrapbooks of the stories about her and the reviews of her pictures in magazines and newspapers. Crandon would have called it idiotic.

It hadn't been so bad when she was making *Love on the Loose*. She worked at the studio all day and was tired when she came home, and Crandon was surprisingly considerate of her. Quite often, unless he'd lapsed into one of his uncommunicative moods, he would have cocktails waiting. He informed her that a cocktail was the only decent drink before dinner, wine during dinner, and brandy afterward. He was teaching her how to drink well.

He was also trying to teach her a good deal else. He presented her with the works of Tolstoy, Hemingway, Fitzgerald, and Faulkner, and told her they would give her a good start in learning. She tried to read them. Her worst experience was attempting to get into *War and Peace*. She was hopelessly bogged down in the long list of characters before she was fifty pages into the huge book. She gave it up shortly after that.

With the picture finished, the days were long and dragging and usually started badly. Crandon was seldom in a civil mood in the morning, and anything he had to say at breakfast was likely to be rude and sarcastic. When she started sleeping later to avoid having breakfast with him, he saw through it immediately and said frigidly that if she didn't want to eat breakfast with him, perhaps she'd rather not have lunch or dinner with him, either.

"What do you expect?" she snapped. "You never talk with me. Just at me or to me."

"I'll talk with you," he said cruelly, "when you start having something worthwhile to say."

She was glad that at least he spent most of the day composing. He was working on a concerto, he said. She asked if she could hear it, and he said certainly not, not until it was right, not until it was finished and perfect. Still, she heard bits of it. His concert Steinway was in the basement in the one soundproof room in the house, but when he opened the window, she could hear him from the pool, where she often spent afternoons, improving her swimming or trying to get interested in one of the books he wanted her to read. More often she lay on the chaise longue, remembering that she was overdue in writing to her mother, occasionally hearing the music, especially the thundering parts, which had an angry quality, like Crandon himself.

In his huge record collection, she found the recording of the movie background score for which he'd won his Academy Award. When he found her playing it, he stopped the record and took it off the turntable.

"I don't want you listening to this. I'm ashamed of it."

"But it's wonderful!" she protested.

"You don't know a damn thing about it! You wouldn't know good music from bad. When I tell you it's bad, it's bad!"

"I don't believe you. They wouldn't have given you an Oscar—"

"*They* don't know good from bad, any more than you do!" he exploded. "The Oscars are awarded *to* idiots *by* idiots. They're the biggest joke of all in an industry that is one colossal joke all by itself."

"If that's the way you feel about it, why did you accept it?"

"I didn't! My God, you don't think I'd stoop to attend an Academy Award presentation, do you? The producer of the film accepted the award on my behalf. Do you know what I did with it? I drove to Santa Monica and threw it off a pier into the ocean."

She gasped. But only for a moment did she find what he had done incredible. Then she realized that it would have been incredible if he hadn't done it.

"Someday they'll see," he said in a different tone. "Someday I'll be greater than Stravinsky."

The way he said it chilled her, and from that moment she thought she was beginning to understand him a little.

Like so much else, the matter of the sculpture of her came as a complete surprise.

The sculptor simply showed up at the house one day, ready to start. He was a middle-aged man named William Annesby. According to what Crandon told Tracy later that day, he was quite well known. By that time he'd made a sketch of her in a swimming suit. The sculpture was to be a nude.

"It would be absurd to do anything else," Crandon said. "Haven't I told you that your one claim to superiority is your body? You should be flattered that I'm having it immortalized in marble when you're at your peak. I'm sure you would never have thought of it yourself. For a movie star, you're surprisingly lacking in ego."

She wanted to please him, and he seemed sincere about wanting this sculpture done, and she could hardly claim not to have the time to pose for it. But she was reluctant. Still, once it was started, there was no walking out on it. The work was being done right on the grounds, in the guest house at the back of the garden, where there was a skylight. The marble was delivered there, and Annesby came every morning at ten to chip away at it for two hours. Tracy felt a certain prudery about posing nude at first, but she soon got over it. The sculptor was obviously untempted by her. She was glad, for she found Annesby as strange and uncommunicative in some ways as her husband.

Though it didn't make sense, she soon began to feel that for some perverse reason Crandon hoped to catch her in a compromising situation with the sculptor. Occasionally he would suddenly open the door and walk in. Somehow she found it embarrassing for him to stand there watching while the work proceeded, and she found increasing unease in seeing the marble slowly forming into a cold white replica of her.

Still, there was a positive aspect. At least she was doing something constructive during the hours she posed. The rest of the day was stagnant. Crandon didn't even want her going off to the movies. He said she'd seen enough terrible movies in the past to last anyone a lifetime.

Then there were the evenings and the nights. After dinner Crandon would put on records, very often Stravinsky, and ask her to identify the music. Was that from "Petrushka" or "The Rite of Spring" or "The Firebird"? After a while she was right most of the time, and at least that pleased him. He talked about ballets, operas, and classical literature. It was always he who talked, she who listened. Sometimes she wanted to scream. Eventually she couldn't endure it without the brandy.

252

There was increasing darkness in his lovemaking. He was as unpredictable about coming to her bed as he was about what he expected her to do in it. She wavered in her feelings about it. Sometimes she lay awake yearning for him to open that connecting door and come to her, even if she didn't know whether to expect tenderness or abuse from him. At other times, particularly when he approached sex with her like a rutting animal, she dreaded it.

She felt more and more brutalized by him, and it filled her with a combination of excitement and fear. She compared him with Cliff. Cliff, the decidedly nonintellectual studio grip, had treated her with gentleness, respect, and consideration when he'd made love to her. He'd adored her body, not punished it. And he'd satisfied her physically if not emotionally.

Crandon, the intellectual composer, also satisfied her physically, but only part of the time, and certainly didn't fulfill her emotionally. He claimed that he respected the beauty of her body, yet sometimes he acted in bed as if he would like nothing more than to destroy it. She didn't understand, and she didn't know how to talk to him about it.

The climax came one night when he came to her, roughly entered her without preliminaries, then suddenly withdrew from her in the middle of the act, slapping her face so sharply that she cried out. He was on his way back to his room before she could get her breath back. "You were thinking about someone else!" he flung back over his shoulder.

"I wasn't, I wasn't!" she cried out, but he slammed the door on her and didn't come back, and he was even more sullen than usual with her the next morning. She said nothing about it and neither did he. She knew it was useless.

The day after the sculpture was finished, Crandon had it moved into the garden.

"It belongs out in the open," he said, "for the whole world to see what Tracy Gordon's body is like."

That day she decided she couldn't stand it any longer. "I'm going to leave you," she announced.

"I've been wondering when you'd decide that," he said tonelessly. "Our ten months together seem more like ten years, don't they?"

"It would be nice to think that wanting to do me over wasn't the only reason you married me," she said.

"It would be useless to try to analyze it at this point. When you get a little older, you'll see that you have to put some time between something that happens and thinking about why it happened before you know what was right or wrong about it."

"I hope that when I'm a little older, I won't make mistakes like our marriage."

He smiled sourly. "You'll always make mistakes like our marriage."

She was packed and gone before the end of the day. She moved into a hotel for a while, and then she found a small house set against a rocky slope in Coldwater Canyon that suited her. Word came from Crandon's lawyer that there would be no contesting of the divorce proceedings. She resolved that she would never marry again.

39

Mike came out from the ocean after his second long swim of the afternoon. Mona had joined him the first time, but this time she'd declined. She was up in the beach house with Pen. Pen was one of the few women Mona liked.

Howard was sitting on the sun deck with Dalton; Robert Erickson, the newspaper publisher; and Aster Bigelow, the Hollywood columnist whom Mike, like so many others, hypocritically pretended to like.

Mike didn't feel like joining them again yet, so he lay down in the sand with his face up to the sun. He was deeply tanned and looked good. He also felt good, because, except for his insecurity about Mona, his life was good.

That was because his career was going well. He'd made six pictures in the three years since he'd returned from the service, and four had turned out well. He'd achieved stardom, and he now had the fan mail, the salary, the special privileges at the studio, and the possessions to prove it. The latter included a maroon Cadillac convertible coupe with a white top, and an elaborate new six-room garden apartment in Brentwood presided over by a fastidious Japanese-American valet.

His agent, Emory Deems, said they would negotiate a new contract for five thousand a week when option time came up again in a few months. Mike was making four thousand now, but certainly he warranted five, in view of the tremendous financial success of *Lisa* in 1947 and the equally fine box office returns from *The Men on Her Mind,* Mike's second co-starring picture with Mona, the following year.

Lisa had removed any doubts that Mike had reached full-fledged stardom, and it had meant even more for Mona. The picture's commer-

254

cial success had positioned her as the studio's top attraction at the box office and had provided a new type of role for her that she'd repeated with great success in *The Men on Her Mind* and would repeat in her next co-starring picture with Mike, *Affair in Rio*. Mona's "good-bad" girl always got slapped around by the man she loved but pretended to hate, a man who didn't find out until the last scene that her "badness" was only pretense and a shield against being hurt.

Mike had gotten Mona at the end of *Lisa* and *The Men on Her Mind,* of course, but the agonizing question persisted of whether he would get her in life. Her divorce had been finalized six months ago, and they'd been lovers ever since. But he was disturbingly aware that he wasn't the only one she was favoring in bed since she'd won her freedom. And she'd repeatedly refused to marry him.

"We're just good friends, that's all," she kept saying every time he insisted that she loved him as much as he loved her, if she would only let herself see it. "I don't want to be in love anyway," she'd also said. "I just want to keep on being a star."

In what pundits of the industry were calling "the new era of the female star," Mona ranked with the loftiest of the new breed of love goddesses gracing the screen. Mike envied Mona because she was a bigger star than he was, but his love exceeded his envy, and he was glad the studio kept teaming them. What he hated was that she was seeing several men right now. He was fiercely jealous of them, and it was difficult for him not to show it. But he was perfectly aware of how delicate the balance was. Until he could make her see that she loved him, he would just have to try to be as rational about the situation as he could. But sometimes he didn't think he could stand the wait much longer without bursting. Not having her was the only thing wrong with his life, but it was a very big thing.

Mike heard someone coming through the sand. He propped himself up and turned. It was Mona, carrying two pillows. She threw them down beside him and sank down on one of them. She was wearing a white sun dress and white sandals. She also wore a big white cartwheel hat to protect her face. Her delicate skin didn't take kindly to the sun.

"The other pillow is for Pen. She's coming down with drinks for us in a minute. We thought you looked lonely down here."

"I was, but only for you. When are you going to marry me?"

"Never. So stop asking me."

"How can I when I love you so much? You're lucky I didn't tell you I loved you when you were still married, because I did, and you knew I did."

"You didn't and don't."

"I've only loved you for seven years, that's all. Only since when we were in the studio's acting school together."

She laughed. "Ridiculous."

"All right, I've loved you off and on for seven years, but mostly on."

"Mostly off. And don't think you're ever going to find any love in me, so stop looking for it. Besides, you don't love me—you just want me. I'm not going to upset the balance of our happy relationship by letting this get more serious than it should."

He was about to protest, but at that moment Pen arrived, bearing three frosted Tom Collinses on a tray. She sat down on the other pillow, and they sipped at their drinks. Pen looked radiant, Mike thought. She and Howard were still as preoccupied with each other as newlyweds, although they'd been married since the fall of 1945 when Howard and Georgina's divorce had become final.

"I think we ought to finish these drinks," Pen said, "and then go up and give Howard some support with the others."

"I suppose so," Mona said, "but I dread it. I never feel at ease with Dalton."

"Who does?" Mike said. "Not even Howard anymore. I think he's the only one who was ever close to him."

"I feel sorry for Mr. Dalton," Pen said. "All that power and wealth, yet he's unhappy, and he's shut everyone out of his life. There he is, all alone in one of the biggest castles in Beverly Hills. Howard wasn't surprised when his wife left him and went East to live, but I was. Good heavens, they'd been together more than thirty years."

"It didn't surprise me," Mona said. "When people no longer find life bearable with each other, what can they do but separate? It doesn't matter whether it's in the fourth or fortieth year of marriage. The end is the end."

"That's one way of looking at it, I suppose," Pen said.

"Mona's going to marry me," Mike said, "and we're going to find life together eternally bearable."

"Wonderful," said Pen, smiling.

"He's absolutely silly," Mona said. She half turned to look up at the house. "Look, Howard's coming."

Mike turned. Howard was approaching quickly. When he reached them, he said, "I need assistance. They're about to eat me alive up there."

Mona laughed. "That's what you get for inviting such guests. Bigelow is a true bitch. I think it's stupid the way everybody kowtows

256

to her because they're afraid of her. If she ever says anything horrible about me in her column, I'll sue her."

"In the meantime," Howard said, smiling, "will the three of you act like nice ladies and gentlemen and go up there and face the music with me?"

They went up to the deck, where the talk soon turned to what television might or might not do to Hollywood if it continued to grow. Dalton insisted that nothing would replace movies as the world's most popular form of entertainment. Aster Bigelow and her publisher argued that the movie industry was shrinking, and if the invasion of television into the American home wasn't primarily behind it, what was? It was all shop talk, and Mike listened idly. He had Mona, and only Mona, on his mind.

Mike started to dial Mona's number but hung up before he was finished. Phoning her was never satisfactory. She would probably tell him that she was busy and couldn't see him tonight, and he didn't want to hear that again.

He left his apartment, got into his car, and drove as fast as the law allowed to her house on the crest of a hill at the end of a winding road. She owned a Moorish castle in a particularly choice location in Beverly Hills. It had been built by a famous director of silents and abandoned by him when, in the early sound era, Hollywood had abandoned him. A succession of owners had followed, and Mona and her husband had bought the place the last year of the war, when prices were still down, and it had gone to her as part of the divorce settlement. The lofty estate looked down superciliously on Los Angeles.

There was a gate at the entrance, but it was open, so Mike drove right on up the long driveway under a canopy of treetops to the courtyard. There was a light on in every room, but the house still conveyed the feeling that no one lived there. Perhaps it was because the fountain in the courtyard, regulated to send up jets of water in changing patterns, was now still.

Mona's protective butler said he would see if Miss Gaillard was in, but Mike didn't intend being put off, and he brushed past the helpless servant and called Mona's name loudly. She appeared at the top of the staircase in a lime evening dress. He bounded up.

"What is this, an invasion?" she asked.

"Yes. I'm not leaving until you say you'll marry me."

"I'm not going to say that. But you'll have to leave anyway. I'm going out to dinner."

"Call him up and tell him you can't make it."

"I'll do nothing of the kind." She turned and started walking away from him. "If you won't leave, then I'm going to ignore you."

He followed her into her bedroom. It was a very feminine room, with satin coverings on the chairs and chiffon draperies at the windows. She sat down at a white dressing table and started brushing her hair, just as if he weren't there.

Mike said, "As I said before, I like your house, and I'm willing to give up my apartment and move in here with you. But this room is too feminine for me."

She didn't answer.

"You'd better talk, Mona. And you'd better call that guy and tell him you can't make it tonight. Otherwise, there's going to be a scene."

She put down the hairbrush and looked at him in the mirror.

"Mike, even if I loved you, I wouldn't marry you. Right now I feel as if I don't ever want to be married again. The last few years with Stewart were unendurable. He wouldn't let me go—"

"What happened between you and him," Mike interrupted, "has nothing to do with what happens between you and me."

"But you don't understand me. I didn't love Stewart, either. I needed his strength in the beginning, and that's why I stayed with him. But when I didn't need him anymore, I wanted to be free of him. It took years to get rid of him, but I was determined. That's the kind of woman I am."

"You won't want to get rid of me."

She smiled. "I remember that when I was a child, I thought things happened in life as they did in fairy tales. I thought I was Sleeping Beauty and that someday my prince would come."

"Well, here I am."

"Don't make a joke of it, Mike. I wish I still believed in fairy tales. But I don't, and I don't believe in love. I only believe in passion."

"I believe in that, too."

"Love is only a dream, and you wake up quickly from it," she said. "Passion passes just as quickly. Passion changes into contempt and then hatred. Is that what you want for you and me?"

"Mona, you're so very wrong." He moved up behind her and put his hands on her shoulders. She trembled a little under his touch. He leaned down and pressed his face against her hair as they looked at each other in the mirror. "We're going to be great lovers, Mona. I promise you we'll turn life into a wonderful dream that will last forever."

She closed her eyes and turned her face to his, and he knew that at last she was going to marry him.

258

40

Tracy Gordon had entered a period of her life in which she was known as "the fun girl of Hollywood." Aster Bigelow coined the name in her column. "Tracy Gordon," wrote Aster, "can be found in Chasen's, Romanoff's, Ciro's, the Mocambo, or *all* of them just about every night of the week, and often takes off for a private party after the clubs close and stays until dawn."

The story was partly true. What wasn't true was the "just about every night of the week." It was more likely to be one or two nights a week, when nobody was due to drop in at Tracy's little house in Coldwater Canyon. If she didn't want to be alone, she would try to round up the "gang" for an outing. The gang consisted of Laurette, Dick, Gail, Bonnie, Roy, Frank, and Mel. Bonnie was under contract at Paramount, but wasn't even on the edge of stardom yet. Gail had been under contract at Universal, had been dropped at her last option time, and was now free-lancing. Neither Laurette nor any of the four men had ever been more than an extra, but they all had their dreams.

Tracy had joined the gang through Bonnie, whom she'd met when Bonnie had been borrowed for a supporting role in *Love on the Loose*. Bonnie turned out to be the best friend Tracy had found in Hollywood since she'd moved out of the Hollywood Studio Club three years earlier. It was strange that although Bonnie was the one around whom the others had clustered to form the group, Tracy was its leader. No one was more surprised than Tracy to find herself leading after always having been led. Bonnie didn't resent relinquishing her position. "We all love you, Tracy," she asserted. "You don't make any demands on us except to be ourselves."

Tracy was grateful that the gang made no demands on *her* except to be herself. They didn't expect her to be witty or brilliant, any more than she expected those qualities from them.

In that sense, Tracy was the "fun girl" that Aster Bigelow had tagged her, a term that caught on and stuck, not at all to the studio's displeasure. But Tracy wasn't nearly the drinker she was reputed to be. It was true that she drank a good deal when she was doing the nightclubbing that got her so much publicity in the columns. But it wasn't true that she began her day with whiskey sours and then guzzled away the rest of it until it was time to go out and do the town again. Neither was it true that she was going to bed with all four of the men in the gang (in rotation, one wag had it) and a lot of other Hollywood men-about-town. The gang got a laugh out of that kind of talk. As Roy said, "Any of us having sex together would be incest."

Tracy occasionally did go to bed with someone, usually some physically compelling type she met at one or another of the Hollywood parties to which she was invited with increasing frequency. Sometimes these sexual encounters were satisfying enough to repeat, but more often they were not. One man even told her contemptuously that she was frigid but didn't seem to know it.

That wasn't true, but she didn't try to explain it, for she didn't intend to see him again. The truth was that she simply didn't like the man, so she was stiff in bed with him. That wasn't her only unsatisfying sexual experience. She recognized that she needed sexual release for contentment, but casual encounters weren't the answer. For any degree of satisfaction, she had to feel a bond with the man she was in bed with. Tenuous as her bond had been with Cliff, she now realized that it had been the main foundation of her satisfaction with him. And despite her problems with Crandon, there'd been a bond between them that had made even his brutal attentions more satisfying than those of a stranger in her bed.

She couldn't forget that what she really wanted was a bond with Howard Stanton. She saw very little of him—although she was now invited to parties at the Stantons' occasionally and was rather reluctantly getting to know Penelope Stanton a little—but she would be seeing him daily soon. They were to do another picture together, another screwball comedy that would attempt—Dalton and Renfew told her—to outstrip the great success of *Love on the Loose* a year earlier and capitalize on her new-found ability as a "natural comedienne," as reviewers had hailed her.

Shortly before beginning that picture, Tracy granted an interview to a writer for a women's magazine, hoping to dispel some of the wild stories about her that were getting into print. She answered the woman's questions honestly, but what came out in the magazine was a series of distortions as exaggerated as Aster Bigelow's, prefaced by the observation that the decor of Tracy's house—filled with ranch furniture and bright Navajo rugs and hangings, with red the predominating color—was, in the author's view, probably a rebellion

260

against her drab childhood in Georgia. The article concluded that the antics of Tracy Gordon, the fun girl of Hollywood, and her gang were an indication that Hollywood, after almost two decades of Depression, war, and postwar adjustment, was at last returning to "normal" and predicted that Tracy would one day outdo those movie queens of the golden age of the nineteen twenties who bathed in champagne, wore ermine swimming suits, and dyed their poodles' hair to match their own.

Dalton called her to his office to congratulate her on the article and to tell her that Fox wanted to negotiate a deal to borrow her for a picture with Tyrone Power. It all showed what a big star she was getting to be, but she was miserable. She kept thinking how humiliated her mother must be by that magazine article. She decided she would never give an interview again if she could avoid it.

Wesley Rainer was noted for hopping in and out of Hollywood, although he had nothing to do with making or financing movies. He was noted for hopping in and out of other places, too, and for his conquests of beautiful women all over the world. So far he'd married only one of them and had presumably settled a million on her when they were divorced. He was reputed to be among the ten richest men in the world, but nobody could be sure of that or of much else about him, even the lieutenants who helped him manipulate his holdings. He was as secretive as he was eccentric.

Tracy met him at the Mocambo the night she was celebrating with the gang the completion of her second picture with Howard Stanton. The party was their idea, not hers. After having seen Howard on the set almost every day for weeks, she certainly didn't feel like celebrating the fact that she wouldn't be seeing much of him in the months ahead.

When Wesley Rainer walked in with two other men and sat down nearby, Bonnie sighed extravagantly.

"Wow!" she said. "There's my cup of tea. Both rich and beautiful!"

Roy made the observation that he looked different from his newspaper pictures.

"He's always scowling in those because he wants to kill the photographer." Bonnie looked at Tracy. "What do you think of him?"

"I don't know," Tracy said, although she'd already noted that he was attractive. Later, when he came over and asked her to dance, she learned that the two men with him weren't companions but bodyguards.

"Do you think anybody would try to harm you here?" she asked.

"I can imagine a kidnapping anywhere," he said.

If his fortune was indeed a hundred million, as one of the gang had said, then she supposed the possibility of his being kidnapped did pose a constant problem.

"I heard I could catch you at one of the clubs," he went on. "That's why I'm here. I'm not a nightclubber ordinarily."

"I don't think I am, either, at heart."

"Then why are you known as the fun girl of Hollywood?"

"It's just a name Aster Bigelow gave me, and it stuck. It's only a little bit true."

"I hate columnists even more than I do the rest of the press. Bastards and bitches, all of them." He paused. "When are you going to start seeing me? How about tomorrow morning at ten? We could fly to Palm Springs. Or Hawaii?"

"Aren't you going a little fast? We just met ten minutes ago."

"I'm going after you. I intend to marry you."

She laughed.

"I'm deadly serious," he said. "You'll see."

She began to see the next morning, when the floral offerings began arriving. He himself arrived early in the afternoon, complete with bodyguards who waited outside in the dark gray Packard limousine while he tried to give her an emerald bracelet.

"This is ridiculous," she said, refusing even to let him put the bracelet on her.

"No, *this* is ridiculous," he said, referring to her little house, amazed that she lived in such simple surroundings, with only her Mexican girl, Maria, to help her. He thought she should be living in the Beverly Wilshire.

"What I like is being myself," she said, "and the Beverly Wilshire has nothing to do with that."

"We'll probably live in Bel Air after we're married."

"You don't want to marry me. You just want to go to bed with me."

"Naturally I want to go to bed with you, but I want to marry you, too."

"I really doubt that," she said. "I've got a feeling it's the chase, not the quarry, that interests you. If I went to bed with you right now, I'd never see you again."

"Try me."

"No."

"Then you *want* me to chase you before we go to bed."

"No again. And please don't try to make this any more complex than I'm going to let it be."

They were an immediate "item" in Aster Bigelow's column. According to the columnist, "the Tracy Gordon–Wesley Rainer romance is the hottest in Hollywood." When Aster Bigelow phoned Tracy about it, asking for a comment, Tracy said stiffly, "I have nothing to say," and hung up.

That caused trouble. Aster Bigelow complained to Regency Pictures that Tracy Gordon was being "uncooperative" and reminded Dalton that Tracy might just not be as big a star as she was today if Aster hadn't given her so many plugs along the way. Dalton called Tracy to his office to remind her that it was getting harder and harder to get people away from their television sets and back into movie theaters, that "selling" pictures through personal publicity about the stars was more important than ever. Dalton was delighted that Tracy and Wesley Rainer were an item. So why not get all the publicity possible out of it? It would not only help Regency Pictures; it would also help Tracy Gordon.

"I don't see how," Tracy said, and she refused to give Aster Bigelow the special interview she wanted about "the affair," as she was now blatantly calling it in her column.

It wasn't an affair. It continued to be a chase, although Tracy asked herself, and Wes, what they really had to talk about after their first few evenings together. She wasn't the least bit interested in the ins and outs of his financial empire, which was his major preoccupation during the moments he wasn't with her, and he wasn't the least bit interested in the movie business.

"It doesn't matter," he said when she pointed that out to him. "Most wives don't give a damn about their husbands' business interests anyway. As for my not caring about the movie business, you won't either, after we're married."

She couldn't help being reminded of Crandon. "I'm never going to get married again. Besides, only a fool would marry you. You consider people your possessions. I've seen how you are with your bodyguards and the others who work for you. You like the idea of owning people, and I don't want to be owned."

"You're talking nonsense," he said, but he frowned, and she knew she'd hit upon a fundamental truth about him.

He kept after her. He didn't like the gang, and acted like a stiff visiting diplomat when he was forced to be around them, resenting the time she continued to devote to them. Periodically he showed up with more jewelry for her, presenting a variety of rings, earrings, bracelets, and necklaces loaded with diamonds, rubies, sapphires, and pearls. She refused them as promptly as she had the emerald bracelet he'd tried to give her the day after they'd first met. He said he would accumulate them all in a bank vault for the time when she finally consented to marry him.

There was a Ferrari, too. She emerged one day and found it sitting

263

out in front of her house, blocking her recently purchased new blue Buick convertible. The rakish Italian car was bright yellow and sleekly beautiful, and she had difficulty returning it to Wes because the ownership papers were in her name.

Then there was the house in Palm Springs. Wes said he wanted to fly her to the desert to show her a new place he'd bought there, and she suspected before they took off that the property was for her.

It was. It was a small adobe house with a tiled roof, surrounded by palms, with a swimming pool in back almost as large as the floor area of the house itself.

"You'll have to use a lawyer to return this to me," Wes said.

"Why do you do it?" Tracy said. "You know I won't accept it."

"I don't give up."

That day, six weeks after they had met, when according to the latest releases from Aster Bigelow the "hot" romance had begun to cool, they finally went to bed.

"What are you thinking about, Tracy?" Wes asked.

Tracy looked over at him. It was the first time she'd looked at him since he'd gotten out of bed perhaps ten minutes earlier. Not a word had been said until now. He looked awkward sitting on the small bedroom chair beside the vanity: he was too tall for the chair and too tall for the low ceilings of the little house.

"I'm thinking your chest is hairier than I expected."

"What were you thinking about before I asked you what you were thinking? What were you thinking about during the ten minutes you lay there looking at the ceiling after I got out of bed? That I was a good fuck? That I was a bad fuck?"

"I was thinking about it, but I wasn't thinking about it that way."

"Don't kid me, Tracy. You don't think about sex in terms of lovemaking. You think about it in terms of fucking."

"I'd think about it in terms of lovemaking if there were love involved."

"All right, we'll talk about it in terms of fucking. What did you think of it? Did you compare it with your other fucking? Was I good or bad?"

"There were moments when you frightened me."

"What does that mean? Good or bad? Come on, Tracy."

"I don't understand this, Wes. People don't talk like this about it afterward."

"I don't do a lot of things other people do. How did I frighten you?"

"You were too rough at times." She thought of Crandon, who'd also been rough sometimes. "I thought you were going to hit me. Or slap me. I don't know. You seemed to want to pound me into the bed."

264

"You like it rough. You like to be fucked by someone who really fucks. It's an art, of course, knowing how to fuck and knowing how to be fucked. We're both artists at it, me giving, you receiving. You quivered and shook with ecstasy, Tracy. You moaned and groaned. Every juice in your body flowed."

She remembered that Crandon had said things like that in the beginning, too. It was true that she felt wild abandon in some sexual situations. She sometimes wondered if it was a kind of delayed response to her prudish attitude toward sex when she was younger. It was hard to explain, just as it was hard to explain why she was beginning to feel a bond with Wes while she was resisting it.

"You're beautiful, Tracy," Wes went on. "Your body is luscious. I don't think I could ever get bored with you. That's a rash statement, I know. But I think I really believe it. I'm looking forward to our marriage. You'll give up the movies then, and that will make things a lot better. I don't like it that you're a movie star, because the world's attention is on you, and that distracts your attention from me. But after you marry me, you won't want to be a movie star anymore anyway."

"Even if I were going to marry you, which I'm not, I don't know that I wouldn't want to be a movie star anymore. I'm not sure I want to be one now, so marrying you or not doesn't really have anything to do with it."

"You're too young to know what you want."

"I don't think age has much to do with how you feel. Maybe with how you think, but not necessarily with how you feel. Besides, I don't think you really want to marry me, Wes. Why should you? You don't love me, any more than I love you."

"I don't believe in love the way you're talking about it, and I don't think you do, either. Strong and independent persons can only love themselves."

"I'd hate to think that was true," Tracy said.

"You like to believe in love, because that's what ordinary people are brought up to believe in. Love, marriage, family, God. But you're not ordinary, and someday you won't believe in any of it."

"You're wrong. And I know that if I said I'd marry you, you'd no longer be interested."

"Now you're wrong. I want you, and I know I'm going to keep on wanting you. Getting you to bed has only confirmed it. Sex can be disappointing, Tracy, but it isn't with you, and I don't think you were disappointed with me." He rose and walked over to her. "We've talked enough for now."

He sat down on the bed beside her. He took her hand, raised it, and

265

kissed the palm. He held it against his face. Then he spread her legs and knelt between her thighs and buried his face there.

They spent four days together at the Palm Springs house. Three bodyguards watched outside, sleeping in shifts in the adobe cabaña out back beside the swimming pool.

The bodyguards didn't go out once, even for meals. They ate in the kitchen, while Tracy and Wes ate in the small dining room. Tracy said she felt as if they were in hiding from the police.

"We're only hiding from the world," Wes said.

He enjoyed hiding; he liked being the eccentric recluse that the press had portrayed. But the world was feeling his impact even now. During those four days in Palm Springs, he was on the phone much of the time, making decisions and giving orders to his associates throughout the world, manipulating the huge business empire he controlled. She soon confirmed that business was more exciting to him than anything else in his life.

Then one morning he told her he had to leave that day for urgent business in London. He wanted her to come along and marry him in England. No, she said. He was patiently not angry. He flew her back to Hollywood and told her that he was going to keep after her until she married him if it took ten years.

The next day, others besides Wes's bodyguards knew they'd spent four days together at Palm Springs. Aster Bigelow reported it in her column. She also reported that Tracy Gordon had instituted legal proceedings to return to Wesley Rainer the small Palm Springs estate he'd "gifted her with to celebrate their union." It looked, said Aster Bigelow, as if the fire fanning Hollywood's love match of the year had been doused.

41

The economic state of Hollywood declined drastically between the peak years at the end of the Second World War and the early nineteen fifties, with disheartening effects on many lives, although many die-hards such as Augustus Dalton refused to face facts. He kept saying that Hollywood's troubles were only temporary and that someday all would be as it had been.

Some Hollywood columnists, trying to buoy sinking spirits, took the same Pollyannish attitude and reported only positive matters to the public. But Aster Bigelow told the dismal truth quite often. Between accountings of the latest liaisons, marriages, and divorces of the illustrious, she reported in 1950 that only thirty-five million persons were attending the movies every week in the United States nowadays as against ninety million a week just five years before.

The next year, the columnist did a special series documenting the low state to which Hollywood's economic health had plummeted. Risking—and incurring—Augustus Dalton's enmity, she used the shaky condition of Regency Pictures to illustrate her points.

In 1951 Regency Pictures had cut its administrative staff to half the figure for 1945 and was producing half as many pictures. It had pared its contract players' list to a third of its size in the days of glory. And although the pictures of its top stars—Mona Gaillard, Michael Baines, Howard Stanton, and Tracy Gordon—still made money, for the most part, the studio had more flops than successes, and the flops were big ones.

Budget cuts had eliminated the studio acting school in 1949, but there were few newcomers to attend it anyway. Furthermore, the formerly bustling writers' building was almost unoccupied these days, and the producers' and directors' building had many empty offices.

The woes of Regency Pictures in recent years had begun with the strike by union members in 1945 that had crippled production, Aster Bigelow told her readers. More bad luck had followed in 1947 from bad publicity engendered when two Regency writers and a producer were called to testify before the House Un-American Activities Committee on the infiltration of communism into Hollywood. As a postscript, the deceased Regency star Timothy Briggs had unknowingly promoted the interests of a Communist front organization in his association with the Anti-Nazi League before the war.

Yes, Regency Pictures had definitely had its troubles, Aster Bigelow concluded in her merciless summation of its vicissitudes in the last half decade. And who knew if the new production chief, Dean Ainsley, would be able to pull the studio out of its financial and artistic quagmire? Ainsley, formerly an executive producer at Superior Pictures, had been hired to replace Alexander Renfew, eliminated in a power squeeze by Nicholas Smetley and Augustus Dalton on the charge that

267

Renfew's misjudgments were the basic cause of Regency Pictures' failures in recent years.

But there were many, stated the columnist, who felt that it was Augustus Dalton's inability to meet properly the challenges of changing times that was really at the root of Regency Pictures' troubles. (It was this observation, more than all the rest, that caused Dalton to order Aster Bigelow permanently barred from the lot and to decline to speak to her publisher ever again.)

And now it was rumored, Miss Bigelow concluded in her last piece on the subject, that the intractable Augustus Dalton wasn't exactly seeing eye to eye with Dean Ainsley on his aggressive ideas for raising the studio from its ashes. Would there be a power showdown between them in the next few crucial years?

Toward the end of their second year of marriage, Mike surprised Mona with the new house. It was a white eyrie built high on a mountainside in Pacific Palisades, approached by a twisting white driveway through a grove of trees, shrubs, and flowers carpeting the precipitous estate. It was a dramatically designed house with sharp lines, great expanses of glass, cantilevered balconies, and rooms dipping down from one to another on various levels. There was no trace in it of the Spanish, Moorish, Tudor, Mediterranean, or other foreign influences that pervaded movie colony architecture. If anyone had influenced the architect, it was Frank Lloyd Wright.

The estate commanded an incredible view. It looked down on the city, the ocean, and the world. The glittering sight that spread below at night was staggering.

The house was under construction for four months. It was amazing that in a town where few secrets were kept long, someone didn't tell Mona about it. But she wasn't only surprised, she was aghast on that Sunday when Mike drove her up and said, "Here's our new house."

"Mike, why did you do this without telling me?" She was frowning. Perhaps the most beautiful view in Southern California was spread before her from the living room window, but she didn't seem to see it.

"To surprise you."

"I'm surprised," she said coldly. "And shocked that you'd do something like this without consulting me."

"I was so sure you'd like it," he said, trying not to sound as depressed as he felt. He hadn't dreamed she would react this way. "I left choosing the furniture to you," he went on awkwardly. He looked anxiously around the large empty room. It probably did look cold and uninviting this way.

"Mike, you've made a terrible mistake. I couldn't live here. I can only live in my house."

"That's stupid, Mona. You lived somewhere else before you lived there, didn't you?"

"Of course. But that's the first house that's been *mine*. It's no use trying to explain. You wouldn't understand."

"No, I don't understand. We're married. Why do you speak of *your* house? Why isn't it *our* house?"

"Because it isn't. Not any more than this house is. Mike, don't try to make out that we're just an ordinary married couple."

"I wouldn't dream of it. I wouldn't even want us to be an ordinary married couple. But I don't want us so different that it doesn't seem as if we're married at all."

"What you'd really like to be is lord and master, wouldn't you? Building this house without my knowledge was one way of trying to establish your authority. Mike, you've known from the beginning that I won't be ruled."

"You've completely distorted my motive for building this house." But he wondered if she wasn't partly right, although he certainly hadn't looked at it from that angle until now. "I built it because I love you," he went on after a moment.

She seemed suddenly on the verge of tears. She moved into his arms and pressed her face against his. "I know you love me. But I can't live in this house."

He decided not to press the matter of the house, telling himself that eventually it would take care of itself. In the meantime he drove up alone once a week and stood in the living room and looked out at the stunning view below him and thought about the time when he and Mona would live there together. One week he found that vandals had broken one of the sweeping walls of glass. He had a servant's bedroom furnished then and installed a caretaker to look after the empty house and the grounds.

He said nothing about any of it to Mona, and she didn't bring up the matter of the house again. It was as if she'd suppressed any knowledge that the house existed. Sometimes she was like that; she wouldn't let herself think about or even acknowledge the existence of things that disturbed her.

The longer they were married, the less he seemed to know her. There seemed nothing left at all of the Mona Gaillard who had come from a small town in Pennsylvania, where her aging father still lived, largely ignored by her. She never mentioned her first husband anymore. Her past seemed to have vanished absolutely and irretrievably. She was a product of the present, of what Hollywood had made of her. She was Mona Gaillard, love goddess supreme. Her identity as Mrs. Michael Baines seemed altogether obscured most of the time, and that hurt Mike.

Yet she seemed content enough with their life together. She was interested in books, music, and movies, as he was, and in keeping herself healthy and beautiful, and she never turned him away when he desired her, as he did often. She even sought him out occasionally by suddenly approaching him, when he was reading, for instance, and leaning down to arouse him with her lips, her hands, and the view of cleavage between her perfect breasts. She was passionate and seemed to relish their sexual relationship as much as he did. They did everything sexual that was possible and left no parts of each other's bodies untouched, and they reached incredible peaks of ecstasy together in bed. That part was perfect.

What wasn't perfect was her attitude about the house he'd built for them and his feeling that she didn't think of their union as a marriage but as a love affair, to be enjoyed but not taken too seriously, for how long could it be expected to last anyhow?

It must last, he kept telling himself.

Mike was proud that Mona was the most beautiful woman at the party. It was a small party, as major Hollywood parties went those days, perhaps thirty guests, and Mona dominated it. She wore the coral evening gown that was her favorite costume from *Woman of Fire,* their most recent co-starring picture, and she talked brightly to the men surrounding her. Mike wasn't jealous of her admirers. He had her, and they didn't.

He talked a lot himself, going from group to group and interjecting himself, giving the impression that he was having a good time when he wasn't. He didn't talk as well as Mona did at these affairs. She talked as if she were following a script with good dialogue. She was always a star, wherever she went. He never saw her show the slightest sense of insecurity, except on those rare occasions when Tracy Gordon was at the same gathering.

Tracy was Mona's sorest spot. Mike wanted badly to do the new picture the studio had planned for him and Tracy, particularly because he'd worked well with her previously, but he'd turned it down because of Mona's displeasure. Thinking about that situation, he stopped moving from group to group and drank alone at the bar. He realized that he was getting drunk again and might make a fool of himself if he kept on, but he didn't stop.

When he and Mona left an hour later, she announced immediately that she would drive them home.

"I'm perfectly capable of driving us myself," he protested loudly.

"The only thing you're capable of in this condition is cracking us up. You can wreck yourself if you like, but I won't let you wreck me."

She was already behind the wheel. He went around unsteadily to the other side of the car and got in. She set off.

"All right, so I drank a little too much," he said. "I was bored. I'm restless. I'm itching to work. You know that. I think it was a mistake to turn down the picture with Tracy. I could see it if it were a bad script. But they'll just go out and borrow someone for it now, and with pictures harder to come by these days, it seems insane. Besides, it doesn't put me in a very favorable light at the studio."

"Do the picture if it means that much to you. I really don't care."

"But you do. It doesn't make much sense, either. Why should you consider Tracy a danger?"

"I don't, not in the tiniest way. I just don't like her, that's all."

He knew it was more than that. She really did consider Tracy a professional threat. He wished she considered her a threat to their marriage instead. But the thought would never occur to her. He hated it that it wouldn't. If she would ever feel the slightest jealousy over him, it would help.

Mike opened the door between their bedrooms. He was naked and so was Mona. She lay stretched across her big round bed, her loose hair covering her breasts, her hands folded over her pubic region, as though in modesty. The room was filled with moonlight. Mona didn't stir, but he didn't think she was asleep. He'd had a feeling she wanted him now, right now, and was waiting for him. He was usually right about such feelings.

He crossed the big room and stood at the edge of the bed. She didn't move. He looked down at her, thinking how beautiful she was, how much he loved her; wishing she would open her eyes and tell him she loved him.

She opened her eyes, but she said nothing. He sat down on the bed. She extended a hand. He took it and pressed it against his face and kissed it. He lay down beside her, just wanting to hold her awhile first, but she turned and pressed against him and kissed him the way he often kissed her. She kissed his closed eyelids, the lobe of an ear, the tip of his nose, the side of his neck, finally his lips. There was desire in it, though that was all. He always hoped for something more, but she never gave it.

271

She turned around on the bed and took his penis into her mouth while he kissed the lips of her vagina and tongued her. They came almost simultaneously, and then rested for a while, and then he entered her and took deep strokes in her. As usual, she seemed to come endlessly while he was building, and he had another powerful climax. He always came copiously with her, even if they'd finished only a half hour before, and he attributed that to the continuing high pitch of passion they generated in each other.

They lay back to rest again, and she said, "We're beautiful."

"You're beautiful. I'm merely handsome."

"We're beautiful. All over. That's why sex is so wonderful between us. Most people have terrible bodies. How can they make love with each other?" She paused and then said in a strange tone, "We mustn't lose it. It mustn't change."

What was wrong with her? Surely she didn't think the success of their marriage rested just on sex? He hated the idea of that.

But he said, "It won't change."

Mona had never looked paler in her life than she did when she told him.

"How wonderful!" Mike said. He meant that, yet he wasn't completely, unqualifiedly happy, as men were supposed to be when they learned they were to be fathers. Then he knew why. It was because Mona wasn't unqualifiedly happy herself. She was frightened.

"I don't know how I really feel about this, Mike. I just know that I have a sinking feeling."

"Maybe most women do," he said uncertainly.

"Most women *don't,* and that's what frightens me. I don't know that I want a baby. The thought of having it appalls me, and the thought of looking bad for at least four months appalls me. I don't think stars should have babies."

"Of course they should."

"You ought to be a very happy father," she said grimly.

She became increasingly withdrawn and moody during her pregnancy, and she kept claiming, during the last months, illnesses that didn't exist. Her outlandishly expensive Beverly Hills obstetrician advised Mike repeatedly, when he made his anxious inquiries, that he could solve most of the problems simply by catering to her whims.

But it was hard to cater to Mona. She exploded the day Ainsley phoned and told her that Tracy had been given the picture Mona was scheduled to do next. She hung up, furious, in the middle of Ainsley's explanation that production couldn't be delayed for six months until she could return.

272

"I don't believe it!" she seethed. "That bitch talked them into it. She was dying for that role."

Mike couldn't persuade her otherwise, and he soon stopped trying. Mona would believe only what she wanted to believe.

In her sixth month of pregnancy, she stopped going out and refused to receive visitors. Mike was excluded from her bed months before it was necessary.

"What am I supposed to do for relief?" he asked angrily.

"Go back to whoever you were screwing before we got married," Mona said just as angrily.

He did exactly that. The girl's name was Janice. She was a secretary in a bank, without movie ambitions. She was the last of a series of similar pretty girls, and two pretty young men, Mike had involved himself with sexually but not romantically since his return from the war. He'd dropped Janice abruptly when Mona had agreed to marry him, but she held no grudges. In the tiny bedroom of her boxy little apartment, she writhed under him willingly that night. He saw her quite often after that, knowing from his previous experience with her that when it was time to walk out on her again, she wouldn't raise a fuss. He stopped seeing her a week before the baby was born.

Mike and Mona's baby girl was born on a beautiful morning in the spring of 1952. A perfect baby, the doctor said. Mike wanted to name her Mona, but they decided on Carolyn instead.

It didn't turn out as Mike had expected. From her past attitude, he certainly didn't expect Mona to be a loving mother. But she worshipped Carolyn with a consuming passion from the first moment she held the baby in her arms, and she was a perfect mother. To Mike's astonishment, she would have willingly given up her glittering stardom to stay home with the child if it had been at all practical.

Guiltily, after the first flush of excitement, Mike realized that he wasn't as drawn to the beautiful little baby as he should have been. Sitting with Mona beside the crib in the nursery while Mona sang lullabies to Carolyn, Mike soon became impatient. He would slip away, go downstairs, pour himself a drink, and wait for Mona. Sometimes he poured two or three or four before she appeared.

"Isn't our daughter the most beautiful child in the world?" she would say, and he would say, "Yes, yes, she is," and would feel guilty because he didn't love her as Mona did.

At times he blamed the baby for deepening the declension that had developed between him and Mona. They'd been lucky with their careers in the course of their marriage, for their pictures—together and starring with others—had been among the studio's top grossers in recent years. But their life together was disintegrating.

It had grown much worse since the baby's arrival. They didn't talk much and they'd stopped making love. Mona had yielded so reluctantly the first night Mike had gone to her after their long abstinence that it had ruined it for him. The most wonderful thing about their lovemaking before had been their total abandon with each other. That was gone, and with it their desire to go to bed together.

Their marriage was ending, and he often thought about what she'd said that time in Malibu when Pen had expressed surprise that Dalton's wife had left him after more than thirty years of marriage. Mona had said that when people no longer found life bearable together, what could they do but separate? "The end is the end," she'd said.

And now it was happening to them, wasn't it? Yet she said nothing about separation or divorce. Was she considering the effect a broken home might have on Carolyn?

He was terribly unhappy. He'd loved Mona so much, and what had it brought him but despair? Or had he really loved her? Had he instead just wanted to possess her? But he had never even done that. He doubted that anyone but her child would ever possess her.

He didn't see how they could continue living together this way, and he asked himself why he stayed on with her. Why didn't he move into the house in Pacific Palisades?

He went so far as to furnish another room in it, a bedroom, and he started taking Janice up there. But their encounters were a release only for his sexual tensions, not relief for his emotional distress. And Janice was certainly no substitute for Mona in any way. He wondered if anyone could be.

He finally allowed himself to face the fact that he did still love her, in spite of everything. What he really wanted was to find a way for them to make their marriage work again.

But then he found that Mona had a lover.

He began to suspect when he noticed that the servants—who were all her servants, and who remained wholly loyal to her—were giving him sly looks as he passed them. The new gardener's look was even more pointed than the others. It was a look of self-satisfied contempt.

Mike wasn't certain about it until he saw Mona come down from the quarters above the garage one afternoon. The gardener's room was up there.

Mike waited in the garden behind a tree. After a short while the man came down from the garage, crossed to the garden, and started raking. His name was Dino. He had an olive skin and curly black hair that

274

shone oilily in the sun. He had a crudely handsome face and a strong body.

Mike moved out from the tree and walked toward him. Dino seemed unsurprised. He stopped work and leaned on the rake handle, his mouth open in a small smile. Mike took out his wallet. There was almost five hundred dollars in it. He took the money out and extended it toward the man.

"Take it and get out," Mike said.

The man's smile expanded. "Why should I get out? You didn't hire me. Miss Gaillard did."

"I'm losing patience," Mike said.

Dino laughed. "I'm real scared." He reached out and accepted the money. "But I can use this right now." He dropped the rake and started toward his quarters above the garage, but he stopped and looked back at Mike. "I could beat you to a pulp, but it isn't worth it. I was going to leave anyway. I've got a better job offer."

He laughed and walked off, and Mike stormed into the house and bounded upstairs to the nursery, where Mona was with the baby. He grabbed Mona and shook her.

"You bitch! You had to fuck the gardener, didn't you?—and make me the laughingstock of this house!"

She stood back from him and looked at him with contempt. "You see how long love lasts, Mike? Not very long."

"I still love you," he said haltingly.

"How hard it is for you to say that."

"Yes, it's hard to say it, because you've made a fool of me."

"Why should it bother you that I find the gardener attractive? It doesn't bother me that you sleep with your sluts."

"I wouldn't sleep with anyone but you if you'd let me. You turned me away."

The contempt left her face. "That's true. What is it in me that made me turn you away, Mike? I don't understand it."

"I don't understand, either, but I'm willing to start over."

"Certainly you're too intelligent to think that's possible. We know too much about each other. The respect is gone. The romance is gone. This is today, not yesterday. We've got to go on to tomorrow."

"We will, together. Do you realize how long it's been since we've *talked*, Mona? But we're talking now, and we're saying things, and we'll work it out."

"It's over, Mike. I'm going to divorce you."

"You can try," Mike said bitterly, "but I'll fight you to the finish."

She nodded. "If that's the way you want it, then that's the way it will have to be. But something tells me you're going to give up long before that."

That night they went out together for the last time. They'd been invited to a party by Howard and Pen, and for them not to attend would have called for explanations neither of them cared to give.

It was a big party, and the house was crowded by the time they made their late arrival.

"But at least that Gordon bitch isn't here," Mona commented as she looked around.

"If there's something Tracy Gordon isn't, it's a bitch," Mike said.

Mona smiled coldly at him. "Have you entertained thoughts of asking her to be your next mate?"

Mike was about to snap back when Howard suddenly appeared. Mona smiled at him. "I see a lot of unfamiliar faces here, and I find that refreshing." She nodded toward the group with whom Pen was talking on the far side of the room. "They have the non-Hollywood look about them."

"They're all from England," Howard said. "Don't you recognize Truscott-Ames?"

"Of course she does," Mike said. "There's no mistaking the last great playboy of our time, is there?"

"I wasn't sure," Mona said. "I don't think he looks much like his pictures."

"That's because he isn't wearing his polo helmet for a change," Mike said.

"Supposedly he's one of the few really rich men left in England these days," Howard commented.

"And he's a real live peer," Mike said sourly. "That's a dying breed."

"I'm sure he's fascinating," Mona said. "Howard, will you take me over and introduce me?"

There was nothing Howard could do but comply. Mike went to the bar and asked for a straight Scotch. Then he had a second and a third as he watched his wife laugh and talk with Lord Clive Truscott-Ames across the room, and finally he walked out and drove home alone, somehow not nearly so angry as he was sad.

The next day he moved out of the house to his place in Pacific Palisades. A few weeks later Aster Bigelow announced in her column that Mona had left for England with Truscott-Ames, and shortly after that, Mike received word from her lawyer that she was instituting divorce proceedings.

276

42

The traffic was bad, but Howard was driving more slowly than necessary, anyway. He was on his way to Mike's place in Pacific Palisades, and he didn't want to go. He wished now that he'd given an excuse when Mike had called about an hour earlier and asked him to come up. Long ago he had stopped feeling at ease around Mike, and they'd seen little of each other in the last two years.

Mike probably wanted to talk about *Smith's War,* which they'd be working in together soon. The picture had already been postponed for a year beyond its intended starting date in the spring of 1953, but was finally scheduled to start production in two months.

Whatever was coming, Howard thought as he turned up the sharply ascending, winding driveway to Mike's house, he was not looking forward to seeing Mike.

Howard looked thoughtfully at the stunning house as he approached. It was perched higher than any other house in sight. Howard supposed that looking down from it gave Mike a feeling of lording it over everything. A god on Olympus. But a god going to pot.

As Howard pulled around back to the parking area, he heard loud music. It was coming from a portable radio at the swimming pool. A handsome young man and a beautiful young woman, both in their early twenties and healthily tanned, lounged in swimming suits. A servant was delivering drinks to them as Howard got out of the car.

Mike appeared simultaneously through a section of sliding glass doors at the rear of the house. He was dressed in a polo shirt and tennis shorts that enhanced his athletic physique, and he was barefoot. He carried a half-consumed drink as he walked toward Howard with an uneasy smile. The sun had streaked his hair, highlighting the tawny richness of it here and there, and he was as glowingly tanned as the young couple at the pool. But up close, the puffiness of heavy drinking showed in his face.

"I want you to meet some friends," Mike said as they shook hands. Then he walked Howard over to the pool and introduced the young people. Their names were Larry Turner and Arlene Maynard. Larry was exceptionally polite, standing up and shaking hands firmly and, to Howard's embarrassment, calling him "sir." The girl simply smiled up at him and surveyed him analytically, as if she were trying to figure out why he was a movie star.

Howard was thankful Mike didn't suggest that the young people join them inside. He steered Howard across to the glass doors opening into his library, and they walked through that room and down three steps to the enormous living room, which rose two stories in one part and one story at the far end, with other rooms climbing out of it like cells in a beehive. The furniture was handsome and modern.

Howard's attention was drawn immediately to a large photograph of Mona in a plain silver frame on the piano. It was the original shot of a famous still that had been used to publicize *Lisa*. Mona had never looked more arresting. Her perfect figure was set off by a plain satin evening sheath so classically cut that it seemed perfectly up-to-date even now, seven years later. Her lustrous long hair fell below her bare shoulders and brushed down toward her marvelous breasts. In the photograph she looked like the perfect love goddess, and Howard knew she didn't look much different these days. Pictures of her and her husband at home on their English estate and at their villa in Cannes, and in assorted poses at Ascot, Deauville, and other gathering spots of the international set, had appeared in *Life* recently.

"If you're wondering about those two outside," Mike said, "I like to keep them around for company."

What did that mean? Howard asked himself. That they were living here? That Mike was making love to the girl? Or to the boy? Or to both?

"Don't you find it hard to talk to them?" Howard asked. "I wouldn't know what to say to young people anymore."

"I was their age when you met me, and you talked all right with me."

"But there's a dividing line. There's ten years' difference between you and them. There's twenty between me and them. And that boy called me 'sir.' It was out of respect for my age, and it made me feel strange."

"It was a different kind of veneration. He respects you because you're a star. But you're right, Howard. It's hard to talk with them. We don't have many interests in common. Except pictures, of course. That's the common denominator for all of us, isn't it?"

"So they're here to get into pictures. Don't they know how impossible it is nowadays?"

"They still hope. You can't kill that."

278

"I suppose not."

Howard looked away from Mike, back at the picture of Mona on the piano.

"It draws you, doesn't it?" Mike said quietly. "If I had any sense I'd put it away in a drawer, but I don't have any sense."

Howard looked back at him. "As you said, it draws you. I can understand why you keep it out."

"You probably think it's a shrine, don't you? But it's just a remembrance. I've been over my unreasonable passion for Mona for a long time."

Howard nodded, but he wondered if it was true. It would soon be two years since Mona had left Mike and gone on ultimately, with enormous publicity, to marry Lord Clive Truscott-Ames, but in Howard's opinion Mike didn't seem to have snapped back at all.

"Of course, I loved her very much," Mike went on. "For years before we married, I loved her. You know that. You know it all. So why am I telling you about it? Why don't I just shut up?"

"It's all right," Howard said. "Talk about it."

"I've tried to blame her, but I can't. Not if I'm to be honest about it. She warned me before we were married that it wouldn't work. She's a tortured woman."

But was she as tortured as Michael Baines? Howard wondered.

"The rumor goes that her marriage with Truscott-Ames is headed for the rocks, too. It wouldn't surprise me. She doesn't love him. She just liked the idea of marrying a peer and playing around in the international set. One of these days she'll drop him and try to pick up her career again, but she'll find it tough going. The love goddess syndrome is dead. We're in the era of the male star now. Men's pictures. Like *Smith's War*."

"There'll always be room for female stars, Mike. Tracy isn't doing so badly."

"No. But her part in *Smith's War* is subordinate. Starring, but subordinate. It's a man's picture. Frankly, I was a little surprised when she agreed to come home from Europe to do this picture."

"Why should that surprise you? Most of us are glad to get a picture these days. I know I need to work again."

"You don't need it as much as I do, Howard. You're stable. You're strong. You're a lot of things I'm not. That's why I drink so much. Because I'm not what I want to be. But I've got to curb it. I don't want to be a lush."

"You'll be all right when someone important comes into your life again," Howard said.

"Oh, I need that, too, I know," Mike said, "because, believe it or not, I don't think booze and raw sex are enough to make life worthwhile."

"I didn't think you did."

"But what's really important is being a star."

Howard didn't answer immediately. Then he said, "It isn't everything in life, but it's a great deal."

"It's more than a great deal, Howard. It matters more than anything else. You know it and I know it, and anyone who's ever had his name over the title knows it."

Howard said nothing.

Howard, feeling a little disturbed, drove away without looking back. His brief talk with Mike hadn't begun to fill the hole between them that had grown larger and larger in the last two years. Mike had spoken of Howard's being stable and strong. How little he knew him nowadays! Howard had come to feel increasingly insecure about both his career and his marriage. He and Pen hadn't talked about it much, but there were strains in their life together these days. Sometimes he thought he just wanted to be free.

But of one thing he was certain: he didn't want his career to end prematurely. Despite Mike's weaknesses, Howard envied him, because it was reasonable to assume that Mike would still be a star after Howard had faded into obscurity. It was largely a matter of age difference. Howard would be forty-four this year. Mike was ten years younger. Given the breaks, Mike could hope to play romantic leads for another fifteen years or more. Howard could hope for five years more, and even that might be stretching it.

The sensible thing would be to retire before he noticeably started to slip, but he undoubtedly wouldn't do the sensible thing. As Mike had said accurately, stardom meant more than anything else.

Howard realized it wasn't fair of him to envy Mike because he was younger. After all, Howard had been a star for almost a decade before Mike had even come into the business.

It wasn't fair of him to envy Mike because he was a better actor, either, but he did. Mike's dissipated way of life hadn't interfered with his growth as a motion picture actor. Howard was convinced that his own artistic growth had stopped years before and remained on a plateau. He knew that continuing stardom had nothing to do with acting ability, but he wished he could have continued to progress as an artist. In a few months he would be working with Mike in a picture for the first time in years, and he was afraid Mike would outperform him.

But it would be good to be working again. After not having made a picture for two years, he needed exposure. *Smith's War* seemed an ideal means of getting back before the public. The book was well known, and a good script had been devised from it. And Howard's role was as strong as Mike's.

Howard was uneasy about the idea of working with Tracy again. They'd made three pictures together in the four years before she went to Europe, and each one had been harder for them. Nothing had ever been said or done about it, but the truth was that they wanted each other.

Tracy had made pictures in Italy and England during the last two years, and had lived in Rome and London most of the time, leaving her house in Coldwater Canyon in the care of a friend. Howard was glad she was gone. He was glad he didn't have to see her.

But he still thought about her often, and now she was coming back again, and he wondered if it would be even harder for them to be together this time than before.

Mike stood behind the bar, pouring Scotch from a decanter over ice in a glass. When the glass was full, he put back the decanter and turned to find Larry walking across the room toward him. Larry looked sullen. He also seemed a little woozy. He couldn't take much in the way of drink. He was a kid, really, Mike thought—a kid trying desperately to grow up.

The boy hiked himself up on one of the bar stools, put his elbows on the bar, and stared at Mike. "You didn't ask us to join you and Howard Stanton. That was rude."

"We had a lot to talk about that wouldn't have interested you."

"Everything you talk about interests me," Larry said.

Mike shrugged and took a long swallow, almost draining the glass. He was long past being embarrassed by such remarks from Larry.

"I got the impression at the pool that Stanton isn't very friendly anyway," Larry went on.

"He's friendly, but he wouldn't be interested in you. He doesn't like boys that way."

"I didn't mean *that*," Larry said with a frown. "I wouldn't want him anyway. I only want you."

"Larry, I've told you that you've got to stop thinking that way. It's nice to have you and Arlene here with me, but I won't have either of you going serious on me. If you can't accept this for what it is, there's the door."

"You don't mean that," Larry said anxiously. "It's Arlene you should be wary of, not me. She wants to muscle me out, but I'm not going to let her."

"The same goes for her as for you," Mike said, finishing his Scotch and pouring another. "She's going to get nothing out of this but temporary bed and board, and the door swings both ways for her, too."

"I wish she'd leave. We'd be a lot happier together if that bitch weren't here."

"I heard that." Arlene laughed coldly as she moved across the room toward them, her breasts bobbing in bizarre rhythm with the clink of ice in the empty glass she carried. "Talk about bitches," she went on harshly to Larry, "who's bitchier than you, my fairy queen?"

"Shut up, you stupid cunt!" Larry said, getting off the bar stool and clenching his fists as if he were going to fight her.

But she only laughed again, walked around behind the bar, and slipped her arm through Mike's. "Essentially, Mike likes only girls. When he lets you at him, it's only for laughs."

Larry's fists were still tightly clenched at his sides. He looked fiercely at Arlene.

"Maybe he *likes* girls, but he *loves* me," he said defensively.

Mike wanted to lash out at Larry for saying that, but he held back. Larry was becoming a problem, but at least he was sincere, or thought he was. Mike couldn't say the same for Arlene. Arlene was definitely a mistake.

In fact, Mike had found he could spend only a short time with Larry or Arlene, or both, before he had to get away from them. He could tolerate being with them for protracted periods only when he was particularly dulled with alcohol.

He escaped them for the rest of the afternoon by feigning need for a nap and shutting himself in his room. Having a liquor closet there, complete with a small refrigerator, made it unnecessary for him to return to the bar for refills. He lay propped against a pillow on his mammoth bed, which was set directly on the floor in Oriental fashion, and drank Scotch. Occasionally he glanced over toward the wall of glass that looked down on the city. From a table there, another of Mona's photographs, a close-up from *Affair in Rio,* smiled over at him. From outside, through the open windows on the other side of the room, came a rising snarl of voices. Larry and Arlene were quarreling again at the pool.

Later, when he heard them in the hall and knew they were going to their rooms to rest, he decided to go for his swim. He stripped and stood naked in his mirror-walled bathroom and confirmed that his physique was still taut and beautiful in spite of his dissipation.

282

He put on a robe and walked downstairs to the pool. He doffed the robe, not caring if the cook saw his nakedness, and took a racing dive into the pool, swimming its length a half dozen times. He pulled himself out, dripping and winded, and offered himself up to the sun.

But he soon went back inside and resumed his drinking, and by the time dinner was served several hours later, he was feeling the saturation of drink to the point of revulsion. They dined on the terrace by candlelight, with Arlene's dusky but shallow beauty enhanced by the soft light. She wore a tight yellow dress with amazing décolletage. It looked as if her nipples might slip into view at any moment.

"That's the kind of dress a whore would wear," Larry said.

Arlene smiled. "You're just jealous."

"Doesn't she look like a whore, Mike?" Larry taunted.

"She's lovely," Mike said.

"And I'm going to be a movie star," Arlene said. "You'll see."

"How are you going to do it?" Larry said sneeringly. "Fuck your way to the top?"

"Stop it, Larry," Mike said. "Try to be nice."

"It's impossible for him to be nice," Arlene said harshly.

They bickered on, and Mike kept thinking that Larry was right about Arlene. She was cheap and demanding. So why did he have her here? It had been far simpler with Janice. Janice hadn't wanted to be a movie star. She hadn't wanted anything from him but his body. It was too bad she'd decided she no longer liked California and had gone back to Ohio or wherever she'd come from. He would probably have a time getting rid of Arlene when he wanted her to go.

After dinner they ran a new picture the studio had sent up, and that kept Larry and Arlene quiet for a while. Mike didn't drink during the picture because it would soon be time for him to perform again.

Sometimes Mike wondered why it didn't disgust him, the three of them together like this in the darkened room. But it didn't, even when he thought about it in the depression of the aftermath. It not only didn't disgust him, it even excited him. Sometimes it excited him so much that he trembled as he pressed against one body or the other, or put his mouth against the mouth of one or the other.

He knew that neither of them liked it. Arlene would have far preferred to have him alone with her, but they were compelled by Mike to perform this way.

Arlene lay beneath Mike, Larry beside them, his hand caressing Mike's back as Mike thrust himself into Arlene. Arlene moaned. Her eyes were closed, shutting out Larry's presence, and her mouth was open. She moaned again as Mike's thrusts quickened and deepened. His chest bored into her breasts. His orgasm rushed up in him. "Oh-h-h-h-h," Arlene sighed. Mike lay still on her, gasping. He was barely aware that Larry had abruptly left the bed.

Mike rolled over on his back. He heard Larry weeping. The boy was at the window, gripping a drapery very hard, as if he hoped to pull it down and with it the whole room, to crush them all and end his misery. He was a stunning vision in the haze of moonlight, a beautiful heartsick child whose passion had been agonizingly thwarted.

Mike wanted badly to call him back and comfort him, but Arlene's presence stopped him. Arlene would only make some stupid remark and make it worse. What he ought to do, he realized, was go over there and put his arm around Larry's shoulder and take him into his own room and stay with him.

Yes, that was what he ought to do, but he hesitated, for Arlene was bound to ruin it somehow. It was taken out of his hands anyway, for Larry suddenly left the room, still sobbing, slamming the door behind him. Mike raised himself on his elbows, listening to Larry's receding sobs.

"Don't go after that silly fairy," Arlene said, putting her hand on his arm as he started to rise. "Stay with me."

Mike flung her hand off. "He's right about you. You're a bitch."

"Don't go, don't go!" he heard Arlene whimper as he crossed the room. He didn't answer her. He slammed the door as he went out.

Time had trickled by. It was only two minutes after three o'clock in the morning but it seemed days, not just a couple of hours, since Mike had slammed the door on Arlene and had come to his room, locking his door on her, ignoring her banging and whining out in the hall, her pleas to return to her bed and her body. She'd finally gone away when he'd screamed through the door that if she didn't let him alone, he'd kick her out of the house.

He'd enjoyed humiliating her. He always did. He enjoyed humiliating Larry, too. He supposed he should dislike himself, perhaps even hate himself, for wishing the same unhappiness on them he felt himself, but he didn't. He was glad he was able to be honest with himself these days, to see himself for what he was, an empty creature without honor, without human feeling, without love.

He rose and went naked into the hall. Far down at the end was the door to Arlene's room. Despite her feverish protestations, Arlene would have long ago sunk into unconcerned sleep and would waken with her wounds healed. It had been a long time since he himself had known a night of untroubled sleep.

He opened the door to Larry's room. The boy lay naked on the bed, absolutely still. He hadn't been sleeping, Mike knew. He'd been crying.

"I didn't think you'd come," Larry said, raising himself on his elbows, "but I've been waiting anyway."

"You should sleep. Things will look better tomorrow."

"They won't be better till you say you love me."

"Larry, you've got to stop expecting that. It isn't going to happen."

"You *do* love me," Larry went on. "I know you do, and knowing it is the only thing that keeps me going."

"Larry, you're going to make yourself sick, hoping for the impossible. I meant what I said today. You've got to get hold of yourself or you're going to have to leave."

"Don't say that!" The boy sprang from the bed, crossed over to Mike, and pressed himself against him, stretching up to meet him. They kissed. "Don't say that ever again," the boy said into Mike's ear, and then kissed the ear. He kissed his way down Mike's body, stooping lower and lower, finally kneeling in front of Mike, wrapping his arms around Mike's thighs. He put his hungry mouth and tongue to work on Mike's hardness, which throbbed up greedily in response to Larry's avidity.

Up and down Larry went on Mike, and there was an awesome intensity about it that made it not vulgar or ridiculous. Larry's intensity was constructed of what he believed to be love.

Mike was near coming very quickly, and Larry stopped sucking just in time and drew Mike over to the bed, where he lay spread-eagled on his back. Larry leaned over him, kissing his eyes, his ears, his nose, and his throat, and then he went down to the groin. His tongue stroked the length of Mike's hardness and his mouth took Mike's testicles into it and rolled them inside.

Larry took Mike's hardness back into his mouth, drawing Mike higher and higher. Mike's body stiffened as Larry brought him to the crest, his hands crushing the sides of the boy's head and his fingers pulling at his hair. He groaned as the spasms overtook him. He came very heavily, but the boy didn't choke. Mike sank back into weakness, but the boy's mouth stayed around the shrinking hardness, holding it captive.

Finally Larry let Mike slip out of his mouth. "You see how much I love you?" he said, and touched Mike's hand with his own.

285

Larry moved even lower then, pressing his face against Mike's thighs, grasping him as if he never intended to let him go. He was crying. The tears were hot on Mike's skin. Mike was sorry the boy was a victim of his own unhappiness. He almost wished he could love Larry, but not quite.

43

Tracy Gordon had been living and working in Europe for two years between the time she finished her third picture with Howard Stanton and returned home to co-star with him and Michael Baines in *Smith's War.*

She'd made two pictures in Europe. The first was an Anglo-Italian extravaganza called *Josephine and Napoleon,* co-starring Tracy with Italian screen idol Carlo Martinelli, with whom she was reportedly having an affair. She wasn't, despite Martinelli's urgings. Except for a few interiors shot on stages at Cinecitta in Rome and battle sequences done on location, the movie was opulently photographed largely in and on the grounds of various villas and palaces rented for the occasion. The picture was noted for its visual beauty and for Tracy Gordon's.

Her second picture abroad was a smart comedy originally slated for Mona Gaillard before her decision to break her contract and leave Hollywood. Ironically, Tracy had worked on the picture in Regency's British studio while Mona, finally freed legally from Mike, waited it out nearby in London while Lord Truscott-Ames waged a court battle to divorce his wife.

Months later, when the picture was released to considerable acclaim, with Tracy enjoying new laurels for "her timing, her glow, her growing authority as a star of the first magnitude," as one noted critic put it, Mona Gaillard, now Lady Truscott-Ames, commented to an inquiring reporter in Deauville, "I could still be the biggest star in Hollywood if I chose to return."

Presumably that was to put Tracy in her place, and she had a private laugh over it in her rented flat near Hyde Park, where Wesley Rainer had visited her yesterday, having flown over from New York for just

286

one day to continue his unsuccessful quest to marry her. He kept on showing up periodically, and she kept on saying no. Wes was having a "private kingdom," as he called it, built in Jamaica, and he said he intended to install her there as queen. She had a laugh over that, too.

Tracy didn't have a happy life in Europe, but she had a busy one. She was popular in London just as she'd been in Rome. She'd found that movie stars were popular almost everywhere but in Hollywood itself these days, and she was greatly in demand at parties, where she did a lot of drinking. She did a lot of drinking alone, too.

The thought of what her mother would think of that disturbed her greatly. Her mother was still often on Tracy's mind, even though they had lived apart for almost nine years, and while Tracy was in Europe during that two-year period, she made the long transatlantic trip home three times just to visit her mother for a few days.

Dean Ainsley himself flew to England to try to induce her to return to California to do *Smith's War.* After reading the treatment the studio had sent her, she'd written that she didn't think the part was right for her, which was nonsense, for the role of the woman who came between two soldier friends, though smaller than those of Mike and Howard, couldn't have been more nearly perfect. The truth was, she didn't want to torture herself working with Howard again. She was better off over here, far away from him.

Ainsley arrived armed with a shooting script in which her role had been fattened, since he'd interpreted "not right" as "too small." Tracy agreed to do *Smith's War,* but her expanded role had nothing to do with her decision. She wasn't sure why she agreed, and on the plane to the States six weeks later, she harbored the disagreeable feeling that she was making a mistake.

Bonnie had been living in Tracy's house in Coldwater Canyon in her absence. Bonnie had changed nothing, although Tracy had told her to make the place her own when she'd departed for Rome more than two years back. Bonnie was the only member of Tracy's gang still around. The others had been discouraged out of the business and had left Hollywood. Bonnie had never achieved stardom, but she was becoming successful as a character actress and was currently working in a television series.

Bonnie offered to move out, but Tracy wouldn't hear of it. Bonnie was one of the few friends left from the old days of five or six years earlier, and her presence in the house was most welcome.

Aster Bigelow reported in her column that "America's favorite sex symbol, Tracy Gordon, has chosen to grace Smogsville with her presence again—but for how long?" The columnist continued with a dissertation on the difference between a love goddess like Mona Gaillard and a sex symbol like Tracy Gordon.

"In ancient times," she said, "a love goddess was a woman who presided over fertility rites—a symbol of propagation, of the perpetuation of life, of posterity. A nicer idea than a sex symbol. What does a sex symbol stand for but raw sex? It seems to me that Hollywood levels are sinking fast in this so-called sophisticated era of the nineteen fifties if we are going to glorify sex instead of love."

Tracy was certain that Aster Bigelow was obliquely calling her a whore again.

Penelope Stanton phoned Tracy a few days after she was back in California and said she and Howard wanted Tracy to drive out to Malibu to spend the day with them. When Tracy hesitated, Howard came on the phone and urged her to come. He sounded as nervous about seeing her again as she was. Tracy decided to face it.

It was a wonderful day and it was a terrible day. She was alone with Howard only for a swim and a short walk down the beach afterward, but it was long enough to tear her apart.

When Howard suggested that they take a swim, Pen said she couldn't go in with them since she seemed to be getting a cold. When Tracy put on one of Pen's swimming suits in the guest room, she found it tight on her. It made her look overripe. It was the way a sex symbol would deliberately get herself up to look, she thought ironically.

As she walked down to the water with Howard, she reflected on how magnificent his body still was. He was forty-four now, but he didn't look it. She thought of him fighting a bare-chested duel in *The Cavaliers,* which she'd seen in the Golden Theater in Abbottsville so many years ago. She thought of him swimming in a pareu in *The Great Typhoon.* She'd been pulsatingly conscious of his almost naked body in those days. She was hardly less so now.

He looked at her as they neared the water, smiled, and took her hand. Her lips quivered as she smiled back. The whole two years away from him were wiped out. His hand tightened on hers. It was as if he understood what she was thinking.

They ran into the surf, hand in hand, and then he let go. The ocean was rough, and she was soon tired. She came out of the water before he did. Pen was up on the sun deck, watching. Tracy waved and Pen waved back. Sometimes Tracy thought Pen sensed how she felt about Howard.

She turned away from Pen and waited for Howard to come out. He soon did so, glistening, smiling. But he was as tense as she was. She'd felt it when he'd so briefly taken her hand, and she saw it in his smile.

288

They walked down the beach a short distance, to dry off in the sun. She wanted to spill out a hundred things. She wanted to tell him about her lust for him as an adolescent, her lust for him today. She wanted to tell him that being away from him these last two years hadn't changed a thing, something she'd known the moment she'd laid eyes on him today. She thought he wanted to spill out a hundred locked-in things to her, too. But neither of them spilled out anything. They talked about how good it was to be together again, how good it would be to work together again. They talked like old friends.

She endured another few hours at Malibu, laughing, pretending, envying Pen her years with Howard, envying them their marriage. She was glad to leave at the end of the day.

"I'm surprised," Tracy said when Mike showed up unannounced at her house the next afternoon and said he wanted to do the town with her.

"And I'm surprised you're surprised," he said, obviously a little annoyed and a little drunk. "I'm glad you're back, and I'm glad we're going to make a picture together again, and I think it calls for some cutting up."

"I used to be known for that, didn't I?" she mused. "The fun girl of Hollywood. I wonder how much fun I really had."

"Not much, if you can't remember. But you probably never stopped to think how disappointing it really was."

"I seem to have a built-in resistance to too much thinking."

"Very wise," Mike said. "Thinking can get you a lot of unhappiness if carried to extremes. We'll do as little of it as possible while we're out together on the town."

"I have a feeling you're in a lonely period, or you wouldn't be here."

"Right. I'm also feeling horny. Don't you think it's time we finally went to bed together?"

"I'm afraid it would ruin our friendship."

"What's the difference, if it works out sexually? I'd rather have you as a lover than a friend anytime."

"You're being a little silly, Mike."

"I've had sex with you on my mind for a long time, Tracy. Ever since the first time I asked you out, and you refused."

"You had Mona on your mind, not me. I wouldn't doubt that you still do."

"That isn't true," he said, a little sharply.

Tracy did go out with Mike that evening, and they had a good time together. They started out expecting to have dinner at Chasen's, but ended up with hot tamales in an obscure restaurant in the Mexican quarter instead. The proprietor made a fuss over them, and several tourists asked for their autographs. Afterward, they went on a drinking spree in various bistros. Throughout their dizzying alcoholic hours together Tracy wondered frequently if Mike would want to go to bed later, and if she would agree.

As it turned out, Mike finally spirited Tracy home at dawn after a mad drive along the coastal highway. Nothing happened except that Tracy went to bed alone, and Mike, too tired to go home, slept on the couch.

Two weeks into *Smith's War,* Mike was almost a happy man. It was wonderful to be working again, making a good picture with a good cast and doing a good job of it under a fine director like John Edsel. Mike was putting in long, hard days, and he hardly missed Larry and Arlene. He'd sent them both away, giving Arlene a few thousand dollars to get rid of her, although Larry had indignantly declined money. Mike was glad they were gone, although he felt bad that Larry had taken it so tearfully.

He was alone now but not lonely. He was seeing Tracy a little, but the real reason he wasn't lonely was that he was working. He was determined to do the best acting job in *Smith's War* that he'd ever done. He wanted to give an Academy Award performance. He wanted to prove to the world that he wasn't a typical standard movie personality type, getting by just on presence, star quality, sex appeal, or whatever they wanted to call it. He wanted to show that he could really act, and here was the best chance he'd ever had to prove it. The role of Lieutenant Smith in *Smith's War* was the kind of role Howard Stanton had been given in *The Young Soldier* more than two decades back, a role of tremendous humanity, the kind of role that came along only once or twice in a career.

Mike expected to do better than Howard had done as *The Young Soldier* because he was a better actor. But he had to admit it was a better role, too. The part fit him like a glove. He could have *been* Lieutenant Smith if so much hadn't gone wrong in his life, if he'd had the love he wanted and the strength he wanted. He could have been as good and clean and bright and brave—and all the other wonderful things—as Lieutenant Smith was.

And Mike was to have top billing. The credits would read "Michael Baines, Tracy Gordon, and Howard Stanton in *Smith's War.*" A few years ago the order would have been "Howard Stanton, Michael Baines, and Tracy Gordon." But the studio had decided to bill them alphabetically because its three biggest stars were involved, "and it just seems fairest that way," as Ainsley had put it. Mike saw it as a comedown for Howard, although Howard probably wouldn't want to look at it that way. They hadn't discussed it. Howard had very little to say to Mike nowadays.

Mike didn't care. All he cared about was that for the first time in quite a while things were going well. He wasn't even drinking much, although cutting down was giving him trouble. He would go home tired from a long day's work and would ache for the burning release alcohol gave him. But he was careful. Two or three drinks were all he would allow himself all evening. He intended that nothing would jeopardize his chances to make the most of his opportunities with this picture. Even if he weren't being billed first, he would still be the star of this picture. He was Lieutenant Smith of *Smith's War*, and he was going to keep it that way.

The company was working late. They were doing a siege scene in the French village on the back lot, and the rigging for the explosions had taken longer than they'd expected. It was after five when they were ready to shoot. Mike had finished for the day and had gone home. Tracy had also finished for the day, but she was still there, sitting quietly near the assistant director. Howard wondered why she was staying around, but he didn't ask. He felt a little strange, because every time he glanced in her direction, he found her looking at him.

They had two rehearsals without the explosions to establish the pace and rhythm of the scene to Edsel's satisfaction. Then the scene was done as a continuous shot, with three cameras shooting from different vantages. The American tank moved into the town square, with Howard and his infantry platoon right behind it. The tank fired at the building where a German Waffen-SS company was holding out. There was answering fire across the square from a German eighty-eight gun crew operating behind a barricade. The tank was knocked out of action. Howard rushed out from behind it with a bazooka and destroyed the eighty-eight and its crew in a blast. The platoon followed, and they rushed the house, firing submachine guns, rifles and bazookas, and throwing grenades, while return fire streamed out at them. Men fell screaming. The scene ended with Howard blowing the door apart with a bazooka shot.

When the company broke for the day, Howard found that Tracy had left. But her car was in the parking lot of the dressing room building when Howard drove in from the back lot.

There wasn't a sound inside. The dressing room building was a ghostly place in these days of underutilization anyway, and particularly so at the end of the day. Howard walked down the carpeted hallway, almost stopping when he saw that Tracy's door was open about two inches, wondering if it was deliberate. But he walked resolutely on down to his own dressing room at the end of the hall, his mind suddenly full of questions. He was nervous and excited. He got out of the Army sergeant's uniform that was his costume for most of the picture and took a shower. He took longer to dress than was necessary. His heart was beating fast. He waited a few minutes more before leaving the dressing room, hoping Tracy would be gone.

But there was still a sliver of light coming out from her slightly open door. He stopped at the door, hesitated, then opened it wider and looked in. Tracy was sitting at her vanity, with her back to him. She was staring into the mirror, and tears were running down her face. Except for the tears she was utterly still. She gave the unreal impression that she'd sat there frozen for days.

He felt unreal himself. He moved into the room and approached her. His heart was beating even harder now. Tracy watched him come up behind her in the mirror, and he watched her watching him. It was as automatic as if they were following a script. He reached her and pressed against her from behind. He leaned down. His arms came around her, his hands folding across her breasts. He pressed the side of his face against hers as they looked at each other in the mirror.

Then they kissed, and what had been building up to happen between them all those years finally happened.

Sometime later they lay side by side on their backs on the white shag rug of Tracy's dressing room. They were naked. Their clothes lay where they'd been quickly dropped on the floor. The door to the hall was still open, for after it had started, there'd been no turning away from it, even to shut out the world. They were resting now. The only sound was their subsiding breathing.

Howard was thinking how wonderful it had been. Quick, irresistible, intense. He'd felt like a young man again. He'd taken her like one, too, and she'd responded with complete abandon. All the years of waiting and avoidance had culminated in a tremendous release of passion.

Tracy was thinking almost the same thing. The man she'd idolized since childhood had succumbed to her at last, and the union she'd thought would never happen had enthralled and fulfilled her more than she'd ever dreamed.

She finally said what she'd been saying in her mind for years. "I love you. You know I do. You've known it for a long time."

292

She didn't expect him to say the same thing, and he didn't. That would take time. But the first high wall had been breached. During the two hours they spent together that evening, Tracy Gordon was almost totally happy for the first time in many years. The only bad moments came when she thought about tomorrow.

44

Tracy always acknowledged that the following weeks would have been much harder, perhaps impossible, if Penelope Stanton's aunt, who'd reared her, hadn't died. Pen flew back to England for the funeral and stayed on for almost a month afterward, visiting relatives. It was a time of opportunity for Tracy and Howard.

Not that they could flaunt their relationship. Neither of them wanted or could afford a scandal. They were conscientiously casual around each other on the set, though it was difficult. Tracy even continued to go out occasionally with Mike, for to refuse him would have prompted questions. But she didn't go every time he asked her, logically pleading a need for rest because picture-making was such an emotional and physical drain. Actually she felt no drain of any kind. She felt renewed energy and zest.

They took no chances of going to each other's houses. Bonnie soon realized that something was going on, but Tracy didn't confide in her. She waited in her dressing room for Howard almost every evening after shooting, and every weekend from Saturday evening to Monday morning they spent at Malibu. They couldn't leave the house during the day for fear of being seen, but they often went out after dark and walked the beach hand in hand.

Tracy kept a secret from Howard. She did not wear her diaphragm when they made love. Until now the thought of ever having a baby had been foreign to her. But she wanted Howard's baby, and the possible consequences didn't bother her in the least.

"I want to tell you about when I began to fall in love with you," she told him one moonlit night as she lay in his arms at Malibu. "I was twelve. I saw you in *The Great Typhoon*. I dreamed that I was your

293

lover. Oh, I know that happens all the time with adolescents. They fall for a star and think they could never love anyone else. In my case it's been true."

"I'm old enough to be your father," he said.

"Seventeen years isn't so much older."

"It's a lot older. But I'm glad you're in love with me, Tracy. And I'm glad you've been in love with me for a long time. The truth is, people always want people to love them, no matter how much heartbreak it might cause." He paused. "I loved you a long time ago, but I wasn't calling it that. I just called it wanting you. Now it's out, and I can call it what it is. I love you. Loving you and being with you is the sweetest thing I know of, and I'm jealous of every man you've ever known."

"It's strange, but I'm not jealous of Pen. It's something other than jealousy, and I'm not quite sure what."

"Don't bring Pen into it, Tracy. Not yet. I'm a coward about that."

"I understand," she said quickly. "We'll take it a step at a time."

She reached down and found him hard again, and she urged him into her. There was no need for preliminaries. She was burning the moment he touched her. He lay on top of her and went into her as her legs locked across his back. It was the most conventional of positions, and they were simply two persons in a sexual embrace, yet it was as new and exciting to her as if it were the first time anyone had ever done it in the whole of human history. She soared. She shivered and shook with convulsive excitement. He brought her to the peak of ecstasy and then released her. Yet there was no letdown. That was the difference. There was never any letdown.

It was different for her with Howard than it had been with any other man, because she loved him.

Mike was more and more suspicious that something was going on between Howard and Tracy. Since it was common enough in Hollywood to finally go to bed with someone you thought you never would, he didn't find it surprising that they seemed to be having an affair after all these years. But he didn't want to believe it. After all, he'd been taking Tracy out, but she hadn't gone to bed with *him* yet.

He was even more suspicious when at the conclusion of Saturday's shooting one week she gave him the same excuse she had the previous Saturday when he asked her out over the weekend. She needed her rest, she said.

Yet when Mike phoned her at home the next day, Bonnie said that Tracy was gone for the weekend, though Bonnie didn't know where. Mike promptly phoned Howard, and a servant informed him that neither Mr. nor Mrs. Stanton was at home. Mr. Stanton had gone to his beach house and Mrs. Stanton had been in England for the past two weeks.

That cinched it in Mike's mind. He could hardly restrain himself from driving out to Malibu and surprising Howard and Tracy together, but it occurred to him that he would be making a bigger fool of himself than of them. He was surprised that he was so upset, and he faced the fact that it was his ego that was hurt the most. That weekend he drank more than he had for a long time.

It had been a cool evening, and it looked as if it would be a cold night. Tracy didn't care. She would be folded into Howard's warmth all night.

Howard was building a fire. Tracy was looking through the phonograph records, many of which were British. There were popular and symphonic selections. She doubted that Howard had selected a single one of them.

"Pen's the music lover around here," he said, as if he'd guessed what she was thinking.

She turned, smiling. He was kneeling in front of the fireplace, a poker in his hand, looking at her.

"Nothing my speed here," she said. "No old Glenn Miller or Tommy Dorsey records."

"It was Paul Whiteman in my day," Howard said.

She shrugged. "Who needs music, anyway? All we really need is for time to stop. Right now, frozen forever. When people find perfect happiness, they should be allowed to keep it. It's only fair."

"There are a lot of reasons why this isn't perfect, Tracy, and sometime soon we're going to have to talk about them."

"But not now," she said quickly. "I'd rather keep my dreams awhile."

"Come over here. I want to touch you. I haven't touched you for five minutes, and it's been too long."

She went to him. He'd slipped down on his elbow. He smiled up at her and extended his hand. She took it and he pulled her down on him. They kissed. They lay back with their heads on the big floor pillows and looked into the fire, his arm around her. They didn't speak for a long time.

Finally she said, "What are you thinking about?"

"My son."

She turned her head to look at him, but he didn't turn his. He continued to look into the fire.

"You're surprised," he said. "It's something very few people know about. Leni Liebhaber and I had a son. They were both killed in a bombing raid on Berlin. For a long time I couldn't get it out of my mind. I'd never seen the boy, but his death grieved me as much as if he'd been with me since birth."

"Of course," Tracy said. "I understand."

"I think I've wanted to be a father very badly. I think I've wanted to make up with a child for what was missing between me and my own father. It's disappointed me that Pen and I haven't had one." He finally looked at her. "I don't know why I mentioned that."

"Because you wanted to. You must always say what you want to with me, Howard."

"You know I won't always. Nobody ever does always, with any-body. You know, Tracy, you still *are* a dreamer. Maybe you always will be. There's a lot to be said for dreaming, but it makes you very vulnerable."

Yes, very vulnerable, she knew. But this dream was going to end right. It must.

Howard was glad Tracy wasn't on the lot that day. He needed time and space to think, and there was too much emotional interference with his thinking when she was around. A clear sense of objectivity in his reasoning was impossible right now anyway, but he was going to have to do better than he had been doing.

It didn't help that his mind kept wandering on the set, either. They were doing a take on stage nine, where a German parlor with lace curtains and Beidermeier pieces had been re-created. The scene was the celebration by Smith's platoon of V-E day in a house they'd commandeered the last day of the war. Howard had only two lines, but he muffed them on the walk-through. He also muffed them on the first two takes. He was embarrassed. He was known for his careful prepara-tion before arriving on the set, and it had been years since he'd botched a scene.

When the company broke for lunch, Mike stepped up to Howard and suggested that they eat together at the commissary. Howard almost asked why they should bother. This was the thirty-fifth day of produc-tion, and it was the first time Mike had asked that they do anything together that wasn't required by the script.

But to be fair about it, Howard hadn't been very communicative with Mike, either. So he said yes, and they went off to lunch together, just as if they'd done it every day. Howard had a feeling from the first that Mike was leading up to something, although he talked only about the picture the first few minutes, claiming that for the sake of authenticity they should be shooting it in Europe instead of on the lot.

"The rushes look authentic enough to me," Howard said. "It's going to be a good picture."

"It would be a better one if you and I had better rapport."

"Our rapport went down the drain a long time ago. You didn't seem very eager to do much about it, and neither did I. I don't think it's affected our work together on the picture one way or the other."

"My God, Howard, rapport or lack of it certainly affects the way we relate to each other in our roles. I don't think this underlying tension between us helps one bit."

"There's tension between us in our roles. Maybe our own tension helps it. I haven't had any complaints from Edsel."

"I just wish we could work better together, the way we used to."

"I don't think you really care, Mike. And I don't think you asked me to lunch to talk about this, either. Why don't you get to the point?"

Mike took a breath. "All right. I know what's going on between you and Tracy, and I don't like it. I don't give a damn that you're not being fair to Pen, but I hate what you're doing to Tracy."

Howard stared at him, stunned that Mike knew. He couldn't imagine how he'd found out, but obviously, from Mike's intensity, it went beyond mere guessing on his part.

Finally Howard spoke. "You don't give a damn about what happens to Tracy. I don't know why you've brought this up, or what you hope to gain from it, but I know it isn't because of that."

"I care about Tracy. I care what happens to her."

"You care about you and about what happens to you."

"I think your guilt is showing badly," Mike said coldly.

"And I think you're sticking your nose in where it doesn't belong." Howard rose. "I don't think we'd better try to finish lunch together. I might just be tempted to knock the hell out of you."

He walked away. Mike's voice followed him. "You're going to hurt Tracy. I know you're going to hurt her."

You're going to hurt Tracy.

It mocked Howard. He kept hearing it, riding on his mind. He even heard it when he bolted awake from a nightmare, a nightmare that vanished from his mind before he knew what it was but must have been terrible, for he was sweating.

That nightmare came before dawn on Saturday morning. Edsel had kept the company late that day because they had to do twelve takes of a particularly difficult scene before he was finally satisfied. Howard didn't get to Malibu until after eight. Tracy had already been there for

297

an hour. She was in the kitchen in an apron, fixing dinner. She had a pitcher of martinis ready. She'd brought a Glenn Miller album and was playing "Serenade in Blue." She looked as if she'd lived there forever. It was incredible. There seemed no trace of Pen left at all. It was a frightening thought that in a matter of weeks they'd wiped her out this way.

Howard tried not to think about that. It was difficult enough without remembering that. He wanted Tracy to be as happy as she could for as long as she could. He danced with her to the ballads of Glenn Miller, his cheek pressed against hers, the way people had danced together in the thirties and forties. He hadn't told her about his set-to with Mike, and he didn't tell her now. He didn't tell her much of anything, but he said "I love you" into her ear as they danced.

He said it, even though it didn't change anything.

Howard had slept only lightly. He'd wakened many times, and this time he didn't drift back into sleep. His hand was pressed over Tracy's. They lay side by side on their backs. They hadn't gone to sleep that way. They'd gone to sleep hours ago on their sides, she backed up against him, his arms around her and folded over her breasts. His last thought before dropping off was how good she smelled, how good she felt against him.

Felt. They were always touching. He supposed they were touching all the time because for so many years they'd wanted to touch and hadn't. They were making up for it now.

He thought of the four women who'd been important in his life: Leni, Georgina, Pen, Tracy. All different from one another, but with strong similarities, too. All sensuous and sensual. All beautiful.

He pressed Tracy's hand slightly, but she didn't waken. He thought about how difficult this last wonderful weekend together was going to be in the end. Time was cruel. It wouldn't let you hold onto your good moments long enough. Time took away from you everything it could.

Howard slipped his hand off Tracy's. She slept on. He moved off the bed. He dressed and left the room, looking at Tracy from the doorway to assure himself that she was still asleep. He went silently out of the house and descended to the beach. The ocean tumbled in toward him. Clouds scudded through the night sky. He started walking. Almost every house was dark, as far as he could see. There was no one on the beach anywhere.

He wished he didn't have to think about anything at all, but he thought about many things. He thought about his fear that he was slipping. He thought about Mike's superior performance in *Smith's War*

298

and his doubts about his own. He thought about the signs of aging he'd noticed in the rushes, the crow's-feet and slight sagging of the jaw, and was aware that they were a harbinger of what was to come. And he thought about Pen's coming home the next week.

Finally he turned back. He'd been walking a long time. A haze of rosiness blended with the darkness in the east. When he was halfway back to the house, he saw Tracy coming. He walked more slowly then, dreading the inevitable. When they reached each other, he even hesitated to touch her, for touching would make it even harder, but of course he did. He took both her hands in his, and they simply stood in the sand and looked at each other for a while. Then he turned her, tucked her arm around his, and they headed back toward the house together.

"I shouldn't have come out after you," she said. "If you'd wanted me to be with you, you'd have wakened me."

"It's all right, Tracy."

"No, it isn't, and I don't know why I panicked and came out here. I knew better. I know that most people have to be alone to do their real thinking."

"That's true. But I've already done my thinking. And my feeling, too. Thinking often wars with feeling, Tracy."

"Yes."

"What do you think we should do about us?"

"I think we should tell Pen what's happened. I want us to be married, Howard. That's the only way I'd ever feel safe about it."

"Tracy, I don't want to give up my life with Pen."

She didn't answer. Her arm tightened around his a little—that was all.

"I don't think it would have saved anything to try to lead up to it," he went on.

"No. And I didn't expect anything else, Howard. I just hoped, that's all."

"I'm not going to say that I won't give up Pen because I don't want to hurt her. I've already hurt her. And you. And myself."

"Pen's going to know sometime, even if you don't tell her," Tracy said.

"I don't know. I'll face that later, if it has to be faced. I hope it doesn't. I'm a coward about a lot of things. That's one reason I don't want to give up my life with Pen. I'm afraid to give up something that's been good for me. Not that it's perfect, by any means. But—" He hesitated. "I suppose I'm afraid of upsetting the balance of my life."

"Or is it that you're afraid of committing yourself to me?" When she

299

looked at him and he didn't answer, she continued, "I don't expect ever to be as unhappy again as I am at this moment."

"Tracy, I just wish—"

"I wish, too," she interrupted. "Oh, how I wish it could be as I want it to be, Howard. But you can't let it be that way. So what we've got to settle is what we expect from each other in the future."

"I'm selfish. I'd like to be with you whenever possible."

"But without a commitment," she said. "That would be torture."

"What then?"

"Nothing then. It will have to be nothing at all. Just as it was before."

Her arm tightened even more closely around his. She didn't want to let him go, any more than he wanted her to, but they were as far apart now as when she'd been a schoolchild in Abbottsville and he her shadowy lover on the silver screen, and they both knew it.

45

The day after Tracy finished her last scene in *Smith's War,* she deeded her house to Bonnie—who was overwhelmed by the unexpected gift—and flew to London, determined that she would return to Hollywood again only when and if she made another picture there.

She returned to her flat near Hyde Park and immediately started accepting the invitations that flooded in, hoping that activity would help her to forget her unhappiness. It didn't, and neither did her increased drinking. When Wesley Rainer flew up from his Jamaican "kingdom" to ask her to marry him for perhaps the twentieth time since she'd met him, she surprised him, and herself, by saying yes.

"But you understand that I don't love you," she pointed out.

He smiled strangely, as if he didn't believe it. She fully expected him to back out, now that he'd at last gotten what he thought he wanted, and at the last minute she wanted to back out, too.

But he didn't and she didn't, and a few days later she found herself in his personal transport plane as it landed on an airstrip he'd had hacked out of the forest on his large private preserve in Jamaica, and she had a foreboding that she'd just made another enormous mistake.

Of the many things Tracy had come to hate about living in what Wes still persisted in calling "paradise," she supposed she hated the relentlessness of the sun the most. It was strange, in a way. The hot Georgia sun of her childhood and adolescence had never bothered her, and she'd cherished the sun in California and Italy. But the sun had meant cheer and hope in those places. In Jamaica it stood for endless boredom and the ruthless repetitiveness of life.

One morning, three months after her marriage, she wakened before her maid came to call her, and although she didn't immediately remove the eye mask she slept in to keep out the light, she was nervously aware that the sun waited beyond the bed for her, pouring into the room through the blinds with slatted viciousness. The pines, palmettos, and oaks were tall and thick around the house, but the sun defiantly worked its way through almost everywhere, and her bedroom was no exception.

She finally slipped off her mask and faced the ribbons of sunlight coming into the room. She got up and was in her bathroom when her Jamaican maid arrived with a tall glass of pineapple juice for her to start the day.

The maid laid out Tracy's white halter dress as directed and left. Tracy dressed and looked at herself in the mirror. Wes would disapprove of her appearing in front of the doctor with her breasts so well accentuated by the halter. She didn't care.

She left her room. Ben's door across the way was ajar, and she wondered whether he was in there and would follow her downstairs, or was already down there, the faithful puppy dog at his master's heels.

She went downstairs and looked into the living room, where the huge Steinway concert grand dominated a corner beside a wall of windows. The heavy piano seemed entirely inappropriate to the house and the room. It didn't respond well to the climate, either, and Wes had already been forced to have a piano tuner flown in from New York several times to put it right again. Tracy loved to hear Wes play. He played as well as Crandon did. She would have been surprised if he hadn't. Everything he did, he did well. In the beginning, he'd even made love well. But now when he came to her bed, it wasn't an act of love. It was an assault. It was possessive rape.

She crossed the room to the front row of windows, all of them open to the porch and the sea breeze. She looked down the long, carefully kept sloping lawn, heavy with its huge palms, to the cove. The yacht was moored out near the breakwater, the million-dollar schooner that Wes liked to play captain on occasionally. That schooner could take them around the world if they had a yearning to go.

But they weren't going around the world or anywhere else. This was prison, and she was Wes's prisoner. There was no other way she could think of it now.

"Mr. Rainer's been asking for you."

She turned. It was Ben, Wes's bodyguard and faithful automaton, who kept turning up everywhere she was, keeping a close eye on her, as Wes had obviously instructed him to do. She'd long ago ceased to be startled at Ben's soundless arrivals. It was as if he walked on pads, like a cat.

"Don't tell me breakfast has gone cold?" she said sarcastically.

Ben didn't answer but turned and walked out of the room. She followed him into the dining room, where the doctor rose. Wes sat heavily, hampered by the plaster cast around his right foot and ankle. But he wouldn't have risen anyway.

"Good morning, Mrs. Rainer," the doctor said with a smile.

"Good morning, Dr. Hallick," Tracy said, smiling back. He was amiable enough, and he'd diverted some of Wes's attention from her. He'd been flown in from Kingston over a week ago when Wes was thrown from his thoroughbred—which had apparently shied at something in the forest—and had broken his ankle and cracked a rib. That the doctor was still here didn't surprise Tracy. Indeed, it wouldn't surprise her if he were appointed permanently to the staff, if only to dispense tranquilizers to Wes when necessary. What surprised her was that Wes, in his initial rage over the accident, hadn't had the horse shot.

Tracy sat down, followed by the doctor and Ben. She looked over at the woman standing next to the buffet, another of the dozen native servants around the house. She couldn't remember this one's name.

"Eggs and sausage, please," she said, and the woman turned to the salvers, filled a plate, and brought it around and set it in front of her. "And coffee," Tracy added. "But of course I'd rather have a Bloody Mary."

Wes looked at the doctor. "My wife has peculiar ideas about how to get the day started."

"Oh, I don't think that's so strange," the doctor said.

"Thank you, Doctor," Tracy said. "Then you might not even think it strange that I find Jamaica boring."

"No, I don't think that's strange, either," the doctor said. "It depends on what you're used to and what you want. Now I like the life here. I like the torpor and the changelessness. I came down from London on a vacation once and found the island greatly to my liking. I only went back home to sell my practice. I had a hard time building up a new practice in Kingston, but it was worth it. It all depends on your definition of contentment. Some people never find it."

"Wouldn't all people have to have at least *some* periods of contentment in their lives or go mad?" Tracy asked.

"Tracy's in one of her philosophical moods," Wes said to the doctor, in a tone suggesting that he was apologizing for the bad behavior of a child.

"But of course she's right. We all must have some happiness or we'd go off our beans."

Thank you, Doctor, Tracy said again, to herself, and decided she would say as little as possible for the rest of breakfast, for it was obviously one of those times—and they were increasing in frequency—when Wes tried to embarrass her as much as possible.

She ate quickly and said she was going for a walk. There were no objections, for she went for a walk down the beach every morning, and what harm could there be in it, since Ben always went with her? She hoped the time would come soon when Wes would acknowledge that she needed neither a watchdog nor a protector, and Ben would stay behind.

For a thug, he had his polite moments. At least he opened the door for her when she stepped out to the porch. They walked down the deep lawn to the white sand beach where the water rolled ashore gently. The cove was comparatively small, and some big rocks jutting out of the sea a hundred yards from shore served effectively as the breakwater, subduing a surf that often broke with real savagery on unprotected beaches down the way. The schooner bobbed quietly out there. There were two crewmen on deck, working with the rigging.

Tracy stopped on the beach and looked back at the house. She'd grown to hate it, but it continued to fascinate her nevertheless. It was modeled after the big old nineteenth-century Caribbean plantation houses, with spacious rooms, a house-wide covered porch, and even a widow's walk around the roof. It looked old, though it had been built less than two years ago. Wes had spotted this area when sailing in the Caribbean a few years earlier, had decided he'd finally found his "paradise," and had told his architect and his building contractor what he wanted. It had been produced promptly at great cost.

She turned away and started down the beach, Ben beside her. They walked in silence. An enormous stretch of greenery along the shore loomed for miles ahead. Buried back in it were the only other estates in

303

the near vicinity, all of them dwarfed by Wes's. The property of the British writer Lyle Jamison and his wife Carlen was the nearest. Tracy wasn't sure why, but she didn't feel wholly comfortable in the presence of the Jamisons. Still, she knew she shouldn't judge them so quickly. She'd been with them only twice in the three months of eternity she'd lived here with Wes. Actually, it would probably help if she could see more of them. It was even possible that she and Carlen Jamison, opposites though they seemed to be, might find some common ground for communication.

Common ground for communication! It seemed impossible for her to communicate with *anybody* lately.

She tried to concentrate on looking for seashells, but her unhappiness had taken over her thoughts, and she couldn't shake it. Suddenly she stopped. They'd reached one of her favorite parts of the beach. She liked it because of its wildness. The sea roared in here, even when the wind wasn't high. With their awesome force the big waves that pounded the beach in times of storm had even undercut the rocky wall that was its backdrop. The waves rolled in heavily now, splashing the beach with fury, then returning with a rush to the vastness from which they had come. Tracy supposed there was a tremendous undertow here, yet she suddenly found herself telling Ben that she intended to go swimming.

He stared at her. His eyes asked the obvious question.

She answered him with a sardonic smile. "Oh, I don't need a suit. Didn't you know that I like to swim in the nude?"

He said nothing. His eyes narrowed as she unclasped her halter and let it drop. She took a deep breath. He was staring at her eyes, but she knew he was seeing only her breasts. He stood stone still. Nothing about him moved but his lips. They began to quiver.

"I'm going in, and I'm going in nude," she said, inviting him to defy her, wondering if he would. But he continued to stand there, staring. She hesitated a moment, then kicked off her sandals and unzipped and dropped her skirt and stepped out of it. She stood facing him. She didn't know what to expect now. Perhaps he would strike her. But he only stared, and his tongue came out a little and licked his lips. It was the only sign of desire she'd ever seen from him.

She turned and walked into the sea. She had to fight it at once. She couldn't swim in this maelstrom. The crushing waves took her over and did what they wanted with her. She struggled, but there was no fighting against the force of the sea. She was so afraid that it was almost thrilling. When she was caught in the undertow of a particularly big wave, and turned over and over before she finally found her way to the surface, she thought for a while that she was going to drown, and wondered why her life didn't flash before her in a single blinding instant.

She was so weakened by her struggle in the undertow that she simply let the next roller carry her to shore. When she came out of the water, she saw that Ben had picked up her clothes from the sand and put them on a rock near the tideline. He was leaning against the rocky wall at the back of the beach, staring at her. He was twenty feet away from her and he would stay there. She knew that now. The possibility that he would try to make love to her, or rape her, had held credibility only briefly.

She sat on the rock while the sun dried her, her back to him. Then she put on her clothes and started back down the beach toward the house. Ben fell in beside her. Again they walked in silence. She wondered if Ben would say anything to Wes about her impulsive behavior. She doubted it. Ben would find it hard to explain why he had simply stood and watched it happen without trying to stop her.

Her thoughts turned to her unhappiness. She'd married Wes, trying to escape from unhappiness, and she'd only fallen into a deeper trap. Wes treated her not as his wife or lover but as his chattel and prisoner. And she knew he'd never let her go. She was trapped forever with him at the end of the world.

She wanted terribly to cry some of this out of her. But she didn't want Ben to see her crying. Besides, she wasn't even sure she could cry anymore. Maybe it had gone beyond that.

46

Tracy kept hoping Wes would decide not to go along with her to the Jamisons' party. Considering her secret relationship with Lyle Jamison, it would be better. If Wes began to suspect, his vengeance would unquestionably be swift and extreme.

But Wes decided he would go, and Tracy could only pretend to be glad about it. After all, it was she who had urged that they see more of the Jamisons. When she had, she'd been looking for relief from the depressing sameness of her day-to-day existence. She hadn't dreamed that socializing with the Jamisons would lead to the growth of a special feeling between her and Lyle.

Even Dr. Hallick came along. Wes's foot and ankle were long out of the cast and functioning normally again, but Dr. Hallick had continued to be retained, as Tracy had expected. The three of them sat in the back of the black Cadillac limousine as Ben drove over the narrow crude road that better accommodated the small British cars that were practically the only automobiles seen in these parts. Dapples and splashes of sun found their way through the flamboyant trees arching the road. At this time of year they were crimson with blossoms, with mimosal perfume hanging heavily on the air.

Tracy heard a calypso band playing in the garden behind the house as they wound up the Jamisons' driveway. Cars were parked all along the porch of the cool, shuttered house. Ben let them out near the front door and then went off to park and wait for them. The Negro butler ushered them into the handsome interior, tastefully arranged with antique pieces Carlen and Lyle had brought down from England when they'd decided, several years ago, that they would live here permanently.

Carlen and Lyle greeted them and introduced them to the people around the room. Dr. Hallick ended up in conversation with another physician in the crowd, and Carlen and Lyle left Tracy and Wes with a middle-aged couple named Yorke while they introduced other new arrivals around. The Yorkes were from the States, and Mr. Yorke was Lyle's American publisher. It turned out that Mrs. Yorke was a movie fan and had seen *Smith's War* in New York just before they'd come down here.

"I don't ordinarily like war movies, but that one was simply wonderful, wasn't it, Amos?" she commented, looking at her husband.

"It was a damned good adventure story," he said.

"*And* love story," his wife added, smiling at Tracy. "You were simply marvelous in your part. What will you be doing next?"

"I don't know," Tracy said.

"I don't think she'll be making any more pictures," Wes said.

Tracy frowned at Wes. He looked hard at her, defying her to protest.

"There's a theory that stars owe themselves to the public," Mrs. Yorke said to Tracy, "but I can understand why you wouldn't want to leave this paradise for anything."

"Paradise is what my husband calls it, too, Mrs. Yorke," Tracy said.

"Yes," Wes said. "Because it's away from the world, and the world is a deplorable place." He looked at Tracy again. "I don't think my wife looks on it quite as paradise yet. But she will, when she's been here long enough."

Tracy felt a slight trembling beginning in her. Wes was building up to

306

embarrassing her again, and as usual she didn't know what to say or do. Fortunately, Carlen came up from behind just then, hooked her arm through Tracy's, and said, "It's time we broke up this clique. There's nothing drearier than a party where people don't circulate."

Carlen steered Tracy into another group. She was glad to be away from Wes, and she tried to act interested in what was going on, but what she was really waiting for was a chance to talk with Lyle. It finally came when she saw him go back into the garden, apparently to give some instructions to the calypso players. She happened to be at the buffet table getting a fresh drink at the time. Before she slipped outside, she looked for Wes and Carlen. They were both talking, with their backs to her.

When Lyle saw her coming, he stepped away from the musicians and strolled back into the depths of the garden. She followed. When she reached him, they were screened from the house by foliage, but they were afraid to reach for each other.

"We shouldn't be stealing even this one moment," he said.

"I know. But you came out here because you thought I'd follow, and I did."

"Why do we make it so dangerous for ourselves? Do we feel our guilt so deeply that we *want* to be caught?"

She hadn't thought of it that way. "I think we do what we have to do."

"We could have stopped what was happening to us."

"Are you saying we should have?"

"No," he said.

"Will you be able to meet me tomorrow?"

"Yes. We'd better go back inside now. If we don't, I won't be able to resist touching you much longer."

They went back in together. It appeared as if they had run into each other in the garden. They laughed as they came in, as if they were sharing an interesting story.

Tracy kept thinking about what Wes had said at the party and how he'd said it, and she couldn't let it go without talking to him about it. An opportunity presented itself an hour after they came home from the party, when she glanced out a front window and saw him standing halfway down the lawn, gazing out at his schooner near the breakwater. He was alone, which was very unusual. Usually Dr. Hallick, Ben, or one of his business assistants was with him.

When she went outside, Wes was surprised to see her. He always was when she came to him without being brought.

"I was just thinking that we ought to take the Jamisons out for

307

another sail one of these days," he said, looking back out at the schooner.

"I'm sure they'd enjoy it."

"They're not boring," Wes continued. "But those Americans at the party were. So were most of the others."

"Wes, it disturbed me when you told the Yorkes you didn't think I'd be making any more pictures. I got the distinct impression you meant you wouldn't *let* me make any more pictures."

He looked at her. "Oh, did you get that impression, Tracy?"

"There's a limit to what I'll endure, Wes. I'm still under contract to Regency Pictures. If a picture comes up that I want to make, I'm going to make it."

He shrugged. "I doubt that it will work out that way."

"If it doesn't, it will be because you won't let it. You think you own me, just as you own this estate and that ship and your gold mine and all those companies you control. The only reason you wanted to marry me was because I was hard to get, and that made me all the more desirable as a possession."

"I married you because I wanted you. And I still want you, even though I see you much more clearly now than I did, and the picture isn't pretty. People marry strangers, no matter how long they've known each other. Marriage is the most elucidating experience possible. Did it ever occur to you that if people reached the point before marriage where they ceased being strangers, they wouldn't marry?"

"Does that mean you're sorry we did?"

"Tracy, I know what's in your mind. You think this is a mistake, and you want to walk out, just as you walked out on your other marriage. Eventually you're going to know this isn't a mistake. And you're not walking out. In our case, 'Till death do you part' means something. I'm never going to let you go."

He'd really given her the answer to her other question, too. He would definitely never let her make another picture.

That evening Tracy was even drunker than usual by dinnertime. Still, if she hadn't been drunk, she wouldn't have been able to be so insistent when she told Wes that she had to go home and see her mother soon, that she'd never before in her life gone this long without seeing her. Wes said what he'd said before, that if she wanted to see her mother, she could have her come here.

Afterward, Tracy went upstairs, locked her door, and lay on her bed in numbed despair. She'd begun to think quite a while back that Wes was more than emotionally unbalanced. She thought he might be going insane. Yet she couldn't accuse him. He would kill her if she did.

She didn't feel she could even talk with Dr. Hallick about him. Or Lyle. She'd turned to Lyle in her growing panic, and that had become far more complicated than either of them had expected, too.

The doorknob rattled. Wes was calling to her to unlock the door. She mumbled something about having a headache. The door exploded open, the lock broken by his heavy foot. He was disrobing as he approached her. His face and his eyes flamed with his anger.

"Don't ever try to lock me out again!" he said as he ripped her dress off.

It was the same savage attack it had been almost every night since his cast had been removed. He said he would keep coming to her bed until she conceived. He had a consuming desire for a child. She didn't think he wanted an heir as much as someone else in his life to rule.

There was nothing left of their union resembling an act of love. He pinned her down and pounded into her. She lay rigid under him, hating it, wondering how she could ever have found excitement from his brutality, wishing for it to be over quickly. It was. He ejaculated and went at once to his room at the other end of the hall.

She lay awake for hours thinking about him and his contempt for her, hating the way he made her feel small and mean in his presence, hating her life with him, fearing his growing madness. She thought that like Crandon, he took his hate for himself out on those around him, and especially her.

Oh, God, how had she gotten herself trapped like this? And how was she to escape?

The day was slow in going. Wes spent most of the morning in his office issuing instructions by teletype, radio, and telephone to various of his enterprises, but after lunch he sat down at the piano and played Chopin. Tracy listened restlessly, wondering if his decision to play after lunch instead of going directly back to his office as he usually did would alter the afternoon schedule much. Usually he spent about an hour in his office in the afternoon and then sat down for a game of rummy with Ben and Dr. Hallick around three o'clock, when she would go for her walk along the beach.

Finally, after he finished playing, he went to his office, but he didn't stay long. By ten minutes after three, when she was getting nervous about the situation, he emerged, and the game was started out on the porch.

She walked down to the beach and started south. For several months now she'd been taking her walks without Ben along. Wes had finally concluded there was no danger in her going alone, and besides, he needed Ben for his rummy game.

She walked more quickly than usual because she was a little late. A half mile below the house, she left the beach by way of a narrow little path leading straight into the mango grove lying on the boundary between Wes's estate and Lyle and Carlen's property.

Lyle was waiting in the grove. He took her hands in his and simply stood looking at her for a while, as he often did, as if she were still a wonderful discovery he'd just made, as if he still couldn't believe any of this.

He unclasped his hands, finally, and put them on her waist, gently drawing her against him. His heart pounded against her, and he was hard below. Yet no matter his urgency, he never rushed. His touch was always a caress, never a weapon. He wanted her for love, not for sex.

He kissed her, then turned her and unzipped the back of her linen dress and let it fall. He unhooked her brassiere and dropped it, then turned her to face him. His hands closed around her breasts and his fingers stroked lovingly. He reached down and pressed his face against one breast, breathing against it, kissing it with tiny kisses until her flesh quivered. Then the other. He nestled against her breasts, loving them.

They undressed and lay down together on the moss. He picked up her hand and kissed the palm. He kissed her breast again. He took the nipple into his mouth, but gently, as a baby would.

He kissed his way down her body. He knelt between her thighs. He wrapped his arms around them and kissed their insides, pressing his face against them. He moved up to her opening, kissing, kissing, kissing as he went. He never tongued. Just those little kisses, so gentle yet so full of passion and love.

He raised himself and leaned over her. His lips met hers. His hand worked below, and he inserted himself. He was in, filling her. Slowly and gently, in and almost out, back and forth he went. Gently he made love to her, always gently, even when he moved inside her deeper and faster. Together they climbed up and up. Their bodies shuddered as his convulsions began and her orgasm radiated through her. Her legs locked over him, holding him inside her as long as she could. He was panting. "Oh, God," he whispered.

He lay back from her, and she rested against his chest. He said nothing, but that didn't surprise her, for usually it was a long time afterward before they talked. They didn't talk easily anyway. He felt

310

his guilt very deeply. Tracy knew their affair would never have started if she hadn't done the seducing. She doubted that Lyle had ever been unfaithful to Carlen before.

Tracy felt a different kind of guilt. She had used Lyle. Her affair with him had offered the only positive emotional relief she'd known in months. She hadn't expected him to go overboard emotionally, but this man who wrote sophisticated novels about worldly men and women had turned out to be terribly vulnerable himself. Tracy couldn't be sure how she really felt about him. The specter of Wes stood between her and any easy reckoning of her feelings about anyone.

"Tracy," Lyle suddenly said, "we've got to talk about what we're going to do about our future together."

She raised herself up and looked at him. "I told you before, Lyle. I don't think it's time yet for us to talk about it."

"After three months of being together like this? I love you—"

"Don't say that," she cut in. "You don't know."

"I do," he said insistently. "I'm sure."

"I've been much too victimized by self-deception in the past, Lyle. I can't let either of us be a victim of it this time."

"It torments me, not knowing what's going to happen. It *must* work out. I couldn't stand its not working out. Wesley and Carlen are going to have to be told, and we must decide how we're going to do it."

"We can't make any hasty decisions," she said, then stopped abruptly, raising her finger to her lips, for briefly there'd been a sound, as if someone had pushed back a bush. Or could it have been just a gust of wind stirring the foliage?

Lyle had gone tense, too. He was looking into the trees as if he expected someone to come bursting out of them. But the sound didn't repeat itself.

Still, they were wary. Just because they met in this secluded spot didn't mean that someone might not walk in on them.

They got dressed, agreed to meet there again the next day and parted. When Tracy reached the beach, the sun had vanished behind scudding gray clouds. The wind had come up so suddenly and forcefully that she had difficulty walking back to the house. When she reached it, the rummy game was finished. Only Ben was on the porch. The corners of his mouth were turned up slightly, as if he were about to smile.

Something was different. Tracy felt it in the unnatural quiet of the house. There were no distant sounds of human activity, yet the house was filled with people. Wes, Dr. Hallick, Ben, and a dozen servants were around, but the only sounds were the whine of the wind and the unusually loud pounding of the surf.

When Tracy's maid arrived to lay out her dress for dinner, Tracy sent her back to bring her a martini. She knew there wasn't a single person on the estate who didn't know she drank in her room, but she no longer cared.

When her maid returned with the drink, Tracy dawdled with dressing. She didn't want to go down to dinner. She had a feeling it would be an ugly evening. Wes was rigid about time, and she was expected downstairs at eight. A little unsteady from a second martini, she was fifteen minutes late.

Dr. Hallick rose with a smile. "Good evening, Mrs. Rainer."

Wes and Ben remained seated. Wes said, "Sit down, Tracy, and get on with your drinking." He nodded at the butler, standing beside the bar. "Bring her another of whatever she's been drinking."

The butler looked embarrassed. Dr. Hallick frowned slightly. Tracy tried to look unconcerned as she sat down and accepted the glass the butler brought to her.

She turned her eyes away as Wes stared uncomfortably at her, saying, "There may be a bad storm coming. The doctor's been telling us what we'd better do to prepare for it."

"A hurricane developed in the Azores and is headed across the Atlantic toward the Caribbean," Dr. Hallick said. "From the radio reports, it's gaining strength. We can hope it will blow right by us, but we must be prepared for the possibility that it could hit us."

"But that wouldn't frighten you, would it, Tracy?" Wes said.

She dared to look at him. "Don't be ridiculous. Of course it would."

"It would frighten anyone, I should think," the doctor said. "A hurricane is the most powerful force of nature." He went on to say that winds in excess of a hundred miles an hour, sustained gusts up to two hundred and fifty miles an hour, and seas running at thirty or forty feet were the usual order of things in a hurricane.

"The point is, if it does come here, we can't stop it, but we can at least be prepared as much as possible. On an estate as large as this, it's important that everyone be told what the consequences could be. If a hurricane watch is issued tomorrow, then we ought to have a meeting of everybody who lives here and issue instructions. We must be prepared for a siege with food, drinking water, lamps, flashlights, camp stoves, candles, and medical supplies. Everything movable from the lawns, gardens, and porches should be carried inside. Let's see. How many people are living in the houses out back?"

312

Wes shrugged. "I don't know. Maybe forty or fifty."

"I know," Ben said, and enumerated them. There were eight schooner crewmen and two of their wives, Wes's pilot, the airplane mechanic, the chauffeur, Wes's two administrative assistants and their wives, and his male secretary. In addition, there were thirty native adults who worked at various tasks in the house and around the estate and the multitude of children who lived with them.

"Over a hundred persons, including those of us in the main house," the doctor said. "That's a lot of lives to be concerned with. But if the storm comes, and we all do what we should, there's no reason why we can't all live through it."

Something was wrong. Tracy had felt it from the moment she'd seen that unsmiled smile on Ben's face the previous afternoon. She was afraid that she and Lyle had been found out. But if that was true, if Wes had sent Ben to follow her yesterday, why hadn't he killed her?

She'd lain awake in fear most of the night, but Wes hadn't come near her. After finally falling asleep near dawn, she wakened at noon with such a headache that she was dizzy when she got out of bed. She took aspirin, put on the dress her maid had laid out for her, and went downstairs. There was no one around.

She stepped out to the porch. Dr. Hallick was down on the lawn, looking out at the water. The schooner was resting quietly. But several crewmen were working with the lines. She walked down to the doctor.

"A hurricane watch has been issued," he told her.

"It has?" She was surprised. The sky was its usual brilliant blue, dotted here and there with a few trailing fluffy clouds, and the water in the cove was its usual shimmering aquamarine, clear and quiet. "It looked like a storm was coming yesterday afternoon, but it certainly doesn't now."

"It's usually like this for the last half day or so before a storm hits," the doctor said. "It's coming straight at us, the radio said. Of course, there's a ninety percent chance it will change direction, but I've got an ugly feeling about it. The birds and gulls have started to leave, and that worries me."

"What about the meeting you're going to have to issue instructions?"

"We've already had it. Preparations are going on right now." He nodded out toward the schooner. "Those crewmen are securing the ship with heavier mooring lines to the anchorage. It's all that can be done except pray, I'm afraid. A hurricane can tear a ship apart just as easily as it can smash a building."

313

"You had the meeting? Why wasn't I called?"

"I wanted to call you, but Wesley said you needed your sleep. Besides, he said you were frightened enough without making it worse."

Yes, she was frightened. And it wasn't just the prospect of a hurricane that was frightening her.

"Tell me, Tracy," Wes said at lunch, "did you sleep well last night?"

"No," Tracy said.

Wes looked at Dr. Hallick. "Isn't it true that people with bad consciences don't sleep well, Doctor?"

"You're entirely too intelligent to believe an old wives' tale like that one, Wesley."

"But I believe Tracy *does* have a bad conscience, Doctor."

"Most of us do, Wesley, about one thing or another. I believe you have, too."

Wes laughed. "The thing I admire most about you, Doctor, is that you say what you think. You're no toady."

"Only part of the time," the doctor said. "I don't say what I think when doing so might harm me. After someone is around you for a while, Wesley, he knows where the line can be drawn. Of course, where the line can be drawn depends on the person involved. I can say what I think to you to a greater degree than Ben can, for instance, because we're on different levels of intelligence and fealty, and you would accept more truth from me than from him."

"This conversation is interesting," Wes said. "That's why I'm glad you decided to stay on with us, Doctor. Because you can talk interestingly."

"That and because I serve as a counterpoint to your regular toadies. But only to an extent. I'm basically selfish, weak, and lazy, and it's easier for me to stay here and be a physician only occasionally than to return to Kingston and resume my full responsibilities. But I do draw a line. Ben doesn't. I believe Ben would kill for you."

"That's quite a theory, Doctor," Wes said.

"He worships you. But worship is hard to come by, and I doubt that your other toadies would go that far. Still, they respect you for your riches and your business acumen, and they're undoubtedly afraid of you."

"Afraid?"

"You inspire fear in most people. Don't act surprised. You know that." The doctor smiled. "I wonder why I'm saying all this. It's dangerous, I suppose."

314

"No, Doctor, it isn't dangerous to be honest with me," Wes said. He looked at Tracy. "What's dangerous is not to be."

"By the way, where's Ben?" the doctor asked. "I've never known him to miss lunch before."

Wes continued to look at Tracy. "He's attending to something for me."

Lunch was over, though they were still at the table. It had been a half hour since Wes had said, with reference to Ben, "He's attending to something for me," and Tracy had kept thinking about it. The words had been innocuous enough, but the edge in Wes's voice and the darkening in his eyes when he'd said them had alarmed her.

"Tracy, what are you thinking about?" Wes said.

"What?" She forced herself to look at him. "I don't know what I was thinking."

"Did you hear that, Dr. Hallick? She says she doesn't know what she was thinking. Do you believe that? I think it means she doesn't want us to know what she was thinking."

"Wes, stop it," Tracy said.

"Stop what, Tracy? Stop thinking *my* private thoughts? At the moment, I don't think you'd want to know them."

"I just want to go upstairs," Tracy said. "I have a headache."

"I must insist that you don't," Wes said. "We'll go into the living room, and I'll play something soothing for your head. Perhaps some quiet Bach." He smiled at the doctor. "Did I ever tell you, Doctor, that I would far rather have matured into a concert virtuoso than a business wizard? The trouble was, the spark of musical genius was missing. One can make millions in the business world with just capital, good judgment, and luck, but to play the piano brilliantly requires innate genius."

"I think we ought to get the latest news on the storm before we do anything," the doctor said.

"Yes, of course," Wes said. "We'll go into the living room and listen to the storm report on the radio, and then I'll play while we wait it out. Naturally we'll serve liquor so Tracy can get drunk. Can't you see how afraid Tracy is of the storm, Doctor, even if she can't be sure it will even hit us? Tracy is afraid of Armageddon, Doctor. She's read the Bible. She's very religious. Would you believe that?"

The doctor nodded slowly, frowning at the same time. Tracy had a feeling that he was as worried about the way Wes was acting as she was. The difference was that the doctor probably couldn't figure out why, but she was very much afraid she could.

315

The afternoon crawled by. Wes kept playing, but it wasn't the soothing Bach he'd promised. It was something heavy and pounding. His face expressed nothing but calm even as he crashed down on the keys, but Tracy knew he was seething inside. All she could do was sit and wait and try not to scream. A bottle of Scotch and a bucket of ice had been put on the table beside her. She drank steadily, but she didn't get drunk. She was too afraid.

They tuned in the radio every half hour to get the storm news. There was more and more static. Outside, the palms were beating sharply in the rising wind, and the cove was a spraying angry sea, bubbling in agitation with troughs of foam. It was announced on the radio that the hurricane watch had been changed to a hurricane warning.

Tracy kept praying silently that Lyle wouldn't set out to meet her today. *Please, dear God!*

The doctor vanished, seeing that what was supposed to be done was done. The porch furniture was being brought inside by the servants. There was scurrying everywhere around the house. Yet here she sat drinking while Wes played the piano. It was madness.

She got up and went to the window. The schooner rocked uncertainly out in the cove. The light was pale, and in the east the sky was turning gray-black, as if night were settling in. Ben appeared suddenly, coming around from the side of the house. She swallowed and looked at her watch as he stepped up on the porch. It was three-thirty.

Ben came into the room. Wes stopped playing abruptly. Tracy forced herself to turn around from the window and look at Ben. He was smiling at Wes. He and Wes stared at each other, and Wes began to smile, too.

Tracy felt herself beginning to slip away.

She came to consciousness slowly. She was on her bed. It seemed to be nighttime. There was a spate of angry rain against the windows. She wondered how long she'd been unconscious. Her head was throbbing. She wondered where Dr. Hallick was. She reached for the lamp switch and turned it on. She almost screamed. Wes was sitting in a chair across the room.

"Good," Wes said. "You're awake. The doctor said he didn't think there'd be any complications. He had to leave for a while."

Wes rose and came over and sat on the side of the bed.

"It's too bad he had to go, but it was an emergency, and a doctor has to go when he's called."

Tracy turned her eyes away. She couldn't stand looking at him.

"Aren't you going to ask me where he was called, Tracy? It was to

316

the Jamisons. Carlen was hysterical when she phoned, and we could hardly make sense of it at first, but it seems that by chance one of their servants was in the forest and found Lyle there. He'd been savagely beaten. Naturally it must have been some vindictive native—"

"You beast, you beast!" She turned her eyes back, forcing herself to look at him. He was smiling at her.

"Beast?" he said. "I'm surprised at you, Tracy. 'Cuckold' is a better word for me, old-fashioned though it is. But I doubt you even know what the word means, do you? You're not very smart."

"Oh, God," she moaned. "You sent Ben to kill him."

"No, I didn't instruct Ben to kill him, although it's true, as Dr. Hallick pointed out, that Ben would kill for me if I asked him to. Ben *does* worship me. If I could have gotten from you one-tenth of what I've gotten from Ben—"

"You're sick," she cut in.

"Not sick. Just looking for justice. And Ben stopped when he was supposed to. I told him just to beat Lyle *almost* to death. I don't believe in murder unless it's worthwhile."

"You're twisted. And I don't believe you. You wanted him to die. If he hadn't been found, he would have. He might die yet."

"Yes, he might," Wes said. "If he did, would that be my fault or yours? Under the rules of logic, it would be yours, for none of it would have happened if you hadn't caused it."

"Oh, God, Wes, there's no reasoning with you."

"What do you expect of me, Tracy? That I'm just going to let you off? That I'm going to almost kill Lyle and not almost kill you? Don't you see that it's all inevitable?"

He suddenly leaned over her. She clenched her teeth as she saw his right arm draw back and then swing toward her. His open hand struck her. She screamed.

The arm swung again. She struggled to turn away and miss the blow, rolling over and falling off the bed on the side away from him. She started struggling to her feet. If she could get to the door and into the hall, there was a chance she might get away from him.

But he bolted around the bed and blocked her. He struck her again. She screamed from the pain. When she tried to turn away from the blows, he grabbed her, pulled her around, and pressed her against him, locking her arms around her back with one hand and repeatedly striking her with the other. She was now beyond screaming. His glaring eyes and clenched teeth blurred before her, and she felt moisture on her face. She was bleeding or weeping or both. She was dying. He was not going to stop hitting her until she was dead.

But then he suddenly turned her and flung her against the wall. She sank to the floor, moaning, weeping, tasting the blood mixed with tears running into the corners of her mouth. She sat cowed and helpless, waiting for the kick to the head that would finish her, but it didn't come. She heard the door slam and his heavy footfalls receding down the hall. She kept tasting her tears and blood. Then everything faded into oblivion again.

Tracy was aware first of the noise—of wind, of rain driving against the window, of palm fronds lashing against the house. And mixed in the depth of it, incredibly, was music. Piano music. Music crashing the way the storm was crashing.

Someone was wiping her eyes. She opened them slowly. The room seemed to be swaying. She was on the floor. The doctor was bent over her.

"He tried to kill me," she said.

"You'll be bruised," Dr. Hallick said, "but you'll be all right."

"Lyle—"

"He'll be all right, too."

"Wes is insane, isn't he?"

"We can't think about that now. We've got to get you down to the cellar. The storm is cresting. It could blow the roof off and collapse the house before it's finished. Do you think you can stand if I support you?"

"I'll try. Do I have any face left? Did he destroy it?"

"Your face will be all right. What's important now is to save our lives. I'm going to lift you up now."

He lifted her to her feet. Every bone in her body was aching, and her head was splitting. The doctor supported her with his arm as he led her into the hall. He was carrying a flashlight. The house lights were out. Painfully, she clung to him as they descended to the first floor. The windows rattled and the house vibrated from the lashing of the storm. From the living room, Wes was producing an eerie obbligato on the piano.

"My God, is he going to just sit there and play the piano while the world comes apart?" Tracy said.

"I tried to get him to come down to the cellar, but he won't," the doctor said. "He's not rational. There's nothing I can do. I told him the room would cave in on him if the wind got bad enough. He laughed and said that if that happened, he'd get under the piano."

"He thinks he's God. He doesn't think anything can kill him."

Downstairs in the fruit cellar, the butler, several of the native

318

household servants, and Ben were huddled on boxes and chairs in the unearthly glow of battery lamps. The doctor told Tracy that the others on the estate were waiting it out in the cellars of the other buildings out back.

"You didn't bring Mr. Rainer down," Ben said angrily to the doctor. "You brought *her* down, but you didn't bring him."

"You heard what he said," the doctor answered. "If you think you can get him to come down, go up after him."

Ben turned and stared at Tracy's face. "You got just what you deserve, you bitch!"

"I don't see you going upstairs after your master as the doctor suggested."

"Shut up, you bitch!" Ben seethed.

"Now just stop this, Ben," Dr. Hallick said. "If you aren't going up after Wesley, then I must insist that you sit over there somewhere and be quiet."

"You're not giving me orders!" Ben exploded. "Only Mr. Rainer can give me orders."

"I'm taking charge down here," the doctor said. "I think I'm better qualified for the job than you are. Now do as I told you."

Ben glared at the doctor. His fists were balled. But the doctor stared him down. Sullenly, Ben turned his back on them.

The storm worsened within minutes. The wind was a steadily rising howl. There were crashing and pounding sounds. The house heaved and shuddered on its foundation. Tracy kept thinking of Wes up there at the piano while the world caved in around him. It sounded as if the house were coming apart. She wondered if this would be the end for all of them.

The tremendous howling and pounding continued for almost an hour, and then the sound died down; but when Ben started for the stairs, Dr. Hallick stopped him.

"The calm might just be the eye of the hurricane passing over. We'll sit tight for a few minutes and see."

Surely enough, in a few minutes the wind rose again, and the storm brutalized the house for another half hour.

This time when it stopped, the doctor said it was safe to go upstairs. They had to force the cellar door to get out, because fallen rubble was heaped against it.

Outside, the schooner had been torn from its mooring, whirled through the water by one of the furious waves, and left on land when the water retreated. Everywhere trees had been uprooted, and some had been hurled against the house like battering rams. One had crashed

319

through a living room window and had struck Wes like a huge arrow. He'd been crushed to death against the piano.

47

Michael Baines hated the thought of being alone at Christmas. Being alone at other times of the year was one thing. Being alone at Christmas was another. There was something unfair about it.

It would help if he at least had a new picture to go into after the first of the year. That would be something to think about, anyway. But there was no new picture, and no sign that there would ever be one. That was cruel irony. *Smith's War* had been a smash, and Mike's performance in it most probably would earn him his first Academy Award nomination, yet the studio didn't have a new property for him.

Three weeks before Christmas he heard from his parents, suggesting that he come home for Christmas. He couldn't bear the thought of Christmas with his parents in Grove Center, Indiana, ever again. He phoned them with the lie that he was too busy reading scripts to get away. He felt they were probably relieved. To this day they were uncomfortable with him, and he with them, although they never discussed it.

He was drinking more than ever these days. He drank away the afternoons, evenings, and nights and sometimes the mornings as well when he couldn't sleep. But there was no one to see but the cook, the housekeeper, and the gardener, who pretended to pay no attention to him, even the day he fell drunk into the pool. He supposed later that it must have looked to them like something out of a slapstick comedy.

That was a day of continuing idiocy. Hardly was he dried out from his unexpected dip than he drove to Beverly Hills and bought almost everything he saw in the way of Christmas decorations. The next day decorators arrived with their truckloads. There was thousands of dollars' worth of the stuff, including a Santa, a sleigh, and reindeer of life size to be placed beside the pool, a Christmas crèche of staggering detail, and three large Christmas trees, including two splendid, be-

320

spangled ones for the roof, which would broadcast his absurdity down the mountainside for everyone to see. The third Christmas tree, another giant, went into the living room, where it was loaded with red Christmas balls, silver tinsel, and a host of multicolored lights.

Mike was engulfed by the Christmas paraphernalia he had forced on himself, and he found the idea of them almost unbearable, yet he couldn't find the words to tell them to take it all away.

That night he did something he hadn't done for a long time. He drove down to Santa Monica and walked the beach. The ocean was unusually quiet. He felt expectant.

A girl passed him, her blond hair loose behind her. Her trench coat obscured the shape of her body, but her fine legs hinted at what the rest of her was probably like. She was tall and very erect and walked without looking behind her. She wasn't the least bit curious about him. He followed her.

Finally she stopped at a pile of rocks at the water's edge and looked out at the ocean. He went up and said hello to her. She turned. Her face was aristocratic and beautiful. Her eyes warned that she was annoyed by his intrusion. He didn't think she was going to answer him. But finally she nodded ever so slightly and said, unsmilingly, "Hello."

Her name was Ria Nicholson, and she wasn't interested in knowing him. But she walked the beach with him that night, and he was at her door early the next day. He kept after her. He soon found that her world had nothing to do with his, and wondered if that was what fascinated him most about her. It was a shock to him that although she'd seen his photograph and recognized him, she'd never seen him in a movie. She didn't go to movies, she said.

She was twenty-six, came of old stock and great wealth, and had gone to Vassar. She was intelligent and autocratic—her father's traits, Mike learned soon enough. She hadn't married, she said bluntly, because she hadn't met a man she considered good enough for her.

"I may never marry," she said two days later as they rode down the beach together on two lively thoroughbreds from her father's stable.

"You're going to marry me," Mike said.

She answered by bursting forth in a gallop, looking back and laughing as he tried uselessly to overtake her.

"My father won't like you," she said the morning she invited him to breakfast. There were just the two of them at a long table with an antique lace tablecloth in a large room hung with portraits, among which was one of her father. He looked as Mike would have expected—tall, handsome, undauntable.

"It won't make any difference," Mike said. But he was glad her

321

father was in New York on business and wouldn't be back until just before Christmas.

Their house was magnificent, one of the largest on the beach, and it was filled with antiques and a multitude of family portraits, including three of Ria, three of her father, and a somehow disturbing one of the two of them together.

Though it didn't make sense, he felt within a few days of meeting her that his life had changed drastically. Her casual attitude toward him had already taken on a disproportionate and disturbing importance.

The day he drove her up to his house he wished he could have done away with the Christmas decorations. She laughed when he embarrassingly explained that he'd done it all on impulse.

"It probably means you never wanted to grow up," she said.

"What do you mean?"

"Christmas is important to children."

"It isn't to me," he said a little stiffly. "I've never thought Christmas seemed right in California, anyway."

She didn't answer. She walked over and looked at the photograph of Mona on the piano.

"Now don't tell me you don't know who she is," he said.

"Yes, I know who she is."

"Did you know I was married to her?"

"No." She turned from the picture and looked back at him. "She's beautiful, but did she have anything more to offer? Did she bore you? Or did you bore her? Did the marriage die of that?"

"No. It died, but not of boredom."

"Some people should never marry. Marriage is a need for most people, but some of us are better off without it."

"You'll change your mind about that after we're married."

"Don't be absurd."

"I'm not. We're both goners already."

"I could walk out of here now and forget within a week that I'd ever met you," she said.

"I don't believe you. You just don't like the idea that you're probably falling in love. Naturally you'd consider it a weakness to feel an emotion like love."

She laughed. "You've been through an unsuccessful marriage—or is it more than one?—and you're talking about love?"

"I believe in love. I think that life with love is better than life without it. I think that's the way most people think about it and that's why most people look for it."

"You have very stereotyped ideas about life," she said. "You're also

322

a dreamer. I don't find that surprising, from what else I've learned of you, but it disappoints me. I was hoping you would be a more basic type. I mean, don't you want sex? So far, all you've done is kiss me. Why didn't you throw me down in the sand when we met and take me?"

"Because I wouldn't want it that way with us."

"But that's the only way it would be good. I don't like sex unless it's earthy."

Why did it annoy him that she admitted having had sex? Why should he have expected her to be a virgin? Still, he felt a pang of disappointment.

He tried to hide it when he answered evenly, "You'll like it when there's a little love mixed in with it."

"A little love? Why not a lot of love? One idea is no more ridiculous than the other. I'll tell you how I like it. The best sex I ever had was with a telephone repairman. He was a wonderful burly brute. He simply threw me down on the floor and took me. It must have lasted every bit of sixty seconds. Sixty explosive, mindless seconds. It was magnificent. And my father was in the next room while it was happening. It added a thrilling element of danger."

She smiled mockingly at him, inviting him to comment. He didn't know what to say. He wanted to believe that her story was a lie, told simply out of perversity to shock and disturb him. He hated the idea of it. He felt like telling her that, but he knew that was what she wanted to hear. He said instead, "Every time you say something about your father, I get the impression that you're afraid of him."

The mocking smile vanished. "I'm not in the least afraid of him," she said coldly. "He's afraid of me, if you want to know the truth."

"It will be interesting to meet him and find out."

"You won't meet him. We won't be seeing each other by the time he comes back. You're beginning to bore me."

He walked up to her. He put his hands on her arms and pressed her back against the piano. She looked at him tauntingly, waiting.

"You want to hurt me," he said, "but I won't let you."

Her eyes still taunted as he leaned down to kiss her, but when he drew away from her, they had softened to thoughtfulness. He hoped it meant she was allowing herself to care for him. He hoped she realized that no matter what she did to resist loving him, it wouldn't make any difference in the end.

The sixth day after Mike met Ria, she gave him his first pangs of jealousy. It got started badly when he drove down early to ask her to spend the day with him and found that she was already out riding, although it was barely nine.

Worse yet, after an hour of impatiently waiting for her, he found that she hadn't been riding alone. She introduced the man with her as Walker Kendricks, an old friend she'd grown up with on the beach. He was associated with a law firm in New York City and had come home for the holidays. He was smooth and low-toned, exuding the dauntless self-confidence that went with inherited wealth. Mike hated him instantly. And he hated Ria as she sat there chatting happily with Kendricks about what fun they'd had together as youngsters.

Ria paid a lot of attention to Kendricks and no attention at all to Mike in the next painful hour. He walked out then, determined not to return until she called and begged him. She didn't call, and he went back to see her sheepishly after two agonizing days of alcoholic self-pity. He found her busy decorating a large Christmas tree in the living room.

"I was afraid Kendricks might be here," he said.

"Would you mind?" she asked with a slight smile.

"Yes. I hope that pompous bore isn't an example of your friends."

"He's a bore but he isn't pompous, and I don't have friends. The truth is, I don't really like anybody."

"I don't care if you like me or not, Ria. Just so you love me."

She tossed her head back, laughing. "You're a fool."

He was hurt, but he hid it. "You already love me," he said evenly. "But you feel you have to fight it all the way. I understand. You want to be stronger than your feelings. But they won't let you. You'll see that in the end."

He moved toward her, and he saw her stiffen. But when he reached her and put his arms around her and pulled her against him, all hint of resistance quickly vanished. Her fingers dug into his back when he kissed her, and she seemed to be pulling him down, suggesting that she would like him to throw her to the floor and take her right then, with the exciting possibility that a servant might come in and confront them while they were doing it.

But he wasn't having it that way. He didn't intend to let her degrade this. He stepped back from her and saw her mouth open slightly with surprise because he hadn't followed through. In a way he'd rejected her, and he knew she wasn't used to that. She frowned. She wasn't so sure of herself now, and that was what he wanted. He told her he would help her decorate the Christmas tree.

Her father came home. Grover Nicholson was as handsome and forbidding as Mike had expected from his portraits. Mike faced him

324

with pulse-racing fear the first time, hopeful that the commanding middle-aged man with the all-knowing eyes wouldn't see that Mike was crumbling inside. Their talk was stiff and difficult because they had no common ground to stand on. There was contempt in Grover Nicholson's eyes after only a few words. Mike hated the way it was going. He was losing the first battle.

But he soon knew there was no winning of battles with Grover Nicholson anyway. Not when the spoils were Ria. Ria was her father's great passion in life. Mike had already concluded that Nicholson had been glad for the premature death of his wife so he could have their daughter to himself.

In that first meeting between them, Mike didn't tell Nicholson his intentions. He didn't tell the tall, domineering aristocrat that he was going to marry his daughter whether she liked it or not—or whether Grover Nicholson liked it or not.

A few days later Mike made up his mind to act. It might have been more appropriate to wait until Christmas Day, but he couldn't and wouldn't. He drove down to the beach and parked behind the massive Nicholson mansion. It was eight o'clock on Christmas Eve when he rang the bell. The maid answered the door, said she would see if Ria was in, and vanished up the stairs. Mike stood in the hall determined to dash up the stairs himself if she returned with the lie that Ria was out.

But before the maid reappeared, Ria's father opened the door from the library and presented himself in a maroon velvet smoking jacket. He was holding a glass.

"Won't you come in and have a brandy with me?"

"There won't be time," Mike said. "Ria will be right down."

"Ria will not be right down. If she comes at all, she'll make you wait." The forceful eyes challenged Mike, said that even if he was a movie star, he was still a nobody in Grover Nicholson's eyes.

"She'll be down, all right, but I'll have a brandy with you in the meantime," Mike said, deciding to accept the challenge, for he was going to have to start standing up to Grover Nicholson, and they'd better get it straight right now. He followed Nicholson into the library. He hated this room because of the full-length portrait of Ria and her father hanging behind the desk. It had been painted ten years earlier, when Ria was sixteen. There was something about the way her father looked at her and held her elbow in that portrait that was subtly obscene. Mike looked quickly away from it.

Ria's father poured the brandy and handed the glass to Mike. "You think you're something special to Ria, don't you?"

"She hasn't said so yet, but she loves me, and I call that special."

"Loves you!" Nicholson smiled. "What an absurd thought."

"I'm going to marry her."

Ria's father put down his brandy glass. He sat down in a chair. He looked coldly at Mike. "She would never marry you. And even if she would, why would you want to humiliate yourself? You'd always feel inferior around her. But she wouldn't have you. She simply wouldn't."

"It's you who wouldn't have me, and you have nothing to say about it."

Ria came into the room. She was smiling. Her eyes shone with excitement. "Who's winning?" she asked.

"I've already won," Mike said. He put his hand on Ria's arm and saw how her father hated that.

"We have some talking to do," Nicholson said.

"Not the three of us, just Ria and me," Mike said, turning her toward the door, steering her out.

"Ria, don't be a fool," Nicholson said behind them.

Ria didn't answer. Mike walked her across the hall toward the door. He intended to take her out of the house, out to the beach, away from the forbidding presence of her father. He knew without turning that Grover Nicholson stood stiffly in the library doorway, watching them go, wanting to come after them, but too prideful to humiliate himself.

The door closed behind them. Mike walked her away from the house, onto the beach.

"He'll hate you even more now," Ria said, "for turning your back on him, for making me walk out with you."

"You wouldn't have come if you hadn't wanted to. You wanted to put him in his place."

"I suppose so."

"And I don't care how much he hates me," Mike said. "He'd hate anybody who took you away from him."

"You haven't. I don't love you, Mike."

"Yes, you do. We're going to be married tomorrow, and nothing is going to stop that."

"You're so foolish. You could just push me down on the sand and take me."

"I don't want it that way, and I don't think you do, either."

"You're wrong, Mike. That's the way I'd like it best. You don't understand me, and you never will." She stopped, and he stopped, too. They faced each other. "I don't love you and I never will," she went on, "but I've decided I'll marry you anyway."

326

48

When Mike and Ria told Grover Nicholson what they intended to do, he was enraged beyond control for the few minutes they stayed with him before walking out together, Ria's eyes glittering with pleasure from her father's unhappiness.

They flew to Reno, Nevada, the divorce capital of the world, and were married there on Christmas morning.

"Feast on me," Ria said in the motel room a little later, naked and perfect, her eyes shining with sexual greed. He did feast on her, time and again that day and night. She was as ecstatic as he was, although he'd been mortally afraid she wouldn't be and might even laugh at him.

She did laugh about Aster Bigelow's item in her column the next day announcing Hollywood's surprise at Michael Baines' "quickie" marriage to a Santa Monica socialite he'd hardly known two weeks.

He suggested honeymooning in Hawaii, but she insisted on Idaho, for she wanted to ski. They went to a snowbound inn in Sun Valley, where he was virtually the only non-skier. He wouldn't take lessons, for he hated the look of a beginner, and he didn't want to be gauche around her. She was a superb skier. When she took off into white space, she soared. He would watch her for a while, then return to the heated swimming pool and drink nervously until she came back. He saw men looking at her all the time, and he was sick with jealousy of them.

They returned to California the second week of January. His servants had removed the excesses of his Christmas decorating venture. He put away the photographs of Mona around the house, although Ria didn't seem disturbed by them. Three days after they were back, they went to see her father. Grover Nicholson was stiff but in control of himself this time.

When Ria went upstairs to see about some clothes she wanted to take, Mike hoped that her father would be willing to discuss what kind of relationship the three of them could have, but when he suggested it, Nicholson only laughed dryly.

327

"No 'relationship,' as you optimistically term it, will be possible or necessary. Just how long do you think she'll stay with you? She's utterly contemptuous of you."

"You're the one who has her contempt."

Nicholson didn't laugh this time. He drew himself up and said, "How ignorant you are, Baines."

There was no more to it than that, and Grover Nicholson made no attempt to see Ria in the succeeding days, but Mike was uneasy because he was so near. Mike suggested to Ria what he'd been thinking about for a long time—moving to New York for a while. He was a little surprised when she agreed readily.

They sublet an apartment on Central Park West, and Mike was immediately glad to be in the city. "New York's as exciting and awful as ever," he said to Ria. "California is clean but boring."

"It can be boring anywhere," Ria said. "But places don't matter to me. Only what's going on in my mind matters to me. That's where I live."

"What does that mean?"

"You mean you don't know?" She shook her head.

"You don't always explain yourself very well."

"Maybe it's just that you don't know much," she said.

"Your father called me ignorant. That made me mad. But coming from you, it hurts."

"I'm sorry if that's so. It's too bad you're so vulnerable, Mike. Is that why your other marriage failed?"

"I don't want to think about my other marriage. All I want to think about is you."

She laughed. "That will change soon enough."

"No, it won't. I'm waiting for the time you admit you love me."

"That will never happen, and you know it. I doubt that Mona Gaillard loved you, either. I have a feeling it's a pattern with you to go after women who don't love you. You're self-destructive. So am I. The difference is that you're self-destructive and weak and I'm self-destructive and strong."

"We're not going to destroy anything. We're just going to build."

"It's much more likely that we're going to run out of things to say to each other. It isn't only that we don't have anything in common. Boredom is bound to set in after a certain period of time anyway."

"You sound as if you expect life to be perpetually exciting," he said.

"You know it can't be. I know it can't be, too. I don't want that anyway. I just want to be happy. I want us to love each other. A week or so before

328

you married me, you said you didn't think you would ever marry. But you married me, and that means you love me. Don't you see that?"

She smiled, and then she laughed. It hurt him that she wouldn't let herself see. But she would, he told himself.

"You're a good lover," Ria said.

The room was dark, but moonlight and the light from the street sifted through the silk curtains and settled softly on their naked bodies. They lay side by side, his hand on her thigh, her hands folded across her breasts. His face was turned toward her. She was looking at the ceiling.

"What surprises me," she went on, "is that we've been together two months and it's still good."

"Why should that surprise you?"

"Why shouldn't it? What stays constant in life? I wonder how many orgasms you've given me in two months. It seems like hundreds. It's hard for me to believe there are so many women who don't have them, if we can trust what the women's magazines say. There must be millions who've never had a good lover like you."

"Being your husband is more important to me than being your lover," he said.

"I don't know why that should give you such a sense of security," she said. "I could walk out anytime."

"I have my sense of security from knowing you won't."

"How do you know I'm not fooling around with telephone repairmen or meter readers?"

"I don't believe what you told me about that telephone repairman taking you on the floor. You knew it would hurt me, and you wanted to hurt me, so you made it up."

"You believe what you want to believe, don't you? I suppose that's true of all of us, to some extent. But maybe I did want to hurt you. I think I like to hurt people."

"I'm not going to let you hurt me—or yourself."

She turned her face and looked at him. "Don't be naïve. People who get too close always hurt one another."

"Don't say that," he said.

"There's only one way you can stop me from talking," she said, "and that's to take me again. Right now."

He pulled her to him.

Mike returned to California for three days in March, leaving Ria in New York, for he didn't want her yielding to any temptation to see her father. He went back for the Academy Award presentations, fully

329

expecting, as the studio did, that he would receive an Oscar for his performance in *Smith's War.* He was surprised and sad when it went to someone else.

He had seen very little of Howard since they'd had their argument over Howard's affair with Tracy. When Howard and Pen had sent a congratulatory wire on Mike's marriage to Ria, Mike had assumed it was Pen's idea, not Howard's. Mike hesitated about calling Howard now, although their disagreement over Tracy seemed meaningless in view of what had happened subsequently. Tracy's affair with Howard had obviously ended traumatically, for she'd left Hollywood and married Wesley Rainer shortly after the completion of *Smith's War.* After her husband's death a few months back, she'd returned to England, where she'd just finished a picture for Regency in the British studio. It didn't look as if she were coming back.

When Mike called Howard, he didn't mention Tracy. He talked about his hope to do a Broadway play and his search for the right script. Howard wished him luck, but there was an edge to his voice, and the conversation was generally awkward. Mike had a feeling that Howard was glad he hadn't gotten his Oscar.

He returned to New York and resumed reading scripts, restless to work again, eager to find a strong role on the stage. Ever since he'd been a student in Konstantin Fedotov's acting class, he'd wanted to prove that he was not a limited actor, that he would be just as much at home on the Broadway boards as he was in Regency movies.

It made him angry that Ria took no interest in what he was trying to do, and when he angrily said so once, she snapped back at him that she could hardly think of anything sillier for a man to be than an actor.

"And what have you done with *your* life that's so great?" he retorted.

"Nothing," she said in a completely changed tone. "I don't like to be reminded of it, but it's true—I've contributed nothing to anybody or anything, and I never will."

That was a bad day, but the next day was worse, because the portrait arrived unexpectedly. The day got off to a bad start anyway because Ria had invited Walker Kendricks to lunch without warning Mike. The man's presence, and his carefree reminiscences with Ria about their set in Santa Monica, gave Mike an almost unendurable two hours.

He said to Ria afterward, "I didn't like him when you inflicted him on me in California, and I don't see why you have to see him just because he works in New York."

"I didn't inflict him on you. You inflicted yourself on *us*, remember? I don't intend to be rude to Walker. He goes back a long way in my life."

"I don't like him."

"You're just afraid I've been to bed with him. I haven't, but if I had, what difference would it make?"

"A lot. I'd be jealous."

She laughed. "You're an idiot, Mike. You'll never find me in bed with anyone like Walker. But you might catch me screwing an Irish cop in the back seat of a police car or something like that."

"Don't talk like that, even jokingly," he said sharply.

"Who's joking? I told you I find it tremendously exciting to be taken by a mindless brute."

"I still don't believe that. You tell me things like that because you want to make me unhappy. It's your way."

"Yes, it's my way, but it's true about me and the telephone man. I just want you to be prepared in case I *do* get a yen for an Irish cop. But I believe in reciprocity. It won't bother me in the least if you screw the maid in the broom closet."

"As long as things are going right between you and me, I won't be turning to the maid or anyone else."

"Didn't you in your previous marriage?"

"Why in the hell are you always bringing up my previous marriage?" he said angrily.

"Because you don't like it and because I'm perverse."

That was when the portrait arrived, and even before it was unwrapped, Mike sensed that it was the one of Ria and her father together, the one he hated.

Ria's eyes lighted with pleasure as she looked at it. "One of us had to do something first, and he did it. It means he's forgiven me."

"Like hell he has. He sent it because he knows I hate it."

"That's ridiculous. Why should you hate it? It's a beautiful portrait. It was painted when I was still an innocent. You say you love me. Then you should like the only portrait of me that's pure."

"Maybe you were pure, but he wasn't. Look at the way he's looking at you. It's incestuous."

"Incestuous?" She laughed, but he was sure she knew what he meant. "I'm going to have this portrait put up. I want to be reminded of myself when I was sixteen."

She had the superintendent come in and put the portrait up over the fireplace in the study, and late that afternoon she phoned her father in

Mike's presence and told him how happy she was to receive his gift. They talked together as if there'd never been a single strained moment between them.

Mike wakened abruptly in the middle of the night. At first he thought he'd been jolted awake from another bad dream. Then he heard thunder. Lightning flashed and heavy rain began to drive against the window.

Ria's bed was empty. He wasn't really surprised. She often didn't sleep well and he would find her out in the living room reading. Tonight he didn't. There was a light under the study door. He opened it and walked in naked. Ria slept naked, too, but she was wearing a filmy negligee now. She was sitting on a pillow on the rug before the fireplace. The portrait of her father and herself loomed over her. She stared at it fixedly and didn't even look at Mike as he slipped down beside her.

"Ria, don't do this."

She didn't move. He turned her face toward him, forcing her to look at him.

"I won't let him have you back," he went on.

"I was just remembering things," she said.

"The wrong things, I suppose. You say you see him as he really is, but you don't."

"You're wrong. I know the truth about him. But I was often happy with him, and that's what I was remembering."

He leaned toward her. He kissed her. "Come back to bed with me."

"No. Take me right here."

He hesitated. He didn't want to take her under the portrait.

"It's here or not at all," she said, obviously knowing what he was thinking. "Either you want to or you don't."

He wanted to. He was hard. He opened her negligee and pressed his hand against her skin. It was very warm. For someone cold in so many ways, she had an intense body heat.

She lay back with her head on the pillow, her thick hair fanning out around her head. He tried to help her out of her negligee, but she stopped him. "I want it on."

He was about to say he wanted it off, but didn't. He leaned forward to lie on her body, but again she stopped him with her hand.

"Eat me," she said. "That has to be first."

He hesitated. He didn't see why that had to be first. What he wanted to do was cover her face with his own so she couldn't see that portrait.

"Eat me." Her hand pressed.

332

He sank back between her thighs and buried his face against her. His tongue and his mouth worked on her flesh. Her thighs pressed against his head. She drew her negligee over his head as if she wanted to trap him with it.

Her thighs tightened and quivered against him and she sighed. Her groin shuddered against his face and she cried out her orgasm. He lay locked between her as she quieted. He parted the negligee over his head as if he were a swimmer coming up for air. She raised her hands to him like a mother beckoning a child to run into her arms. He collapsed on her, kissing her. Her legs parted and crossed over him. He went into her and came quickly and intensely.

But there was no joy in it.

He'd been out for a walk in Central Park, just strolling around and thinking. He hadn't been gone much more than an hour, but when he returned to the apartment he knew at once when he looked at Ria that something had happened. She was smoking, something she seldom did. With her face framed in a little cloud of cigarette smoke, she seemed a frightening combination of allure and evil.

"Father was here today," she said.

The smoke drifted away. Her beautiful golden doe's eyes challenged him to show surprise and indignation. He wasn't at all surprised. This had been certain to happen sometime.

"Is he coming back?" Mike asked.

She looked a little disappointed that he hadn't responded more forcefully. But he refused to let her use her father as a weapon against him, as she'd used him as a weapon against her father.

"Perhaps he'll stop by when he returns from Europe." She gave a little smile. "I'm afraid my reunion with Father would have disappointed you."

"I just wish he'd stay the hell away."

"The surprising thing about it was that it was nothing. We just talked, and it wasn't the least like it was when we used to *say* things when we talked, say things that mattered, I mean. My father and I talked the way you and I do, Mike. We said nothing. 'Nothing' is such a descriptive word. It describes our marriage and life together very well, doesn't it?"

"Why do you keep goading me, Ria? Do you want me to beat you up?"

"I might respect you more if you did. What keeps us together, Mike? There's no reason for it anymore. Even the antagonism isn't interesting any longer."

"Don't talk like that, Ria. We've been happy together most of the time. We can't be happy together all of the time. Most people are lucky if they're happy together once in a while."

"Happy. Is that what you think you are?" She laughed bitterly. "I don't think you've ever been happy, with me or without me."

"I've been as happy as most people," he said.

"You're a fool, Mike. That's all you are. Just the world's biggest fool."

He clenched his fist. He'd never felt more like hitting her. But he didn't do it. His fist unclenched as she smiled defiantly at him.

Still, there were moments like they had together that night, when their life together seemed right.

Somewhere, above his head, in the distance, he heard her. Her moans and sighs were those of a woman beyond control of herself. This was one human thrall she couldn't resist. He kissed and licked her vaginal lips, his tongue churning the pink flesh.

He moved up on her, irresistibly. A breast. The other breast. He suckled them like a babe. Her nails raked his back, and there would be long thin red lines tomorrow, but he didn't care. She moaned and sighed, one erogenous zone from head to toe. There was no understanding her. She was cold in so many ways. She was all fire in this.

He reached her soft, beautiful neck. His face nuzzled there. He could stay this way eternally. But her nails raked insistently, urging him to take her to the top. He entered her. Her vagina sheltered him, consumed him. He rose rapidly. Spasms shook both of them. They shuddered into quiescence.

He rolled off her, thinking how close they'd just been—as close as two human beings could be. Yet it would soon be as it always was. Soon she would be a million miles away.

Howard felt depressed within moments after he had driven through the gate. Where were all the people who used to roam the streets of Regency Pictures in costume as they made their way to the sound stages? Where were the trucks scurrying about, containing parts of sets to be delivered through the yawning doors of the stages?

Where were the signs of life?

There were a few people, a few vehicles here and there, and of course pictures *were* being made, but Howard had heard that most of the current shooting on the few sound stages in use was being done by independent producers and television production companies who were renting production facilities from the studio.

Howard parked in the space that had been reserved for him for more than twenty years beside the dressing room building. He walked across to the administration building where Ainsley occupied the big suite where Alexander Renfew had held sway for almost three decades before his ousting.

"Would you wait just a moment, Mr. Stanton?" the senior member of Ainsley's battery of secretaries asked, after checking on the intercom with the production chief.

Howard sat down, trying hard to conceal his irritation when the "moment" stretched into ten minutes before he was ushered into the vast office. Ainsley rose from behind the big desk, circled it, and met Howard with a handclasp and a smile. After Ainsley had poured them drinks from a bar that swung out of a panel in the wall, they sat down in armchairs facing each other across the table.

Ainsley was still smiling. He gave the impression that he didn't have a trouble in the world, although the word was around that he and Dalton were getting along less and less well and that real trouble lay ahead if Ainsley continued going directly to Smetley concerning issues on which he and Dalton were at odds.

"What did you think of the script?" Ainsley asked.

"Fine," Howard said.

"Mike just phoned from New York. He's wild about it."

No wonder, thought Howard. Mike's role was the best in the picture.

"It's going to be a very big picture," Ainsley went on. "The whole works. An even bigger budget than we had for *Smith's War*. We're making half as many pictures these days, but they're twice as good as they used to be."

That seemed to be Ainsley's favorite remark. Howard had heard it quoted many times. It was a distortion. Regency wasn't making a fourth of the pictures it had in its prime days, and some of them weren't very good.

"If *Safari* does half as well as *Smith's War*," Ainsley said, "we'll have a winner."

Howard nodded. *Smith's War* had been the studio's biggest domestic grosser in five years, and the foreign returns were holding up.

Ainsley talked on, saying that one particular reason why this picture was so satisfactory from a star's viewpoint was that the leading roles were equally strong. That was certainly not true at present, but Howard didn't say so. Although he felt Mike's part was better than his, that could change by the time the script was reworked another few times.

"With Veda Morell sewed up and Tracy Gordon filling out the star complement, we'll have the greatest cast of the year," Ainsley said.

335

"Is there any possibility the production date will be moved up?"

"I'm afraid not. We begin in four months."

"By the time this is finished, it will have been over two years since my last picture. Do you realize that I sometimes made four pictures a year in the thirties?"

"Of course. But few stars make even one picture a year these days."

That was true, and it was also true that Howard's popularity had held up in spite of the long periods between his pictures in recent years. He realized that he was lucky still to be on top, though it was a wavering top, after more than two decades of making pictures and considering that he was now nearing forty-six.

"We've tried a lot of different approaches to get the public back into the theaters," Ainsley was saying, "and I'm now convinced that the only way to do it is to give them good stories with their favorite stars. Stories and stars. That's what it takes. We did it with *Smith's War* and we'll do it again with *Safari,* and then we'll do it with something else."

The interview was over. Ainsley was smiling again, and he had risen. Howard rose, too. He was walked to the door. He passed the battery of secretaries and made his exit, glad to get out. It was never going to be the same at Regency Pictures again, he thought as he drove away from the studio. No matter what anyone wished or dreamed.

Mike was very excited about the prospect of making *Safari*. He was preparing for his role in a way that would have made Konstantin Fedotov proud. He'd steeped himself in African lore and had read the novel so many times by now that there were parts he could probably have quoted almost verbatim. He'd been over and over the latest script the studio had sent him.

With the picture coming up, he'd stopped looking for a play. It elated him that he was getting another big picture, after not having had a picture for a long time, and it annoyed him that Ria showed no interest or enthusiasm about it. She laughed when he suggested that she at least read the book the picture was based on.

"I'm sure it would bore me," she said.

"Damn it!" he exploded. "Aren't you the least bit interested in my career?"

"Why should I be? Because we're married? To me that isn't a valid reason."

"My career is at least half my life. I don't see how you can ignore it."

"But your career isn't half my life. That's how I can ignore it."

He kept telling himself that she would change her mind about that

336

and other things, but when he faced the truth, he acknowledged that their marriage wasn't getting better. She was restless and moody. She talked to her father on the phone more and more. Finally it got to be every day. At first it was her father who called her. Now, more often than not, she would phone him. Mike didn't know what to do about it.

Then the schedule for production arrived, along with relevant information pertaining to the accommodations Regency Pictures would provide the cast, production people, and spouses both in England, where interior work would be done in Regency's British studio near London, and in Africa. It worried Mike a little that spouses would be excluded from the location site in Kenya but would be accommodated in Nairobi, to be visited on weekends only, but he understood why it was necessary.

He postponed telling Ria about the arrangements for almost a week.

"I wouldn't even consider going along," she said at once. "I think you knew that even before you brought up the subject."

"You're coming with me," Mike said. "I'm not going to let you get away from me, Ria."

"You wouldn't even put it that way if you didn't know it's over."

"I love you and I won't let you go."

"Letting me go is a ridiculous idea, Mike. You never had me. I'm going to leave you. I'm going home."

When Mike stepped inside the apartment, he heard sounds deep in the back. They were unidentifiable sounds, yet his dread told him what they were.

He walked slowly through the apartment to the door of the bedroom. The sounds from beyond the door were unmistakable now. They were the sounds of groans, of heavy breathing, of the slap of flesh against flesh.

He stood with his hand on the doorknob, listening, hesitating to see what he was certain to see. He finally turned the knob and slowly opened the door. Ria was naked on the bed, her legs spread. There was a stocky, powerful, partly dressed man on top of her, pounding into her. The man's wrinkled pants, shorts, and shoes were on the floor beside a pool of Ria's discarded clothes. He was wearing his shirt, his socks, and a cap.

When Mike entered they stopped and turned their faces toward him. The man was moustached and coarse-looking. He looked startled but unafraid. Ria's expression was fathomless. Then she smiled and turned back to the man.

"Don't pay any attention to him."

The man grinned at Mike, then turned back to Ria, thrusting heavily into her. Mike watched rigidly, unable to turn away from it, unable to move or shout or scream, almost unable to breathe. The man pounded Ria's flesh even more mightily at the end, and grunted as his body shook in paroxysms of orgasm. When he was finished, he simply withdrew from her and got off the bed. He had a big uncircumcised penis. He picked up his clothes from the floor and dressed quickly and wordlessly. He walked past Mike and out of the room. Mike stared at Ria, who was propped up on her elbows, smiling at him. In the distance a door closed. The man was gone.

"A telephone repairman?"

"A taxi driver," she said. "And you don't care. If you did, you would have killed us."

Mike turned and left the room. He heard her laugh, and when he was in the kitchen, getting the knife, he heard her laugh again. He went to the study and ripped the portrait up and down and across a dozen times. He didn't stop until the canvas was nothing but strips hanging grotesquely out of their frame like flayed skin.

He walked out and went to the nearest bar and got drunk. When he got back to the apartment, Ria was gone. She'd left almost everything behind, but she'd taken the shredded portrait. She was going back to her father.

49

Their base camp was on a grassy knoll overlooking the river, screened in by trees, baobab and creepers, thorn and underbrush, with an umbrella of mimosa hovering over the area where the stars were quartered. Out beyond was the plain where zebras, wildebeest, kudus, gazelles, lions, rhinos, and a hundred other animals ran; and fringing the plain was the bush where Larkin had almost been killed the other day, where he'd followed a wounded rhino in to finish it off. Beyond the bush were the serrated hills that gave way to the purple mountains.

In Howard's eyes it was Eden, a place of peace and well-being, the beginning and the end of the world. But he knew that Mike was impatient with it and that Veda Morell hated it. He wasn't sure how Tracy felt about it. After a month of shooting interiors in England and almost six weeks of shooting on location in Kenya, there was still little communication between him and Tracy.

But he was much more aware of Tracy's proximity here than in England, for Pen had been with him there—she'd stayed on afterward to visit relatives rather than wait out the African filming in Nairobi—and here he lay awake many a night thinking about Tracy in the tent across the way, wondering if she was thinking about him, too. He wasn't sure to this day that he'd made the right decision on the beach at Malibu to turn Tracy out of his life. He supposed she was a fool if she didn't hate him for it.

His concern over Tracy was the only thing clouding life for him in Africa. The picture was going well in spite of Mike's wavering performance and Veda Morell's frequent displays of temperament. The director, Elton Lamson, had done another African picture, for the Rank organization, and seemed to know what he was about. And Howard had found an immediate friend in Ian Larkin, the white hunter the company had retained to provide meat for the camp and to trap the animals used in scenes. Howard had obtained a hunting permit and hunted with Larkin those mornings when he wasn't being filmed.

The production company's camp, said Larkin, who had been a professional hunter for a quarter of a century and had seen all kinds of them, was the most elaborate he'd come across yet. Three hundred tents of varying sizes housed the stars, supporting players, production crew, African help, offices, laboratories, dispensary, hospital, messes, and warehouses. A special recreation marquee was fitted with a library, a game section, and the facilities for showing pictures. The tents housing the stars, the director, the producer, and the white hunter were in a private enclosure on the edge of the camp, with its own mess tent and a superb view of the river.

"I must say," Larkin said one evening as he and Howard walked away from the mess tent, "I don't give Baines much in the way of decent taste."

"You're right," Howard said, still annoyed at Mike's obnoxious behavior at dinner, when he'd slurringly asked Larkin how many of his clients' wives he'd "fucked" over the years "in the tradition of the white hunter." Howard cringed now, thinking of the embarrassing moment and the stunned silence that had followed. "He was drunk," he went on.

"That bloke's drunk too bloody much," Larkin said.

"His wife walked out on him a few months ago," Howard said. "He doesn't seem able to handle it."

"I'm being paid more for this than I would be for a hunting safari," Larkin went on, "but I couldn't take two Baineses, no matter how much I was paid."

When they reached the edge of the enclosure, they stopped. A canopy of wild figs and acacias loomed over them, and the night spread out grandly and sweepingly before them under the brilliance of a full moon. The gleam of a native's fire flickered like a star a half mile away. A hyena cackled; a jackal shrieked. Larkin took out his pipe, packed it with tobacco, and lighted it. The pungent aroma blended exotically with the sharp night smells of greenery and musk and the hides of animals.

"Actors are a strange lot," Larkin said. "So are actresses. That Veda Morell is an odd fish. As cold and unfriendly as Tracy Gordon is not."

"It might be professional jealousy. Veda thinks Tracy's part is better than hers. It isn't. But Tracy comes across better."

"I wouldn't want to tuck Veda into my sleeping bag. Frightful temper."

"She's pent up," Howard said, deciding not to mention that Veda was a lesbian and that part of her trouble here was that Tracy and the few other women in this camp—the nurse, the script girl, and some wardrobe women and secretaries—were not.

"She certainly takes her unhappiness out on everyone around her. But Tracy Gordon doesn't."

Howard looked at Larkin cautiously. "What makes you think Tracy's unhappy?"

"Oh, just a feeling I have. I know she smiles a lot, but she has a yearning look in her eyes and she drinks too much and—" Larkin stopped and grinned sheepishly. "I'm embarrassed. I sound like one of your Hollywood gossip columnists. That isn't like me, really."

"I know it isn't," Howard said.

"Are you gunning with me in the morning?"

"Yes."

"Good. We'd better turn in, then."

Tracy sat in darkness in her tent, waiting for Howard to return to his tent across the way. She'd seen him stroll off with Larkin, as he usually did after dinner, but didn't think they would be long. So she waited. She would have preferred having the light on, but if Mike blundered out of his tent down the way, she wanted him to think she was asleep. She'd had just about as much of Mike as she could take.

340

She saw Larkin and Howard walk up. They were silhouetted against the opening of Howard's tent. She could see Chabani, the native servant assigned to Howard, waiting inside. She hoped Chabani wouldn't stay around long.

Larkin talked for a moment, then went on to his tent down the way. Howard went into his. Finally Chabani emerged and headed toward the rows of tents in back where the natives were quartered. Tracy stepped out of her tent and crossed to Howard's. She paused at the flap. Howard wasn't immediately in view inside. The bed was turned down under a white cone of mosquito netting, and white pajamas were laid out, folded, on the foot locker. On the table nearby, under a ring of light from the carbide lamp, was a gin bottle with two tumblers. Two canvas chairs were pulled up to the table.

Howard stepped into view. He was wearing a robe. She knew now why it had taken so long for Chabani to come out. He'd been busy pouring cans of heated water into the canvas tub so Howard could have his bath.

"Your flap was up," Tracy said. "I thought that might mean you're receptive to a visitor."

"Come in, come in," Howard said, looking a little wary, as she'd expected.

She stepped in, nodding at the gin and tumblers. "It looks as if you were expecting one."

"Chabani sets that up for me every night. Sometimes Larkin comes in for a drink. Let's sit down and have one together."

"I'll sit down, but I won't have a drink. I don't have a taste for neat gin, and I can't imagine why the British like it that way." She sat down, and he sat down across from her. "I just need to talk, Howard, and I think you do, too. We've done a very good job of not talking since we began this picture. We've thrown a lot of words back and forth between us, and we haven't said a thing."

"Tracy, I don't see how it's going to do any good to talk about us."

"Are you telling me you haven't been thinking about us? I believe you have, Howard, just as I have."

"But talking about it won't change anything."

"I remember very well what you said when you let me go, Howard. That you didn't want to give up your life with Pen, because it had been good to you. You said you didn't want to upset the balance of your life. I said you were afraid of committing yourself to me."

"It's still true, Tracy."

"I don't believe it! I believe you love me and want me, just as I love you and want you! Still! And that's all that should matter. It's all that should ever have mattered. My God, think of the way life would have been if we'd let it happen. I wouldn't have had another loveless marriage, and—"

She couldn't go on. She was suddenly crying. Her face went into her hands and her body shook. She heard his chair move, and then she felt his hands on her trembling shoulders. She continued to weep helplessly. Suddenly his face was against hers, and she felt herself being turned. He was kissing her.

God damn them to hell! Mike was thinking as he sat sagged over the table in his tent, his hand clutching an empty tumbler that had been filled with gin less than two minutes ago. The script lay open before him. He'd looked and looked at it, because he didn't want to fumble tomorrow's difficult scenes the way he'd been fumbling most of his role, but he was still far from prepared.

God damn them to hell! he thought again as he pushed the script away. God damn Ria and Tracy and Howard and practically everyone he could think of at the moment. He was quite sure he'd never felt more lost and alone in his life than he did now. Ria was divorcing him, and Tracy and Howard were shutting him out. Worst of all, his unhappiness was reflected in the poor work he was doing on the picture.

So much was wrong!

One thing particularly wrong was that he didn't like Africa. He didn't like the intense heat of the African day and the extreme cold of the African night, and he didn't like the choking alkali dust that settled on him each day like an extra skin. He didn't like the smell of hyenas or the rotten breath of lions, and he didn't like the idea that he was in real physical danger making this picture.

He'd hoped that he and Howard would be able to improve their relationship while working together again, but instead it had worsened. It galled Mike that he was being outperformed by Howard for the first time ever, though he knew it was his own fault.

He was drinking more than ever to try to escape his unhappiness, although he was perfectly aware that the camera was recording his deterioration with ruthless accuracy. The rushes were shown regularly in the recreation marquee, and they didn't lie. It was ironic. He'd wanted and needed this picture so badly, yet now that he had it, he couldn't handle it. He seemed to be bobbing on the crest of a tidal wave hurtling toward a sea wall where he would finally be smashed apart.

He kept having that thought, and every time he had it, he poured himself another drink. As he did now.

He downed the drink, rose unsteadily, and stepped outside into the sharp clarity of the African night. The stars seemed as relentlessly bright as the sun. He stared up at the dots of glitter in the night sky for a long time. Then he started down to Tracy's tent. He didn't know whether he wanted to try to make love to her or talk to her or what. He just knew that he wanted to be with her. But when he reached her tent, the flap was down and there was no light inside. It was the same with Howard's tent across the way.

Mike's fists clenched as he gathered his thoughts. His reason told him that they were alone in their tents, asleep. His intuition told him that they were together in Howard's tent, making love.

He was filled with hatred and jealousy. He felt an urge to burst in on them and wrench them apart. He never knew later why he didn't do it. The next thing he knew, he was drinking in his tent again. He kept on drinking until he passed out.

They had both dreamed of being together like this again, and to both of them it had seemed an unfulfillable fantasy, a memory caught irretrievably in the past.

But this was no dream. Howard Stanton and Tracy Gordon were wide awake to the wonder of their naked embrace under a cone of mosquito netting in a jungle clearing in Kenya. It was no dream that he was moving up on her, kissing her body, stopping to bury his face against one breast, then the other, before he reached her lips, and their mouths opened to each other.

His penis pressed against her groin, and when she took him into her, it was glorious: it was the same as before, with the lost years wiped away. Only this moment mattered, and it was beautiful. It was a moment of pure love. They were both thinking that, in different ways. He wasn't a controlled middle-aged man but a resurrected youth overwhelmed by sexual wonder. She wasn't Tracy Gordon, movie star and recent unloving wife, but a virgin whose prince had come.

There was no holding on to such passion for very long. His climax rose quickly, while their mouths melted together. Her orgasm commenced a moment before his, and she screamed joy silently in her mind while his mouth against hers shut off all sound. He came in her then and their bodies shuddered and they wished it weren't ending. When it did, he lay panting on her breast.

Tracy said softly against his ear, "I love you."

Yes, she loved him, and he loved her, but the other things she'd said remained true. He didn't want to commit himself to her or upset the balance of his life. Reality had returned with a jolt.

He had to make her understand. He raised his face from her breast and looked at her. Even with the lamp out, enough starlight seeped through the canvas so he could see her face clearly. The eyes that had been weeping a few minutes ago were bright with happiness. He didn't know how to say what had to be said. But the way her eyes changed, he knew she understood. She was full of pain again, and so was he—pain after such joy. He sank against her breast again.

"Go to sleep," she said softly in his ear, and eventually he did. When Chabani came to waken him before dawn for his hunt with Larkin, she was gone.

Tracy kept thinking about last night all day long while the scenes on the plain with Mike and Veda were shot. She muffed her lines so often that Elton Lamson, the director, was irritated with her for the first time since the picture began. She knew that both Mike and Veda were pleased. Veda disliked her, and Mike was spiteful about anyone who gave a decent performance in this picture.

There was no opportunity to talk to Howard until late that evening, because a movie was shown in the marquee. Afterward, he fell in beside her as they walked to their tents.

"Last night was my fault," he said.

"Your fault." She was angry. "What a way to put it!"

"I'm trying not to be any more selfish than I was last night. I'm trying to stop us from making another mistake. Last night was certainly a big one, Tracy. It wakened too many questions—"

"My God, they were already wakened, Howard. They've been burning in me. The question now is, Will the *important* question ever be answered?"

"I'm not going to let us repeat last night, Tracy. It would be too selfish of me. I want it, but it wouldn't change things, so it wouldn't be fair to either of us. It would have to end when the picture does."

"I think I could change your mind about that."

"I don't think you really believe that, Tracy."

"I hate this," she said. "You don't want me to love you, and you don't want to love me—"

"You're right, I don't," he cut in.

"That isn't saying you don't love me, Howard. You told me in Malibu that you did. I prefer to believe that."

"Have you ever asked yourself whether you'd still want me if I were free?"

"Of course I would. You're all I've wanted through everything."

"You obviously believe that, but I'm not sure it's true, Tracy."

They'd reached their tents. They stopped and faced each other.

344

"If we can't have anything more," she said bitterly, "we can at least have each other for the rest of the time we're together here."

"No, we can't. I'm going into my tent and you're going into yours, and that's the way it's going to stay."

"You're afraid," she said.

"I am afraid." He turned and stepped up to his tent flap.

"Please come to me tonight," she said. "I'll be waiting for you."

He stepped into his tent without looking back, and she went into hers and waited for him to come and right the wrong. He didn't come. For the first time in quite a while, she drank herself to sleep.

It was an extremely hot afternoon. The company was out on the plain shooting, and Mike had been left behind because he wasn't in any of the day's scenes. He began drinking even before lunch and was a little resentful that there was no one important around to give him dirty looks about it.

He wandered out of his tent in the middle of the afternoon without his boots on, although they'd all been cautioned not to, and when he stepped into some high grass at the edge of the camp, suddenly something spat at him. There was a sharp pricking sensation in his ankle, and he looked down in blurry horror at a green thing slithering away.

A mamba had bitten him, they told him much later, when he drifted out of his coma in the hospital tent, and it was sheer luck that one of Larkin's men was near and heard his cry. It was even better luck that the company's doctor was on hand instead of out with the shooting crew, as he usually was. And it was great luck they'd had the mamba serum to give him immediately, for if you didn't get it immediately, you were very dead.

Yes, it had been an extremely close call. But he wondered if anyone besides his parents would have cared much if he'd died. God, how alone he was! It was unreal. His life seemed as unreal to him as a fantasy movie. It was a series of scenes going nowhere, with angry characters warring with one another, hating one another. It was unreal that he'd loved and married one woman who hadn't loved him and had ultimately made him miserable, and then had repeated the tragedy with another one. It was unreal that he was letting the advances he'd made as an actor go down the drain in this picture. It was unreal that he was hostile to, even felt he hated sometimes, the man who'd helped him get started in pictures by asking for him in an important supporting role—but he did, for reasons he didn't understand but knew were rooted in guilt.

345

Howard came to see him in the hospital, and they made a pretense of hiding their hostility. But they couldn't easily pretend it away. Still, it was clear that Mike's close brush with death had shocked Howard. Mike had a feeling that at this moment, at least, Howard probably wanted to do something to improve things between them. Mike wished it were possible. He wished something could be right.

Tracy came to see him later that evening, and he didn't believe her cheery performance at his bedside for a moment. She was wishing him well, but she was thinking about something else, he was sure. She was deeply sad about something. It showed glaringly through that false cheer. He wondered if there had been trouble between her and Howard. He hoped so.

Howard was out long before dawn, helping Larkin trap a leopard, because he no longer stayed in camp when there was an excuse to leave it. He was alone in his tent too much as it was. With a seemingly uncrossable barrier between him and Mike, with the distance deepened between him and Tracy, he found his only companionship with Larkin.

Howard was depressed. He was paying dearly for that single night of abandon with Tracy, and he knew she was, too. Their weakness that night, and his firmness in rejecting any repetition of it, had ruined any chance for an easy relationship between them during this production. He remembered all too well a line of dialogue he'd spoken to Tracy in *Smith's War:* "Something that can't have a happy ending shouldn't have a beginning."

Howard thought about going home, about going back to Pen, as he and Larkin waited in a blind at sunrise for a leopard to be lured to the rotting gazelle strung in a tree to trap him. And he thought about death after not having thought about it for a long time. He thought about Leni and the son he'd never seen and his friend Barney and his friend Tim, all dead. He wondered about his own death. How would it come?—and when? Why was he thinking about it? Was it because death was all around him here in Africa? Here the bigger and swifter animals killed the smaller and slower ones, every moment of the day.

Howard felt a harbinger of death the morning they filmed the buffalo charge. He didn't know whether it was because death was on his mind or because Larkin had said that there was no more dangerous beast in Africa than the Cape buffalo.

The scene had been prepared with difficulty. It had taken Larkin and his men days to locate a herd of buffalo, and then they'd had a hard time hazing it to a water hole, where they were finally able to surround and corral it. Cameras had been set up on the sides of two hills, and the

346

animals were to be stampeded through the valley running between them. There could be only one take for the scene, for the animals would charge out into the plain at the other end of the valley and be lost forever.

It was Howard and Tracy's scene. The action called for them to be trapped in the path of the raging herd. In running for the safety of the hillside, they would barely escape being trampled. Distance and timing had been carefully calculated and rehearsed so they would reach the hillside just in time.

But no one could have anticipated that the herd would split in two as it raced down the valley, preventing escape on either side. Worse yet, to his terror Howard saw that the herd had not entirely split. The rear of it formed a solid phalanx stretching completely across the valley, thundering at unbelievable speed toward him and Tracy, trapped between the two wings of rampaging animals.

Tracy screamed and clutched him, and he had to push her away to raise his gun. Barely in time he remembered a story Larkin had told about how he'd saved his own life when he'd been trapped in a charge of these beasts. Howard fired, hitting the nearest of the onrushing buffalo, which was fortunately several lengths ahead of the others. The huge animal dropped dead just short of them. Tracy's screams trailed away as Howard grabbed her. She was limp with terror as he half carried, half dragged her atop the mammoth carcass. They made it just in time as the rest of the herd thundered by on both sides, leaving them choked with dust but alive.

Three days later, after he'd viewed the rushes in Hollywood, Ainsley sent a cable. He said that shot was by far the most exciting scene in the picture, so why didn't they try more things like that?

50

After *Safari* was finished, Tracy returned to her flat near Hyde Park in London and took up the life she'd led after her return from Jamaica following Wes's death. In her thirtieth year, Tracy was at the crest of her beauty and still a top box office draw, although in these days of waning moviemaking, she often didn't know where her next picture was coming from. With two million coming to her from Wesley's estate, she didn't have to worry about money, anyway. But she was unhappy and unfulfilled.

It didn't show on the outside. As before, she was invited many places, and when she had enough to drink, which was most of the time, she was usually the life of the party. Many of the men she met wanted to go to bed with her, but she went with few of them, though gossip had it otherwise.

On the eve of Mona Gaillard's departure for the States after the end of her four-year marriage to Lord Truscott-Ames, Tracy saw her at a party. They didn't acknowledge each other's presence. Mona had announced to the press that she was returning to Hollywood to make a comeback picture with Howard Stanton as her co-star.

Tracy was going to the States herself. It was time to see her mother again. Afterward she would appear at the world premiere of *Safari* at the Regency Grand in New York and then go to Hollywood for a short time to discuss a possible co-starring picture with Mike that the studio was considering.

The night before her departure, she attended a West End party where she noticed a slim, dark, striking-looking man on the other side of the room. She soon identified him, for his picture had been appearing in the international press for the past two years. He was Juan Olivares, one of Spain's leading matadors. They met and talked, and Tracy felt a strong attraction to him. When they parted, Juan Olivares kissed her hand and expressed his hope that he would see her again soon. Tracy certainly hoped so.

Tracy looked at the world twinkling below. And above. Millions of twinkling lights below, millions of twinkling stars above.

"I'm sure this is one of the most stunning views in Southern California," she said.

"How stunning it is depends on your mood when you're looking at it," Mike said. "I don't look anymore. California is crapland, Tracy. I'm going to get rid of this eagle's nest and move to New York permanently one day."

She turned and looked at him. He was sitting in a chair, holding a drink. There was a drink in hers, too. She'd been Mike's houseguest for a week now, and there had been strong innuendoes about that in Aster Bigelow's column. Tracy and Mike had laughed at them, partly because Aster seemed so delighted to have a decent scandal to report in these days when fewer and fewer Hollywood people were still in Hollywood to create scandals, and partly because the innuendoes were true. They were sleeping together. It had started in New York, while they were there for the premiere of *Safari,* and they saw no reason for not continuing it out here, because it was going well.

As Mike said, it had been inevitable for years, and the truth was that Tracy found Mike comforting. He seemed safe, because he was as weak and vulnerable as she was. The photographs of Mona he displayed around the house attested to that.

She thought about Mona when she wakened beside Mike late the next morning. What did Mona think of their affair? Surely she knew, as everyone must know by now. Mona was living with her daughter by Mike and her son by Lord Truscott-Ames in a rented house not a mile away, but Mike said he'd seen her only once since her return, in a stormy interview in which she'd said he'd have to sue for visiting rights to see his daughter, since he'd been so uninterested in her in the past.

And what did Howard think of the affair? Tracy liked to think he hated it. She'd been pointedly casual with him at the premiere in New York, and she thought his stiffness toward her was centered in his disturbance about what had started between her and Mike.

Mike suddenly snored, and Tracy smiled. It seemed a little gauche for anyone as beautiful as he to be caught snoring. She cradled her head in the crook of her arm and watched him sleep. He looked magnificent naked, and he knew how to make love. The whole world could see how handsome his build was, of course, but the whole world didn't know the perfection of his body in nakedness or how well he made love. He made love like a lover, not like an assaulter, although he was highly sexual. He was a lover much like Howard, but she didn't allow herself to think about that.

She put out her hand and stroked the flat hollow of his midriff and let it lie there. He didn't move. She wished he would waken and take her, as he had done twice during the night, but she didn't pursue it. She let him sleep away his pain.

Tracy was lying on her back on a lounge beside the pool. The beads of water on her skin were evaporating in the sun. She hadn't stayed in the water long. She didn't like to swim with Mike because he was so much better than she, and he was always trying to show her that. She didn't resent it, because she understood. She watched him now as he swam back and forth in the pool. "Streaked" back and forth would have been a better way to put it, she thought. It was amazing that he could do it, the way he drank.

349

They'd talked about many things in the last few days: Mike's difficult childhood in Indiana; his failure ever to find real rapport with his parents; his struggle to be an actor in New York City; his early days in Hollywood when Howard had helped to get him his first real break; his fear that he wouldn't survive the war, or, worse yet, that he would not be able to get started again in Hollywood afterward; his aching longing for Mona over the years; their tumultuous marriage; his failure to love his daughter; his disastrous second marriage to an enigma he still sometimes thought of as more a dream than a reality; his continuing descent into deeper and deeper alcoholism; and his growing conviction that there was no such thing as happiness.

Tracy had talked about growing up with difficulty in Georgia; her endless and useless quest for her mother's approval; the fateful trip to New York that had set off the chain of events that had brought her here; her first loveless marriage; her second loveless marriage; her aching longing for Howard; her brief fulfillment of it and the bitter aftermath; her own descent into deeper and deeper alcoholism; and her feeling today that she could no longer fight life, that it would do with her what it wished.

They'd learned more about each other in the past ten days than they had learned in the previous ten years, Tracy told herself as she watched Mike swim back and forth in the pool as if he were trying to break the world record for speed and endurance. Yet they'd only scratched the surface, and she wondered how much deeper the probe would go.

Mike suddenly stopped his mad race, hauled himself out of the pool, and lay dripping on the lounge beside Tracy.

"I'm glad we're together, Tracy. I think we need each other, don't you?"

She looked at him. "What do you mean?"

"I mean we're good together, and not just in bed. We don't bore each other, even when we're sober. I think we ought to get married."

Tracy laughed. "Mike, people don't marry each other just not to be bored. Especially when they've already been unsuccessfully married."

"You're not about to hand me that old cliché that love is the only reason for marriage?"

"I think it's the only good one."

"I've found that love is an overrated emotion. Besides, after it's been around a while, it changes into something else."

"Not always, Mike. I believe it can be beautiful and lasting, if you're lucky." She paused. "I think we ought to stop talking about this."

350

"Not talking things down to the end is a common malady of cowards. Do you want to be a coward all your life, Tracy? Of course, the way never to talk things down to the end is to drink the way we do."

"Shall we stop drinking and see what difference it makes?"

"I don't think either of us could, even though we know what it will probably do to us eventually."

"Then we're not very good for each other, are we, Mike? We're not the weak leaning on the strong; we're the weak leaning on the weak."

"We are good for each other, Tracy, and I want to marry you."

There was nothing Tracy wanted less than another loveless marriage. She wanted marriage with no one, since she couldn't have it with the one she wanted. Her life was better without it.

They were married a few weeks later in Las Vegas. The irony didn't escape her that she was beginning her third marriage in the very city where her first had gotten off to such a terrible start. It was on her mind in the suite at the hotel while they were giving a champagne party to a roomful of strangers Mike had collected from the casino. The strangers all thought the giddy, impromptu celebration was wonderful and typical of what Hollywood stars did. Tracy pretended to have a good time. She drank a lot of champagne but didn't get very drunk, because she was thinking too hard.

"This is going to be a very good marriage," Mike said when he took her to bed that night.

Tracy kept thinking that it didn't seem like a honeymoon and it didn't seem like a marriage, but in the course of their three days in Las Vegas, Mike said three times, in slightly different ways, "Having affairs is only half enough. People who are good together ought to get married. Marriage is the best state. It's the only security there is."

Soon after they returned to Hollywood, Pen called and said that she and Howard wanted to give "you newlyweds" a party. It was the sort of thing Pen did. It was the sort of thing Howard would ordinarily do, too, but he certainly must have hated the idea this time. Tracy didn't handle herself well on the phone with Pen. Pen even asked her if something was wrong.

Mike didn't want the party any more than Tracy did; he said if he'd answered the phone when Pen called, he would have given an excuse. Tracy didn't believe him; Mike was a big talker and a small doer.

"All right, we'll go," he finally said after a lot of arguing back and forth, "but we're not going to invite them here. I don't think either one of us is going to feel at ease around them now."

That was true, and Tracy dreaded the party.

351

The guests were mostly people that Tracy and Mike had worked with; the studio brass was represented by Dean Ainsley. Dalton's absence wasn't surprising, since he'd become notably strange and didn't even show up at the studio much anymore.

"We're absolutely delighted about your marriage," Ainsley beamed as he pumped their hands, meaning the studio was. And for good reason, for aside from all else, this was an extra fillip of publicity for *Safari* at a propitious time, when the picture was going into general release throughout the country and was about to begin its international run.

The party went quickly from bad to worse. Mike drank too much, talked too loudly, and in general made a fool of himself. Tracy drank too much, too, but she was sober with tenseness. She and Howard kept avoiding each other after the first awkward moments when he wished her happiness and they briefly clasped hands, and she almost cried from the falseness of it.

But the time came when she turned away from a group just as Howard turned away from an adjacent group, and they faced each other, alone together and very vulnerable.

She said quietly, "You think it's a terrible mistake."

"I think you think it's a terrible mistake or you wouldn't be saying it," Howard said.

"You want it to be a mistake," Tracy said.

"You're wrong. I think you've done what you had to do and wanted to do. Most people do just that."

"The strong don't," Tracy said. "The strong do what they should do. Mike and I aren't strong. You are."

"If you need me, I'll be here."

That wasn't true. She needed him and always had, and he wasn't there and never would be.

Tracy kept feeling the presence of Mona Gaillard in her new house, even though Mike prudently put away her photographs. The irony was that Mona had never lived in the house that Mike had built for her, but she haunted it. Tracy thought about it a lot, but actually it didn't bother her. What did bother her was that it didn't.

It also bothered her that she thought too often about Howard, although she didn't see him after the party, and she seldom mentioned his name. When Mike did, it was usually in a tone of resentment. Mike was chafing because Howard had drawn better notices for his performance in *Safari* than he had.

"I was at rock bottom emotionally when we made that picture," he

352

said, "or it wouldn't have happened. But it will never happen again, because I expect my emotions to be in a far more civilized state the longer we're married, Tracy."

He wanted the marriage to work, and he said it would if they would let it. Maybe so, she thought. It had gotten off to a good start, which her other marriages hadn't; and, impossible though she would have considered it at the beginning, she even began to harbor a hope that they might fall in love. Maybe love was waiting down there, inside them, if they could just push away their devils and get to it. Mona was Mike's devil. Howard was hers.

They didn't talk much about trying, but they did try, and Tracy was a little surprised at how comparatively contented they both were. She even took an interest in cooking for him, and they both cut down on their drinking. They didn't give parties and didn't attend them, and when they were seen around town less and less frequently, Aster Bigelow felt compelled to comment in her column, "Usually when a couple vanishes from the scene, they're hiding something. Could it be that there's trouble in paradise for Tracy Gordon and Michael Baines after just four scant months of marital bliss?"

They had a laugh over that. There was no trouble. Actually, there was nothing in particular to be disturbed about and nothing in particular to be happy about. On most days life went along on an almost even keel. Usually they stayed up most of the night, reading and drinking and playing honeymoon bridge, and then slept until early afternoon. Mike would swim before lunch, and Tracy would watch him. Tracy let the housekeeper prepare lunch, but she cooked dinner herself, preparing the meals her mother had taught her. Mike liked her cooking almost as much as he liked Scotch, bourbon, and gin.

There were few visitors to the house, and although Mike wouldn't have minded letting reporters come to interview them about their marriage, as the studio kept urging, Tracy was against it.

"I don't know why you're so reluctant," Mike said lightly. "We wouldn't even have to lie. We're even a sexual success together. Not a dud screw between us yet."

It was true that sexual excitement still ran high between them, although Tracy sometimes expressed more ecstasy than she really felt, because she knew how important it was to Mike to know that he was a good lover.

"Some experts would lead you to believe that sex is the least important factor in a really meaningful relationship," Tracy said.

"It's important to you and me. What do you think about having a baby?"

"I think it's far too early to think about it."

"I don't know why I brought it up. I'm a lousy father already. Why should I try to top the record?" He drew her to him. "We don't need a baby to make us whole. We're getting closer and closer to each other, Tracy."

But they weren't, really, and soon Tracy had to admit she was becoming restless. Their drinking began to increase again. Mike was more and more annoyed when one postponement after another was announced for the picture he and Tracy were scheduled to do together. A series of revised scripts had been sent to them over the past few months, each worse than the preceding one, and when Ainsley called one day to tell them that the studio had decided to shelve the project, Mike exploded.

"Why did it take you six months to decide that? My God, what kind of judgment do you people use?"

Their judgment had been bad about Mona's comeback picture, although that was Dalton's mistake, for Ainsley had been against filming the script that had been scheduled for Mona when she'd run off with Lord Truscott-Ames, saying it was no longer suitable. He was right. Although the ads for *The Adventuress* read, "Gaillard and Stanton are together again and it's dynamite!" the picture was described by reviewers as a dated, makeshift, and strained vehicle, with lackluster performances by its stars.

"This will finish Mona," Mike said, "and I'm glad."

"I know you don't mean that," Tracy said. "I also know that there's only one woman in the world you really want to be married to, and that's Mona."

"No!" He banged his fist heavily down on the table beside his chair. "No, God damn it, that isn't true."

"I see it isn't," Tracy said.

"It's not!" he insisted. "She made a fool of me."

"She was honest with you," Tracy said. "She told you she didn't love you, and you accepted her on that basis. She didn't make a fool of you. You made a fool of yourself."

"What the hell do you know about it?" he said angrily.

"Only what you told me, Mike."

"I don't tell you everything, Tracy, and I'm going to tell you less, now that I know how you twist things around to suit you."

"We all twist things around, Mike. Do you think that if we live a lie long enough, it becomes truth? Do you think if we tell ourselves our marriage is happy often enough, it will be?"

"Our marriage is working," he said.

"It was working a month or so ago, if you can accept half measures," Tracy said. "I suppose half measures are endurable, Mike, but anything less is strictly shortchanging ourselves."

"What are you getting at?"

"I think we've reached the shortchanging stage."

"Crap! You're just looking for ways to be difficult."

"Let me remind you that you started this, Mike. The emptiness has gotten to you. It's surfacing."

"For God's sake, don't go psychological on me! You don't know what you're talking about."

"I know that I'm beginning to realize how unhappy I am. I think the same is true of you."

"That isn't so," he said, but he was frowning, and his tone was unconvincing.

"Mike, I've been asking myself why we married each other. I think we did it because we both felt a need to be close to someone again—"

"It was much more than that," he broke in defensively.

"I don't think so—and it certainly isn't a solid basis for marriage. I'm afraid the old cliché is right. To succeed, a marriage has to have good bedrock to build on."

"Ours would have if you'd let it!" he said angrily.

He refused to try to understand what she was saying, so she didn't go on with it. A few days later, when Ainsley phoned to ask her to come to the studio, she didn't tell Mike she was going. When she arrived home with a script for a picture Ainsley wanted her to do at Regency's British studio, Mike was adamant.

"No! You're not going to make a picture until we can make one together."

"You sound like a jealous kid, Mike."

"What the hell's the matter with that idiot Ainsley? He comes up with a picture for you, but nothing for me!"

"It's really a little hard to believe that you're so worked up because I might have a new picture to do and you don't."

"Why shouldn't I? Making pictures is what our lives are about. Being and staying a star is what matters. You take that away, and what is there?"

"That says a lot about what you really think of our marriage."

"My God, Tracy, it takes more than marriage for people like us to be happy. Our work has to be right. I don't like sitting here on this mountain with nothing to look forward to but opening bottles of bourbon."

Tracy turned her back on him and crossed to the large front window that stretched across most of the room. She looked out at the panorama spread below her. It blurred through her sudden tears.

"We're going to have to end this mistake, Mike," she said.

"So you're going to walk out."

She turned and looked at him. "Yes, for our own good, so we can save what we have; so it won't end in hate."

"Hate? God, Tracy, I could never hate you. I can only love you."

"But you don't love me, Mike. And you never could."

"You still think you love Howard, don't you?" he said. "Face it, Tracy! If you could really have him, you wouldn't want him. I hope not too much happiness goes down the drain before you realize that. Tracy, let yourself love *me*. If you'd only love me, we could be so happy together!"

"Mike, you're wrong about so much. And especially that you want me to love you. You only want Mona to love you."

They looked at each other for the last time in that house. The next day Tracy started arrangements for a divorce and then left for England.

51

Howard hadn't been to Dalton's house in years. He went this time only because he thought it would be less of a strain to talk to him there than at the studio. He didn't really want to talk to Dalton, but it seemed important to express his views.

As Dalton's old butler led him down the hall, Howard noted that nothing seemed changed in the place: the same portraits lined the walls, the same huge oriental rug ran down the marble floor. When he was led into the living room, he saw that it was the same there, too. It was as if Dalton were holding the past in abeyance in this vast old place just in case Eunice Dalton might return to resume her rightful role as mistress.

But of course Eunice Dalton would never return, and the real reason Dalton kept his house unchanged was to keep his immediate environment rooted in an era he'd loved. But outside this house, that era was gone, and time had passed Dalton by. Obviously he'd forgotten the period in his life when he had asserted that the man who didn't change with the times was doomed.

Dalton had been generally unwilling to accept change at the studio, and the result was growing conflict with Ainsley and Smetley. But Ainsley's efforts to accommodate Regency Pictures to the demands of change hadn't achieved much, either, Howard realized. Ainsley had tried one thing after another to meet the challenges of the new Hollywood, but the studio's operations had remained in the red most of the years he'd been in power as production chief.

"Well, well," Dalton said, rising from the recesses of a huge barrel-backed chair long enough to shake Howard's hand before he sank back down. "Good God, but it's been a long time since you were here!"

"It looks just the way I remembered it," Howard said as he sat down.

"I don't suppose you've changed your house much, either."

Howard nodded. That was true enough.

"Why should we change what we're used to and like, anyway?" Dalton commented.

"Maybe we don't have to in our homes," Howard said, "but what about our outside interests? Some say that it's resistance to change and reactionary attitudes that have brought Hollywood to its low state."

"Those who say that are wrong. Hollywood has been brought to its low state by the combined forces of television, union trouble, bad publicity from the House Un-American Activities Committee hearings, and that formidable tax England put on American pictures right after the war. Why, the returns in England used to mean the difference between profit and loss on many a Regency picture."

"There are some who say that Hollywood could have handled it a lot better. Especially this matter of trying to ignore television instead of trying to compete with it."

"Hindsight! I've said it before and I'll say it again: Hollywood will again be as great as it was. And Regency Pictures will be in the vanguard. We'll lead the way with *Paris and Helen*. M-G-M has seen the light. They're going to remake *Ben-Hur*. We're entering an era of very big pictures on epic themes. They will cost a great deal of money, but they will make a great deal of money, too, because who could enjoy an epic on a pea-sized television screen even if TV *could* program them? Pictures like *Ben-Hur* and *Paris and Helen* will bring movie audiences back into the theaters where they belong."

357

Howard thought about various gimmicks Regency had tried to lure audiences back into the theaters since early in the decade, including wide-screen, third dimension, and stereophonic sound, plus various content approaches, including all-entertainment pictures and pictures with social significance. Nothing yet had helped much to fill the theaters. Now the all-star epic was on the horizon. Howard doubted that it would succeed, either.

Dalton smiled. "I told Smetley three years ago we should make this picture, and now we're finally going to do it, even though Ainsley doesn't like the idea. Ainsley's been wrong too many times, Howard, and Smetley at last is seeing the light."

"I'm seeing it, too. I don't want to do *Paris and Helen.*"

Dalton looked surprised. "You can't be serious. This is going to be the biggest picture of the decade."

"It's the role, not the picture, that's stopping me. I had a slightly lesser role in *Safari* than Mike did, which didn't make much difference in the long run; but the role of Hector is much weaker than the role of Paris, and it will make a lot of difference."

"Howard, Hector is a hero."

"But he's not the big hero. Paris is. Oh, it isn't that I think I should be Paris. I'm too old for the part. I'm forty-seven. But the truth is, Mike and Tracy have the starring roles in this picture, and I'm just supporting them, because my role is much smaller and far less important than theirs."

"If you feel that way, we'll have Hector built up."

"That wouldn't help. Hector's a good character as he is. It's just that he's a supporting character. And if the public sees me in this role, they're going to say, 'Why doesn't Howard Stanton get the girl in this picture? Must be slipping.' The public scorns slipping stars, and you know it. They love you when you're on top and laugh at you when you're going down."

"You're serious about this, aren't you? You really don't want to do this picture."

"No. I did *The Adventuress* with Mona against my better judgment, and it flopped. I don't want to repeat the mistake."

"It might mean suspension, Howard. You know how Smetley feels about temperament in these tight times."

"I'm prepared for that," Howard said. "My contract expires in a couple of years anyway, and I don't expect a renewal. Why should I be different?"

"Suspension is risky. Independent producers don't want to hire

358

uncooperative stars any more than studios do. Howard, I don't want to see you throw away such a long and successful career after all these years."

"That's what I'm trying not to do." He paused, then said, "I don't think you really care what I do."

"On the contrary. I realize that our relationship changed many years ago, but I still care about what happens to you. And I care about what happens to Regency Pictures. The studio is my child. I don't care what else I lose in life if I still have the studio."

Howard nodded toward the painting of Eunice Dalton looking down from the mantelpiece. "Is that why her portrait is still up there? Is that why this house is just as she left it?"

"This house is as it is because it's the way I want it. I'm perfectly content here alone. I don't even care what Eunice is doing, so long as she doesn't try to take the studio away from me. If she does, I'll fight her."

"What do you mean?"

"She was well paid in the divorce settlement, Howard. I settled a big chunk of Regency stock on her. It was a mistake. She holds a great deal of power through that stock, and if she and Smetley combined forces, they could force me into a corner."

"Surely you don't think she'd do that."

"I hope not, but it worries me sometimes. I don't want to lose my power. Think of the studio heads who've lost power in the last few years. That isn't going to happen to me."

Wasn't it? Howard wondered.

A few days after Howard's formal refusal to undertake *Paris and Helen* and the studio's immediate suspension of him under contract terms, there was a surprise coup at Regency Pictures. Dean Ainsley was forced out as production chief, his exit made more palatable by a full settlement of the balance of his contract, which still had three years to run. He was the third studio production chief to fall from power that year. His replacement was Denton Taylor, a businessman from the East with no experience in the movie business, who had been brought in by Smetley on his record of having taken over two faltering manufacturing businesses in the last decade and making successes of them by weeding out the dead wood, insisting upon efficiency, and introducing fresh ideas.

As soon as he arrived at Regency Pictures, Taylor had Dean Ainsley's office redecorated to remove all traces of its previous owner and announced that production on *Paris and Helen* would move forward as scheduled but that other future production plans were in for modification.

"Regency Pictures is going to be revitalized," the new production chief announced to the press.

Howard recalled that Dean Ainsley had said something like that his first days on the job, too.

52

Mike was glad to get *Paris and Helen,* because he hadn't had a picture since *Safari* two years back. He was also glad that Howard had declined a role in it; he didn't want to work with Howard again. He didn't want to work with Tracy, either, but he couldn't quarrel with the studio's choice. Who better fit the concept of the beautiful Helen of Troy, for whom nations went to war, than the beautiful Tracy Gordon?

Except perhaps the older but still beautiful Mona Gaillard, who, according to an interview she gave Aster Bigelow, felt that she should have been offered the role. The columnist's piece in her still-extant but less flourishing column indicated that Mona had considered herself grossly misused and abused by Regency Pictures in her comeback, and felt it necessary to remind the public and the industry that her pictures had made more money for the studio in the nineteen forties than those of any other star.

Mike knew that the studio didn't give a damn about that in the late nineteen fifties, and he knew that Mona was aware of it, too. She was no longer a star—she was an ex-star; and according to Aster Bigelow, she was facing her situation in a realistic manner by seeing a great deal of a multimillionaire land developer. Aster hinted that Mona flew down to Acapulco to spend weekends at her lover's lavish estate and commented that she thought America's former favorite love goddess was at last really in love for the first time and would marry soon for the fourth time.

Mike reacted to the news by getting drunk, as he had done a number of times in the year since Tracy had left him. It had been an empty year of drinking and taking to bed a lot of young women and a few young men. But he'd come to a decision. He was selling his house in California, and after he had finished making *Paris and Helen* in Spain, he would either live in Europe or settle in New York City. His Regency contract ended in another year and a half anyway, and he had no illusions that it would be renewed. Nowadays no one's was.

He reported in Spain, determined to make as much of his role as possible, though he already had misgivings about the turgid script. He took an immediate dislike to the British director, too, and soon decided that Vivian Kennicott—retained for this project because he'd made several moneymaking historical spectacles in Italy recently—wasn't directing either him or Tracy very effectively. Kennicott was expert at directing mob scenes, but he was too unsubtle to evoke good performances from individual actors.

Mike felt awkward with Tracy, too. He'd known about her affair with the Spanish matador Juan Olivares before he'd come here, for it was common gossip in the scandal magazines, but he hadn't anticipated the distaste he felt for the situation. He wasn't sure whether he was jealous or concerned. Whatever, Tracy's situation was no joke. Olivares was married, and Spanish marriages were for keeps; Tracy was just getting herself into a mess.

Olivares was around a lot during the six weeks they were shooting interior scenes at the studio in Madrid, and even went along on location on a plain in Andalucía, where the set of the city of Troy had been erected and the battle scenes and the siege of the city were being filmed. Mike didn't like the matador, but he saw at once that he was a gentleman. Mike kept away from Olivares and Tracy most of the time. He'd told himself that he would keep his drinking down while they were making this picture, but it was soon out of control. He felt terribly lonely.

Though the location camp for most of the crew was out on the plain, the stars, principal featured players, director, producer and a few other important persons were quartered in a fine old inn in the town.

One morning Tracy wakened at dawn to hear doors opening and closing down the hall, and then the sound of vehicles departing from the courtyard. They were driving out to the location camp for today's shooting of a battle sequence. Her presence wasn't required, so she could have a whole lazy day here with Juan, and maybe tomorrow, too.

361

Juan had said he would return to his family tonight, but he'd said that on other occasions, and she thought he would stay this time, too, if she encouraged him. She thought he loved her, though he hadn't said so yet.

She looked at his beautiful face on the pillow beside her. He hadn't awakened even once during the night after their lovemaking. He always slept deeply and contentedly unless there was a bull to be fought the next day. He was twenty-six years old and she was thirty-one. She didn't know why that came to mind as she watched him sleep.

When he wakened an hour later, he kissed her but didn't make love to her. He was conventional about many things, and for him lovemaking was for the night. She watched him dress with pleasure. She loved his slim, strong body.

And she took pleasure in being seen with him in public, in being identified more and more not just as a movie star but as Juan Olivares' lover. His people idolized him: not the crowd he traveled in socially, not the aristocratic circle he'd been born to, but the middle- and lower-class Spaniards. They would greet him everywhere he went with bows and smiles: *"Buenos dias, matador!"* There was excitement in this village right now not because a movie company and two American movie stars were in its midst, but because Spain's greatest hero, the torero who had restored bravery to the corrida, was present.

This morning they walked out of her room together, arm in arm, down the shining hall of ornamental tile to the heavy carved wooden staircase; then down to the main room, with its huge stone fireplace and shuttered windows. *"Buenos dias, matador. Buenos dias, señorita!"*—with bows and smiles from the employees of the inn.

Outside, in the neat, quiet ancient square, it was the same. Everyone looked at them; everyone greeted them.

"Spain is so different from what I expected," she said as they walked across the cobbles toward a little café on the other side. "I don't just mean that Madrid is so modern. I mean even ancient places like this village aren't what I expected. I thought there'd be women in mantillas everywhere, duennas looking after their children, castanets clicking in gypsy caves."

"There is still much of that in Spain," Juan said.

"Yes, I suppose there *is* a feeling of the past preserved here. But not so much as in Italy. Someone tried to tell me about the feeling of the past in Italy, but it didn't seem important then. It does now."

"We will go to Rome together sometime. And Venice. They are two of my very favorite places." He paused. "I want to be with you everywhere."

362

But not forever, she thought, with a feeling of hurt she knew wasn't justified. Why should she expect *him* to believe this could be anything more than a short affair when she couldn't believe it herself?

"Juan, do I make you happy?" she asked as they ate breakfast in a café garden where colored umbrellas shielded the tables from the sun.

He smiled. "Do you need to ask that? I thought I showed you how happy you make me."

"Oh, yes, you do. But hearing it said is important, Juan. Americans like to be told."

"Yes, Americans talk when they do not need to talk, and they like to be told what they should not need to be told. You make me very happy, Tracy. That is why I am here with you instead of with my family. I would like to be with you all the time. That is how I feel."

"I'd like that, too," she said after a moment.

After breakfast they walked to the river, where a park, gardens, and orchards ran into one another. They took a path by the water's edge, shaded by plane and sycamore trees, to the farthest corner of the park, and there they looked out on a distant scene of fields where men moved with donkeys and carts. Sunlight trembled on acres of golden grain, and Juan gently touched Tracy's arm, turning her to him.

"I am going to say it, Tracy. It pains me not to have said it before, because I feel it so deeply. I love you. I love you." He drew her to him. "You are the first and last one I will ever love."

She didn't know why she was suddenly weeping. She clung to him hard, pressing her tears to his face.

The morning shooting hadn't gone at all well, the first trouble coming when Paris' chariot had upset and thrown Mike into the midst of hundreds of Trojans and Greeks, making reshooting of a large segment of that action necessary. Then the scene had to be shot again after a number of horses that had thrown their riders suddenly stampeded, dividing the battle scene into unscheduled halves.

When the company broke for lunch, Mike heard the news from the producer that Augustus Dalton had resigned as studio head of Regency Pictures and Denton Taylor had been named by the board of directors to fill his spot.

Later, Mike learned that Dalton's terse announcement to the press gave as his reason for resigning his intention to go into independent production. Still later, the real truth made its way from Hollywood to the plains of Andalucía: Nicholas Smetley had persuaded the major stockholders, including Dalton's ex-wife, to join with him to force Dalton out, "for the good of the studio."

363

It made no difference to Mike, who had never liked Dalton anyway, but he knew it would make a difference to Howard. Howard would care.

In the time that Juan had been Tracy's lover, she'd come to dread Sunday afternoons. In the beginning she had found a certain dramatic beauty in the colorful pageantry of the bullfight. Now the corrida represented three hours of endless dread. Every Sunday, all over Spain, toreros were gored in bullrings. Sometimes they died. Because of his bravery, grace, and skill, Juan Olivares was the most popular matador in Spain, but his popularity would never preserve him from the possibility of death in the arena.

Today as she sat waiting in her seat in the plaza de toros in Madrid, Tracy was particularly apprehensive. Today was Juan's most important fight of the season. It was also the most important *mano a mano* of his career; he was to compete in the ring with Luis Galindo, the ranking matador in Mexico. There wasn't a single unoccupied seat in the entire bullring.

When the president of the bullfight arrived at his box near where Tracy was sitting, the signal was given to begin. In the opening ceremony the matadors and their quadrillas marched into the arena to processional music. Juan, in a gold suit of lights, was the most beautiful man in Spain. In the hours of high tension ahead he would try to outperform his rival as between them they fought six enormous black fighting bulls.

Tracy prayed silently for him. His wife Elena, far away on the Olivares ranch in Andalucía, was unquestionably praying for him at this moment, too. One of the few things Tracy knew about the wife of Juan Olivares was that she couldn't bear the agonizing suspense of watching her husband in the bullring. But she assuredly still prayed for him.

Two hours had passed and the matadors had each fought two bulls. It was incredible how well matched they were, Tracy kept hearing around her. Whose cape work was so superb as Juan Olivares'—unless it was Luis Galindo's? Who worked so close to the bull as Juan Olivares—unless it was Luis Galindo? Who made so superb a kill as Juan Olivares—unless it was Luis Galindo?

The contest was clearly a draw as the matadors prepared to face the final challenge of the afternoon.

Luis Galindo fought magnificently almost to the last. But he was slightly off when he plunged the sword into the bull's neck at the

364

moment of truth, and he hit bone instead of the aorta. The second try was perfect, and the bull fell dead. But it *was* the second try.

Still, Tracy knew all too well that something could go wrong for Juan with his third bull, too. He could be tossed—or worse—from a single moment of miscalculation. She clenched her hands tightly in her lap as she watched him make his breathtaking passes, with the bull brushing perilously close to him as he followed through. The crowd cheered its approval as their favorite matador gave them yet another superb performance of stunningly choreographed movements.

In the final moments, its head heavy from pics planted in its huge neck, the bull swayed hypnotically through Juan's muleta passes. And now the moment of truth! Juan raised his sword high over the sagging horned head, pointed toward the vital area in the heavy neck, and plunged the sword to the hilt. The beast stood stock still for a single moment and then fell.

The arena was filled with screams as wineskins and flowers were tossed into it. Juan walked about, smiling at the crowd. Music played. The judges awarded Juan the tail and both ears. Few matadors were so honored.

It was over, and Juan Olivares had bested Luis Galindo in the last act of a *mano a mano* that would be ranked among the best of the decade by the critics and the aficionados.

It was over, and Tracy Gordon's lover was still alive to fight another Sunday, to live and love for another week. It was over until next time.

There was always a party after the corrida. Juan joked that still being alive and in one piece was cause enough to celebrate. It was really no joke, of course. But Juan never talked of his fear of death. He thought it improper, and Tracy understood.

Juan's quadrilla always attended the parties. So did his business manager, his personal manager, and others of the entourage that traveled with him during the season. So did some members of the press and certain of Juan's friends.

Often, Juan would hold the party in a café. If the party was large enough to fill the place, Juan would simply buy it out for the evening, and they would all sit around drinking and watching the flamenco dancers. Once Juan had persuaded Tracy to dance the flamenco, and the crowd had cheered her wildly, but she was embarrassed, feeling that she hadn't done very well. She'd learned the dance for a scene in *The Gypsy and the Baron,* which she'd made here in Spain shortly after completing *Paris and Helen,* but for the filming she'd performed the dance only in pieces, which was far different from doing it whole for an audience that knew mediocre flamenco when they saw it. She'd asked Juan never to ask her to perform like that again.

Today Juan had decided to hold the party in his apartment. There was a buffet of shrimp, mussels, and lobster. The crowd was much the same as usual except for the long-retired matador Chavo Varona, who was old enough to be Juan's grandfather and had been famous in his day. Juan was greatly pleased that the old man had traveled all the way from Cadiz to see him fight.

"I hope Juan will quit the ring while he is still on top," Chavo Varona said to Tracy in his good but heavily accented English. "The way down can be swift."

"Isn't that true of most things where people find unusual success? It certainly is of the movie business."

"It is also true," the old matador continued, "that most people recognize it when they have started down; yet how many stop before it is too late? There is something in them that will not let them."

"It's something called hope, I think. From the way you're talking, Señor, I don't think you stopped when you were on top, even though you knew you should."

"No, I did not. There came the time, when I was thirty-five years old, when I was not as brave or as good as I had been. When you are no longer as brave as you were, you cannot let yourself come as close to the bull as you did before, and the aficionados like you less for it. When you are not as good in your movements as you were, your cape work is not as good, either, and the aficionados like you less for that, too. And then, when you finally do step down, their memory of you becomes their last impression of you, not of how great you were before you declined."

"Yet knowing that was the way of it, you still didn't step down."

"Few do. I do not think Juan will, either, no matter how intelligent he is. Yet he knows, as we all do, that if you are a great bullfighter, there are only two ways to remain great and to be remembered after you are no longer active—to be killed in the ring at your peak, as Manolete was, or to go out when you know you should."

Pray God, she thought, that Juan would not be killed and that he would go out when he knew he should.

An hour later the apartment was silent and dark. Out beyond the closed bedroom door were reminders of the party—half-filled glasses, filled ashtrays, the remains of the buffet. And beyond the open bedroom balcony door could be heard the soft evening sounds of the city.

366

Madrid was a somber city, Tracy thought, and its noise levels matched its solemnity.

Juan was undressing her piece by piece, kissing her almost everywhere his hands went. But he didn't kiss the vaginal flesh. Tracy had concluded that Spanish men, even those of Juan's sophisticated background, never did that.

When she was naked, she lay watching him disrobe. He undressed as gracefully as he did everything else in life, and she loved seeing his beautiful, lithe body become progressively nude. When he was naked, he paused at the side of the bed and smiled down at her, his brown eyes glowing with his love for her.

He lay down beside her. His hand caressed her left breast and then slid down with adoring fingers to the lips of the vagina that his own lips never touched. His lips were on her breast now, kissing it softly. She began to feel as if she were floating.

He raised her hand and kissed the palm. He kissed the inside of her arm, up and down. She lay quietly, aching to respond, to be a partner, not just a receiver. But she couldn't. When she'd tried that in the beginning, it had disturbed him. A woman was to accept love, not make it herself. It was the role of the woman in Spain.

Her impulse was to show that there was a better way for her, and that if it was a better way for her, it would be better for him, too. But she'd been afraid to reassert herself, to try for partnership in their love-making, until she was more certain of him, until she was sure he loved her.

She was sure of that now, but she was still afraid to try to change her ways in bed with him. Besides, it was beautiful his way, because *he* was doing this to her, because *he* was filling her body with himself. She could lie almost unmoving under him and come simply because he was inside her.

She cried out at the end. As usual, he didn't make a sound. He kissed her, then slipped out of her and off her, pressing against her side, his hand clasping hers. Soon he was asleep, but she lingered in wakefulness for a while, wondering if she would ever have him all for herself.

Tracy sat in darkness on the balcony. Juan slept heavily in the bedroom, exhausted with the emotion of the fight, the party afterward, and their lovemaking.

Tracy's thoughts went unbidden to his wife, the woman named Elena who'd come of a family as distinguished as Juan's, whose marriage to him had been "arranged," who had borne him two children, both boys, with a new child on the way. A woman who lived on the vast Olivares ranch in Andalucía all year long, who never accompanied her husband on his tours, who was afraid to watch him fight, who'd never seen her husband's apartment in Madrid, but whose framed photograph was kept on a living room table to remind Juan of her faithfulness and his faithlessness. A woman who was all faithfulness, all goodness, who loved Juan no less than Tracy did, who would give him up no more willingly than Tracy would.

In the last year, Tracy had buried much of her past. She'd been back to London only once, to close her flat and put its contents up for sale. And she'd been back to the States only once, to visit her mother for a few days. Her mother assuredly knew of her relationship with Juan, since it was more than an occasional matter of attention in the press, but they hadn't discussed it. They'd found it no easier to talk to each other than before.

In Spain Tracy officially lived in a small rented villa on the outskirts of Madrid, but she spent little time there. She usually stayed with Juan in his apartment when he was in Madrid and often traveled with him to the bullrings of Barcelona, San Sebastian, Seville, Valencia, and Zaragoza, where she watched him fight with the same dread she had felt today. Death in the afternoon! How well that had been put.

She loved him but she couldn't have him. That was the saga of Tracy Gordon, movie star and sex symbol. She loved men she couldn't have, and married men she couldn't love. She sometimes wondered what a psychoanalyst would say about that.

Hearing a rustle, she turned to find Juan coming out, barefoot and wearing one of his beautiful silk robes. He sat down beside her. He pushed back her hair at her ear and kissed her just below it.

He took her hand in his. "I will not ask you what you have been thinking out here while I have slept. I think you have been thinking secret thoughts."

And he respected that. He respected *her.* He never made her feel like a fool, as Crandon and Wes often had, and sometimes Mike. He wasn't in any important way like the men who'd been her husbands, and he wasn't like Howard except in his respect for her. It wasn't surprising that the only two men she'd really loved respected her.

"Yes, but only partly secret," she said. "I've been thinking about loving you, too."

"Have you thought about my loving you?"

"I think about it most of the time," she said. "And I wonder what's going to happen to us."

"I love my children, and I love my father and my mother," he said

368

slowly, "but the time I could spend with them, I no longer do. I spend it with you, Tracy. What does that mean?"

"Not that you love me more. If it became a question of giving me up or giving them up, you'd give me up. But I don't want to think about that. I just want us to be happy together as long as we can."

"You ask no more than that? I do not believe it."

"I believed in fantasies for too many years, Juan. I'm much more of a realist now. Besides, I don't think what a person will or won't give up is a proper measure of his love. Anyway, it isn't going to become a question with us. I don't want to think about what might happen tomorrow or next week or next year. Day by day, Juan. That's the only way to take life."

"I do not believe you really mean that," he said. "I think you want me to love you tomorrow and next week and next year, exactly as I want you to love me tomorrow and next week and next year. It is what we all want."

She sank against him and he kissed her. She wished she could believe in that tomorrow he hoped for. She clung to him, holding the moment as long as she could.

Tracy knew, even before he announced himself, that the man at the door was Juan's father. He was simply an older, graying version of Juan. He was even almost as slim. There was the same warmth in the deep-set brown eyes, the same nobility of carriage. Don Felipe Olivares was an aristocrat. Naturally he would have the bearing of one, as his son did.

Tracy wasn't surprised to see him. In the back of her mind she'd expected Juan's father to show up here someday. What seemed strange was showing him in to Juan's apartment as if it were hers. He didn't even look around, although he'd never been here before. He just looked at her.

"Juan does not know I am here," he said.

She nodded. "I didn't think so. He's already left for Malaga. He's fighting there tomorrow."

"Yes. That is why I am here today. I know that you usually go with him when he fights. I hoped that you would not this time, and it is good that you have not. I think we must talk, and I do not think we could if Juan were here. Perhaps later, the three of us. But not until you and I have talked."

"You want me to give Juan up," Tracy said.

Don Felipe nodded. "I have hoped all these months that the affair would end, but since it has not, I am here to talk about it."

369

"Would you believe that I've loved only two men in my life?" Tracy said. "And Juan is one of them."

He nodded again. "And I believe that you are not just a passion with Juan. I believe he loves you."

"Yet you'd like to see us give each other up."

"You do not have the same values we have, or the same traditions. Love is not everything in our world, Miss Gordon."

"It's not everything in any world, Señor Olivares, but it's important to me. It's important to Juan, too."

"What do you expect to get from this, Miss Gordon? You know that Juan can never marry you."

"What I expect to get from it is happiness, for as long as it lasts."

"It is tearing my son apart. He can never be comfortable living two lives. Guilt will weigh heavily on him as long as this continues."

"Juan was living two lives before I met him. He's an international figure."

"What means the most to him is his family."

"You mean, what means the most to *you* is his family, or you wouldn't be here. If his family were that important to him, he wouldn't spend so much time with me."

"He is wracked with misery," Don Felipe said.

"He feels guilty, but he's not miserable, Señor. He's happy more often than he's unhappy. And I'm happy with him. You're wrong if you think I'd willingly give him up. You haven't given me a single valid reason for giving him up. I don't think you even really expected me to."

"I felt I must try."

"Did you expect me to feel guilty about his wife and children? It happens that I do—but not enough to give him up."

"You are very beautiful. I understand why Juan has done what he has."

"I like to think that Juan and I are together for more important reasons."

"I see that my visit here has failed. But time is on my side. So is our religion, Señorita."

"I hope you're wrong," Tracy said.

"And now I shall go." Don Felipe rose. "I think in time Juan will come back to us willingly. I think he will choose us over you. But even if he does not, I think you will choose to leave him. What is not right does not endure, Miss Gordon. In the end, God will determine it all."

Tracy felt a chill. It could have been her own mother talking.

53

Until the day she phoned him with the shocking news that Dalton had died in New York City, Howard hadn't talked with Eunice Dalton once in the more than twelve years since she'd left Dalton and gone back East to live.

"A heart attack," Eunice Dalton said thickly. She went on to say that apparently it had happened when a stock coup Dalton had engineered to gain control of Regency Pictures had backfired.

"How did it happen?" Howard asked numbly.

"I don't quite understand it, but it seems that Nicholas Smetley was going to put a large block of his shares on the market to help refinance the studio. Augustus' plan was to put up his fortune, plus everything he could borrow, to buy the shares secretly through a covering broker. But Nicholas found out about it and withdrew his shares, and when Augustus learned that he couldn't buy the controlling shares of stock, he was dead within minutes. He couldn't stand the shock of the final disappointment."

She went on to say that she'd never been able to forgive her husband for preferring another woman to her. "And now he's dead," she said in a strained voice.

Howard could find nothing to say. Long ago, Eunice Dalton had left her husband because he'd taken a mistress, and she'd remained bitter over the years long after Dalton had dropped the woman. Now she was suffering deep regrets over the role she had played in forcing Dalton out of the studio.

"Will you be bringing him back to Hollywood to bury him?" Howard asked after a moment.

"Yes. Hollywood is the only place he would want to rest, no matter how unhappy it finally made him."

Howard hung up. He was alone in the house; but he felt alone in the world. Soon he found himself crying quietly. Then he was sobbing uncontrollably, unable to stop. He hadn't cried when his own father

371

had died, but this was different. Even though their relationship had changed in the last decade or so, Dalton had once been the only real father to him he'd ever known.

Tracy's penthouse apartment in a pink stucco building on the Janiculum Hill in Rome was sleekly modern, its walls lavishly decorated with the works of its owner, a prominent artist who had leased it on a month-to-month basis to Tracy while he was in the States on a commission. Tracy had been in Rome for three months working on a new picture being filmed at Cinecitta.

When the picture was finished, she decided to stay on in Rome rather than return to Spain. Juan was with her at least half the time here, nearly as much as he'd been with her in Spain. He flew to Rome for a few days each week, and when he didn't have a bullfight scheduled, he was usually there on weekends. Although he didn't say so, she knew he preferred that she continue to live in Rome. He was afraid his father would come to see her again if she returned to Spain.

Tracy hadn't told Juan about his father's visit; his father had. The visit had weakened the father-son relationship and had strengthened Juan's and Tracy's. Juan went home to the Olivares ranch in Andalucía even less often now than he had when Tracy had lived in Madrid.

Tracy was happy with Juan as long as she didn't think about the uncertainty of their future together. She tried to be patient. She understood the conflicts Juan was fighting. His father had put them to her very well.

Mike tried not to show it, but he was disappointed at Tracy's response when he called her shortly after arriving in Rome to start his new picture. She seemed not to care one bit that he was going to be in Rome for the next three months, and was quite vague about when they could get together.

Mike went to the bar at the Excelsior, where he was staying, and had a few drinks to mull that over. It was true that their marriage had ended badly and she'd subsequently flaunted her affair with Juan Olivares when they were making *Paris and Helen*. But that was a long time ago, and he wanted to see her, to talk about what they had both been doing for the last couple of years and about the world that had collapsed under all of them—the world of Hollywood, of Regency Pictures.

Howard was the only one from the old days who still lived in California. He hadn't made a picture since he'd been unlucky enough to co-star with Mona in her comeback picture a few years earlier. It had been Mona's last picture, too; she had announced when she married her

372

multimillionaire lover and went to live in Acapulco that she was retiring from the screen for good.

She wouldn't have had a contract anyway. Regency Pictures didn't have a single star left under contract. Nor did the other studios, except for M-G-M, which still had Robert Taylor; and Paramount, which had Elvis Presley.

Mike's house in Pacific Palisades was now owned by an aircraft company executive. After finishing *Paris and Helen,* Mike had gone to live in New York and had searched unsuccessfully for a play. He'd been there for the premiere of *Paris and Helen* and had seen it flop grandiosely, panned universally as a dragging bore. The losses from the epic, reported Aster Bigelow, put the final sad touches on Regency Pictures' record of red ink operations during the nineteen fifties. The company was at its lowest ebb; it had even decided to demolish the last symbol of its former grandeur—the sumptuous Regency Grand—in favor of a much more profitable office building to be raised on its choice location at Broadway and Fiftieth Street. Aster Bigelow observed that the recently deceased founders of Regency Pictures— Augustus Dalton, followed shortly in death by Nicholas Smetley— must surely be turning in their graves.

More news was released about the company just as Mike signed with Otto Steinbrugge to do *The Iron Gunfighter* in Rome. Denton Taylor had been ousted as studio head, and Noel Jordan, a television executive, had been installed in his place by the board of directors. Jordan made the expected statements about getting the studio back on its feet. Mike didn't care whether it got back on its feet unless it meant a new contract for him. He felt very insecure without his Regency contract, and it was little consolation to him that the collapse of the Hollywood studio system meant that practically no one else had a contract, either.

The deal to make the Western at Cinecitta in Rome was Mike's first professional hope in a long time, and he intended to make the most of it. This Western promised to be more important to him than the ones he'd made for Regency Pictures. Steinbrugge was a new type in the movie industry. A businessman from Philadelphia, he'd come to Italy in 1957, had bought the rights to an Italian adventure picture for a half million, had taken it to the United States and released it in a saturation booking supported by an advertising campaign costing a million and a half, and had grossed ten million. He'd followed this astounding success with the profitable exploitation of two Japanese horror pictures and now had formed his own production company.

Mike had signed for the Steinbrugge picture on a percentage basis, and if the picture was a success, he stood to gain considerably more than was possible under a studio contract. But although he began the picture in high spirits, for the script was good and his role was strong, he was soon discouraged. Steinbrugge ordered substantial changes in the script as they went along, with the picture being rewritten scene by scene as they shot it, and Mike recognized that both the focus of the picture and the strength of his role were being eroded. He quarreled with Steinbrugge about that and about his dissatisfaction with the director, an Italian who hadn't the proper feel for making American Westerns. He got no satisfaction from Steinbrugge, and their relationship steadily deteriorated. As the picture went downhill, so did Mike. He could see the reflection of his discontent in the rushes. He didn't need another poor picture and another poor performance, but he was getting one and giving one. He felt trapped. To forget what was happening, he began to drink more and more.

His life off the set reflected his dissatisfaction on it. The irritants of life were magnified, and he often found himself acting rashly. One night he threw a scene in the bar of the Excelsior Hotel over the "pimps, whores, and phonies" that occupied the famous sidewalk tables out front under the mimosa trees of the Via Veneto. He was asked to vacate. He moved to a hotel across the street.

He'd liked Rome at first, but the constantly honking, madly racing traffic, little controlled by policemen, frequently marked by collisions and fist-shaking exchanges between volatile Italians in the middle of the clogged streets, became a nerve-wracking experience to Mike as he drove to Cinecitta in his rented car. Battling the more organized tumult of traffic in New York City had seemed easy by comparison.

It turned out that he saw Tracy only once in the three months he was in Rome. She asked him to come to her apartment for dinner one night, but she didn't tell him that Juan would be there. It was a revealing and saddening evening for Mike. He saw that Tracy and Juan were really in love with each other. He didn't know why he shouldn't have expected it, since the affair had been going on for more than two years. He was jealous of their happiness together—a happiness beset with problems, to be sure, but happiness nevertheless. He could hardly remember ever being happy himself.

It seemed to Mike that Tracy had given him a message: she didn't want him tampering with her life again, if that was what he had in mind. Maybe it *was*. He was selfish. He wanted love. He wanted to be happy.

Mike picked up the copy of *Life* at a newsstand near his hotel that sold foreign publications. He was arrested by the cover: the picture of a blond young man with fine features, sparkling blue eyes, and a dazzling smile. The headline read: *Wells Corlen, The New Hollywood Breed*.

Inside was a four-page spread on Corlen, who was twenty-one years old and about to become a movie star. He was already the most popular singer in America, eclipsing even Elvis Presley in the polls, after a soaring rise to fame which had begun only three years earlier with his first appearances in the Catskills hotel circuit.

Like Elvis Presley, Wells Corlen played the guitar. Unlike him, he wrote most of his own songs. Most of them were about love. Some had earned him gold records. Corlen was the top recording star in America. There had been teen-age riots at his concerts, but the youngsters of America weren't his sole audience. He packed in record-breaking audiences at Las Vegas, too.

"No movie star in history," ascertained *Life,* "has been so besieged and beloved by his legions of fans as has Wells Corlen."

He'd recently signed a multimillion-dollar contract tied to percentages with Regency Pictures, whose new studio head had honestly admitted that they all hoped Wells Corlen could do for them what Elvis Presley had done for Paramount. Corlen had accepted Regency Pictures' offer over similar ones from M-G-M and Fox because the company had prepared the script he liked best. Corlen's first movie for Regency Pictures was to be called *The Performer*. It was about a magnetic singer who takes America by storm. It was Wells Corlen's own story.

The article concluded as it had begun: he was the new breed; he and the few others like him were the only hope Hollywood had.

"The old kind of movie star is dead," the article said. "Long live the new kings!—Presley and Corlen."

Mike closed the magazine and threw it across the hotel room. It slapped against the wall and fell to the floor, the cover shot of Wells Corlen face-up. Mike walked over and put his foot on it. He ground the cover until the taunting smile was destroyed.

54

Mike stood at his hotel window, looking across the Grand Canal at the pink, pearl, and *verde antico* palaces of Venice, basking in the strong sun. One of them, like this hotel, was vivid with frescoes and ornamentation, but it didn't look gaudy. The palaces doubled themselves in the water below, Technicolored images in the green mirror that was the canal. A water-bus passed, leaving a considerable wake, followed by two gondolas, one of them black and gold and manned by a liveried gondolier. A police launch, a motorboat, and a vegetable barge overtook and passed them. Life was moving on the Grand Canal, and it was a quiet life, except for the sound of boat motors.

Mike had noticed the quiet of Venice right away. It seemed so strange after the noisiness of Rome. Italians in general were naturally noisy, but it was impossible for Venetians to be as loud as their other country-men, because the water muffled their effusions, absorbed and drowned them. And there were no automobiles with honking horns and squealing tires.

Mike had come to Venice after finishing *The Iron Gunfighter,* had picked up with some American expatriates in Harry's Bar, and was still here after a month. He'd been thinking about returning to New York, but there was no urgency; he faced the same hollowness of existence there that he'd known before.

There was the light, timid tap on the door he'd been expecting. He turned from the window and crossed the room. When he opened the door, Giorgio was looking nervously up and down the hall, fearful as usual of being caught. Relatively speaking, it would be much more serious for Giorgio to be caught entering the room of Michael Baines for any but hotel business than for Michael Baines to be caught asking him to enter. Jobs were difficult to find in Venice, especially at high-class hotels like this one, and Giorgio knew when he was well off. He was only a busboy now, but, as he'd told Mike in his halting but acceptable English, he hoped to be a waiter like his father someday.

It was one of the few things Giorgio talked about, although he'd been with Mike several times now. The boy had an hour off from his kitchen duties late in the afternoon, and he would come to Mike's room for that period when asked.

Giorgio stepped inside and Mike closed the door behind him. The boy looked up at him, smiling glisteningly, his perfect teeth shining white against his satiny olive skin. Giorgio was sixteen years old. He had beaming brown eyes and very thick black eyelashes. He was as beautiful as a girl. Mike bent down and the boy brought his face up. Mike kissed Giorgio's lips. He'd never known softer ones.

He invited Giorgio to sit beside him on the silk-covered couch and poured vintage wine for him. They drank together. Giorgio licked his lips, savoring the fine wine. He put down his glass and took Mike's hand and kissed the palm and pressed his face against it.

They drank the rest of the wine while they continued embracing and kissing on the couch. Finally they undressed. Mike lay down on the bed on his back and extended his hand to Giorgio. The boy came to the bed and sat on the side, taking Mike's hand, kissing it and pressing it against his face again. He looked dreamily at Mike. He stroked Mike's thigh with his hand. He leaned over and kissed Mike's penis and then caressed it with his hand. He made love to Mike as if he loved him, not as if it were a business with him.

Mike felt helpless under it. What happened between them happened because of what the boy did, not because of what Mike did. Mike did nothing but lie yielding under the narcotic of the boy's warm sensuality. Giorgio covered his skin with little kisses. Mike trembled under the subtle erotic touch, but his body hardly moved. Time had stopped. He was lost in a sea of ecstatic oblivion. His body was under the paradoxical strain of an overall calm countered by a strong urge to convulse and explode.

Giorgio was ready to take Mike into him now. He straddled Mike's pelvis and lowered himself on Mike, the brown eyes still beaming their love, that magnificent deception that so thrilled and warmed Mike. A fleeting sign of pain appeared in the eyes when Giorgio began to take the rigid organ into his depths, but when he'd accepted its fullness and bigness and had accommodated it, the fantasy of love returned.

Up and down Giorgio moved, slowly, deeply. There was joy in the loving look now, too. Mike began to build. He clutched the bed sheets. He felt as powerful as Hercules. The wave over the top overtook him. He ground his teeth and gasped for breath as he came. It was like a climax of youth, as long and as strong. Even at that, it was over in moments.

They lay side by side then, hand covering hand. Giorgio's warmth radiated to Mike. Mike gathered Giorgio to him and kissed him, and the boy's heart thumped against his chest. Mike looked into Giorgio's eyes, wondering what he was thinking, wondering if he was thinking anything at all.

They lay together until the last possible moment. Then Giorgio dressed hurriedly while Mike watched. Giorgio was as beautiful in his white cotton busboy's jacket as if he'd been dressed by the best tailor in Rome. Mike handed Giorgio the lira notes, and he put them in his pocket and left.

Mike sighed, feeling a little depressed now that Giorgio was gone. He didn't like the side of him that made him take up with boys and men. He wished it would stop. It had never brought him happiness, and it never would.

Juan had been tossed on the horn of a bull and had suffered a cornada, the most dreaded word in the lexicon of the bullfight. The horn had entered Juan's groin and inflicted a serious wound. He would fight no more this season. Juan phoned Tracy the news from the hospital in Barcelona. Tracy had her own news, which she'd just learned, news that she certainly couldn't tell Juan yet.

She flew to Barcelona. Juan's father and his wife were at the hospital when she arrived. She waited and waited. Juan's father looked coldly at her when they came out of the room. There was a flicker of surprise in Juan's wife's eyes, then nothing. They both turned away from Tracy without a word.

Tracy went in to see Juan. They didn't let her stay with him long. She took his hand and wept with relief that she was with him. He asked her to return to Rome and wait; he would come as soon as he could. She wanted to stay in Barcelona with him, but she understood; he feared another confrontation between her and his father. Perhaps he even feared one between her and his wife.

She returned to Rome and waited for him to recuperate at the family estate in Andalucía. Tracy was full of fear of what might be happening there, even though she received reassuring letters from him almost every day. She had her news to use as a weapon, but she didn't use it.

She still hadn't told him two days after he'd returned to her, six weeks after his accident, although she wasn't sure why.

She decided to tell him one day when they had been visiting a museum filled with treasures of ancient Rome on the top of the Capitoline Hill. Afterward, they crossed the piazza to the parapet behind the senatorial palace and looked down at the huge wasteland of the Forum far below.

"It was the most important part of the ancient world," Tracy mused. "And now it's just a hole in the ground, with a few broken walls and columns."

Juan nodded. "The Palatine Hill across the way was once the site of the palaces of the Caesars, and now it is just a hill with stone pine and ruins on it. That is the way the world goes." Juan sighed. "The Italians make a shrine of what they have lost. That is the way of people. We do it in Spain, too. We look back on times of glory. Spain was once the greatest power in the world, just as Rome once was, just as England has been more recently, just as the United States is now. We look back to our glory because what we were is our heritage, and it is important."

"It doesn't seem important to me," Tracy said.

He looked at her. "What is important to you, Tracy? Being a movie star?"

"I won't say it isn't, although I would have said it once. I'm older now, and I know it's as important to me as it is important to you to be a matador. I suppose it takes away a little from the way I love you."

He nodded. "Any imperfection of life takes away from love, Tracy. But the way we love each other is the finest thing that has happened in my life. We have been happy with each other and unhappy with each other. But we have loved."

"You say it so sadly, as if we don't anymore," she said.

"I am sad only because of the great injustice I have done to you. I have asked you to love me and sacrifice for me because I was too weak to give up my family and my life as I have known it, because though I am a brave man in the bullring most of the time, I have been a coward with you. I have come to a decision, Tracy. You know that I cannot be divorced in Spain. So I will be divorced outside Spain. I am leaving my wife and my family."

Tracy took a deep breath. "I didn't expect this, Juan."

"I should have come to this decision long ago. I finally have. I am no longer a coward."

"Oh, darling!" She stepped into his arms and pressed her face against his. "I'm so happy. I don't care about your wife or your children. I'm the one who's selfish. I just care about us and our child. Juan, I'm pregnant!"

Tracy was in the kitchen finishing dinner. Juan still found it astonishing, even after all this time, that she so often wanted to cook for him.

She was roasting veal the Italian way, having rubbed juniper berries into it to give it a special flavor.

As she worked, she thought about the future. Tomorrow was no longer just a dream for her. The prospects for the future were now very real. She was going to have a child, and she was going to be with Juan all the time, not just part of the time. He was giving up his world for her because she meant more to him than that world did. She didn't understand why she felt a persistent guilt about it; their relationship had been tested over a period of time and remained solid, and he'd made his decision before she'd told him about the child, so he certainly hadn't been blackmailed into it.

She didn't want to think about guilt. She just wanted to think about how happy they were going to be. She hoped that Juan would want to settle in Rome. Perhaps they could build a smart modern villa out on the Appian Way where the Italian movie crowd was settling nowadays. It would be nice to rear a child outside the city, too.

She left the kitchen. There was nothing more she could do for another half hour. She walked through the living room, where Spanish fandango music was playing on the phonograph. Juan was out on the terrace, stretched out on a lounge, watching the sunset. When she sat down in a chair beside him, he reached over and caught her hand.

"I hope our child will be a girl and that she will be as beautiful as you and as good as you when she grows up."

"I hope it's a girl, too," Tracy said. "Most pregnant women say they don't care which it is. I'd rather it be a girl, and I don't mind admitting it."

He squeezed her hand. "We are going to be very happy together. I am only sorry that I could not bring myself to face the decision I needed to make long before I finally did. I feel very guilty about that. You were so patient! You would have been justified in leaving me."

"Most of us are basically selfish, Juan. I didn't leave you because I love you, and that helped to compensate for the insecurity I've felt until now. I gave up on love before, and maybe I shouldn't have. This time I didn't, and I'm glad."

"I will make it up to you for the insecurity."

"Let's not even think about making up for anything. And let's not think about guilt, either. There's been too much guilt in my life already."

"We will not think about it. I only want to think about how much I love you."

She told him then that she hoped he would want to make their

380

permanent home in Rome, since they both liked it so well and since they had so many friends here.

"You won't even miss Spain after a while," she said impetuously, "and you won't be sorry about retiring from the bullring, either."

"No," he said, but he turned his eyes away and fell into silence. She knew she'd made a mistake. He wouldn't be ready to think about things like that for a long time yet.

The Barkers were very rich Americans who spent their summers in Venice. They occupied an ornate Gothic palace on the Grand Canal, with decorated balconies, and bronze lions peering out from the façade. Mike had met Hilary Barker at Harry's Bar and had accepted her invitation to cocktails, even though he'd thought her a little silly.

Now he sat in the Barkers' sweeping drawing room, with its frescoed walls and gilded ceiling, while Hilary talked effusively on one forgettable subject after another. Mike was not listening; he was completely caught up with her visiting cousin, Sheila, who had such a quietly elegant presence that she captured attention by sitting in silence. She was absolutely lovely.

She obviously knew what was on his mind, and took advantage of a break in her cousin's spate of frivolity to ask him if he'd like to see the rest of the palace. He accepted gratefully.

"I had a feeling Hilary was making you uncomfortable," she said when they were out of earshot of the others, "and I didn't want you to run without giving us another chance. Hilary means well, but she gets carried away."

They ended their tour in the garden, where they sat in white chairs among a profusion of honeysuckle, wisteria, pomegranate, and palm trees.

"I used to like you in the movies," she said.

"I have a feeling you didn't see me in many."

She smiled. "I've never been much of a movie fan."

"I don't think you're much like your cousin Hilary, either."

"I don't suppose so."

"I've been wondering," he said, finally getting around to what he'd been thinking about almost since the moment he was introduced to her, "if perhaps we might see Venice together."

"I think that would be lovely," she said.

Venice was beautiful, and so was Sheila Renslow.

Mike saw much more of the city after he met her than he had before.

She wasn't one just to sit at an outside table at Florian's and watch the world go by, or to drink herself into forgetfulness in the smoky silences of Harry's Bar. She was alive and vital, and she wanted to see everything and know everything. She was young—only twenty-five—which probably accounted for her verve. What astonished him was his own at the age of forty. He hadn't been this eager about life in years.

She persuaded him to start out virtually at dawn the first day they spent together. It was an opalescent morning that proved that summer dawn in Venice was as stunning as summer sunset. During those early hours they simply poked around, wandering the meandering short streets, eating shrimp and admiring the neat displays in vegetable stalls in the small piazzas they wandered into here and there.

"We ought to go to the top of the Campanile and look at the city from there if you haven't already done it," she said when they reached St. Mark's Square.

"I haven't. Why is it the Campanile looks as if it's leaning?"

"Because it probably is, slightly. Venice has been noted for her leaning towers. Some of them have even toppled into the street. But don't worry. They always know well in advance when it's going to happen. The last time one fell early in the century."

They went up into the tower and looked down at the city beneath them, tucked away under brown roofs. The small canals were hardly visible from this perspective, but the graceful curve of the Grand Canal plainly split the city down the middle. The Adriatic lay gray and murky out beyond the lucid blue lagoon with the dots of green that were its multitude of islands, and far to the north were the snowy peaks of the Alps. But the stunning view was lost on Mike; he was looking at Sheila.

They hired a guide with a speedboat for a tour of the lagoon and flitted in and out among launches, barges, ferries, and yachts, and even passed an ocean liner putting in to the city from the Adriatic Sea. On their way back Mike wondered, as the blue water sprayed in their wake and he looked at Sheila for the hundredth time that day, if he was falling in love again.

Before another week had passed he was sure of it. More than that, he needed her. He had learned that he couldn't really go it alone, for when he tried to, he sank into emptiness and depravity. He'd proved that to himself and the world entirely too often, and now it was time to take himself in hand—for good.

He asked her to marry him.

382

55

Tracy was full of fear. Things had gone from bad to worse for both her and Juan. The torment in Juan's soul kept growing, and the more he tried to hide it, the more she saw it. And the feeling of well-being she'd known when Juan had told her of his decision to give up his world for her had crumbled and vanished.

They didn't talk about their mutual uneasiness. Instead they went ahead making plans, and the decision was finally made to fly to Mexico for his divorce and their marriage next month because it could be done quickly there.

Juan was restless. He read the Spanish newspapers and went for walks alone. He went to Sunday Mass and returned with troubled eyes. He turned down most of the invitations they received, although he knew and Tracy knew that it would have been far better for them to go out socially more often in this troubled period. His worst times were after he'd had a letter from his father. He never spoke of what his father wrote, but the torment in his eyes showed that he was taking it very seriously.

Tracy went often to an American interdenominational church near the church where Juan went to Mass and confession.

"Do you find peace in church?" Juan asked her one Sunday after service.

"I want to, but I don't," she said honestly.

"I do not, either," he said solemnly. "I keep going back, hoping for it, but it does not come. God is punishing us."

Tracy took a deep breath. "No, Juan."

"You have a deep feeling for God, Tracy. You know it is true."

She saw that there could be no reasoning with him when he was so overwhelmed with guilt. The real Juan Olivares was a different person from the brave matador and international sophisticate the world knew from accountings in the press. The real Juan Olivares was a man so full of sense of country and family and church and honor that he found the burden of love he was bearing in total conflict with it.

Tracy didn't know how to fight it any more than he did. She drank more and so did Juan. They fell into long silences.

Three days before they were to fly to Mexico, she saw Juan writing a letter. She was sure it was to his father, telling him what they were going to do, closing off his former life forever. The pain in Juan's eyes as he wrote told her how unbearable this final act was for him.

The night before they were to leave, they decided to have champagne on the terrace to celebrate.

"To our new life," Juan toasted, looking solemn and unnatural in the almost palpable heavy red light of the Roman sunset.

"To our new life," Tracy repeated, smiling tautly as she raised her glass and touched it to his.

But it was as false as a bad script, she kept thinking as they drank in lingering silence. The champagne was making them anything but gay. Tracy weighed a risk in her mind. She knew if she said what had been in her thoughts for a long time, she might lose everything.

But she said it. "Juan, you don't want to go tomorrow. It's upon us, and you don't want to do it."

"You are right, Tracy. I do not want to do it. But I will. I must."

"We can turn back from it. We don't have to go. We can think about it some more. You're not happy, Juan. We've got to talk about it."

"I will be happy again when this is over," he said. "I am sorry I have not been myself. I know it has been difficult for you. I will make it up to you."

"I'm not worried about your making anything up to me, Juan."

"There is a good deal to make up to you. You waited for over two years for me to take the measures I am finally taking."

"I've never expected or wanted anything more from you than you've given me," Tracy said. "And you're giving up a great deal more than I am when we get on that plane tomorrow. I want you to be sure—"

"Tracy, I am sure!" he interrupted. "What it sounds like to me is that *you* are no longer sure."

"I'm not sure that we shouldn't wait and think about this some more before we act."

"There is only one thing to think about. We love each other, and we are going to have a child and spend the rest of our lives together. I hate hurting my family, Tracy, but it must be. That decision was made, and there is no need to talk about it anymore."

"We haven't talked about it nearly enough, Juan, and that's why we must now. We've been trying to find peace with God, and we haven't found it. How can we, if we can't find it with each other? I'm afraid of what we're doing tomorrow. Why have we talked so little about it? Why have we been hiding from it?"

"Hiding from it? I do not understand you. Tomorrow we fly to Mexico. Tomorrow we are doing something about all the rest of our tomorrows."

"I've seen you become another person in the last few weeks, Juan. I think that deep inside you, you resent me for tipping the balance of your life, for leading you to this point where you have to give up so much—"

"You are wrong!" he cut in. "Do not say such things!"

"How can you honestly say you aren't bitter? I wouldn't expect otherwise. And I'm afraid it will get worse. I'm afraid you'll end up hating me!"

"No, no, no!" he said. "You are the only woman I have ever loved, and that will never change."

He reached for her and pulled her to him. He trembled against her as they embraced. Even his lips trembled on hers. She clung to him. Her only hope was that he really felt as he said he did.

Juan's face was pressed against her breast. He was folded against her like a child. They had lain in silence for a long time. The champagne bucket and the glasses sat beside the bed. Tracy couldn't remember how many bottles they'd drunk since sunset. But she remembered how many times they'd made love. Three times. She'd heard, and she believed, that emotional problems were never resolved with sex. But were they when it was lovemaking, not just sex? No. She felt no more confident now than she had hours ago when she and Juan had talked.

She stroked his hair with her free hand. "I think we ought to put the light out and go to sleep."

"No. I want to take a drive."

"But Juan, it's after one."

"The night is just beginning." He raised himself on his elbow and smiled at her. "We will drive out to the water gardens at Tivoli. They are very beautiful at night. All those beautiful fountains spraying all that beautiful water colored by all those beautiful lights."

"Juan, you've had too much champagne. So have I. We need to sleep. Besides, the gardens will surely be closed by now."

"Then we will open them, and we will turn on all those colored lights, and we will make love on that knoll where you can see the lights of Rome in the distance."

"Be practical, Juan."

"Who wants to be practical? I just want to stay as happy the rest of the night as I am right now. I want to make love to you in Tivoli, and then I want to bring you back here to watch the sunrise from the terrace."

385

"I still don't think we ought to go," she said, but she got up and dressed, hoping that he'd change his mind and turn back long before they reached Tivoli.

They went downstairs and got into his new car. It was a white Alfa Romeo rakishly set off with wire wheels. It had leather seats and a convertible top. Juan put down the top and they started out. There wasn't much traffic, and there was even less when they got out on the road to Tivoli. Juan was going too fast. He always drove too fast, and usually she asked him to slow down. Tonight she didn't. Her hair streamed out behind her in the night wind, and tears stung her eyes. She looked straight ahead. Even if she'd wanted to talk, he couldn't have heard her over the shriek of the wind. She had nothing to say, anyway. She felt a numbing sense of inevitability that she didn't understand.

She heard an explosion above the sound of the wind, and the car began to weave wildly, tires screaming. She knew immediately that they'd had a blowout. She looked at Juan. He was trying desperately to control the steering wheel. The car resisted him and flew off the road like a plane taking flight. She was screaming, but she hardly heard it over the panic in her mind. The car was gone from her. She was flying herself. She met the ground with a terrific jolt. Her ears roared, but through it she heard the crashing of the car. Where was Juan? She was sinking into death. Darkness crept through her mind like an incoming tide. She fought to hang on, but she was helpless. The darkness washed over her.

She was aware of blinking red lights in the night. Men knelt beside her, speaking Italian. She opened her mouth to ask about Juan. Nothing came out. "You are going to be all right," a man in a white coat said. She didn't believe him. She was in terrible pain. She was certain she'd lost the baby, and she thought she was dying. The darkness washed over her again.

When a little light crept in, she heared voices again. She opened her eyes and saw blurringly, and wondered if she was looking through blood. She seemed to be inside an ambulance. A siren screamed. They were racing, racing. She turned her head. There was someone across from her, hovered over by a man in a white coat, just as she was hovered over by another man in a white coat. Juan's profile took shape in the blur. His face was dead white and still. Oh, God, was he dead?

But if he was dead, why was the man in the white coat working on him? If he was dead, why wasn't the sheet pulled up over his face? No, he wasn't dead; he wasn't dead.

She didn't quite lose consciousness again the rest of the way in to

386

Rome. She was aware of being taken into a hospital. She was aware of doctors working over her. Juan had vanished; she wondered where they'd taken him. She wanted to think but she couldn't. Tubes were attached to her and tape was being wound around her. The snout of an X-ray machine pointed down at her. Needles went into her, and the pain drifted away. She fell into deep sleep.

When she wakened, a doctor and a nurse were at her bedside. The doctor spoke English. He said she'd lost her baby. He said she'd suffered shock, two broken ribs, and deep cuts and abrasions, including a long cut from her left eye down over her cheekbone almost to her mouth which would probably require surgery.

"Juan—what's happened to Juan?" she asked in a weak voice she hardly recognized.

Juan's injuries were much more serious. Both his legs were broken. He'd smashed against the steering wheel, and a rib had penetrated his lung. He'd suffered a severe concussion and was in a deep coma.

Tracy prayed that Juan would live as she drifted off to sleep under heavy sedation.

Juan's father came to see her the next day. He said the doctors had told him she was going to be all right, and he was glad. He said Juan's wife was here with him. He told her that they'd prayed and prayed that Juan would live, and now it seemed he would. The crisis had passed.

"Thank God," Tracy sighed.

"You prayed for him, too, of course," Olivares said quietly.

"I prayed for him," Tracy said.

"I understand how you feel—"

"No," she cut in. "You understand how you feel, Señor Olivares. That's quite different."

"We are here to take Juan back to Spain with us when he is able to go. I think you know that."

"Yes, I know it."

"You can stop it if you want. I hope you will not. In the long run, it would ruin Juan's happiness to stay with you."

"You're not thinking of Juan's happiness. You're thinking of yours." She paused. "And of the happiness of Juan's wife."

"Of course that is true. But you will understand that I must try to do what I can."

"Juan is the only one who should decide on his own happiness, Señor."

But she knew the decision had been made long ago. The climax had been the accident. It was exactly as Juan had said. God had punished them. God had made them see.

She was allowed to go in to see Juan a week later. They didn't really talk much about what had happened and what was still to happen. It was all inevitable. She knew that Juan wanted to go home to his family, to stay, and she wasn't going to stop him. It didn't mean that they loved each other less. It just meant that other demands upon them were more powerful.

He took her hand and kissed the palm just before she left him. She didn't look back. Outside, she saw his father and his wife down at the end of the corridor, waiting. She turned away. The end of this seemed so unreal. It hadn't ended the way a movie would. It had ended the way life did.

56

In the beginning, Mike was quite content in his marriage to Sheila. When he stopped to think about it, he supposed that was partly because he felt secure with her and partly because she fit the traditional concept, in his eyes, of what a marital partner should be. Sheila was lovely, she was comfortable to be with, she was passionate in bed, and she was interested in what he wanted from life. Most important, she loved him and gave him peace.

They were married in Venice just two weeks after they'd met. Sheila's parents flew over for the ceremony. They were Oyster Bay aristocrats, but they didn't make a point of it, any more than Sheila did, and Mike felt at ease with them.

When Mike and Sheila were in Switzerland on their honeymoon, the news flashed that Tracy and Juan Olivares had been badly injured in an automobile accident. Mike tried to get through to Tracy by telephone but couldn't, for she was still on the critical list. He sent daily wires of inquiry and finally received an answer through the hospital, thanking him for his concern and assuring him that she would recover.

Mike felt greatly relieved. It occurred to him that one of these days he should sit down and write Tracy a long letter about the things that should have been said between them and never were. He owed Howard a letter like that, too.

Back in the States, Mike and Sheila purchased a large penthouse apartment in New York City and furnished it partly with antiques that Sheila's doting parents provided from their Oyster Bay mansion, which had been in the family for three generations and would be coming to Sheila one day.

Mike and Sheila had a good and full life together. They usually spent their weekends at Oyster Bay with Sheila's parents or at the beach house they bought at East Hampton; but wherever they were, they were in heavy demand socially because of Sheila's connections. Mike found himself moving with ease in her circle. Strangely, he found that he didn't miss show business talk.

But then he began to change. He yearned for the companionship of show people, and he started dropping in at Sardi's and Downey's. But encounters with working actors only reminded him of how much he still wanted to do a play. Sheila recognized his deep need to perform and kept encouraging him to continue his search for a good role.

He wasn't getting any movie offers. Much had changed in the movie business recently, but the axiom still held that you were only as good as your last picture. *The Iron Gunfighter* had proved a critical dud in its recent saturation release. But it had still netted Mike two hundred thousand dollars on his percentage deal with Otto Steinbrugge, because, bad as it was, the picture had done well in the small towns.

He didn't have to worry about money anyway. He wasn't nearly so rich as Sheila, who had come into six million from her paternal grandfather when she was twenty-one, but he was rich enough. His broker had invested well for him. He doubted that he was as rich as Howard, who was unquestionably a millionaire several times over by now, or Tracy, who'd inherited a fortune from Wesley Rainer, besides doing well in her investments and her percentages for pictures she'd made abroad, but he was rich.

Michael Baines recognized when he took stock in the spring of 1961 that he had much to be thankful for, but he wasn't professionally happy, and there were many times when he didn't feel like a movie star anymore. When he walked down the streets of New York City these days, as often as not, no one paid any attention to him. That hurt.

Howard rose late that morning. He'd been awake for over an hour before he finally got up. He found himself listening for sounds in the house, and there weren't any. It was as if the servants had gone, too.

A bird sang distantly in one of the gardens for a while. Pen would have known what kind of bird it was from its song, for Pen knew such things. Howard thought about Pen for most of the hour he lay awake in

389

bed before finally getting up. She'd been gone for three months now, and she wasn't coming back. It continued to surprise him that after fifteen years with her, he didn't miss her more than he did.

He got up, dressed, and went downstairs to his study. The maid appeared with coffee almost at once. She was efficient, as were the rest of the servants. Pen had trained them well, and the household went along as smoothly as it had when Pen had been running it. Pen would probably be hurt to know that.

A magazine lay on the desk, and Howard opened it again as he drank his coffee. It was a cheap scandal magazine, with an unflattering candid picture of Tracy Gordon on the cover. There was a cruel story inside suggesting that Tracy was sleeping around Rome now that her long-time affair with Juan Olivares had ended and he was back in Spain attending to his family and his bullfighting career. The article also suggested that Tracy was deeply worried about what the facial scar she'd suffered in her terrible accident with Olivares might do to her faltering screen career. It seemed that despite expert plastic surgery done by a top surgeon in London, a trace of the scar could still be detected in certain lighting and at certain angles.

With the article were several pictures of Tracy, and none of them, even the recent ones, revealed the scar, although this might have been because none were close-ups. There was an old picture of her dancing at a ball with Olivares and a recent one of her having lunch with independent producer Otto Steinbrugge, discussing a possible picture deal, according to the caption. She was also shown with an Italian prince at a garden party, with Italian screen idol Carlo Martinelli—her co-star in *Josephine and Napoleon* several years earlier—at the Excelsior Bar, and alone in the Roman Forum, looking thoughtfully at a pool in the ruins of the House of Vestals.

Howard closed the magazine and wondered if today he would be able to write to Tracy. He'd tried to many times, and he'd been unable to do it. There was so much to say, but he didn't know how to start. The truth was that he didn't want to say anything at all. He thought it was too late for him and Tracy, and she probably thought so, too. Otherwise, why hadn't she written? Why hadn't she asked him to fly over there? He would have taken the next flight if she had.

Wouldn't he?

He wasn't sure.

The maid brought him the mail, and there was a letter from Pen. She said she was doing nicely. She'd bought a cottage in the rolling green country of Kent near her birthplace. She had renewed her ties with her relatives and was making new friends. She was content, and she hoped Howard was, too.

390

Yes, he was content. His and Pen's decision to end their marriage had been a long time coming, but it was the right decision. Since they had ceased to fulfill each other's needs and no longer had anything to give each other, they were better off apart.

Howard took his two German shepherds out for a walk around the grounds, then sat for a while in the sun beside the swimming pool, the dogs at his side. He'd bought the dogs after Pen had left, and they were fine companions.

After lunch he went back to his study and did something he hadn't for a very long time. He looked through the scrapbooks that Georgina had begun when they'd first married. Pen had continued them right up to the last, although there hadn't been much to put in them in recent years. The books contained most of the multitude of newspaper accounts of his activities over the years, supplied by a clipping service; most of the many magazine articles; and stills from all of his pictures.

In all there were two dozen crammed scrapbooks. Howard quickly leafed through them, lingering over the stills of him and Tracy together. He finally put them aside with a feeling of satisfaction mixed with sadness. The scrapbooks epitomized how very much he'd done with his life, after all, even though in retrospect it sometimes seemed so little. They also epitomized where he'd ended. Nowhere.

He suddenly felt that he could now do what he hadn't been able to do before—write to Tracy. He pulled out paper from his desk and started.

Dearest Tracy, I want to tell you how much I still love you, how much I regret all the minutes and hours and days and months and years we've lost from each other, the endless moments between. And I want to tell you about my burning jealousy when you were married to Mike and how I despised Juan Olivares because you were with him and . . .

On and on he went, through four tightly written pages, and then he simply tore them up. It was far, far too late.

Mike was having one of his glad-sad days. It excited him that the play was set, that rehearsals would begin soon, that he had a tremendous opportunity for real acting achievement with this role. But there were ripples in his happiness, too. His drinking was getting out of hand again, and he attributed it mostly to his growing irritation with Sheila. She was obsessed with the idea of having a child, and there was hardly anything he wanted less. He'd already proved, with his lack of interest in his daughter by Mona, that he was the world's most inadequate father, but Sheila was so in love with the idea of motherhood that she kept telling him—and herself—that he would change his mind about fatherhood when he held *their* baby in his arms.

Her persistence with this issue was his only dissatisfaction with her,

391

but it was enough to start him off in directions he didn't want to take. Soon it was more than an increase in drinking with him. He'd begun to cheat on her, too.

He felt all the more guilty about it because she trusted him so implicitly. In general their lives were centered around her world, but if she'd been asked to give it up for him, she would have. She was thrilled about the play. She wanted him to regain all the glory he'd lost, and she would have made any personal sacrifice if she could have helped him to do so.

He knew all this, knew how very much she loved him, how deeply and significantly; yet, even knowing it, he didn't want to give her the only other thing in life that was as important to her as he was—a child.

Tracy wakened when Angelina, her maid, came and opened the white silk draperies at eleven o'clock. For a few minutes Tracy lay in bed, thinking. As she did every day, she thought about Howard Stanton and about her scar. She also thought about Juan and Carlo Martinelli and Otto Steinbrugge and about the duplex apartment she'd bought in a converted palace on the Janiculum near the apartment she'd shared with Juan. And she thought about having turned down the role in the new Fellini picture about modern life in Rome, the role that had subsequently been played by Anita Ekberg.

She thought about being tagged "fun girl" again after all these years. The scandal magazines were calling her "the fun girl of Rome." "Fun girl" was even less fitting now than it had been twelve years ago. At thirty-four, she could certainly no longer be considered a girl, and she didn't believe the small pleasures she found in life nowadays really qualified as fun.

Carlo was coming by today. They were going to spend the afternoon together and probably the evening—and possibly the night; Tracy wasn't looking far enough ahead to be sure of that at this point.

She got up and went into her pink marble bathroom, which was illuminated with pink lights, and studied her face in the mirror. There was a darkness under her eyes, forecasting a probable shadow problem that she sometimes worried about, but it was the scar that concerned her the most. She looked at the scar in the mirror many times each day. She'd come to realize that it symbolized her ultimate destruction to her.

She acknowledged that it was barely visible in the flattering pink light of her bathroom, but it was several minutes before she stopped looking at her face. She stepped out of her nightgown and into her pink marble shower. Minutes later she emerged, feeling much better about herself. She patted herself dry with a huge towel and looked at her body

392

in the full-length mirror on the door. Her body was still beautiful, smooth and totally without sag. Even the scandal magazines that derogated her said that her figure was still second to no other star's, even Marilyn Monroe's. Of course, if she did another picture, she would have to take off at least five pounds.

She dressed and went downstairs. Angelina brought her a Bloody Mary, disapprovingly as usual. She also brought a tray of melon, rolls, and cappuccino. Tracy ignored everything but the Bloody Mary, sipping it slowly as she looked through the copy of *Variety* Emory Deems had airmailed from the States. Emory always mailed copies of the trade papers when there was an item about her. This particular item was short. It announced that Otto Steinbrugge was still planning to make a big picture starring Tracy Gordon when the right script came along.

Tracy put down *Variety* and picked up the Spanish magazine with Juan's face on the cover. Juan smiled, but his eyes were sad. The cover caption said that Spain's most honored matador, Juan Olivares, was having his most glorious season in the bullring.

There was a piece inside with a picture showing Juan sinking his sword into a bull's aorta at the moment of truth. The text said that less than a year after he lay near death from an automobile accident, Juan Olivares was fighting so brilliantly that he was now being hailed as the greatest matador since Manolete. It went on to say that Juan Olivares was no longer the international social figure he'd been in the recent past. Sundays he spent in the bullring, but the rest of the week he spent with his family.

Tracy put aside the magazine and closed her eyes. She must have looked at this magazine twenty times, and she didn't know why she tortured herself like this. She'd said good-by to Juan a long time ago in the hospital, and she was never going to see him again. She was sure that Juan was still convinced, and always would be, that God had made their decision for them. At times she thought so too.

The mail arrived, and Tracy was disappointed as usual that there was no letter from Howard. It had now been more than six months since she had heard that Penelope Stanton had left Howard and had gone home to England for her divorce. Tracy had waited and waited for a word from Howard, but there was none. Why did she keep hoping? If he loved her, he would have come for her long ago.

Tracy was on her second Bloody Mary when Carlo arrived. When she and Carlo had made *Josephine and Napoleon* together years before, there had been published rumors that they were in love and having an affair during the production of the picture. They hadn't been, although Carlo had wanted to. They were now having what Tracy thought of as a "friendly" affair, and Carlo, who had left his wife but couldn't divorce her, was Tracy's usual escort at parties.

Carlo almost immediately launched into one of his favorite subjects: how much better he could have done the lead in *La Dolce Vita* than Marcello Mastroianni if Fellini had only had the sense to cast him in the picture.

There were times when Tracy didn't think she could stand Carlo's monstrous ego another instant, but now she let him babble on. She didn't even protest when he wanted to go to bed before a half hour had passed. Why not? He was a good screw, as could be attested to in many quarters in Rome, and she was envied because he'd stayed with her so long. And when you couldn't have love, having a good screw was good enough, wasn't it?

She lay back on her pink sheets and took him into her, and it was as exciting as ever in a strictly sensual way. She thought about *La Dolce Vita*. The sweet life. It would have been better to call it the empty life, she thought.

57

Mike was awake for more than an hour before he finally got up, a little after noon. He knew Sheila was scheduled to attend one of her charity meetings immediately after lunch, so he deliberately stayed in bed late so he wouldn't have to see much of her. He would rather not see her at all today. He felt that way sometimes, yet none of it was her fault. It was his. He had to face that.

He had a headache. There had been celebrations almost every night since he'd received the Tony a week ago Sunday. Last night the producer had given another party, at Sardi's, right after the performance. Sheila hadn't come to the performance, so she'd missed the party. Mike had gotten very drunk and had probably made a fool of himself. He couldn't remember much about it except that there'd been the usual empty talk and the producer's wife had felt him up under the table. He couldn't even remember coming home or what hour it had been. But at least he hadn't wakened in a strange bed.

The Tony medallion was propped against his cuff-links case on his dresser next to piles of congratulatory wires—among them Howard's and Tracy's—and it seemed to mock him as he crossed to his bathroom. The thrill of having it was all gone now. He'd thought he would go to pieces when he heard them announce, "And the best actor is—Michael Baines for his performance in *Rising Wind.*" He closed his eyes for a moment and remembered it—the wild applause as he rather unsteadily made his way, just slightly drunk, from his seat to the stage—then standing there like a fool, thanking the playwright and the director and the producer and a lot of other undeserving persons for making it all possible when he should have said, "I owe it all to myself and Konstantin Fedotov!"

He opened his eyes and passed on to the bathroom. The truth was he didn't give a damn for the Tony, no matter how prestigious the award was supposed to be. He would far rather have had an Oscar for his performance in *Smith's War,* as he should have. He would far rather be a movie star than a Broadway actor.

He gazed at himself in the bathroom mirror. Puffy, veined eyes, bags under them, a drying skin, a hint of hair recession, muscles going soft. It all screamed at him. He was almost forty-two years old and he looked almost forty-two years old, and if anyone was ever going to ask him to play a thirty-five-year-old hero in a movie again, he was going to have to cut down on his drinking and start swimming daily at the club again.

He shaved and showered, got dressed and walked toward the front of the apartment. Sheila was in the library, reading the mail. "You have a letter from Regency Pictures this morning," she said.

The letter was signed by the most recent studio head, Noel Jordan, former wonder boy of the television industry. It informed Mike that Regency Pictures was commemorating its fortieth anniversary next November with a special celebration and intended to bring its stars back home at company expense. Jordan stated that in the months ahead there would be further correspondence on the studio's plans, but right now Jordan wanted Mike to set aside that date in November, because this was going to be a great opportunity for all of them to get together to glorify the past and plan for the future.

"To hell with it," Mike commented after he'd given the letter to Sheila to read. "I'm not setting aside any dates. Who knows what I'll be doing half a year from now? Maybe the play will still be running. Maybe I'll be making a picture in Europe. I don't know that I'll want to go even if I'm not doing anything."

"Oh, I'm sure you will," Sheila said.

"What makes you so sure?" he asked a little irritably.

"Because your association with the studio was so important to you. It was the best time of your life, Mike. Please don't try to tell me otherwise. It's been adding up that way for quite a while."

"That isn't true. Now is the best time of my life, Sheila. I may not act like it all the time, but that's the way it is."

"You don't act like it most of the time, Mike."

"My God, Sheila, why is it you don't believe me when I say something?"

"I believe you when you're believable."

"I get the impression you expected our honeymoon to last forever, Sheila. You've got to expect to be unhappy part of the time. You've got to expect to have some doubts."

"Oh, I expect that, Mike. But I would also expect to talk about them, which we don't." She paused. "Answer me a big question, Mike. Do you want to leave me?"

"No."

"Your assurance comes as a great relief to me," she said. "I just hope you really feel that way."

He knew he hadn't really eased her doubts, but he couldn't face going into it more deeply. He didn't want to talk to her about it because he didn't know how. He didn't understand her much, but he understood himself even less. One moment Sheila and his life with her were everything to him; the next he didn't want her or it at all. Sometimes he only wanted back what had been lost from the past. He felt himself to be an empty person and was contemptuous of himself because of his ambiguous feelings, and he drank more so that he would feel less helpless about it.

He drank two whiskey sours during lunch and dared Sheila with his eyes to say anything about it. He knew she was as relieved to go to her charity meeting as he was to see her go. He took another whiskey sour into the study and turned on the television set for the Matinee Movie. *The Great Typhoon* was playing, with Howard Stanton and Georgina Fox making love in the South Seas in Technicolor. Mike had first seen the movie over twenty years ago when he was in college. The story seemed dated in 1962, but Mike hadn't the least doubt that there were plenty of middle-aged women glued to their sets right now dreaming they were Georgina Fox, being made love to by the young and handsome Howard Stanton, bare to the waist, on a palm-hung beach. Howard was called a "durable" star because his old pictures appeared so often on television. Sheer irony! He was a "durable" star who could no longer get a picture to do.

Mike turned off the set before the picture was half over and took a taxi to a bar near Times Square where theater people hung out. He ordered a drink at the bar. Several people stopped and congratulated him on his Tony, but no one lingered. Finally a striking young man stepped in beside him and started to talk. He was blond and blue-eyed and reminded Mike somewhat of himself in his youth. The young man's name was Derek. There were other parallels between Mike and Derek besides a physical resemblance widely separated by time. Derek was studying for the theater.

"But what I really want to be is a movie star like you," he said.

A movie star like him! A movie star without a contract or a picture in sight!

But Mike was grateful for Derek's exuberant admiration. Four drinks later he was in bed with the young man in his grimy little apartment on Eighth Avenue. He lay naked with him for the rest of the afternoon, sobering up with a pot of coffee before he had to leave for the theater. He knew Sheila would be worried at his absence, but he couldn't bring himself to phone her with another lie. That evening his performance suffered because he couldn't concentrate properly. He was too often interrupted with persistent thoughts of how rotten he was.

The dogs came into Howard's bedroom and wakened him by licking his hands. He wasn't angry with them. Howard knew what they wanted. They wanted to run on the beach. They didn't care that it was scarcely seven in the morning.

He got up, dressed, and set out with the dogs, walking toward an undeveloped part of the beach area, considerably north of Malibu Colony, that he liked because of its wildness. The dogs kept running ahead, then running back to him. From time to time he threw a piece of driftwood and let them scramble to retrieve it. A jumble of thoughts drifted through his mind, revolving around Mike's winning a Tony award, and the envy he'd felt; the studio's letter announcing the fortieth-anniversary celebration they were planning for November; the letter he'd started to Tracy last week, and had torn up, as he had so many others over a long period.

He finally reached the wild area that he liked so well. A palisade rose sharply at the back of the beach. A steep path led to a plateau covered with lemon groves, palm trees, and the weedy remains of a former estate. Sometimes Howard went walking up there with the dogs, far away from the world.

This morning he decided he wasn't up to scaling the cliff. He sat on a rock close to the tide line, with the dogs beside him. He looked out at the sea glistening under the new sun. Suddenly he felt as if he were sinking. He *was* sinking, slipping off the rock. Was he fainting? He felt

397

pain then, a sharp stabbing in his left side, and he realized that he was having a heart attack. Was he going to die? The idea terrified him. He crumpled onto the beach. He was aware of the dogs' barking, then of nothing at all.

58

Howard was recovering: that was what the doctor kept telling him. He wanted to believe it. But a few years ago the world had been told one day that Clark Gable was recovering nicely from his heart attack, and the next day he was dead in his hospital bed.

Howard didn't want to die, in or out of his hospital bed.

"I think I understand now what wanting to live means," he said to Emory Deems, who had called at the hospital every day after Howard was permitted to have visitors. "Yet when I woke up in this bed the day after the attack, my first thought wasn't gratitude that I was still alive but a feeling of emptiness that I was alone."

"Perfectly natural," Emory said. "But you've got your friends. And there'll be someone special in your life again. You'll see."

Someone special. Leni and Georgina and Pen had all been special to him, and they were lost to him. And Tracy, the most special of all, seemed as much lost to him as the rest of them now. But he couldn't talk to Emory about that.

"You'll be on your feet in no time," Emory continued, "and I've got a feeling we'll have a picture deal for you soon."

"Emory, you know nothing I'd want is going to come up."

"Sure it will. We might even think about television for you. More and more of the big stars are considering series, now that so few theatrical movies are being made."

"Am I still a big star, Emory? I don't think so."

"You'll always be big, even if you never make another picture—which you will. Some of your classics like *The Cavaliers* will still be showing when the public has forgotten this so-called new breed of star like Wells Corlen."

Howard smiled. "A good agent makes his clients feel good. You've always been tops at that, Emory."

398

"I don't bull you, Howard. We've had a good relationship for thirty years. I expect us to continue together for at least twenty more."

When Emory left, Howard began to look through the cards, letters, telegrams, and cables that had arrived during the morning. The table on the other side of the room was heaped with piles of them that had arrived during the early days when his life had hung in the balance. Among them were two telegrams and a long letter from Georgina, still in Chicago with her second husband and wishing him well. Pen had cabled almost every day from England, and so had Tracy from Rome.

Tracy had phoned, too. A week ago, when the doctor had allowed him to start receiving calls, Tracy was among the first to be put through. It was a bad connection, and, on top of that, he thought she was crying. She said something about wanting to come to him, and he said something about waiting until he was up and around again. It was awkward. He didn't think she really wanted to come, and he didn't think he really wanted her to come. It was simply much too late for them, wasn't it? He wanted to ask her whether it was and hear her say it wasn't, but he was afraid to.

She hadn't called back since, and when the phone rang just then, he thought it might be Tracy. But it was Mike. Mike had called from New York almost every day.

"You sound a lot better today," Mike said.

"Do I? I'm surprised. I've been thinking a lot about death."

"Don't. Think about love. It's the best thing in life, next to being a star."

"That sounds like something the old Mike would say."

"Good. I'm aiming to be more like the old Mike and less like the recent one. I don't want to embarrass you, but our friendship means a lot to me, Howard. I keep thinking of that, and of what I've done to knock the pins out from under what I really want to preserve. It doesn't make sense."

"A lot of what I've done in my time doesn't make sense, either."

"I'm looking forward to seeing you, Howard. If I could duck out of the play for a couple of days, I'd fly out right now."

"Our reunion can wait, Mike. You keep on giving those Tony-award performances as long as you can. I always did say you were the best actor we ever had around Regency Pictures, and that still stands."

"But my personal star never shone like yours, Howard."

That was just about the finest thing Mike could possibly have said. Howard thought about it a long time after they hung up.

Tracy kept saying no to people who called, wanting her to do this or do that. She gave excuses even to Carlo, who understood even less than

399

most of the others why Tracy Gordon, the fun girl of Rome, suddenly wanted to be alone. No one would have dreamed, she was sure, that it was because she was mortally afraid that one of the two men on this earth whom she had truly loved was going to die.

Tracy did something she hadn't done for a long time. She went often to church and prayed that Howard Stanton would live. She prayed at home, too, but it didn't seem so significant as praying at church.

She phoned the hospital in California every day, and finally she got through to him. She wept as she talked to him and hoped he couldn't detect it over the static of their bad connection. The horrible thing was that she wanted to go to him, and he didn't want her to come.

She thought of the months and months she'd waited, after he and Pen had separated, for him to come to her, and he hadn't. That had been agony enough. This was worse. In the last analysis, was what Howard Stanton felt for Tracy Gordon at this point in time just a remnant of love? Or even less? Perhaps just a morsel of friendly affection?

She hated the thought of it. Briefly, she even wished she could hate Howard. But that didn't last. She continued to pray that he would live, and one day she stopped wanting to be alone. She called Carlo, and he was glad to see that she was out of her "mood." They started partying again. It was back to *la dolce vita,* the sweet life, the life the scandal magazines said Tracy Gordon had practically invented, the life that was all lighthearted gaiety. But with all that gaiety around her, there were nevertheless many nights, with Carlo sleeping obliviously beside her, when Tracy Gordon sobbed quietly into her pillow until she finally went to sleep.

Rising Wind closed its Broadway run in August, and the national company went out on tour without Mike, although the producer had urged him to continue in his role. Mike had even considered doing the tour for a while, grind though it would be, because there was nothing else in the offing for him.

A possibility came up when a pilot script and an outline for a television detective series were submitted to him. He gave the material careful consideration before he made his decision, and then decided he would fly to the Coast to talk to Emory Deems about it, since this would also give him a chance to see Howard, who had been out of the hospital for three months and was apparently completely recovered.

Mike flew out of New York on a hot and humid morning and found Los Angeles clamped under a pall of smog when he landed a few hours later. It seemed ages since he'd left. Actually, it had been barely four years.

400

He rented a car at the airport and drove to Emory's office in Beverly Hills, a larger and even more lavish place than the agent had occupied the last time Mike had conferred with him. Agents enjoyed considerable influence in the new Hollywood of the nineteen sixties. Since they, rather than the studios, now controlled the talent, it was said that they now had as much power over what happened in Hollywood as the studio czars had in the past. Emory's first important client thirty years back had been Howard Stanton. Subsequently, he had also represented Michael Baines, Tracy Gordon, and a dozen other important stars. Today he was one of the most successful agents in the business. He was heavier and grayer than when Mike had last seen him, but Mike told him he looked the same.

Emory laughed. "That's nonsense, but I must admit that *you* look better than you have in years."

"I'm happier than I have been in years," Mike said. That was true, in spite of the restlessness and doubts that had crept unwanted into his life again. "I'd be happier still if something came along in the way of a feature film. But I've decided I'm not interested in testing for that TV series. I don't want to be a detective. Besides, if the series turned out to be a success, I'd no longer be a movie star but a television star."

Emory nodded. "You didn't have to fly out to tell me this decision. You could have phoned me."

"I wanted to come anyway. This was home once. I wanted to see how much it's changed in the last few years."

"It's changed, and it'll keep on changing. The soothsayers have it that if Southern California isn't finally destroyed by forest fires, landslides, or a colossal earthquake, it will be completely taken over by mystics, evangelists, and freeways."

Mike laughed. "I'd never live here again."

"Never say never. If you ever do a TV series, this is where you'll do it, because this is the center of the television universe."

"I doubt that I'll ever change my mind about doing television."

"I don't blame you for not taking the plunge right now, Mike, but don't shut your mind to it. With picture-making cut back the way it is, and with the outlook for the rest of the sixties already looking bleak for feature movies, I think a lot of stars who looked down their noses at television five years ago are going to reconsider their viewpoint."

"I'll wait and see how I feel."

"Well, it's settled then, for the present at least. Will you be staying long?"

"Just a day or so, I think. I'm going to see Howard, and I may take a look around town."

"Are you going to stop at the studio? Maybe we could arrange for you to meet Jordan."

"I'm only interested in going to the lot again to make pictures."

"I'm afraid that making pictures is something Regency's been doing less of than any other major studio, and they're all in bad shape. The company was in the black last year, but only because Wells Corlen's picture was a smash hit and two TV series were successful."

"I saw Corlen's picture and hated it. I find him a big pain in the ass. If he's the next James Dean, as they say, then I'm the next Laurence Olivier."

"But he's very big, Mike."

"He won't last," Mike said, but with doubt in his voice. "They'll be making my type of pictures again. You'll see."

"I hope they'll be making your type and lots of other types again."

When Mike left Emory, he drove to the Beverly Wilshire and checked in, then phoned Howard, who told him to come right over. Howard was tanned and glowing, with the look of fine health, with no outward reminder that a heart attack had laid him low just a few months back.

"I can see you've been spending a lot of time at Malibu," Mike said.

Howard nodded. "I'm out there for a while, then back in here for a while. It doesn't seem to matter where I am. My life doesn't amount to much these days, Mike, but that doesn't seem to matter, either. I'm back where I was in the beginning, alone. But so what? I've always been selfish. I've always lived largely for myself, even when I've been with others, so it isn't unpleasant for me to be alone. I don't live an exciting life nowadays, but it's satisfying. I don't expect excitement, and I don't expect any more love."

"You don't have to expect it. If it happens, it happens. For a lot of us, love just comes and goes, like other important things in life."

Howard shrugged. "I think about it, but I don't think about it much. I don't have burning hopes for tomorrow anymore, and that doesn't seem to matter, either. My heart attack has slowed me down, but I could work again if there was work, my doctor tells me. I don't go out much. I see a lot of my neighbors, and that's about all. There hasn't been a party here since long before Pen left. I don't go out to movies at all anymore, even premieres. I watch them on TV. There was a time when I didn't like to see myself, young and full of vigor, on TV. Now I don't mind watching my old pictures."

402

"A new picture would help, wouldn't it?"

"I don't even think about making pictures anymore."

"I don't believe that, Howard. Movie people think about making pictures up to the last gasping breath."

Howard smiled. "You're absolutely right."

"I don't think the last reel ever really runs out on anything important we do in life, Howard. I have a lot of regrets about things I've done, and I don't believe that old cliché about doing things the same way if I had a second chance. I'd do them differently in most cases."

"I think most of us would," Howard said.

"As I get older, I find myself bogged down in the same weaknesses as before. Guilt should be running as thick as blood in my veins, but I just wash it out with liquor. I've never felt guilty enough, Howard. Take my daughter. Carolyn is ten years old, and I hardly know her and don't want to. I don't want to have another child, and I should feel guilty about it because Sheila wants one so badly. But I don't. Do you understand?"

"Yes."

"Can you understand this, too, Howard? I don't want Mona to be happy, and I don't think she is. Oh, I know she's supposed to be living in a fairy-tale paradise with that rich new husband of hers in Acapulco, but I'd bet my life it's turning sour already. In the end, she only wants what the rest of us want—to be a star. And I'm glad. Because she didn't love me."

Howard said, "You sound as if you're emptying your soul, Mike."

"There was a time when I could empty it to you freely, Howard, and I want it to be like that again. You know one big thing wrong with my life? I don't have anyone to spill things out to. Sheila tries to help, but usually she can't. She doesn't go back deeply enough into my life to really understand, much as she'd like to."

"And I go back deeply into your life."

"Yes. You and Tracy."

"The three of us," Howard said.

Mike nodded. "The three of us. Somehow, in the end, it gets down to just the three of us."

59

Tracy wasn't a hundred feet away from Mike, but it might as well have been a million. Physically, only a patch of grass and garden separated their bungalows at the Beverly Hills Hotel, but emotionally the distance was vast. Tracy wasn't going to sleep with him tonight, any more than she had last night. She wasn't even going to have dinner with him, or drink with him, or do anything else with him. She was going to sit in her bungalow and wait for tomorrow. Tomorrow they were going to Malibu as Howard's guests, and that was what Tracy wanted—to be with Howard.

Mike didn't want to think about that. He didn't want to think about today, either, but he did anyway. It had been a lousy, humiliating, unhappy day. The fortieth-anniversary celebration of Regency Pictures had set a new low in depressing events for Michael Baines. It had revealed all too glaringly what he'd once been, no longer was, and probably never would be again.

He'd hated it. He hoped Tracy and Howard had hated it, too. They'd been used and abused by the current regime of Regency Pictures. The birthday celebration of the studio where they'd been stars in an era when stars were stars, movies were movies, and Hollywood was Hollywood hadn't been held for the sake of sentiment or nostalgia but to tout their gold mine, this horse's ass named Wells Corlen, who, along with Elvis Presley, seemed to be cornering the whole movie industry in this inglorious year of 1962.

God damn Wells Corlen! thought Mike again, perhaps for the dozenth time in the last hour. He drained his glass, put in fresh cubes from the ice bucket, and filled the glass with Scotch again. He stared at the book he'd looked through on the plane coming out here two days ago and had put down in anger and resentment—*Portrait of a Superstar: The Story of Wells Corlen.*

Mike drained the glass again and refilled it. The quart of Scotch he'd started on about two hours ago was now less than half full. Mike was

404

beginning to feel woozy but not happy. The liquor was betraying him even more than usual. He was thinking about what he didn't want to think about. He wasn't forgetting what he wanted to forget.

The phone rang sharply. He let it ring six times before he answered it. He'd become apprehensive of answering phones, because so often there was someone at the other end of the line he didn't want to talk to, or someone saying things he didn't want to hear. He finally answered it, hoping it would be Tracy wanting him to come over to her bungalow. But it was Sheila. He immediately lied to her and said he'd been just about to call her. He doubted that she believed him.

Sheila asked him how today had gone.

"It was fools acting like fools in a fools' paradise," he said, and then he told her a little about it, about the red-carpet reception at stage seven, with those silly Regency pages accompanying the guests to the door, and then about the cocktail party inside against a background of blown-up stills from the more famous Regency movies, and finally about the endless luncheon where scenes from Regency movies were shown on a huge screen, where boring speeches were given and endured, where Wells Corlen swiveled and sang, where chorus girls came bursting out of a huge papier-mâché movie camera to perform a number that had originally graced the screen in a 1929 musical kicking off the all-singing, all-dancing, all-talking era at the studio. "And all the while," Mike continued, "the cameras kept recording our agony."

But he didn't feel he was really getting it across. Try as she might, Sheila could never really understand this aspect of his life, and he could never explain adequately to her how he really felt about today and the hopelessness it had left in his heart.

"I wish you had come along out here with me," he said.

Her voice brightened. "I wish I had, too. But I thought—"

She'd thought she wouldn't fit, and she wouldn't have. He'd encouraged her not to come, and now, suddenly, he regretted it and felt guilty about it.

"You'll come along next time," he said, "and we'll go on to Hawaii from here."

"That would be lovely," she said.

When she hung up, he had another drink. Then he had two foolish impulses, one after the other. He thought of phoning Ria, and then he thought of phoning Mona. But he hadn't the least doubt that Ria would simply hang up on him; and although Mona probably wouldn't do that, the chances that she would be glad to hear from him were only slight.

He finished his drink with a burning swallow and poured another, noting that the bottle was down to less than a third now. He picked up the book and stared at the smiling golden face of Wells Corlen on the cover.

He rose and walked to the door with the book under his arm and the glass of Scotch in his hand. He stepped outside. He glanced over at the drawn draperies of Tracy's bungalow, and then he started toward the swimming pool, drinking as he went. He felt quite unsteady. The book almost slipped out from under his arm, and he pressed it against his side to secure it. He reached the pool. A few people were sitting nearby. There was a buzz of talk and laughter.

He stood at the edge of the pool, so close that he could easily have fallen in. "Be careful," someone said nearby, and laughed, and he was unreasonably angry with whoever it was, but he didn't turn to see. He suddenly threw his glass. It crashed against the other side of the pool, the pieces falling into the water. Then he threw the book into the middle of the pool. It sank like a stone.

All talk and laughter had stopped. He turned and walked weavingly away, knowing what they were all thinking—there goes Michael Baines, Tony Award winner, faded star, and complete fool.

Tracy was seated at her dressing table, a glass of vodka and orange juice at her elbow. Looking straight into the mirror, she couldn't see the scar, even under the merciless light from the dressing table lamps. But when she turned her face a quarter of a circle, the light caught the delicate tracery of curved line that had been a vicious gash in her face before the plastic surgeon had made his delicate repairs. Even at this angle and in this light, few would notice the scar, Tracy realized, but somehow that knowledge didn't help.

Picking up her drink, she went into the living room and turned on the recording again. For the third time in the two days she'd been here, she listened to Howard Stanton being interviewed by Aster Bigelow on her radio program fourteen years earlier, heard him tell the Hollywood gossip columnist that the up-and-coming Tracy Gordon was a joy to make pictures with, was a much better actress than she thought she was, and was going to be a very big star.

Tracy finished her drink and refilled the glass. She thought about tomorrow. She and Mike would drive out to Malibu to be with Howard, and they would all pretend to be happy together, as they had pretended today at the studio. But they weren't happy. They were sad. The three of them.

The day after tomorrow Tracy would leave, and she would never come back again. She would return to Rome and be a fun girl again, and she would take up with Carlo again until someone else came along, and she might consent to make the picture about George Sand that Otto Steinbrugge wanted her to make if she could have the cinematographer she wanted, if she could be sure she would be photographed properly. She would be busy. She would forget about coming back here and the agonizing frustration of it.

The phone rang. Tracy frowned. It was probably Mike, drunk and maudlin in his bungalow, wanting her to come over, or wanting to come over here. She hesitated to answer. She didn't enjoy telling Mike no.

She answered. It was Howard, phoning from Malibu.

"I just took a long walk on the beach," Howard said, "and now I'm sitting here in front of the fire. Remember how we sat in front of the fire together?"

She swallowed. She remembered more than that. She remembered their making love in front of the fire, remembered it as vividly and as cuttingly as if it had only happened yesterday.

"I'm looking out at the beach," Howard continued. "It's cold and dark and dazzling. The ocean is roaring in, and there's a wind. It's beautiful and exciting, and I wish you were here with me, Tracy."

There was a terrible grabbing at her throat. "Oh, my God, Howard. I *want* to be there with you," she managed to say, though it was difficult trying to speak when she felt like laughing and crying at the same time.

"Why haven't we said to each other what needs to be said?"

"Because we're both cowards," she said. "Because we're afraid to hear truths we might not want to hear."

"What do you want to hear from me, Tracy? That I still love you? I do."

"Oh, my God."

"What does that mean?"

"It means I love you, too, and always have and always will."

"Life races away, and people waste themselves so badly. We were finally in the position to do something about us over a year ago, Tracy. Why didn't we?"

"Cowards and fools."

"Yes. I thought it was too late for us."

"So did I, so did I."

"That was stupid of both of us. Why should it be too late? I want us to be married, Tracy. I want to finish out the rest of my life with you. I want us to be together, loving each other and being happy. Will you?"

"Will I? Do you hear that funny sound? It's me, starting to cry. I want to come to you right now, Howard."

"Tomorrow, Tracy. We'll tell Mike together. He'll be happy for us."

Tracy didn't think Mike would be happy for them, but she didn't say so. "Tomorrow," she said sighingly.

Howard was too excited to sleep. He'd even decided he was going to stay up to see *Love on the Loose,* which was being shown on the late movie for the first time on television tonight. It was the first picture he'd ever made with Tracy. It was ironic that it was being shown the night he finally asked her to marry him.

There was an hour left before it started, and Howard decided to take another walk on the beach with the dogs. The dogs ran and played, as usual, barking occasionally but disturbing no one, because the beach was deserted on this cold night. The wind slapped at Howard, but he hardly felt it. He felt exhilarated. He felt like a young man, looking forward to life.

He looked forward to living with Tracy, loving her, being happy. It wasn't outside the realm of possibility that they would even make pictures together again.

It was ironic. He had thought he was finished, but he wasn't. He'd been offered a television series today, and now he was going to marry Tracy and was thinking about making pictures with her again. No, he wasn't finished by any means. He was fifty-two, but he still had a face and a build, as Barney had pointed out so long ago. And more than that, he had Tracy.

He returned to the house and warmed himself before the fire. Then he went to the window and stood looking out at the beach as the dark waves, shining with moonlight, threw themselves onto the sand, then receded to the depths of the world. He had gazed at this stunning scene hundreds of times over the years. It had never looked more beautiful than now. He'd never been happier than now.

He was thinking that when he began to sink. It came as suddenly as it had come last spring on the beach. There were the sharp pains, and then he crumpled. He heard the dogs barking. His vision fogged and the room slipped into darkness. As sound and sight drifted away, he had a last thought. Would he wake up in the hospital this time, too, or was this really the end?

When Mike and Tracy arrived for the funeral services, there was a crowd outside and the church was full. They saw few familiar faces as they looked around. They sat in what would have been the family pew if there'd been a family. The closest to it was the deceased star's divorced wife, Penelope, who had flown over from England to see her ex-husband buried. Howard Stanton's other living ex-wife, the former Georgina Fox, had wired her regrets from Chicago.

The other occupants of the family pew were Howard Stanton's agent for three decades, Emory Deems, and his friends and neighbors in Beverly Hills.

Alexander Renfew, former production chief of Regency Pictures, and the only studio executive still around from the days thirty years back when Howard Stanton became a star, gave the eulogy. The aged movie executive mentioned the irony that Howard Stanton, who had contributed so much to the glory of Regency Pictures in its finest days, had died on the studio's fortieth anniversary.

In Hollywood Memorial Cemetery, the body of Howard Stanton was placed in a fine black marble tomb near the resting places of Douglas Fairbanks and Rudolph Valentino. *Howard Stanton, 1910–1962, requiescat in pace.*

In the distance, a small plane flew over the studio again, trailing its long streamer behind it:

REGENCY PICTURES, 1922–1962
40 Years of Glorious Past, 40 Years of Glorious Future

Tracy was finishing her packing, but Mike wasn't. It wouldn't be necessary now. He'd just talked to Sheila. She was going to fly out tomorrow, and then they were going on to Hawaii.

"We might end up flying clear around the world," he said. "I'd like to go back to Venice, where we met."

Tracy nodded. "You've decided you want to make it work. I wish you luck. If we could only manage not to put ourselves first always, I think a lot in life would work that doesn't."

"I seem to have put myself first in all my relationships," Mike said. "When do we grow up, Tracy?"

"Maybe when someone dies."

"You didn't cry," he said. "But I understood. You were crying inside. You still are."

"But you aren't. You didn't really love him."

"I was jealous of him. I admired him terribly. He was a man of true depth, a real hero, a shining star. His kind of hero has just about vanished from the scene, and they don't make his kind of pictures anymore, but I'd bet a lot that his pictures will still be showing twenty years from now when most of the pictures they're making nowadays are rotting away in vaults. It was the people in the pictures who made the pictures great in Howard's time."

Tracy looked at him. "Nobody could have put that better."

He smiled. "So what do you do now, Tracy?"

"Take life from day to day. I'll be happy part of the time and sad part of the time. That's what happens in life, and that's what I expect. I'm going to make a picture for Otto Steinbrugge, and I'm going to try to stay beautiful. I want to be a sex symbol as long as I can. I want love again, too. It's almost as important as being a star."

"Almost."

Mike took Tracy to the airport, and as they waited for her plane to be announced he said, "Hollywood people are terrible takers, Tracy— all taking, no giving. The fight for survival makes us that way, I suppose—the terrible need to be stars."

Tracy nodded. Her plane was announced, and she smiled at Mike and left. He turned away. He had the uncanny feeling that he was never going to see her again—or any of the other dreams that had once made up this golden world.